JIM C. HINES

TERMINAL
PEACE

Book Three of the Janitors of the Post-Apocalypse

T0002130

DAW

Cover design by Katie Anderson
Cover illustration by Kieran Yanner
Edited by Sheila E. Gilbert

DAW Book Collectors No. 1922

DAW Books
An imprint of Astra Publishing House
dawbooks.com
DAW Books and its logo are registered trademarks
of Astra Publishing House

Printed in the United States of America

ISBN 9780756412814 (mass market) | ISBN 9780756412821 (ebook)

First edition: August 2022
First mass market edition: July 2023
10 9 8 7 6 5 4 3 2 1

For the survivors.

1

Human beings, once the worst of their feral instincts have been cured, are an undeniable military asset. However, the recent decision to allow the humans of Earth to govern themselves is the most tentacle-knotting foolishness to come out of the Alliance Judicial Council in decades.

Humans are little more than animals. I say this not out of malice or racism. Indeed, I'm quite fond of human beings. But after years of study, I've found them to be an evolutionary quagmire of inefficiency. Scientifically and objectively, humans are a primitive species.

They have redundant lungs and kidneys, but only a single brain or heart, as well as seemingly "optional" organs like the appendix. Even more absurd is their reproductive system. Half the species keep their genitalia on the outside of their bodies! Then there's the human gastrointestinal tract, an evolutionary abomination if ever there was one.*

Recently discovered research from the Library of Humanity suggests one of the greatest threats to human health in pre-contact years was their own immune system. Much like humans themselves, their immune system was vicious and undiscerning. It attacked external pathogens with moderate efficiency, but assailed the host body as well.

A sampling of human immune disorders includes arthritis, diabetes, lupus, gastrointestinal inflammation, multiple sclerosis, and countless more. While human medicine was able to manage many of these diseases, their physiology was a disaster waiting to happen. The so-called "Krakau Plague"—an inaccurate and offensive misnomer—was but the latest in a long list of pandemics to ravage this primitive world.

Indeed, one could argue that the Krakau Plague resulted in a stronger, more resilient breed of human. Just as Krakau government has produced a stronger, more stable human society.

*—From "A Defense of Krakau Oversight in
Human Evolution and Government"
by Krakau physician Aberdovey Bells*

---

*The human GI tract is more than seven and a half meters long. Despite this absurd length, humans regularly emit foul-smelling exhaust as a byproduct of inefficient digestion. Krakau biochemists have tried for years to reduce these emissions through a carefully controlled diet, but their efforts have met with minimal success.

CONTRACTORS AND SPECIALISTS FROM the Krakau Alliance had completely overhauled the *EDFS Pufferfish*, including "human-friendly" upgrades to the medical facilities. Brand new medtanks gleamed like oversized aquariums beneath light strips designed to mimic the spectrum of Earth's sun rather than Dobranok's. The walls and storage lockers were a gentle blue instead of the sandy brown the Krakau preferred. Cheerful images of baby Earth animals with encouraging text decorated the ceiling.

None of it eased Captain Marion "Mops" Adamopolous' impatience. Every minute she spent here, lying in what the Krakau called "a perfectly balanced restorative

medical bath solution," brought them one minute closer
to interplanetary war—a war with Earth at its center.

She stared up at the picture of a kitten clinging to a
tree branch with its front claws. The text, in Human, read,
Continue dangling in your present location!

"How long?" she asked for the sixth time.

Azure turned so one large eye faced Mops. "I'm analyzing your test results as quickly as I can."

Mops dug deep, scraping for the last dregs of patience.
Azure was young for a Rokkau, roughly equivalent to a
human in her late teens, and while she was a genius when
it came to biochemistry, that didn't make her a trained
physician.

Azure stood a bit over a meter tall, her cylindrical body
resting on thick, snakelike limbs. Four long, dexterous
tentacles paged through the medical information displayed
on the wall-mounted console. One of those tentacles was
slightly shorter and skinnier than the rest. Mops had shot
that one off eight months ago, and it hadn't quite finished
regrowing.

Thick, overlapping shells covered most of Azure's body.
Like the skin beneath, the shells were mostly black with
irregular splotches of blue.

The ever present salt-and-alcohol smell of Krakau an-
tiseptics threatened to give Mops flashbacks to the first
time she'd woken up in a medtank. That had been years
ago, on Earth. Antarctica, though she hadn't known it at
the time. She hadn't known anything. No language, no
identity, no idea who or what she was. No memories, save
for nightmarish flashes of hunger . . .

Back when Mops had been in charge of Shipboard Hygiene and Sanitation, she'd tried everything to minimize
that smell. Odor-absorbing minerals, upgraded air filtra-
tion systems, air-freshening sanitary scrubs . . . nothing
worked.

She turned onto her side. A painted gorilla grinned
down at her from the wall. Colorful writing arched over
the creature's head like a rainbow: *Have you groomed
your dental protrusions today?*

"I'm not sure about the artwork."

"I'm told the style is designed to mimic the décor of an old human medical facility specializing in tooth care. Are the posters not comforting?"

"I don't think 'comforting' is the right word." In fairness, Mops doubted anything would bring much comfort today.

Azure hummed and clicked to herself as she pored over a computer console. "Perhaps a trained doctor would be better for these tests. The Alliance has—"

"I don't trust the Alliance with this." Bad enough the Krakau—and, to be fair, their Rokkau kin—had been behind the infection that transformed humanity into shambling, near-unkillable monsters all those years ago. The Krakau Alliance claimed to have searched for a cure, but the truth was, they *wanted* the monsters. What they called a cure was just enough to turn the monsters into obedient soldiers in their war against the Prodryans.

And then, four months ago, Mops had discovered a Krakau admiral working to infect and weaponize other races. To deliberately do to them what an accident of biology had done to humans.

Mops wasn't alone in her distrust of the Alliance. These days, only escalating Prodryan aggression kept the whole interplanetary organization from crumbling like wet sand. She wasn't sure how much longer that would be enough.

"You don't trust them, but you trust me?" Azure's stuttering clicks were the human equivalent of wry laughter.

"Why not? You haven't attempted any acts of bioterrorism in eight months."

Azure waved a tentacle. "That was the impetuousness of youth. Who hasn't incapacitated a ship and tried to wipe out a planet's population when they were a child?"

"Some of us spent our youth trudging about a ruined planet, eating anything that moved." Fortunately, Mops had no memories of those years before the Krakau had "cured" her. "Speaking of children running wild, how long has it been since you called your mothers?"

"Three days." The translator on Azure's beak managed to convey her eye-rolling exasperation, though Mops wasn't sure if it was directed at her or at Azure's parents. "They got matching shell-etchings last month: three-color line art of silver wave-skimmers perched on coral blooms." At Mops' blank expression, she explained, "Wave-skimmers are like shimmering dragonflies. They mate for life. The coral blooms are just pretty."

"That sounds nice," said Mops.

"It's *embarrassing*. They're old enough to be grand-parents. Do you know what they said to me when I asked about getting an etching, back on the lifeship? I thought they'd burst an air bladder . . ."

Azure's skin darkened. One large, black eye continued to watch the console. The other shifted to focus on Mops.

Mops braced herself. "What is it?"

"I've finished comparing your test results to Alliance diagnostic criteria." Azure's lower limbs undulated with distress. The melody of her words—before translation—was off-key as well. "It appears your body's immune system has begun to reject the Krakau cure."

Mops had been dreading those words. Hearing them now was almost a relief, an end to weeks of uncertainty.

For close to a month, she'd felt *off*. She had trouble sleeping, and when she did drift off, she spent her nights twitching and sweating, jolting awake from half-remembered dreams.

At first, she'd told herself it was nothing serious. Humans were practically unkillable, immune to most diseases and able to shrug off injuries that would destroy another species. It was one of the things that made them such useful soldiers. But as her symptoms increased, she'd started to suspect the worst.

"Well, shit."

Azure gave an exaggerated full-body nod. "A fecal analysis was part of the diagnosis, yes. Your nonstandard diet presented challenges, but the sample's pH was abnormally high. In addition, your white blood cell count is up, your adrenal glands are overproducing, your neurotransmitters—"

"I'm reverting."

"It appears so," Azure said quietly. "I'm double-checking the results."

Mops sat in the tank, acutely aware of her body. The wrinkled skin on the pads of her fingers. The medbath lapping against her skin. The recirculated air raising goose bumps on her arms. She felt . . . hollow, like an old tree rotting from the inside. "What's my prognosis?"

Azure's beak clicked. "I don't understand your question."

"How do we treat this?" Mops snapped. "What are my odds?"

"There is no treatment." Azure spoke slowly, as if to a child. "I've reviewed the latest medical research, what little there is, but . . ."

"There's not much there," Mops guessed.

"This particular area of study is remarkably barren."

Why wouldn't it be? If the occasional human reverted back to its feral state, there were millions more where that one came from. Cheaper to round up and cure a new batch from Earth than to try to troubleshoot and fix whatever had gone wrong with one random human.

"What triggered this?" asked Mops. "Why is it happening now?"

"It's impossible to say."

"Could it be deliberate? A form of biological attack? You and the other Rokkau developed a drug to trigger immediate, temporary reversion. If the Prodryans got hold of that, they could have used it to—"

"All humans were inoculated against that formula seven months ago," said Azure. "I've found no trace of any external agent causing your reversion. This is a result of your body's own actions. Your immune system is rejecting the cure."

"In other words, my body screwed the pooch on this one."

"Bestiality would not cause reversion either," Azure assured her.

"It's an expression." Mops touched the controls on the side of the tank. The med fluid drained away, and warm air blasted her from above. The transparent walls lowered. She swung her legs over the side and stood. "What about natural immunity, like Gabe and the others? Could we use their genetics to help me fight off the effects?"

She was stretching, grasping at any grain of hope.

"I'm sorry, Captain."

Meaning Mops was facing not one, but two unwinnable wars: one against the Prodryans, and one against her own illness.

It had been a joint Krakau/Rokkau contact mission to Earth a hundred and fifty years ago that inadvertently triggered the end of human civilization. Rokkau venom, combined with humanity's ill-advised attempt at a cure, had created an unstoppable outbreak.

Shame had driven the Krakau to cover up their part in Earth's downfall. They publicly blamed the Rokkau, even going so far as to banish the Rokkau from their home world. A handful of Rokkau, like Azure's great grandparents, escaped into hiding. The rest were imprisoned where it was believed no one would ever find them.

The Krakau returned to Earth a century later. The first explorers from that mission to set their tentacles on the planet's surface were promptly swarmed and eaten by Mops' ancestors.

Poetic justice, considering.

A minuscule fraction of Earth's population had proven immune to the plague. They'd hidden all those years, doing what they could to survive and preserve Earth's history and knowledge in what they called the Library of Humanity.

Their bodies had fought off the changes wrought by the plague. Mops' body had fought off the fucking cure.

She gathered her things from the fold-down shelf in the wall and dressed slowly, hands trembling with fury. Slipping into the familiar black jumpsuit eased her nerves a little. Every movement was disciplined. Routine.

Mops had helped design this uniform. One shoulder sported the gleaming pufferfish insignia of her ship, the other a rotating image of Earth. The globe was the official emblem of the Earth Defense Fleet—currently a fleet of one. Yellow stripes above and below the pufferfish marked her as the captain of that lone ship.

She donned her equipment harness next, then pulled on her boots. Finally, she slid an oval memcrys lens from a padded pocket and placed it over her left eye. It jumped from her fingers, aligning and connecting to the magnets implanted within the orbital bones.

"Your pulse and respiration are both up." Doc "spoke" through the speakers in Mops' collar. The AI's voice was pitched low, for her alone. *"Skin conductivity suggests increased perspiration. I take it the results weren't good."*

Mops pushed the shelf up until it locked flat. "Azure confirmed reversion."

"Well, shit."

Trust Doc to make her chuckle, even on her worst day. "My words exactly."

"Alliance medical records have fifty-six known cases of reversion. Given Krakau secrecy surrounding their role in infecting humanity, there's an excellent chance they've classified additional information that could be useful in treating your condition. We could—"

"The instant we start digging into secure Alliance data, they'll want to know why."

Azure paused, clearly piecing together the half of the conversation she could hear. "You don't want anyone to know about your condition?"

"How long until the effects become debilitating?" Mops' words sounded distant, like she was listening to someone else speak. Someone far more calm and clinical. Buried beneath those words was the real question: *How long until I lose myself and try to eat my own crew?*

"The rate of progression varies from patient to patient," Azure said slowly. "Judging from the tests we've done so far, you could have anywhere from two weeks to two months. Running additional lab work in the coming week should give us a better idea."

Two weeks. Two months if she was lucky. "What should I expect in the meantime?"

"It varies," said Azure. "Your thinking will probably

get cloudy. You may have blackouts. Appetite will increase. Emotional regulation could become more of a problem. Digestive complications are likely."

"Digestive complications?"

"Certain internal processes are trying to recalibrate. Intestinal calibration may go too far, or not far enough."

"Lovely."

"Should I continue?"

Mops shook her head. "Upload the list to Doc. I'll review it later." She rotated her arm until the shoulder popped. "Am I fit to continue commanding the ship?"

"For now." Azure slid closer and twined a tentacle around Mops' forearm, a gesture of fondness and support. "I'm sorry, Captain. I assume I should keep this secret from the crew?"

"They deserve the truth." That much, Mops was sure of. "I'll tell them at this morning's briefing. I trust them."

And if . . . *when* . . . she lost herself, when she reverted to the mindless savagery she'd been born into, when she fell too deep into hunger to claw her way back, she trusted them to do whatever was necessary to stop her.

Just like Medical, the bridge had gotten a months-long upgrade. Mops barely recognized it anymore.

The personnel stations circling the center chair looked brand new, with all their exposed circuitry and wiring fixed and sealed away. The notes Kumar had scrawled on the walls at Navigation were scrubbed clean. Gone were the video game controllers Grom had spliced into Navigation and Tactical. Even the old methane smell from spilled alien slushees was gone, replaced with a faint hint of lemon and pine.

At Mops' request, the engineering team had also installed a permanent cupholder at Grom's station.

The bridge was empty save for her second-in-command and a Krakau engineer on loan from Stepping Stone Station who'd adopted the Human name Johnny B. Goode. Both were engrossed in their work and quiet enough for her to hear the low hum of the air vent fans hidden in the walls.

"Good morning, Captain." Commander Monroe vacated the captain's station in the middle of the bridge and moved to his customary seat at Tactical.

He'd recently straightened his shoulder-length white hair, draping it to the right and tying it off with a static bead, a small sphere of alien design with just enough of a charge to help hold the hair in place. It wasn't exactly regulation, but it partially obscured the damage done by a Prodryan grenade during his infantry service.

Monroe blew a bubble of brown gum that smelled like barbequed ribs as he studied Mops. "What's wrong, sir?"

"I'm changing our schedule." She missed the upholstered lounge chair Grom had welded into place after the loss of the ship's original Krakau captain. This new seat was too stiff, and had the faint chemical stink of freshly extracted polymers. She settled in and pulled up the latest repair logs. "How's my ship, Johnny?"

Johnny rippled all three of her primary tentacles in annoyance. "The *Pufferfish* is ninety percent repaired. Despite the extensive damage your crew of semi-evolved primates inflicted upon her."

"That's not fair," chided Mops. "Grom inflicted a good chunk of that damage, and they'd spine-slap you silly at the suggestion they had primate ancestry."

Monroe chuckled without looking up from his station. "Hey, Captain. Remember when our crew of semi-evolved primates and one Glacidae fought off a Prodryan attack force and saved Johnny's home world?"

Johnny let out a series of annoyed, guttural clicks. "The remaining repairs should be complete within nine days. We'll need an additional four days for final testing and inspection, after which you can get back to your chaos and bloodshed."

"Mostly chaos these days," said Mops. "We're trying to cut back on the bloodshed."

"You mentioned a change of schedule," said Johnny. "I've received no such orders."

"I haven't issued them yet."

The engineer was young for a Krakau. Her rubbery green-and-white skin gleamed like wet glass. The skin around her beak and eyes was a soft, flexible gray.

Despite her youth, she was a skilled engineer. Her team had thoroughly cataloged every centimeter of damage to the *Pufferfish*. She had the typical Krakau disdain for humans, but Mops had dealt with worse.

Mops' only regret was that she'd looked up the song that had inspired Johnny's Human name. Now, every time the engineer fell behind in her repairs, Mops had to repress the urge to sing, "Go, Johnny, go!"

Mops studied the display at the front of the bridge. Earth and Stepping Stone were centered on the large, curved screen. A small blue icon represented the *Pufferfish*, one of several ships docked at the station. To one side of the screen, a live feed from the system's security satellites listed current threats.

It was a very long list. Hundreds of Prodryan warships waited in the darkness, far enough out to evade any offensive from Earth, but close enough to take advantage of any opening that might present itself.

Mops turned her attention back to the *Pufferfish*. Her ship looked like a chubby rocket with a slender outrigger jutting from the side. She'd originally carried three matching weapons pods, but only one had survived the abuse Mops and her team put the ship through.

Maybe Johnny had a point . . .

Mops focused on the weapons pod. Her monocle tracked her eye movement and sent a quick query to the *Pufferfish*'s system. The pod's inventory list popped up on her monocle an instant later. The ship carried a complete complement of missiles, A-gun slugs, and fully charged batteries for the energy weapons. "Your team has been working through the repairs in order of priority, yes?"

"Of course," said Johnny.

"So that last ten percent is relatively nonessential?"

Johnny drew herself taller. "*All* of my work is essential."

"What would happen if we took the *Pufferfish* out sooner than expected?" asked Mops. "Say, today."

Monroe turned in his seat. He kept his face expression-less, but Mops could see the unspoken question in his eyes.

In contrast, Johnny looked frustrated enough to tear off her own wriggling limbs. She snatched a curved visor from her webbed harness and placed it over her eyes, pre-sumably checking the latest updates from her team. "Two entire decks lack redundant fire-suppression systems. In-ternal scanners still insist on misidentifying Tjikko as sixty-eight individual servings of broccoli. We haven't yet tracked down the source of Nusuran skin lotion seeping into the pool in Recreation."

"We don't have any Tjikko in the crew, and we can go without swimming," said Mops. "Are the decks with the fire-suppression trouble in use?"

"Not currently, but once you take on a full crew—"

"Have both decks sealed off and pump out the air. No oxygen, no fires." Mops switched the main display to a tactical overview of the solar system.

Green splotches were scattered about the edges like mold creeping across an unsanitized shower unit. Each smear represented a hostile Prodryan squadron. "Any chatter from our would-be destroyers?"

"Nothing new," said Monroe. "Most of what the Alli-ance has been intercepting is a mix of goading and gloat-ing. Which clan has the most kills, which captain has the biggest wings, that sort of garbage."

Space was just too damn big. The closest Prodryans were almost ten AUs away, almost an hour and a half for light-speed transmissions, and far longer for ships or weaponry. "Johnny, are we combat-ready?"

"Weapons were our second priority, after life support. Both offensive and defensive systems are up to code." The Krakau followed Mops' attention to the screen. Her skin darkened. "You're considering an attack against the Prodryans?"

"Not all of them. Not all at once."

"They would see you coming, giving them more than enough time to prepare a counterattack."

Mops magnified the fleet closest to Jupiter. The screen brought up additional information on the number and type of ships, presumed armaments, speed, crew size, and clan affiliation.

"My sisters used to talk of human bloodlust." Johnny slapped a tentacle against the floor. "If you were determined to blow yourselves up, why the depths couldn't you do it *before* I poured my hearts into fixing this ship?"

Mops ignored her. "Monroe, we're moving up the morning briefing. I want the crew in the Captain's Cove in twenty minutes."

"Yes, sir." He knew better than to argue.

Johnny didn't. "This is madness. They'll either scatter before you reach them, leaving you floundering impotently in empty space, or else they'll welcome your lone ship into their claws like a tangler crab and crush you. You can't—"

"This is a bad day to tell me what I can't do." Mops stood, anger flooding her blood. "These Prodryans have been circling my home like sharks for weeks. Any one of them would happily burn my planet if given the chance. They're escalating on a scale we've never seen before, a scale the Alliance can't hope to match. I'm—*we're* running out of time. The Tuxatl mission can't wait another two weeks."

"But the final tests and inspections . . ."

"Inspect quickly." She stepped closer, fists clenched. "You and your team have one hour to finish what you're working on and get off my ship. Anyone still on board is coming with us."

"Yes, Captain." Body flattened to the floor, Johnny slunk toward the lift with surprising speed.

Monroe waited until the lift doors closed, leaving the two of them alone. "Captain—Mops—what's wrong?"

Monroe had been her second-in-command for two years. He'd earned her trust again and again. He was the closest thing she had to family.

And if she told him the truth now, she wasn't sure she'd be able to pull herself together before the rest of the crew arrived. "I'll tell you in twenty minutes."

2

Throughout recorded Prodryan history, twelve Supreme War Leaders have commanded the loyalty of all clans. Each one united their people during a time of exceptional chaos or opportunity. None have had as broad or long-lasting an impact on Prodryan culture as the first.

In typical Prodryan nomenclature, the first Supreme War Leader of Yan went by the name "Supreme War Leader." History describes him as a prodigy, born nine hundred years ago in a remote hive in the icy wastelands of Yan's southernmost continent. The only survivor of a barbarian raid, Supreme War Leader set out on a mission of vengeance at the age of eleven. For three years, he tracked and slaughtered those responsible for the attack on his home.

During this time, he revolutionized military tactics and invented seven new distance weapons, including the barbed bola and the wing spear. His poetry from this period was collected and published as Supreme War Poems, Part 1, and remains on the Prodryan bestseller list to this day.

By the time Supreme War Leader finished his mission of vengeance, he had gained many disciples, drawn by his tactical genius and innate charisma. He spent the following *eight years traveling the world at the head of this personal army, bringing law and order and civilization to the surrounding lands. Early battles were difficult, but as his reputation and his army grew, other clans surrendered more quickly. Soon, Prodryans were eager to submit to his leadership.*

At the age of twenty-four, Supreme War Leader received his name and title by a unanimous vote of Yan's surviving clan leaders. (Six clan leaders voted against him, but they were promptly killed, so are not included as survivors.)

His wings were said to be powerful enough to blow a grown Prodryan warrior to the ground. His mandibles could crush stone. His mating habits were so prolific that more than ninety percent of modern-day Prodryans claim a direct family link.

It should be noted that most information about Supreme War Leader's life comes directly from his own writings. As such, the general consensus among Krakau historians is that the story of Supreme War Leader is "a giant trench of whale shit."

TO JOHNNY'S CREDIT, SHE had clearly researched human history and culture before her team began work on the Captain's Cove, the small, private room just off the bridge, traditionally used by the Krakau captain to meet with her officers in a relaxing saltwater pool.

The transformation was . . . thorough. Johnny had created a perfect, chaotic storm of ideas lifted from various Earth cultures and historical periods, all blended into a gaudy mix of eye-burning light, color, and design.

Fluted columns of white imitation marble bordered the door. The primary lighting came from a crystal-and-gold chandelier hanging from the center of the ceiling. Each of the chandelier's hundred-plus individual lights had been programmed to flicker like real candles. The ceiling was covered in stamped metal tiles, with every square depicting an identical Japanese painting of an ocean wave.

The walls were dark blue, printed with a lacy gold scallop pattern. And then there was the carpet: pea-green shag, so deep Mops' every step felt like wading through ankle-high seaweed.

By comparison, the desk was almost subdued. A large rectangular block of glassy resin encased an ocean scene, complete with neon coral and what Mops hoped were imitation tropical fish frozen in the imaginary currents just below the desk's surface. Coral handles marked cleverly fitted drawers of different sizes.

Johnny claimed it was a highly popular design from the mid-twenty-first century.

Mops settled into her chair—a ridiculously high-backed throne with a velvet cushion. The desk's console activated automatically. A thin screen slid up, its edges bordered by decorative blue seaweed. She skimmed her recent messages, then pulled up the latest Alliance scans of the Prodryan fleets.

She was reviewing the specs for the enemy ships hovering beyond Jupiter when Sanjeev Kumar arrived, early as always. He cringed as he entered. Knowing him, he was probably imagining every alien mold, fungus, and parasite that could thrive in the dark depths of that carpet. His hand twitched toward the canister of sanitizer he always carried on his equipment harness.

Kumar had been the most thorough and careful member of Mops' SHS team. He wasn't the fastest worker, but when he finished a job, every square centimeter had been cleaned to Alliance specs and beyond. His broad shoulders and muscular build came mostly from endless hours of obsessive scrubbing. These days, he was an equally thorough and careful pilot.

He sat in a chair and crossed his legs to keep his feet off the floor.

"The room is sanitized twice a week," Mops assured him. "It's as clean as anywhere else on the ship." She thought about Grom's quarters and added, "Cleaner than some."

"I know, sir. I review the cleaning logs each night." He didn't lower his feet.

Vera Rubin entered next. She was one of the newer members of Mops' team, an ex-security guard from a space station of questionable legality. She checked every corner of the room before taking the seat next to Kumar. She gave his hand a quick squeeze.

Mops studied the glistening purple tube coiled around Rubin's left forearm. "I don't think I've met this one."

"She's a rock eel from Dobranok." Rubin ran her index finger along the back of the tube. It raised a spherical head, opened a trio of large yellow eyes, and undulated whisker-like tendrils.

"Does she have a name?"

"Eel."

Mops should have known. Rubin kept a number of pets, though she preferred the term "companions." Naming them had never been a priority. If animals had names of their own, she'd explained, what right did she have to rename them? If not, then any names were just random and arbitrary sounds to them anyway.

"They thrive on Krakau wastewater," said Rubin. "When we take on more crew, I thought they might be able to help with waste processing." Noticing Kumar's cringe, she added, "I bathe her before I take her out of my quarters."

"Much appreciated," said Mops.

One by one, the rest of the crew filled the room. Monroe and Azure stayed near the back. Grom coiled their body and settled by the wall to wait, the small limbs around their head fiddling with a portable gaming console. Grom's spines lay flat along their back, creating a yellow stripe against the dark, oily sheen of their segmented body.

"Sorry I'm late, Captain." Gabriel Naudé stepped through the door and froze, eyes wide as he took in the room. This was his first time seeing the Captain's Cove. His head turned this way and that. "Wow . . ."

Gabe was one of the few humans with a genetic immunity to the Krakau plague. He'd spent most of his

young life working for the Library of Humanity under the
de facto leader of Earth, a woman named Eliza Gleason.

These days, Gleason was technically Mops' commanding officer. When she'd asked to assign one of her people
to the *Pufferfish*, Mops hadn't argued.

Whereas the rest of the crew—the humans, at least—
wore the standard black uniform, Gabe had brought his
own wardrobe. Today's theme was red: red shirt, red vest,
red suit jacket, and red pants. The colors were so bright,
Mops half-expected a Quetzalus to come along and try to
mate with him. The only exceptions to his color scheme
were the rank and ship insignia strapped to his arms, a
necklace of black wooden beads, and his polished black
shoes.

Everything was modeled after genuine Earth garments,
produced by a Merraban who worked in textile fabrica-
tion on Stepping Stone.

His head was shaved smooth, and his brown skin had
a strange warmth to it, a result of his natural red blood.
As far as Mops could tell, he hadn't stopped grinning
since the day he set foot on the ship. He'd spent the past
month working through the ship's vast collection of communications tutorials and training simulations.

Mops surveyed her people. "Where the hell is Cate?"

*"He's currently in the acceleration chambers on Deck
3,"* said Doc.

"What the hell is he doing there?" She really needed
to broaden her repertoire of Earth profanity. Since the
discovery of Gabe and his fellow survivors, Mops had
been actively trying to purge Krakau curses from her vo-
cabulary. Gabe had been happy to help, but suggestions
like "zounds" and "scumber" and "turtle-head" made her
suspect he was messing with her. "Cate, this is the captain. You were ordered to the Captain's Cove. If you're
not here in ninety seconds, I'm sending a security detail
to fetch you."

An icon on her monocle indicated Doc had relayed the
message through the ship's internal comms network.

Kumar perked up. "We have a security detail?"

"We have Rubin," said Mops. "Doc, remind me to run

a diagnostic on the acceleration pods to make sure Cate didn't sabotage anything."

She knew her crew questioned the choice to keep a Prodryan spy on board, especially with the Alliance/Prodryan conflict growing like flames in an oxygen feed. There were times Mops second-guessed her decision too, but so far, Cate's usefulness had outweighed the threat he presented.

Most significantly, he'd helped uncover and stop Fleet Admiral Sage's illegal biological experiments on Earth. True, he'd done it to undermine faith and trust in the Alliance, as well as to keep the Alliance from developing bioengineered soldiers to use against the Prodryans, but in the process he'd prevented an atrocity that could have twisted millions of sentient beings. His knowledge of Tuxatl should prove helpful in their upcoming mission as well.

Privately, Mops had another reason for keeping Cate close. She wanted to see how long he could suppress his instinctive Prodryan hostility toward other races. The Krakau had always taught that Prodryans were incapable of overcoming their drive to destroy anything alien. But Mops had learned to question much of what she'd learned from the Krakau.

The door slid open, and Cate entered—eighty-six seconds from the time of Mops' ultimatum. He wore form-fitting organic-looking plates that armored most of his small body. His yellow-and-blue wings hung behind him like a stiff cape. Thick antennae curved forward in what Mops had come to recognize as an expression of haughty superiority. Since this was default Prodryan body language, she didn't take offense.

"I want to hit one of the Prodryan fleets lurking around our system," said Mops. "Maybe it will make the rest back off. What can you tell me?"

"You're asking me to betray my people?" Cate scoffed. "Even if I helped you, your desperate actions will do nothing to prevent our ultimate triumph."

Behind him, Gabe rolled his eyes and used one hand to pantomime flapping jaws. Or mandibles, in this case.

Cate didn't notice. "Allow me to offer a counterproposal. As a certified legal advocate and spy, I'm authorized to accept your immediate and unconditional surrender. If you'd like to save yourself the humiliation of—"

"I'm tired and not in the mood," Mops interrupted.

"Your human fatigue is yet another paving stone of weakness on the road to Prodryan victory. The Alliance's time grows short . . ." His antennae rose, and he leaned closer to peer at the display on Mops' desk. "Are those drones?"

Mops magnified the formation of small ships that had caught his attention. "We think so. We haven't picked up any identification beacons, but one of the satellites managed to get a shot of the hull markings."

She called up a grainy image of a larger ship built like a chubby caterpillar with blotchy red-and-orange skin. A triangle of three giant green Prodryan skulls decorated the side.

"I thought as much." Cate rubbed his forearms together. "These drones belong to Strikes from Shadows, a coward and a disgrace to the Prodryan people. He is, in your parlance, an anus of epic proportions. I once had the pleasure of prosecuting his brother for six counts of undercooking cracked mudworms in poisoned cloud gravy."

Gabe cleared his throat. "I'm not sure my translator got that. You went after him for poisoning the gravy?"

"Poisoning one's enemies is legal," said Cate. "Improper food preparation is another matter. Thanks to my efforts, he was sentenced to six years imprisonment and renamed Undercooker of Worms." His mandibles scraped together as he thought. "Strikes from Shadows is a blight upon our people. The argument could be made that his elimination benefits all Prodryans." He straightened. "I shall assist you in this service to my people."

"Thank you for your cooperation," Mops said dryly. "What else do you know about him?"

"Shadows comes from the Torn Wing Clan, a weak family from a third-wave colony world. He has few victories to his name. His resources were inherited, not earned in battle. I doubt anyone from his clan was summoned to Yan to participate in the war conclave."

That explained why he was here. According to Prodryan law, which Cate had explained at mind-numbing length, any Prodryan warrior was technically eligible to become Supreme War Leader. But for someone like Strikes from Shadows to be considered, he'd have to prove himself, presumably by killing lots of humans and Krakau.

Given the number of Prodryan fleets poised to pounce, he'd have to stand in line.

The only benefit of all these would-be warlords sniffing around Earth was that it had briefly slowed Prodryan attacks on other worlds.

Once the Prodryan conclave selected a new Supreme War Leader, those attacks would increase tenfold. Even at its strongest, the Krakau Alliance couldn't hold against a unified Prodryan offensive. With Krakau leadership in disgrace and other races grumbling about withdrawing their membership, the Prodryans would cut through their enemies like hydrogen peroxide through bloodstains. "What else can you tell us?"

"He has foul manners," said Cate. "He believes his coarseness makes him appear strong, but he comes across as boorish and immature. Also, his stench is repulsive. It's said he once executed his executive officer for daring to suggest he should wash his thorax joints more than once a month. I pity anyone trapped with him on his command ship."

"What else can you tell us that might be relevant in a fight?" Mops clarified.

Cate stroked his mandibles. "His few victories, such as they were, have been on distant worlds with limited resources. He is inexperienced. Impulsive. A poor representative of Prodryan superiority and an ideal target for your newly refurbished ship. I would be happy to help you develop an attack plan in the coming days."

"We're doing this today." Mops checked the latest update from Johnny's team, making sure they were keeping on schedule. The decks with fire-suppression trouble were locked down, and all but three of Johnny's engineers had already returned to Stepping Stone. "Hitting Strikes from Shadows will serve as our shakedown run. Assuming the

Pufferfish holds together, we leave for Tuxatl before the end of the day."

"You're changing the mission schedule, Captain?" Kumar drummed his fingers on his thighs. Sudden changes in routine made him anxious.

Cate's antennae flattened. "Captain, I strongly suggest you avoid that accursed—"

"Alliance intelligence reports the final clan representatives have arrived on Yan for the conclave," she interrupted. "We were hoping the infighting would drag things out a while longer, but we're running out of time."

Azure and Monroe both watched her, waiting for the rest of it.

"You're stalling." Doc's words were gentle. Mops had invested in countless upgrades for him over the years. His personality had developed well beyond that of most AIs. Beyond that of many of the officers Mops had served under, for that matter.

"Yes, I am," she subvocalized. She'd gone over this next part again and again in her head, trying to make it sound matter- of-fact, and to eliminate any hint of self-pity. She needed her people focused on the mission, not their dying captain.

"Is it because of your condition?" asked Rubin.

Mops stiffened. She glared at Azure, who scooted backward in alarm, spreading her tentacles and lowering her body.

"I told nobody," Azure protested. "Please don't shoot me again!"

"Wait, what?" asked Gabe. "You shot her?"

Mops ignored the question and turned toward Rubin. "What condition do you mean?"

"Reversion."

Grom's spines rattled in alarm. Cate spread his wings and stumbled back, slapping Kumar with one wing in his hasty retreat.

Monroe rose from his chair. "Mops . . . ?"

"She's right." Mops gripped the edge of her desk. "How did you find out, Rubin?"

"Your appetite has changed. You're continuing tube

feeding protocol, but you've been snacking more frequently, in the mess and on the bridge. Mostly items high in fat and protein. Also, your movements are different."

For a moment, curiosity overpowered Mops' other emotions. "My movements?"

"Your limbs are slightly . . . out of synch. It's subtle, but it's the same pattern you see in feral humans. Probably caused by the gradual decay of higher neurological function." Rubin looked around. "I thought everyone knew, and we were keeping silent out of politeness."

"Everyone did *not* know," snapped Cate.

"How long do you have?" asked Monroe.

The room fell silent.

"It could be weeks, or it could be months," said Mops. "As the disease progresses, Azure should get a better idea how quickly—"

"Reversion isn't technically a disease." Kumar's words were flat, and he stared at the far wall, avoiding eye contact even more than usual. "It's more like your body's natural state reasserting itself, fighting off the cure."

Rubin touched his arm and whispered to him. His shoulders hunched, and he lowered his gaze, muttering, "Sorry."

"If your body's rejecting treatment," said Gabe, "can it be managed with immunosuppression? The library has records of old medicines that suppress the immune response to foreign bodies."

"Traditional human medicine is generally ineffective in ferals, cured or otherwise," said Azure. "They're resistant to most drugs and other chemicals. Immunosuppressants have been tried, along with a litany of other Earth treatments."

"I'm sorry, Mops," said Gabe. "I mean, Captain Mops. That bites."

"Yes, it is the biting that frightens me as well," said Cate.

"Should Captain Adamopoulos be transferred to the medical facility on Stepping Stone?" Grom curled into a tighter coil. "I mean no offense to Azure, but they have real doctors."

Azure clicked an obscenity.

"I'm not stepping down yet," said Mops. "Earth and the rest of the galaxy are staring down the gullet of the Prodryan war machine. Tuxatl could hold the key to stopping this war."

"What exactly does Tuxatl have?" asked Gabe. "You've all talked about it, but nobody's given me a straight answer about what we're hoping to accomplish there."

"That planet holds nothing but death for all who trespass," said Cate.

"What kind of death?" asked Mops. When Cate refused to answer, she turned back to Gabe. "We don't know what we'll find. Admiral Sage's files had flagged Tuxatl as a potential weapon against the Prodryans."

Cate hunched his back and brought his forearms together. "Sage was, by your own standards, a criminal. Hardly a reliable source of information."

"We've verified parts of her data," said Mops. "It's the one planet the Prodryans have come across that they neither colonized nor destroyed. From the recon drones and security platforms spread through the system, whatever's on that planet, the Prodryans don't want anyone else to find it."

"Sounds like a long shot," said Gabe.

"It is," Mops admitted. "The top stripes in the Alliance agree. But if there's a chance something on Tuxatl could give us leverage to help end this war, I'm willing to spend my final days hunting for it."

Nobody spoke.

"You're the only ones who know my condition," she continued. "I'd like to keep it that way until we finish our mission. But if anyone would prefer to leave—"

Cate straightened, his wings snapping open in his eagerness. "I prefer to leave!"

"If anyone who isn't an enemy combatant and spy would prefer to leave, you may," she clarified.

"This is madness." Cate spun to face the rest of the crew. "Bad enough you mean to visit a planet so dangerous even my people avoid it, but to follow a dying woman who's falling into primitive madness is suicide. If Tuxatl and its inhabitants don't kill us, the captain will!"

"I trust her," Monroe said evenly.

Cate glared at him. "Sentimental foolishness. Another example of human inferiority."

Grom slid closer. Their spines had mostly settled. "How predictable is this condition? How do you know you won't make contact with the natives and end up eating their leader's face?"

"Or infecting them," Azure said quietly. "Like the Rokkau did to your people."

"A reverse *War of the Worlds*," added Gabe.

Mops frowned. Doc whispered, *"A nineteenth century science fiction novel by H. G. Wells. Invading aliens were defeated by human germs. I'll add it to your reading queue."*

Her reading list held far more books than she'd be able to get through in the time she had left. Doc knew that as well as she did.

"That's one of the reasons I'm telling you." Mops' throat knotted, a dam threatening to block her words. She forced them through. "According to Azure, I should have time to finish this mission. I want you all watching me in case she's wrong. Doc will monitor my vitals and relay them to Azure and Monroe. If I start to slip away, you're authorized—you're *ordered*—to take whatever steps are necessary to relieve me of command and ensure the success of the mission."

She looked from one face to the next, checking their reactions. Shock, grief, sadness, fear . . . the same maelstrom she'd been swimming through since Azure told her. Her gaze stopped on Kumar, who stared unmoving at the floor, fists clenched at his sides. Tears dripped down his cheeks. Softly, she asked, "Are you all right, Sanjeev?"

He slashed a sleeve over his face. "Fine, sir."

He lied worse than a Prodryan, but Mops chose to respect the lie. She called up what information they had on Tuxatl. "Admiral Sage's records included the initial biological survey from the Quetzalus. They say there's minimal chance of cross-contamination with Alliance species—or with the Prodryans. Admiral Pachelbel's people have reviewed their work and concluded the same. Azure, I want you to double-check anyway."

"Yes, sir."

"Kumar, take charge of the pre-departure checklist." He'd do better with a checklist to work through. "I don't want to get halfway to Tuxatl and discover we forgot toilet paper."

Gabe chuckled and shook his head. "It's 2252, you have a spaceship that goes faster than light, and we're still using toilet paper."

"Technology breaks," said Monroe. "It's a universal truth. So when it comes to vital functions, you keep things as simple and straightforward as possible."

"Despite the strenuous protests of the Tjikko," added Grom.

Gabe cocked his head in a wordless question.

"You haven't encountered the Tjikko yet," said Mops. "There aren't currently any on Stepping Stone. They're essentially sentient trees. You can understand why they might find the concept of toilet paper offensive."

Gabe whistled softly. "Got it."

"Monroe, I'd like you to look over my preliminary notes for the attack on Strikes from Shadows. The rest of you have your duties." She waited for further questions or objections. None came.

Mops had planned to say more, to thank them for their trust in her and in each other, and for how they'd spent the past eight months adapting to challenges no SHS team ever expected to face. She'd planned to tell them there was no crew she'd rather be with, no ship she'd rather be on, for her last mission.

She got through, "Thank you," and then her throat tightened again.

From the looks on their faces, it was enough.

Mops swallowed hard. "Dismissed."

Krakau Alliance General Session 126.14b

Agenda Item #2: Reprimand and Vote of No Confidence in Alliance Military Council

Secretary General: The Nusuran representative may proceed with the introduction of zir proposed resolution.

Niko-Rakalak-Si (Nusuran): Thank you, Secretary General, and thank you to everyone here who supported our resolution. I would be happy to express my gratitude in person after the session.

Secretary General: Point of order. The Nusuran representative is warned, again, to refrain from seducing other members.

Niko-Rakalak-Si: For a species with such flexible tentacles, you Krakau have no sense of fun. All right, fine. Solikor-zi and all colony worlds call for the Alliance Military Council to be censured for their negligence in the matter of Fleet Admiral Belle-Bonne Sage and her crimes against Alliance species.

Further, the Nusuran people note that the Krakau have controlled the Alliance Military Council since its formation. Under their leadership, the war with the Prodryans has lasted more than a hundred years. During this time, the Krakau concealed the fact that their human mercenaries were created by Krakau and Rokkau bioscience. The Krakau are also accused of the attempted genocide against the Rokkau people.

Therefore, we formally demand the leadership of the Alliance Military Council immediately step down and go fuck themselves.

Zixal Quellos (Quetzalus): Seconded.

Eliza Gleason (Earth): We've heard rumors of a Rokkau prison planet. When will the facts of this alleged prison, including its location, be made public? When will the Rokkau be given Alliance representation?

Secretary General: The Rokkau situation is being discussed in another committee. Rest assured, the reintegration of the Rokkau is proceeding—

Zixal Quellos: We're supposed to take a Krakau's word for that?

Eliza Gleason: I've been working closely with Admiral Pachelbel in the reintegration discussions, and can confirm that things are progressing. However, neither Earth nor the Rokkau are satisfied with the speed of that progress. I would like to propose an amendment to Niko-Rakalak-Si's resolution. The Krakau must present a specific plan, with deadlines, for full reparations to the Rokkau.

Niko-Rakalak-Si: Why have humans been privy to these discussions when the Nusurans were excluded?

Eliza Gleason: Maybe because humans didn't insist the Subcommittee for Cultural Relations immediately establish a pornography exchange with the Rokkau.

Longarm (Merraban): With all respect to the Secretary General and her people, I'm afraid I have to concur with my human and Nusuran colleagues. I support both the original resolution and the proposed amendment.

Niko-Rakalak-Si: Excellent. Let's get on with the voting. I have an important diplomatic orgy to attend this evening, and I need time to stretch and warm up.

A DMIRAL PACHELBEL, COMMANDER OF Stepping Stone Station and Alliance Military Council representative to Earth, appeared visibly older than the last time Mops had seen her.

The bridge screen magnified the white, flaking skin around Pachelbel's eyes and beak, the pale splotches near the ends of her limbs, and the dullness of her skin. Ever since Mops' crew had uncovered Admiral Sage's crimes on Earth, Pachelbel had been working nonstop to clean up the mess. Sometimes it seemed like she was trying to hold the Alliance together with the strength of her tentacles alone.

"I'll be blunt," said Pachelbel. "We have seven EMC warships patrolling the system, but given your reputation, the presence of the *Pufferfish* has been an important deterrent. The Prodryans may decide to probe our defenses once you're gone."

"I'm hoping our attack on Strikes from Shadows will teach them what happens when anyone gets too close to Earth," said Mops.

Despite the toll the months had taken, Pachelbel's mind remained sharp. "The plan is sound. What I don't understand is your insistence on swimming out without a full crew, and without sign-off from the repair team."

"The longer we wait, the closer the Prodryans get to unifying their military against us," said Mops. "Johnny has certified the *Pufferfish* battle-ready."

"I hear she's staying aboard?"

Mops spread her arms helplessly. "She says she put too

much work into this ship to let us smash it up again."
Johnny might not care for Mops and her team, but she'd
clearly come to care for the *Pufferfish*. It would be a relief
to have a qualified engineer on board.

Grom spoke up from their station at the rear of the
bridge. "For the record, it was other people smashing our
ship, not us. Usually."

Both Mops and Pachelbel ignored them.

"There's more, isn't there?" asked Pachelbel. "What
aren't you saying, Captain?"

Not only was Pachelbel the sharpest person on Stepping Stone, she'd been Mops' commanding officer for a
year before her transfer to the *Pufferfish*. Pachelbel knew
her, and she knew damned well when Mops was lying or
holding back.

"It's personal, sir."

Pachelbel didn't move. "If I order you to tell me?"

"I'll remind you that I'm no longer part of the Earth
Mercenary Corps. I report to Eliza Gleason of Earth."

"I figured as much." The Admiral's familiar clicking
laugh eased a little of Mops' tension. "Be careful, and
take care of yourself, Captain. I'll alert Jupiter to be
ready. Pachelbel out."

The *Pufferfish* was prepping for departure when Cate arrived on the bridge. He took everything in, then strode to
the center chair to peer over Mops' shoulder. A light dust-
ing of shed scales fell from his wings onto Mops' sleeve,
like brightly colored dandruff. She brushed them away
and turned her chair, but Cate failed to take the hint. His
people weren't big on subtlety.

Mops cleared her console and stood. "Kumar, we need
a course out of the system, one that takes us past Europa."

"Already plotted, sir." He kept his head bowed. "Stepping Stone has retracted docking tunnels. Tethers and
maglocks are clear. At top acceleration, we should pass

Europa in just over four hours. No, wait. Sorry . . . What's Europa's orbital speed around Jupiter?"

"Once every three and a half days," Gabe said brightly. He was struggling to catch up on his galactic knowledge, but when it came to the local solar system, he was almost as good as the ship's computers.

Kumar ran a quick calculation. "Four hours travel time . . . that's seventeen degrees of a full orbit, which comes to two hundred thousand kilometers. That shouldn't have a significant impact on our arrival time."

"Don't forget Jupiter's moving too," said Gabe.

"I know *that*," he snapped. "I just hadn't accounted for Europa's movement."

Mops coughed quietly.

Kumar flushed. "We're all set, sir."

"What makes Jupiter a superior location to engage Strikes from Shadows?" Cate demanded.

Most of Mops' crew knew exactly what waited on Europa. She could see it in Monroe's tight smile. Only Gabe shared Cate's ignorance, looking blankly from Cate to Mops.

"I like the view," said Mops. "Kumar, take us out. Monroe, how long will Strikes from Shadows need to reach Europa from their current position?"

Monroe double-checked his console. "They're farther out, but his drones can accelerate faster. Roughly five hours."

"Kumar, reduce acceleration to give us a five-hour trip." Mops felt better for being able to act, but this next part of the plan was about as appealing as cleaning up after a Nusuran coming-of-age celebration. She turned to face Cate. "Are you sure about this script?"

Cate's demeanor changed in an instant, from suspicion and defensiveness to twitchy anxiety. "My script is flawless. I would have preferred the opportunity to coach you on your delivery, however. Have you taken the time to practice your lines with an audience?"

"I read it to Doc while I was in the head."

His antennae twitched. "Captain, a machine is hardly

qualified to judge your performance. I, on the other wing, am supremely experienced in preparing witnesses to testify before the highest courts."

Mops didn't know how much time she had left before the reversion caught up with her, but she knew she wanted to spend precisely none of it working with a Prodryan acting coach. "Gabe, we'll need a broad-beam transmission to Strikes from Shadows' position."

"Wait!" Cate looked her up and down. "What about your wardrobe? Where are your weapons?"

"I don't think I can shoot him from here."

Cate fluttered his wings, making the implanted blades around the edges peek out like tiny metal teeth. "If you want Shadows to take you seriously, you have to look the part. Can your uniform be programmed to a better color scheme? Your blandness makes you too easy to overlook. Of everyone on this ship, only Gabe displays the sartorial sense of a true warrior."

Behind Cate, Monroe fought to hide his laughter.

"What color would you recommend?" asked Mops, her voice dangerously soft.

He studied her more closely. "The blazing orange of your sun. I always wore sky-themed armor when I worked in Prodryan courts, and as you know, my record of success was most impressive."

"So you've said." She took a calming breath. This sort of advice, no matter how obnoxiously delivered, was exactly the reason she'd kept the Prodryan on board. "Doc?"

"Preparing smart fabric updates now."

Cate turned to Monroe. "Commander, fetch the captain a sidearm and combat baton."

Monroe folded his arms and raised one eyebrow, an unspoken warning that probably would have gone over Cate's head even if he hadn't been focused on Mops' uniform.

The change began at her collar and flowed swiftly downward, the black brightening to a brilliant orange.

Mops raised her arms. "I look like a signal flare."

"I agree," said Cate. "You haven't the stature to pull this look off. Have your AI add sky-blue trim."

Blue splotches appeared on her shoulders, chest, and legs, a symmetrical pattern split down the center. Her insignia became a bleached white. If she squinted hard, she could see how the additions made her look vaguely like a stocky, thick-limbed Prodryan with her wings wrapped around her body.

"Better." Cate circled her. "The rest of the crew should remain silent and submissive at all times to emphasize your power. Keep the men offscreen if possible so their superior strength and size don't detract from—"

It was then that Rubin entered the bridge carrying a pistol and baton. "Commander Monroe said you needed these for props, sir?"

"Very good." Cate hurried over, plucked the weapons from her hands, and brought them to Mops. "Make sure they're displayed as conspicuously as possible."

Mops hooked the pistol to the front of her harness, then hung the baton from her left hip. Not where she'd normally carry them, but they should be hard to miss. "Rubin, in the future, please avoid handing guns to the enemy spy."

"It's a dummy pistol from the combat range," said Rubin.

Mops checked the gun more closely. She should have noticed that herself. "Good work, thank you."

"I don't suppose we have time to recolor your weapons? No, I suppose not." Cate completed another circle, his mandibles clicking and scraping. "Human eyes are so puny. The monocle helps a little . . . I suppose that's all we can hope for. Would you be willing to shave your head fur? My people find it repulsive."

"I think we're done." Mops returned to her chair and checked their status. The *Pufferfish* had departed Stepping Stone five minutes ago. "You heard him, people. Not a click or a whistle once we start broadcasting. Understood?"

Gabe cleared his throat. "On Earth, we'd say 'not a peep.'"

"Noted. Put me through to Strikes from Shadows."

The tip of Gabe's tongue poked from his mouth. It

happened often when he was concentrating, to the amusement of the rest of the crew. He double-checked his settings, switched the viewscreen to a split display, and pointed at Mops to signal they were broadcasting.

Mops squared her shoulders and tried to ignore her garishly magnified form on the screen. "Attention, Strikes from Shadows. This is Captain Marion Adamopoulos of the *Earth Defense Ship Pufferfish*."

The text of Cate's script scrolled slowly up her monocle. She forced herself to keep reading.

"Bow your head and flatten your barbs at the mention of my name, for I am the victorious flame who burnt Heart of Glass' fleet to ash at the Battle of Dobranok. I am the slayer of Falls from Glory. I am the destroyer of Admiral Belle-Bonne Sage of the Krakau. I am . . ."

From the side of the bridge, Cate made a lifting gesture, encouraging her to continue.

"I am the cleanser who disinfects the galaxy."

"I like it," whispered Doc. *"I think the crew should address you that way from now on."*

"You and your cowardly drones trespass in Alliance space," Mops continued. "If you do not immediately surrender to me, then the mighty *Pufferfish* will destroy your pitiful forces. Your remains will fertilize our worlds, and your name will be spoken no more, save in the recitation of my victories."

She gave a small nod to Gabe, who tapped his console and said, "We're all clear, Cleanser. I mean, Captain."

Mops shot him a glare that would peel hull paint, then turned to Cate. "You're sure this will draw them in?"

"I don't understand how you continue to doubt me." Cate ruffled his wings. "The *Pufferfish* has an impressive battle record. Your destruction would bring honor and prestige to any Prodryan, enough to possibly earn a voice in the conclave. I'd exterminate you all myself if such actions wouldn't result in my death as well."

"Naturally," said Mops.

"Strikes from Shadows will assume he has a greater chance of success against a single cruiser, commanded by a human, than he would against Stepping Stone or Earth.

He won't be able to resist your challenge, especially with the other clans having heard your transmission. He will fight."

On cue, Monroe said, "Strikes from Shadows' fleet is powering up their engines."

Cate eased closer. "Assuming he sends everything, the *Pufferfish* appears to be outgunned roughly thirty-to-one."

"I concur," said Mops.

"You haven't yet shared your plan for defeating Shadows and his fleet."

"Correct." Mops stood and stretched. Five hours to reach Jupiter and Europa. Five hours of waiting. "Monroe, you have the center chair. Gabe, try to listen in on Prodryan chatter. Let me know if you hear anything interesting. Kumar, keep us on track for rendezvous."

"Where will you be, Captain?" asked Cate.

Mops drew the practice pistol. "I want to shoot something."

Mops had set the combat range to labyrinth mode. Configurable display partitions from the walls and ceiling divided the ten-by-thirty-meter room into a dimly lit two-story maze, creating a passable illusion of Glacidae ice tunnels.

Hunching her shoulders, Mops moved up a slight incline of rippled blue ice. A two-meter silhouette popped up ahead. She sighted automatically, but the figure was blue. Hostiles were green. She kept an eye on this one, though—targets could shift color without warning.

The tunnel split in two directions. Mops checked them both, spotted a flash of green to the right, and fired twice. The hostile vanished.

"Cate is once again snooping around the acceleration chambers," said Doc, making her jump. *"This time, he's examining the brig units on deck eight."*

"Why wasn't that area locked down?" Mops calmed her breathing and started down the right-hand tunnel.

"It was. Cate overrode the security lockout."

"What's he doing?"

"I'm not sure." Doc sounded annoyed. *"The security feeds aren't working. That was part of the nonessential ten percent of repairs Johnny's team didn't finish."*

"Put me through to Rubin, please." She waited for acknowledgment. "Rubin, do me a favor and haul Cate out of the brig on deck eight. Or lock him into one of the cells. I don't care either way."

"On my way, sir."

"And see if you can figure out what he was doing down there."

A flash of green from the corner of Mops' vision made her whirl. She squeezed the trigger a hair early. A dot on the wall showed where her shot had gone half a meter wide. Before she could shoot again, there was a bright flash.

The silhouette froze. Green text blinked onto her monocle.

```
You were shot and killed by a Merraban
with a plasma-bazooka.
Your score: 13,180.
Your high score: 204,100.
Would you like to see a slow-motion
replay of your death?
```

"No, thank you." It had been Grom's idea to add features like high scores and instant replay. Mops had been skeptical, but crew time on the range had tripled. To her surprise, she had found herself enjoying the challenge of trying to match her best score. "I would have gotten that one if you and Cate hadn't broken my focus."

"Because most real-life combat situations are so *quiet and distraction-free."*

As the panels retracted, she returned her pistol to the weapons rack in the wall, slamming it home harder than necessary. Had she really just been distracted, or was this another aspect of the gradual mental and physical decay that came with reversion?

"Are you all right? This is when you usually tell me to go format myself."

"Doc, analyze my marksmanship for the past four hours. How does it compare with my usual performance?"

"Everything is within normal human variance."

"That's a non-answer."

"It's a perfectly acceptable response to your query."

"Doc . . ."

With a simulated sigh, he said, *"Your accuracy is down four percent from your mean. Response time down six percent. Overall time to complete a course is up forty-nine seconds. All of which is perfectly normal, considering the additional anxiety of impending battle and the stress of your recent diagnosis."*

"Or it could be part of my neurological decline. We know it's having an effect. Rubin said she could see it in my movements."

"Rubin talks too much."

"She's the quietest person on the ship," Mops said with a snort. She grabbed a towel and wiped the sweat from her face. She closed the weapons locker, powered down the range, and was about to leave when Doc spoke up.

"There's a matter I've been struggling with. Though it pains me to admit, I could use your input."

She started to tease him about asking a human for help, but his tone was flatter than usual. Whatever the problem, he was devoting so much of his processing power he'd neglected his conversational emotion overlay. "What's wrong?"

"All personal AIs are encoded with basic instructions for the death of our partner. Things like security precautions to prevent an enemy from accessing our data. Transfer protocols that allow us to grant access to the appropriate ranking officer. Algorithms for filtering out personal information and other private, nonessential data to be reviewed and deleted."

"That's good. Nobody needs to know how often I scratch my ass in private."

"Three-point-four times per day, on average," he said

immediately. *"For most AIs, these instructions are more than adequate. Humans tend to invest their earnings on things other than software and hardware upgrades for their computerized partners, so those AIs are, frankly, primitive."*

"What are you getting at, Doc?"

"Nothing in my programming tells me how to process such a loss. I've run many simulations, attempting to model my future after you've reverted. None of them are acceptable to me."

Mops draped the towel around her neck and leaned against the wall. "I've been running simulations of my own. Trying to imagine what's going to happen to me. Trying to prepare myself."

"Has it been effective?"

"Not yet. I guess my programming has some gaps of its own."

"Perhaps you should request a firmware update."

She smiled. "Monroe might be a better person to ask about this. He doesn't talk about it much, but I know he lost people when he was infantry."

"Monroe found new connections. New family. Should I attempt to do the same?"

"Yes." Her eyes watered. "Yes, you should."

"But they won't be you."

If he'd had a physical form—one larger than a memcrys lens—she would have hugged him.

"It will be difficult to—" His tone sharpened. *"Incoming shipwide announcement."*

Commander Monroe's voice filled the range. "We've cut engines and will begin hard deceleration in sixty seconds. Projected time to intercept the Prodryans is one hour. All hands to battle stations."

Mops tossed her towel into the laundry chute and left the range. As the door closed behind her, she rubbed her eyes, trying to settle her thoughts.

"You're functioning well within parameters," Doc assured her.

"What?"

"Your hesitation suggests uncertainty."

"You'd be uncertain too."

"I would not." He sounded offended. *"My judgment is based on data, not emotion. My data shows you to be a highly effective captain. And despite the unusual nature of your crew, their success rate is undeniable. Therefore, in my judgment, your doubts are illogical and uncalled for."*

"If your judgment is so great, maybe you should be captain."

"I agree," he said primly. *"I could make you my second-in-command."*

Mops stumbled abruptly forward. For several seconds, it felt like she was on a steep hill. She dropped to one knee to steady herself as her brain fought to reconcile her sense of balance with the evidence of her eyes.

A faint tremor passed through the ship, and the world righted itself. "What the shit was that? The Prodryans shouldn't be close enough to attack yet."

"From the timing, I believe it was an effect of our deceleration."

The ship's gravity plates were supposed to compensate for such maneuvers. "Monroe, what's going on up there?"

"Stand by, Captain." His response was terse. She heard Gabe swearing in the background and Grom chittering with low-key panic.

She sprinted for the closest lift.

"The purpose of a test run is to discover any problems before commencing the larger mission, yes?"

"That's right."

"I suspect this has been a successful test run."

Mops stepped into the lift and hit the controls for the bridge. "Doc?"

"Yes?"

"Go format yourself."

4

Dear Grandmother,

Thank you for your latest databurst, and congratulations! My new aunt is adorable, and she has your coloration! I'm so happy for you.

I've been spending most of my time lately studying human biology. One of the humans on board is immune to the Krakau plague, which means I've been able to compare him to "cured" humans. We have a good understanding of how humans were changed into their present form, but nobody knows how to reverse the process. That will take many years yet.

The Pufferfish has a Krakau now, an engineer. We try to avoid one another, but that's difficult with such a small crew. It's strange how much easier it is for me to trust the aliens on board than someone from my own planet of origin.

To answer your question, yes, I've been making friends. A Glacidae named Gromgimsidalgak invited me to join their co-op gaming league. I play a Comacean pirate named Fisheye. And I've been talking to Vera Rubin, one of the humans. She's not *a trained biologist, but she's taught herself a lot, and she's been to many different worlds. She even has a small branch of glow-coral from Dobranok. She said she'd give me a nodule the next time it blooms.*

I can't tell you where we're going when we leave the human system. It's secret. But I can tell you it's not supposed to be a combat mission. Don't worry about me. Captain Adamopoulos takes good care of her crew. I'm sure we'll be safe.

I'm worried about her. I'm not supposed to talk about why. But if you get the chance, please sing a song for her strength and health.

I'll send another burst as soon as we're back in-system. And yes, I'll write my mothers before we go.

> *Love,*
> *Azure (That's what the*
> *humans call me)*

MOPS STEPPED OUT OF the lift and paused to take in the chaos on the bridge. Kumar was struggling at Navigation, his face sleek with sweat. Monroe and Johnny were shouting at one another. The engineer had swelled with anger, and Monroe's finger twitched like he was squeezing an imaginary trigger. At Communications, Gabe sat very still, like prey hoping to avoid the attention of predators. His wide eyes moved from Monroe to the viewscreen and back.

Mops checked the screen. There were no hostiles in range, no proximity alerts. They hadn't hit anything. They hadn't been shot. The lack of level one alarm messages meant they weren't in imminent danger of exploding, which was reassuring.

Less comforting was the oblong object tumbling away from the ship, jets of white gas shooting from its broken pylons. "Isn't that the *Pufferfish*'s weapons pod?"

The bridge went quiet.

"Yes, sir," said Monroe.

"I remember it being attached to the ship when we left Stepping Stone." Mops walked slowly toward the center chair. "Where do you think it's going?"

"Jupiter," said Kumar. "If it continues on this course, it should orbit the planet twice before tumbling into the atmosphere." He paused. "Or was that a rhetorical question?"

She continued to watch the screen. The pod rotated slowly end over end, leaving a double-helix of dissipating gas in its wake. The movement was hypnotic, like a Nusuran kinetic sculpture. "Well, people?"

Monroe pinned Johnny with a glare. "Tell the captain what you told me."

Johnny raised herself higher. "This is *not* my fault."

"Not that part." Monroe's prosthetic fist tightened with an audible creak. "What happened?"

"The engineering principles are complex. Because of the reduced crew, much of the *Pufferfish* is in standby mode, operating on minimal power. Now, even in standby, the gravitational plates on every deck are supposed to provide acceleration compensation to maintain structural integrity. In other words, they counter the effect of sudden changes in velocity to protect the crew and, more importantly, the ship. Do you understand so far, Captain?"

Mops eased into her chair and clasped her hands together. She was used to this kind of condescension from non-human races. It still made her want to tie Johnny's tentacles in knots, but she quelled the urge. For the moment. "I think so."

"I'll need to review the logs and run a number of complicated tests to confirm my theory," Johnny continued. "But it appears that internal compensation wasn't strong enough for the suddenness of our deceleration. I'm merely pointing out the facts, not criticizing your navigator. Considering his lack of formal training, he's done an admirable job overall."

The unspoken "for a human" hung in the air like Glacidae flatulence.

"Because of this miscalculation, structural stress increased too swiftly for the backup systems to compensate.

The tension was greatest at the pylons connecting the weapons pod to the rest of the ship. When that strain exceeded certain preset limits, the emergency separation protocols were triggered. Those protocols worked as designed, safely shedding the weapons pod before the stress could tear the ship apart."

Mops pulled up her console and set it to mirror Navigation. According to the flight log, their deceleration had certainly been stronger than acceleration. As Gabe would say, Kumar had hit the brakes a lot harder than he'd hit the gas. But everything was well within tolerances. "Kumar?"

"I followed every step of the navigation tutorial for a variable-speed intercept with an enemy ship," he said tightly. "I ran eleven simulations before we left Stepping Stone. I've been going over each second of our decel, and I can't find any problems. We've done maneuvers with almost twice the delta-vee before, and I've never broken the ship."

"Perhaps you've been lucky," suggested Johnny. "It may be that your prior maneuvers caused stress fractures to develop over time, and today's mishap was the end result. I would be happy to review your logs to help find your error, once I've finished inspecting the *Pufferfish* for additional damage."

"Are we safe to continue maneuvering?" asked Mops. Coasting toward Europa was fine for the moment, but it would help to be able to steer before Strikes from Shadows arrived.

"You should be," said Johnny. "For prudence, I recommend staying under fifty percent of the ship's stress tolerances. I will look over my team's work as well, though I don't expect to find any problems. I personally verified acceleration compensation throughout the ship, calibrating every deck's grav plates to within one ten-thousandth of a percent of specs. That's two orders of magnitude better than regulation, Captain."

To Mops' left, Monroe winced. He'd heard it too, then.

"I'm impressed," said Mops. "I assume you were using the latest official specs for an EMC cruiser?"

"Naturally."

Mops watched her ship's arsenal continue to float away. "Remind me, how many weapons pods does a standard EMC cruiser carry?"

"Three, of course." Johnny stopped, her beak half-open. She turned to stare at the screen. Her skin darkened as her body instinctively tried to disappear against the sandy floor of an ocean light-years away.

"And how many do we have—" Mops smiled, "—forgive me, how many *did* we have on the *Pufferfish*?"

A single note, barely audible, squeaked from her beak. "One."

"I'm not an engineer," said Mops. "I know the principles we're talking about are complex. But wouldn't that mean the *Pufferfish* had significantly less mass than a standard cruiser, and that the distribution of that mass would be completely different?"

If Johnny sank any lower, she'd melt out of her shell. "That's correct, sir."

"I see." Mops let the silence stretch. "Kumar, maintain course for Europa. Keep a light touch. Under fifty percent of tolerance."

"Yes, sir."

Mops should have been furious. Instead, she felt almost lighthearted. It helped to focus on her ship's damage instead of her own. And she doubted the crew would know how to handle a mission where *something* didn't immediately go wrong. "What would it take to go after the weapons pod and reattach it?"

"Two tugs to retrieve the pod and a minimum of eleven days in a repair bay." Johnny straightened. "Captain Adamopoulos, I take full responsibility for the situation."

"Yes, you will." Mops continued watching the departing pod. "What about controlling it remotely? Could we maneuver and fire it from here?"

"Negative," said Monroe. "Weapons controls are hardwired to minimize the chance of enemy hacking."

Mops nodded. She knew that, dammit.

"We're defenseless," said Grom.

"Not true." Kumar turned around. "Our energy dispersion grid remains functional, and electronic missile countermeasures can be broadcast from here. It would be more accurate to say we're offenseless."

"Should we turn back, Captain?" asked Monroe.

Even if she'd wanted to, such a spectacularly embarrassing failure would only embolden the Prodryans. "Johnny, make sure the separation went as perfectly as you say. Inspect everything. If we took the slightest microfracture, I want it documented and fixed. When you've finished there, you'll review every repair you and your team completed. Make sure everything is up to specs and calibrated *correctly*. The next time something falls off my ship, I'm sending you out to bring it back. Without a suit. Is that clear?"

"Perfectly transparent, Captain." Johnny brought one tentacle to her head in a passable salute, then raced toward the lift, her lower limbs squelching in her haste.

"Strikes from Shadows is signaling us," said Gabe.

Naturally. No way had he missed the *Pufferfish* breaking in two on the way to battle. "Doc?"

"One wardrobe upgrade, coming up." Mops' uniform once again took on the orange-and-blue color scheme. This time, Doc added a flickering edge of brighter orange running down her sides, like a stellar corona.

A trio of Prodryans appeared on the main screen, superimposed over the tactical display. The frontmost—presumably Strikes from Shadows—wore armor of yellow and pastel green with an excessive number of polished silver barbs. He probably stabbed himself every time he sat down. He spread his wings, blocking out the other two in a display of black-striped green meant to intimidate. To Mops' eyes, the wings were simply . . . pretty.

"Captain Marion Adamopoulos of the *Pufferfish*, I am Assault Commander Strikes from—"

"From Shadows, yes, I know," Mops interrupted. "You have thirty minutes to surrender."

Strikes from Shadows paused, then turned to speak to his crew. Mops couldn't hear everything, but from what she picked up, it sounded like he was ordering his communications and linguistics specialist to confirm the translation. With his wings out of the way, Mops could see the two closest Prodryans shifting uncomfortably.

After a brief back-and-forth, he glared at Mops and said, "I believe I understand. Your reputation is well-known among my people, human. This is a deception. You are attempting to make me underestimate you and your crew."

"Twenty-nine minutes."

An update appeared on Mops' console, sent from Monroe's station. Approximately one-third of the Prodryan drones had changed course to intercept the weapons pod. She tapped an acknowledgment.

"This 'accident' does not fool a trained Prodryan warrior," Strikes from Shadows continued. "I presume your weapons pod is some form of automated defense platform, set to flank us when we attack your ship?"

"Such keen tactical insight," said Mops. "I'm astounded to find you here instead of on Yan, taking your rightful place as Supreme War Leader."

He started to respond, then gnashed his mandibles and turned to consult again with his communications officer. When he turned back, his antennae were rigid with anger. "You mock me, Captain?"

"I do indeed." Mops was impressed. Prodryans had almost as much trouble with sarcasm as they did with lying. "But I'm sincere in offering you one final chance to retreat. Leave our system in peace."

Behind her, Grom added, "Or leave in pieces!"

Mops sighed. "Grom? Don't help."

"This is no longer your system," said Strikes from Shadows.

"Cocky little zounderkite, aren't you?" Mops glanced at Gabe, who gave her a thumbs-up on the profanity.

"Earth will fall to the Prodryans soon enough, but that's not what I meant. This place hasn't belonged to humans for some time. It was taken from you by the Krakau. Now, my people will take it from them. It's the way of things."

"Why?" Mops massaged her temples. It was all so *pointless*. "You've got an entire galaxy. You could spend a million years exploring and colonizing uninhabited worlds, and you wouldn't reach a fraction of what's out there. Why pour so many lives and resources into killing the rest of us?"

She wasn't sure her question could even be translated into Strikes from Shadow's language. The instinctive Prodryan hostility and aggression toward non-Prodryan life was a central pillar of their mindset. Asking a Prodryan about peace would be like asking the tree-like Tjikko to discuss competitive roller skating.

Cate's presence proved those instincts could be controlled, but he was the first to admit he allowed the *Pufferfish* crew to live only because he believed it would give him the long-term opportunity to kill far more non-Prodryans.

Speaking of Cate . . . "Where is our resident spy?" she whispered.

"I believe Rubin locked him in the brig on deck eight."

Eventually, Strikes from Shadows responded. "We're merely purging your infestations before they can spread further. As inferior species, you would die out eventually, even without our intervention. Gunners, launch first salvo."

The transmission ended.

On the screen, green sparks, each representing a long-range missile, spat from the drones and crept toward the *Pufferfish* weapons pod. At this range, a target had plenty of time to disrupt and destroy incoming missiles. This type of salvo was about taking the measure of your target's defenses.

Or lack thereof, in this case. A short time later, the lead sparks struck the weapons pod in quick succession. The pod disappeared. The remaining missiles flew through the debris and circled like a swarm of confused fireflies.

The screen flickered. Missiles seemed to jump from one spot to another as the scanners refreshed and updated.

"External interference," Monroe reported. "Someone's trying to jam us."

"Oh, good," said Gabe. "I thought it was me. Communications are being affected as well, Captain."

"Understood. Expect it to get worse." Mops doublechecked their position relative to Europa. "Monroe, do what you can to scramble those leftover missiles before Strikes from Shadows can redeploy them toward us."

One by one, the missiles winked out. The same signals interfering with the *Pufferfish* would play havoc with guidance systems. With the *Pufferfish* adding to the electronic confusion, the missiles had no chance.

Strikes from Shadows' drones increased speed. The *Pufferfish*'s scanners did their best to track them. Enemy ships turned from green to yellow, meaning the positions were approximations based on last-known course and speed. Every few seconds, a new fragment of data would come through, causing the drones to turn briefly green and jump to their realtime positions.

One such flicker revealed another batch of missiles launching toward the *Pufferfish*.

"Take us out of their path please, Kumar. Drop us five klicks straight down and adjust course twenty degrees to port. Monroe, make sure none of them follow."

A cluster of missiles vanished.

"That wasn't me," said Monroe. "Two missiles must have collided. I'll try to mop up the leftovers."

If they were having this much trouble seeing what was happening, this entire area should be nothing but static to the Prodryans watching from farther out. "Gabe, send a message to Europa."

"Europa? I mean, yes, sir. What do you want to say?"

Mops waited as the last of Strikes from Shadows' ships came into range. "Happy hunting."

Her breath quickened. This was her only gambit. If anything else went wrong . . .

Additional shapes appeared on the screen: irregular blue spheroids clustered around Europa. Only a handful at first. Then dozens. Then more than a hundred, ranging in size from a few meters wide to a monster half a kilometer in diameter.

"Holy shitwaffles," whispered Gabe. He jumped, then turned to Mops. "Um, Europa says to maintain course if we want to stay in one piece."

"Too late for that, but keep us steady, Kumar."

"What are those?" asked Gabe as the first wave of Strikes from Shadows' drones began to wink out of existence.

"Those are some of the stealth security platforms the Krakau put in place around Europa over the years. They're packed with cutting-edge weapons and signal-jamming tech. You've heard about the civil war between the Krakau and the Rokkau? When the Rokkau lost, the survivors were locked away in the oceans beneath Europa's surface. The Krakau deployed a rather obscene amount of military hardware to make sure they stayed put, and to keep it secret from the rest of the galaxy. Four months ago, Earth's leadership became aware of that secret. The public doesn't know it yet, but the Rokkau were granted full control of Europa. And its defenses."

"Strikes from Shadows is retreating," said Monroe.

Half the drones were gone, with more vanishing every second. Strikes from Shadows himself had held back, keeping his ship out of range of the *Pufferfish*'s weapons. The weapons the *Pufferfish* used to have, rather.

"The Rokkau figured out how to interlink the platform targeting systems," said Mops. "It doubles their accuracy and gives their guns three times the range of an Alliance cruiser."

The last of the drones was gone. Only four larger ships remained, all accelerating away on full burn.

"They're showing off," said Monroe. "I'm not picking up the spikes of any energy weapons, and the debris patterns don't look like missile damage. They're doing all this with A-gun fire alone."

One of the ships twisted and fell out of formation, then exploded. Monroe whistled softly. "Pinpoint targeting, right through the engines."

Mops stood and stretched. Tension had locked her shoulder again. She rotated the arm until the joint popped.

The screen went black. When it came back again, only

one ship remained. It was coming about, firing all weapons. Strikes from Shadows had chosen to go out fighting. In the end, he'd proven himself a true Prodryan.

It didn't make the slightest difference to the outcome.

Six platforms fired in unison. Two seconds later, the final ship disappeared.

"Why don't we put some of those around Earth?" asked Gabe.

"We did," said Mops. "Rather, the Krakau did. Not this many, but enough to boost Earth's defenses. And the Alliance has seven warships ready to go after anyone who makes a run for Earth. It should be enough to keep the Prodryans at a distance."

But for how long, she couldn't say.

Gabe's console clicked. He wrenched his attention from the aftermath of the battle, if such a one-sided conflict could be dignified with the term. "Signal from Europa, Captain. Voice only."

Visual would be useless with so much interference. "Go ahead."

A mechanical, crackling voice said, "Greetings, *Pufferfish*. We saw—weapons pod. Do you—medical assistance?"

"We're fine," said Mops. "No casualties. Thank you for your help, Europa."

"—pleasure. I've been wanting—test those platforms."

"I'd call that a successful test. How long until you can cut the jamming?"

"Another five min—weapons to cool down."

"Understood. Thanks again."

"Tell Azure—grandmother says hello."

"Will do. *Pufferfish* out." She watched as, one by one, the weapons platforms began to disappear from the screen. "Monroe, any stragglers from Shadows' fleet?"

"It looks like Europa got everything. That was . . ."

"Depressing," said Mops. "It's all so bloody pointless."

"I was going to say efficient."

In five minutes, the other Prodryan fleets would see the aftermath: Strikes from Shadows' fleet utterly annihilated, and the *Pufferfish* untouched by Prodryan weaponry. "Gabe, record a message and broadcast system-wide as soon as we're clear."

He flipped through a paper notebook, skimmed a page, and tapped his console. "Recording now. Go ahead."

"This is Captain Adamopoulos of the *EDFS Puffer-fish*. Please relay my thanks to Strikes from Shadows' clan. We've been looking for the right time to debut our new weapon." She frowned and shook her head. "Stop recording. It needs a name."

"What new weapon?" asked Grom.

"The one that took out an entire Prodryan fleet in under a minute." Mops pointed to the screen. "If we convince the rest of the Prodryans that the Alliance has a new superweapon, maybe they'll hold back longer."

"What about 'Death Blossom'?" suggested Gabe.

"Because nothing instills fear like flower-based weaponry," said Grom.

Gabe flushed. "It's from an old Earth entertainment vid."

"I like it." Mops signaled Gabe to resume recording. "Death Blossom exceeded expectations. If you'd like more intelligence on Death Blossom's capabilities, by all means, stick around. I'm sure any of the remaining Alliance warships would be happy to arrange additional demonstrations."

Gabe ended the recording and turned to ask, "What if they call your bluff?"

"These are the dregs of the Prodryan military," said Mops. "Their best and brightest are back on Yan. I suspect at least a couple of these fleets will turn tail and race home, wanting to be the first to bring word of the Alliance's terrible new Death Blossom."

She checked Navigation. "Kumar, do we have a course out of the system for the jump to Tuxatl?"

"Yes, sir. Three hours, and we'll be clear for the jump."

"We're still going to Tuxatl?" asked Gabe. "With no weapons?"

"Strikes from Shadows had plenty of guns." Mops pointed to the screen. "It didn't do him much good."

"No offense, Captain, but I don't think your logic tracks."

"Whatever's waiting for us on Tuxatl, a single ship's weapons pod isn't going to make a difference," said Mops. "This is an exploratory mission. We'll be contacting the natives and searching the planet. Diplomacy and negotiation will be more important than military force."

"Not our greatest strengths," said Grom.

Mops chose to ignore that. "I'd call this a successful test drive. Good work, people. Doc, have Johnny get me an updated status report before we jump."

A private message icon appeared on her monocle. Mops focused on it, and the message appeared.

```
Monroe: Was this a test run for the
ship, or for the Captain?
```

Mops touched a swollen dot of fresh scab at the base of her neck, one of many sites where Azure had implanted subdermal medical scanners to better monitor Mops' condition.

```
Mops: Yes
```

Advocate of Violence: Mission Progress Report

Captain Adamopoulos persists in her determination to reach the world of Hell's Claws, which the Alliance calls Tuxatl. She has ignored all warnings and wisdom. I'm beginning to suspect my objections make her more determined to seek out this planet. Human nature is contrary and confusing.

It's unclear whether Adamopoulos' stubbornness is related to her condition. The Rokkau Azure has confirmed that Adamopoulos is reverting to her feral state. Current timeline is unknown, but not expected to exceed two Earth months. My hope is to seize control and slay Adamopoulos myself before she succumbs. For a non-Prodryan, she has been a worthy adversary, and deserves a better end than this disease would give her.

The Red Star Clan will be pleased to know I personally arranged the elimination of Strikes from Shadows, who was stationed on the outskirts of the human system. The Pufferfish was quite thorough in destroying him and his drones. I haven't yet discovered exactly how this was carried out. See attachment "Death Blossom" for additional information and speculation.

I've completed most of my preparations for our jump to Hell's Claws. Unfortunately, such preparations were interrupted by the human Vera Rubin and her fully charged combat baton.

I will make one final attempt to help Captain Adamopoulos, but I have little hope of making her see reason.

THE CLOSER THEY GOT to the jump point, the more Mops' doubt grew, rising around her like the tide.

Under better circumstances, the Alliance would have sent a proper contact and exploration team to Tuxatl. Instead, they had their tentacles full building up their fleets and trying desperately to hold the Alliance together. Sending even one ship to a quarantined world based on the hunch of a disgraced admiral was out of the question.

That left Mops and the *Pufferfish*.

"Have you finished reading yet?" asked Cate.

Mops rubbed her eyes and turned away from the 6000-word legal brief displayed on her desk. Another screen showed the Prodryan blockade around Tuxatl. Various satellites, mines, and drones covered the projection like pepper on an overspiced Tjikko nut. Larger icons marked suspected fighter hives. She slashed a hand through the air, clearing both screens. "Legally speaking, am I allowed to just shoot you?"

Seated opposite her, wings hanging awkwardly to either side of his chair, Cate tilted his head. "According to Alliance law, not unless we're in an immediate military conflict and I commit an act of treason or insubordination that causes direct harm or risk of harm to others. Or if I use a stolen bubbler for purposes of seduction."

"What?"

"It's an old law, enacted ex post facto more than a century ago following a diplomatic incident involving a Krakau admiral's pet."

"Were Nusurans involved?" guessed Mops.

"Surprisingly, no. The thief was a rogue Tjikko, believe it or not. I'd be happy to send you the relevant legal analyses." He brushed his mandibles. "Back to your question. By Prodryan law, given my various activities and stated intentions, you'd be disciplined for *not* having killed me yet. The trouble is that this is officially an Earth ship, and Earth law hasn't been fully codified or documented. Without statute or precedent, it's impossible for me to provide an accurate answer to your query."

"I see."

He paused. "I take it your question wasn't an inquiry, but a threat?"

"It was."

"I'd hoped my logic would persuade you, not aggravate you further." He let out a chittering sigh. "You still plan on going through with this mission? Despite the many thorough and compelling objections I've presented?"

"Correct." She could see his Prodryan bravado warring with genuine fear. His limbs glistened, a Prodryan threat response. The barbs on his forearms twitched rhythmically, and his antennae quivered. "What is it about Tuxatl that frightens you?"

"Only the Alliance calls it Tuxatl. The planet's official name is Hell's Claws. All contact with the planet or its people is forbidden."

"Why?"

He didn't answer.

Mops pulled up an old mission log on her desk display and spun it so they could both see. "Eleven years ago, the Quetzalus sent an exploratory party to Tuxatl. They called the natives 'Jynx,' describing them as small and primitive, with a mostly nomadic society. Unfortunately, the Quetzalus were slaughtered by a Prodryan war fleet before they could learn more about the Jynx and their culture."

"Slaughtered in proactive self-defense!"

"That's the most Prodryan phrase I've heard all week," Doc said quietly.

"The Quetzalus should be grateful," Cate continued. "Better a quick and efficient death by Prodryan warriors than whatever fate Hell's Claws held for them."

"Two years later, the Alliance sent a larger force to investigate," said Mops. "The Prodryans launched a joint fleet—warships from at least four clans—to chase them away. I assume that escalation was proactive self-defense as well?"

"In my expert legal opinion, yes."

Mops cleared the reports and pulled up a projection of Tuxatl, a ringed world slightly smaller than Earth. She let it complete a full rotation between them before asking the question Admiral Sage had asked again and again in her notes. "The Jynx's most advanced weapons are single-shot firearms. A lone warship could orbit the planet and burn the continents one by one at their leisure. Why haven't the Prodryans wiped out the Jynx and either claimed or destroyed this world?"

Cate's wings sagged. He fidgeted with his mandibles, a sign of uncertainty.

Mops sighed. "You don't know that, either."

"I know the Prodryans discovered Hell's Claws years before the Quetzalus. The details are classified, but nobody who touched down on the planet ever returned." He turned away. "Captain Adamopoulos, my superiors believe Hell's Claws and its inhabitants to be more dangerous than the entire Prodryan military."

"That must be hard to admit."

"It's a serious blow to our pride, yes." He leaned forward. Dust drifted from his wings onto Mops' desk like colored snow. "This planet killed the finest Prodryan warriors. It baffles the finest Prodryan minds. How can you hope to triumph with only a broken Alliance cruiser and a desiccated crew?"

"Desiccated?"

"I believe it's the Prodryan equivalent of 'bare-bones,'" Doc whispered. *"Essentially a skeleton crew. Whereas the internal skeleton is generally the last part of a human to decompose, dead Prodryans rot from within, leaving an empty husk."*

"Our mission isn't to fight the Jynx," said Mops. "I intend to talk to them. I want to understand them, and maybe find a way to cooperate for mutual benefit."

Cate stared at her for so long she started to wonder if his translator had malfunctioned. "You mean to *befriend* the Jynx?"

"That's the goal. Or are you going to tell me that won't work either?"

"I . . . don't know." He looked shaken. "We've never considered such a radical and unorthodox approach."

"Unorthodox is the *Pufferfish*'s byword."

"This ship and crew have been unexpectedly effective under your command," Cate admitted. His antennae curved forward attentively. "How do you think their performance will be affected by your impending death?"

Mops expected to feel anger at the casual cruelty of the remark. Instead, after a moment of shock, she realized she was *chuckling*.

"Laughter in the face of death is a sign of courage," Cate said approvingly. He leaned closer, examining her expression, and added, "Or madness."

She laughed harder. "Thank you, Cate."

"For what, exactly?"

"For not light-stepping over the truth like a Glacidae crossing thin ice. For seeing me as broken and dying, but not *fragile*." Sure, it was because Cate was an asshole who simply didn't give a shit about human feelings, but it was refreshing nonetheless, like that first breath of open air after spending an entire shift sealed in an environmental suit. "As for the crew, I expect them to continue performing to the best of their abilities."

Cate gave an exaggerated nod. "In other words, we're doomed."

She couldn't tell if it was intended as a joke. The translator didn't capture nuance well, and she didn't think she'd ever heard Cate make a joke before. She laughed anyway.

Maybe he was right. Maybe there was an undercurrent of madness to her thoughts. She'd have to watch for that.

Cate stood. "If you won't be dissuaded from this suicide mission, there are matters I need to take care of before we jump."

"Like sabotaging the ship's acceleration pods?"

He froze. "As I explained to Rubin, I was simply inspecting the technology. The only sabotage I've committed on this ship was to Grom's personal audio device. Glacidae opera is not to my taste, and the bass makes my exoskeleton vibrate."

"Thank you for that," said Mops, and meant it. "Humans can't hear sounds that low, but I feel them in my teeth." She pulled up an inspection report. "I know you haven't sabotaged anything yet. Johnny went over every pod you touched."

"Johnny also inspected your weapons pod."

Mops tilted her head, acknowledging the point. "At first, I thought you were looking for a way to disable the crew's pods. The instant we jump, everyone else gets crushed to organic pudding, leaving you to take the *Pufferfish* for yourself."

Cate scoffed. "Even had I considered such a plan, and this should not be construed as an admission, the *Pufferfish* has too many built-in safeguards and pre-jump checks that would alert you to such alterations. To bypass them all would require reprogramming four core subroutines, physically rerouting the primary and backup power lines, and disabling the redundant sensors that monitor power usage.

"It would be simpler to leave the pods intact and adjust the autoinjectors to administer a fatal overdose of pre-jump sedatives and medications, but I would need another three and a half days and access to secure medical supplies to carry out such a plan." His left antenna twitched. "Hypothetically."

"Much easier to adjust a single variable in a single pod's software." Mops scrolled through Johnny's notes, but kept most of her attention on Cate. "The end-time, for example."

Cate didn't move.

"Instead of trying to keep the rest of us from waking up, you could set your own pod to rouse you mid-jump. Given the distance to Tuxatl and the duration of the journey, you'd have almost half a day to leave your pod and roam the ship before you had to go back down. Two rounds of jump sedatives and stimulants would be hell on your body, but it could be worth it."

"Did you know certain Earth laws give the accused the right to refuse to answer questions? Prodryan law would never allow such foolishness, but I believe in this case, I'd like to invoke that right by requesting a fifth."

"You could shoot every one of us while we slept."

"I have no intention of shooting anyone." Cate looked away. "Not since I learned you'd locked me out of the ship's armory."

Mops smiled. So much for refusing to answer. "Then how did you plan to kill us?"

"I'm offended you think so little of me, Captain." He appeared to mean it, but continued before she could respond. "I'm no thick-shelled ground-walker like Strikes in Shadows. Living prisoners are too valuable to waste. I simply liberated several canisters of your hull sealant compound, which I could use to trap you in your pods after our arrival. Thus giving me total control of the ship and crew." He brushed a bit of dust from his arm. "Hypothetically."

"That's not a bad plan," Mops admitted.

"The hull sealant was inspired by your own tactics. You and your people have a remarkable ability to think against the wind, and to take advantage of your limited knowledge and expertise. It's doubly impressive, coming from humans."

"How would you like to become one of my people, officially?"

His head tilted to the side. "I don't understand."

Mops brought up the projection of Tuxatl and known Prodryan defenses. "We know the Prodryans are entrenched, ready to attack any ship that jumps into Tuxatl space. But if your plan worked, that would change everything. A captured Earth ship commanded by a Prodryan spy? That's a prize they'll want to keep intact."

"You . . . you want me to join your crew and turn against my fellow Prodryans by *pretending* to take over your ship?"

"I'm not asking you to betray your people. Not all of

them. I just want your help reaching Tuxatl without getting blown up."

"What about the weapon you used to so thoroughly obliterate Strikes from Shadows' stench from the galaxy? Why not use your Death Flower to overcome our defenses at Tuxatl?"

It was good to know Mops and her team could keep a secret even from a trained Prodryan spy. "I'm afraid the weapon doesn't work that way. We need your cleverness and expertise to get us through the blockade."

"Direct deception is not our strength, as you well know. Unlike weaker races, we don't turn away from reality. Prodryans are taught to face the truth, not to fear it. Lying is alien to us."

"Monroe will coach you. As for the rest, consider it a test of Prodryan security. If we successfully reach Tuxatl, you'll have discovered a weakness you can report to your superiors. That should give your clan leverage over whoever's in charge at Tuxatl, right?"

"True." He rubbed his forearms together in thought.

"Report to Monroe." Mops shooed him toward the door. "But first, turn that stolen hull sealant over to Kumar!"

Sound carried differently in an empty bridge. Mops' footsteps were sharper. Louder.

Control consoles were on standby, and the main viewscreen was off. The only exception was Navigation, which displayed the countdown to their jump.

Mops circled the bridge one final time, enjoying the quiet. Everyone else was secure in their acceleration pods. For the bridge crew, this meant their seats had recessed into the floor, where they had been partially encased in gelatinous cushioning. A series of pre-jump injections prepared their bodies for the stress of faster-than-light travel.

The A-ring had been deployed twelve-hundred meters

ahead of the ship and was spinning up to speed, warping gravity and distorting space.

A-ring tech always made Mops' brain hurt. She understood the basic concept of directionally compressing space. Each ring had a depth of roughly a meter, but in passing through that ring, a ship was actually crossing many kilometers of space.

On an interplanetary scale, kilometers were nothing. What mattered was the acceleration the ship acquired in the process. A-rings were essentially acceleration cannons, shooting ships at speeds significantly faster than light. A second A-ring decelerated the ship at the end of the journey.

Watching the simulated swirl of space on screen, all she could think was that it looked like an oversized toilet preparing to flush the *Pufferfish* halfway across the galaxy.

"Not the most flattering image," she muttered.

"What's that?" asked Doc.

"You don't want to know." She turned her attention downward, toward Tactical. Her monocle brought up Monroe's vitals. Beneath the floor, he was conscious and alert. His heart rate and respiration were both slower than usual, courtesy of the preparatory sedative he'd received.

One by one, she checked the rest of her crew, making sure they were secure. Grom was out cold. Rubin was listening to a xenobiology lecture.

She spent extra time looking over Gabe's readings. This would be the first time sending an unmodified human through an A-ring. Stepping Stone's doctors and engineers had subjected poor Gabe to a litany of tests, adjusting medications and reducing thresholds for gravity compensation to make sure the G-forces wouldn't give him a stroke or an embolism or collapse his lungs . . . Unmodified humans were simultaneously tough and fragile. Injuries that would inconvenience Mops or the rest of her human crew could kill Gabe instantly.

"How are you doing down there, Gabe?"

"Never better." His response over her comm sounded

tense. She imagined sweat beading on his dark skin. "These acceleration rings, they work better than your weapons pod, right?"

"Don't worry. Every A-ring comes with a money-back guarantee. This should be the safest part of the mission."

"From what I've heard in your mission reports, that's not as comforting as you think." He sighed. "I read so much from Earth scientists and physicists. They all agreed FTL was science fiction, not fact. Obviously, we had it wrong. But there's still a part of me expecting relativity to catch the ship in a headlock. Time slowing down, my mass becoming infinite, every atom in my body transforming to energy. I suppose if I have to go, turning into a miniature supernova would at least be quick . . ."

"I don't believe anyone has ever spontaneously exploded from an A-ring jump," Mops assured him. "You might throw up, though."

"How many jumps have you made?"

She chewed her lower lip, trying to think back—

"Forty-six," said Doc.

Mops relayed the number. "I haven't exploded yet, and the only mass increase I've noticed was because of this wonderful Merraban restaurant on Coacalos Station."

His respiration and heart rate were slowing. "This past month has been a dream. I've been living on a spaceship, working with people from other planets. Now I have the chance to see another world . . . I never dreamed I'd be so lucky. I know we're at war. I know about the Prodryan raids on colony worlds. I've seen the casualty reports, the lists of ships lost in combat. But . . . *damn*, you know? I've felt like Charlie in the chocolate factory. I was so caught up in the wonder, I didn't have time for the negative."

"I thought chocolate grew from a plant."

"Sorry, it's a reference to an Earth book and movie. Three movies, actually. Most people prefer the Gene Wilder version, but I've always liked the 2048 remake with Zendaya as Wonka."

His response did nothing to clear her confusion, but she let it go. "I felt some of that same excitement and amazement the first time I came back to Earth," she said.

"When I wasn't busy running from wild dogs or feral apes, I mean."

"Now I'm trapped in this mechanical coffin, and it's like a month's worth of fear and anxiety are hitting me all at once. I can't stop thinking about everything that could go wrong." He exhaled sharply. "I'm sorry. I know you've got bigger things to worry about."

"That may be, but I can't do a damned thing about any of them right now." Mops returned to the center chair and sat back. It reclined automatically and descended into a shallow rectangular chamber. The walls here were dull brown tile. Overhead, the floor—now ceiling—slid back into place, so close she could lift her head and bump her nose against it. Light strips along the edges flickered to life. "Tell me what it was like growing up on Earth."

"I don't have much to compare it to. It was all right, I guess. There weren't many of us kids, so we all spent a lot of time together. Most days you did your chores, studied with the librarians, and if you had time, maybe played a few games of chase or feral tag."

"Feral tag?"

"One person is feral. They chase the rest of us, trying to tag someone. Whoever they touch turns feral too. And on it goes, until there's only one human left. It was morbid, but we didn't know any better. When you're a kid, it's all normal. Then you get older and start to understand life wasn't always like this. I read so many books, but it didn't click that the world had ever been so different. The idea of living in Paris or New York or even on some suburban cul-de-sac was as alien and fantastic as living on Pern or Arrakis."

Mops had no idea where most of those places were, but his vitals were continuing to calm down, so she didn't interrupt.

Nozzles at the base of the walls extruded a thick gel that enveloped her legs and torso. She grimaced. The stuff was supposed to be body temperature, but it always felt a little on the chilly side. Sharp pressure in her lower back signaled the injection of her pre-jump meds.

"When I turned twelve, I started doing rotations in

cataloging, preservation, translation, audio/visual," Gabe continued. "We all needed to find how we could best contribute to the library's mission. I ended up in A/V. Watching those old films, listening to the books, I discovered another 'alien' experience from old Earth."

"What's that?"

"Hope." He chuckled. "Until your crew showed up and all hell broke loose with Admiral Sage's experiments, I figured I'd live and die in that shelter, never traveling farther than a camel could take me. You know we weren't preserving all those books and records for ourselves, right? It was for whoever found them after we died out."

"I understand. But try to hold onto that hope if you can. We're not dead yet." Mops removed her monocle and slipped it into its padded pocket. "And you should probably brace yourself."

"Huh?"

Technology could only do so much to compensate for the sudden acceleration as the *Pufferfish* passed through the A-ring and shot into deep space. It felt like a Quetzalus had sat on her chest.

She knew it was pointless, but she fought to remain conscious, just as she'd done for the forty-six jumps before. She exhaled hard, tightened her core, and listened to her heartbeat pounding slowly in her skull.

For the forty-seventh time in a row, she lost that fight. Her vision narrowed, a rumble like distant thunder filled her ears, and darkness took her.

6

Until recently, Earth had been considered a Krakau colony world, falling under the jurisdiction of Krakau Colonial Military Command. Despite this, the trio of CMC officers glaring at Admiral Pachelbel from her holomist projector had never bothered to adopt Human names. They'd probably never seen a human in person.

Like most of the galaxy, they nonetheless had very strong opinions about humans.

"Adamopolous is chasing ghost currents," said the center figure, a large warrior whose red-and-orange shell made her look like molten rock. Her name was a series of clicks, musical whistles, and color changes that transcribed roughly as °°—%/orange/—°. She was the second most powerful Krakau in the entire CMC, and for as long as Pachelbel had known her, she'd been swimming hard for the top spot. "But in the unlikely chance there is something useful on Tuxatl, why would you entrust it to humans? They'll probably just try to eat it."

"They would not." Honesty forced her to add, "Most of them. Regardless, neither the Pufferfish nor her crew report to the Alliance. I have no authority over their mission."

"Stop bubbling my sac, Pachelbel." Orange spat the

*name, disdain dripping from her beak. "Bad enough you
gave away an entire world. You could have reclaimed
that ship any time you wanted under emergency wartime
powers."*

*"The Alliance didn't give Earth away," Pachelbel corrected, trying to keep her coloration neutral. "We ceded
control to the native sentient race."*

"Barely sentient," said the rightmost Krakau.

*"If Captain Adamopoulos discovers anything on Tuxatl, it could benefit the entire Alliance, including the
Krakau. You've seen her record."*

"Yes," said Orange. "Including her history of mutiny."

"I'm curious how you learned the details of the Pufferfish's mission," said Pachelbel.

*"That's not your concern. All three branches of Krakau
Military Command agree that our priority is the protection of Dobranok and our colony worlds. To that end,
you're ordered to share all information and communications related to the Pufferfish with me."*

*Pachelbel had been expecting something like this. "CMC
has no authority over the Alliance."*

*"The Alliance is dying," clicked Orange. "You'd be
wise to consider your future, Pachelbel. Assuming the
humans don't get themselves killed, I expect you to make
sure anything they find is delivered to our tentacles. Otherwise, you'll find yourself sent to the shallows faster than
you can spit."*

MOPS' MOUTH TASTED LIKE sand. Unpleasant, but better than the alternative. Sand-mouth
meant she hadn't puked during the jump.

"Good morning."

Doc's voice was uncomfortably loud and intolerably
cheerful. One day, Mops was going to pay a programmer
to put Doc through a simulated jump cycle so he could
see how he liked it. She tried to sit up from the gel that
partially cocooned her body. "What's our status?"

Her words were little more than a croak, but Doc understood. *"Happily, we haven't been blown up, and nothing else has fallen off the ship."*

"The day is young."

"The Pufferfish *decelerated four hours and twenty-one minutes ago on the outskirts of the Tuxatl system. We were spotted immediately, as expected. The closest fighter hive is roughly two AUs away. They've launched two squadrons. At this range, we have another eight hours and sixteen minutes before they reach us. Longer, if we maneuver to avoid them."*

Mops strained to pull her right arm from the gel. One by one, her fingers peeled away, each with a quiet squelching sound. Once her hand was out, it was easier to lever the rest of her arm free. She retrieved her monocle and clicked it into place. "How's the crew?"

"Vital signs all within normal range for their various ages and species. The other humans are beginning to stir, with the exception of Gabe, who remains unconscious."

"How is he?"

"Medical sensors detect minor capillary damage, but nothing serious. His eyes will be a lovely shade of red for the next day or two."

"Good. And Cate?"

"Normally, he'd be out for another eleven hours, minimum. However, his pod was programmed to administer the equivalent of human adrenaline to speed the process. He's conscious, but groggy."

"Make sure nobody else opens their pods." Everyone had been briefed on the plan, but your thoughts coagulated after a jump, flowing more slowly than usual or clogging your brain altogether.

She rubbed her other eye, then focused on the display controls directly above her head. Her arm tingled as she opened a line to Monroe's pod. "Nap time's over, Commander."

"How are you feeling, Mops?"

Normally, she appreciated his informality when they were speaking privately. Today his words were irritatingly gentle. Careful and delicate, like he was defusing a damned bomb. "My eyes are crusty, my mouth tastes like shit, and my shoulder's throbbing like a celibate Nusuran. But being stuck in a pod hasn't turned me feral, if that's what you're asking."

"It wasn't, but that's good to know." The familiar pop of his gum made her wish she'd thought to swipe some of his supply to wash the taste from her mouth.

Mops licked her cracked lips. "Will Cate be able to handle communications on his own?"

"He said he could, and Puffy's queued up to assist. He should be fine. If not, Kumar preprogrammed our backup plan into Navigation."

Puffy was the ship's tutorial, programmed to cheerfully advise on everything from advanced communications tech to personal hygiene. Humans fresh from Earth didn't always understand the need for regular showers...

As for the backup plan, it involved turning the *Pufferfish* around and jumping the hell out of there before the Prodryans could reach them.

"Cate has left his pod," said Doc.

"Show me the bridge." Her display lit up with a top-down view of the bridge. "Monroe, you didn't tell Cate about the backup plan, did you?"

"As far as he knows, he either makes this work, or else we all die."

"Good." Cate would happily muck everything up if he knew it meant retreating safely back to Alliance territory and away from Tuxatl.

The lift opened, and Cate staggered out. He managed one step before toppling to the floor. Only the reflexive spread of his wings slowed his fall. He lay facedown for several seconds, limbs twitching, before pushing himself into a sitting position.

"He doesn't look so good," said Mops.

"He has a lot of drugs pumping through his system to keep him up and moving. Or down and moving, in this case."

Cate turned his head, convulsed, and hacked up several soggy pellets. "That's better."

Mops touched the communications icon on the display. "Don't just leave that mess on my bridge. Kumar will have an aneurism."

He wiped his mandibles. "According to *your* regulations, it's my bridge now."

Technically, he was correct. As part of the plan, she'd officially drafted him as a member of the crew, albeit at the lowest-possible rank. As long as everyone else remained inside their pods, Cate was in command by default. It had been Monroe's suggestion, a way of sidestepping his species' inability to lie when he addressed his fellow Prodryans.

Cate pressed one hand to the wall, wobbled to his feet, and adjusted his armor. He'd added several decorations Mops hadn't seen before: a bright silver sash, a braided circlet around his head, and a heavy chain bracelet. He stumbled to center of the bridge and sat in the captain's chair.

Rather, he sat where the captain's chair would have been, if it wasn't currently two meters below the deck, serving as part of Mops' acceleration pod.

He jumped to his feet and glanced around, as if to make sure nobody had seen his fall, then glared at the empty floor. Chittering to himself, he moved to one of the empty stations at the back of the bridge, pulled up the console, and activated the communications module.

Mops needn't have worried. He manipulated the controls like he'd been raised on them.

Or maybe she should worry. Cate's boisterous and self-aggrandizing rhetoric made it easy to underestimate him, but he'd pulled the strings to bring about Admiral Sage's downfall and, with it, the backlash of distrust washing through the Alliance. He'd probably spent countless hours studying the *Pufferfish* until he knew enough to take control for real if the opportunity ever presented itself . . .

"He's signaling an orbital platform around the fifth planet," said Doc.

Cate brushed his arms and turned to face the main screen. With partially spread wings, his voice buzzing with haughty pride, he said, "This is Advocate of Violence of the Red Star Clan. I have taken control of this enemy vessel. The *EDFS Pufferfish* is classified as an apex-level target. Under Amendment 108 of the Articles of War, I order you to cease any and all offensive action against my prize.

"The *Pufferfish* crew are helpless in their acceleration pods. Their knowledge and secrets will speed the inevitable triumph of the Prodryan empire. Be aware that continued aggression against a properly identified apex-level prize will put you in violation of sixteen laws and three inter-clan treaties. As a certified legal advocate, I can detail exactly how you will be stripped of rank, humiliated, and executed if you do not comply with my orders."

Cate ended the transmission and sat back, resting his head gingerly on the console to wait.

Mops touched the intercom function on her console. "Not bad."

Cate clicked disdainfully. "This was nothing. I once argued a case for seventeen straight hours before the supreme inquisitors of Yan, only half a day after molting."

The distance to the fifth planet meant it took more than twenty minutes to receive a response. A group of Prodryans appeared on the main screen, their wings and armor mostly shades of yellow, red, and black.

"Advocate of Violence," said the largest. "I am Guardian of the Abyss, Outpost Commander of this system. I'm authorized to defend Hell's Claws from all intruders. Our mission priority overrules Amendment 108."

Cate pushed himself upright and muttered, "I'd hoped he wouldn't realize that."

"My communications specialist is sending instructions for real-time signal link," Guardian continued. "Comply immediately or be destroyed."

"Does Cate know how to set up an FTL link?" asked Monroe.

Cate attacked the console again. Like the ship itself, communications broadcasts could be accelerated through an A-ring, then decelerated and processed by a receiving ring, but the process required precise synchronization.

Cate reached for the communications pod alignment controls and entered distance and frequency.

A harsh squeal filled the bridge. Cate jumped so hard he nearly toppled over backward. He struck the controls again, and the noise died. "*Alliance* units of measurement," he muttered, clearly annoyed with himself. "Everything in base nine. Savages. What was the charred conversion factor?"

A dot of light appeared in the center of Cate's console. It grew into a cartoonish, personified animation of the *Pufferfish* with overlarge eyes and a frightening smile.

"Hi there," said Puffy. "You look like you're trying to configure faster-than-light communications with an enemy of Earth and the Alliance. This could violate regulations. Are you sure you want to continue?"

"I am," said Cate.

"All right." Puffy beamed. "Let's start by reviewing the fundamental principles of accelerator ring technology and how that technology affects various forms of energy. Please enjoy this informative video clip. You'll be asked nine questions at the end. If you're confused about any terms, tap the—"

"As acting commander of this vessel, I order you to help me synchronize communications at once. If a link is not established within the next minute, I will have you transferred to the plumbing systems and repurposed to fecal output analysis."

Puffy's eyes grew even wider. A red light flashed on Cate's console. "Press that button."

Cate did so.

"Now import these A-ring settings," Puffy continued, illuminating a different section of the controls. "I've set up automatic Prodryan-to-Alliance unit conversion for you."

There was something to be said for Prodryan command style.

Once again, Guardian of the Abyss and the other Prodryans appeared on the screen. For a moment, Puffy stood among them, seemingly part of the Prodryan force. The cartoon icon quickly fled.

"Advocate of Violence," said Guardian. "I have confirmed the status of your ship. Rather than destroy such a valuable prize, I will permit you to surrender *Pufferfish* and her prisoners to me. You will remain here in quarantine while I deliver the ship and crew to Yan."

"And abandon your post?" Cate replied. "As I recall, this sector is of the highest importance, and the penalties for dereliction of duty are quite strict. I could list them for you, if you like. But perhaps a compromise could be reached? You possess superior force, but I possess superior knowledge of this ship. Without me, you'd be likely to miscalibrate a jump and spread your atoms halfway to Yan."

"Anything would be better than remaining in this cursed system," said Guardian.

Cate paused, then leaned in, rubbing his forearms together. "Your tour of duty protecting Hell's Claws has been unpleasant?"

"Yours is the first ship to approach in five months. We have nothing to fight, no communication with anyone outside of the system. Almost everything is automated or run by AI. These fools behind me abandoned their posts to join me at Communications, all out of desperation to see a new face."

"I see," said Cate. "Perhaps I can find a solution that doesn't result in you stealing the *Pufferfish* and exploding. I may have mentioned I'm a certified legal advocate, licensed to practice throughout Prodryan territory?"

"You did."

"I have extensive knowledge of military rules and regulations. I'm certain I can find a way to have you reassigned. Transmit all contracts and conditions of your assignment to me and allow me three hours to review them. In the meantime, you will call off your fighters and allow me to travel freely."

Guardian rubbed a mandible thoughtfully. "Travel where? If you've captured the ship, why come here at all? Why not jump directly to Yan?"

"I took the ship while en route to Hell's Claws," snapped Cate. "It's following a preprogrammed flight plan to the planet. I have no desire to get anywhere near that horrid world, but I need time to override the navigational lock-out. Do we have an agreement, or will you spend the rest of your life guarding this damned place?"

"You have three hours," said Guardian. "I'll have the contracts sent over."

"Three hours from the time I *receive* the contracts."

"Agreed."

"I'll be waiting." Cate killed the connection. "I've saved your life and the life of your crew, Captain Adamopoulos. You are now free to throw them all away with this mission to Hell's Claws."

Mops touched the comm. "Good work."

"For the record, your acceleration pods are a nightmare for exoskeletal species." Cate stumbled toward the lift. "I'll be in my quarters sipping a very old, very fermented pouch of night-clover nectar and waiting for every bristle on my body to stop hurting. Forward Guardian of the Abyss' information to me as soon as it comes through."

"The fighters are decelerating," said Doc. *"Judging from their course change, they're returning to their original hive."*

Mops entered the code to open her pod. The overhead panel slid open, and her chair raised her to her customary place in the middle of the bridge. The last of the gel began to evaporate upon exposure to the cooler bridge air.

One by one, the rest of the bridge crew rose into view, all but Gabe and Grom.

"I'll be damned," said Monroe, slicking back his white hair with one hand. "For a Prodryan, he's got quite the gift for improvisation."

"That wasn't part of your coaching?" asked Mops.

"He was light-years off script." Monroe watched the fighters continue to retreat. "You know, the closer we get to the planet, the harder it will be to get back out if things go to hell."

"'If'? You've gotten optimistic with age." Mops grinned, but there wasn't much humor behind it. "Kumar, maintain course and speed to Tuxatl."

Tuxatl was prettier than Mops had expected.

She'd seen the pictures and videos from the ill-fated Quetzalus colonists, as well as tactical scans from Alliance military ops, but nothing was the same as seeing a new world for the first time through simple optical magnification. No enhancement. No annotations or labels. Nothing but a ringed, cloud-painted planet dominating the bridge viewscreen.

The broad ring was aligned to the planet's equator and sparkled in the sun, all except for a black arc where Tuxatl's shadow blotted it out. Lighting flashed between the inner edge of the ring and the planet below.

The distribution of land and water was similar to Earth's, but the land was a more vibrant green, broken by patches of black. Swirling white clouds covered most of the oceans. Both poles were capped with white-and-blue ice.

"Those trees . . ." Rubin whispered.

From this distance, most of the vegetation was an undistinguishable mass of green. The only exception were the skytrees.

The Quetzalus had described them as "enormous" and "humbling." Their reports didn't capture the half of it.

Thousands of skytrees were scattered across the planet like green-and-black skyscrapers averaging between one and two kilometers in height. Most grew on land, though a few sprouted from the oceans. Both the trees and their shadows were clearly visible.

"They're incredible," Mops agreed. "Any signals from the surface?"

Rubin was covering Communications until Gabe woke up, but she didn't seem to hear. She stared at the screen, entranced.

"Rubin?" Mops prompted.

She jumped. "Sorry, sir. One moment . . . I'm not getting any airborne transmissions. No radio or anything else we could use to contact the Jynx."

"That's expected. According to the Quetzalus, the Jynx were beginning to experiment with some form of biological telegraph, but that's as far as they'd gotten."

"Captain, you should see this." Monroe made several adjustments to his console, then sent a new image from Tactical to the main screen. He'd filtered some of the light, removed the glare from the planetary ring, and highlighted electrical activity.

Mops whistled a Krakau curse under her breath.

The Quetzalus referred to heavy storms in the equatorial region," said Doc.

"Quetzalus have a gift for understatement." The lightning Mops had seen before was now revealed to be a wall of electricity dancing between the planet's ring and the equator. It stretched away in both directions, presumably encircling the entire planet. Where the lightning crossed ocean, it created enormous clouds of steam.

Kumar raised a hand. "I respectfully request we avoid landing near that."

"Agreed," whispered Mops. "Is it a natural phenomenon? The Prodryans couldn't have engineered anything like this, could they?"

"I can't imagine how," said Monroe. "Or why, for that matter. It looks like the inner ring skims the top of the planet's atmosphere. That builds up a constant electrical imbalance, which discharges as lightning."

"What stops the inner ring from losing kinetic energy and falling into the atmosphere?" asked Kumar.

Monroe raised his hands and shrugged. "I have no idea. Lots of glue and repair tape?"

Mops tried to process everything she was seeing. "I need a sense of scale."

"Those bolts can be as high as forty to fifty kilometers," said Monroe. "I can't begin to calculate the amount of energy discharge."

"I can," Doc said smugly.

"The majority of the lightning strikes are confined to a region roughly twenty kilometers wide," Monroe continued. "We're seeing an average of at least one bolt per square kilometer per minute."

The lift opened, and Cate wobbled forth. He was once again dressed in all of his "bells and whistles," as Gabe would say. He jumped back upon seeing the screen, making a crackling, hissing sound Mops had never heard before. "This planet means to kill us all."

"Sounds like you and the planet have a lot in common," said Mops. "How's it coming with Guardian's paperwork?"

He spread his wings and leaned against the wall, keeping one wary eye on the screen. "Guardian of the Abyss is a fool. It's obvious he never had competent legal counsel review the terms of his assignment. The only termination clause involves the literal termination of Guardian and his crew. However, I believe I've found a solution that should satisfy all parties."

"What's that?"

"Normally, I'd be happy to regale you with tales from my successful hunt through the tangled clauses and loopholes of Prodryan military contract law, but that will have to wait. I set my alarm to wake me before our three hours had expired. Guardian will be contacting us momentarily."

"To *wake* you?" Mops repeated. "You've been sleeping this whole time?"

"Not at all! I needed a full twenty-three minutes to discover a way to free Guardian from the bonds of this assignment. I only slept once my work was complete. I am a professional, after all. And don't worry, I only intend to bill you for those twenty-three minutes." He made a shooing motion with his arms. "Leave my bridge, all of you. I need to speak with my client."

Mops and the others crowded around her desk in the Captain's Cove, watching a split display of Cate and Guardian of the Abyss.

"This is a boilerplate contract of service," Cate was saying. "You appear to have done little to no negotiating on your own behalf. As such, the default assumption is that the superior has no obligation to the inferior."

"Are you suggesting *I* am inferior?" demanded Guardian.

"It's not a suggestion." Cate gently massaged the base of his antennae. "The contract explicitly says so in Section four, Paragraph two. Did you read any of this?"

"I read the pay rate," Guardian muttered. "Do you have a solution for me or not?"

"I do." Cate paused, clearly basking in Guardian's eagerness. "I believe our best chance is to argue unintentional fraud. If we can do that, it would nullify the contract as a whole."

"How?"

Cate shifted his balance. He'd taken Mops' chair, but couldn't sit comfortably since it wasn't built for Prodryan wings and exoskeleton. As a result, he had to crouch on the front edge, teetering precariously in the seat of power. "Your contract specifies certain prerequisites, including a minimal level of competence as a warrior. I propose we demonstrate your incompetence."

"Insult me again, and I'll rip the wings from your back," Guardian snarled.

"Thus proving your prowess as a warrior and condemning you to serve out the remainder of your contract," Cate said smoothly. "The duration of which is . . ."

"Six more years."

"You foolish, foolish man." Cate clicked his mandibles in amusement. "Six more years, *with an optional extension* that can be exercised by your employer as many times as they like."

Guardian's wings slashed out. "*What?*"

"See Section twenty-three. According to this, they can choose to keep you here for the rest of your natural life." Cate paused, double-checking something on his console. "On the bright side, it also says you're entitled to a half-percent pay raise with each ten-year extension, assuming you pass your performance review."

Slowly, Guardian sagged. His wings drooped, and his antennae fell limply over his brow. He looked like his armor was about to slough from his body. Mops had never seen a Prodryan appear so utterly defeated.

"How do we prove my incompetence?" he asked.

Cate made a show of reviewing his notes before answering. "According to the contract, your primary responsibility is to keep all unauthorized ships away from Hell's Claws. Logically, the simplest solution would be to allow such a ship to reach the planet. I had initially planned on taking the *Pufferfish* directly to Yan once I gained full control. However, for a small retainer, I could delay that journey and allow the ship to continue to Tuxatl, thus proving your lack of competence and invalidating your contract."

Guardian's head bowed lower. "Agreed."

"Holy fuckwaffles," whispered Mops. She wasn't sure the profanity was right, but she didn't care. "Did he just convince Guardian of the Abyss to not only let us pass, but to pay Cate for the privilege?"

"He did," said Monroe.

Mops shook her head in disbelief. "That could be the most frightening thing I've ever seen."

"Why?" asked Rubin.

"Because it means Cate might be as clever as he thinks he is."

7

*Official Notice of Grievance: Working Out of Class
Filed by Advocate of Violence, PV3, Earth Defense
Fleet*

This letter serves as notice that Private Third Class Advocate of Violence of the EDFS Pufferfish was ordered to perform duties beyond the scope of his rank and assignment, including but not limited to:

- *Assuming command of the aforementioned EDFS Pufferfish while in hostile territory, despite the captain being healthy and able to perform her duties;*
- *Comprehensive legal review of a hostile soldier's duty contracts; and*
- *Extensive consultation regarding the planet known as both Tuxatl and Hell's Claws.*

Per Alliance law, Advocate of Violence hereby requests an immediate reclassification to Chief Warrant Officer 3, *complete with increased pay retroactive to the start of his additional duties.**

Signed,
Advocate of Violence, PV3

———

*The Earth Defense Fleet does not yet have a procedure for WOC grievances. Alliance law should thereby take precedence, as established in Nokala-Tinian-Si v. Lieutenant J.G. Disney.

SELF-GUIDED PRODRYAN MINES CREATED a distant, deadly shell roughly three light-seconds around Tuxatl. The *Pufferfish*'s defensive systems registered more than five hundred individual sensor pings as the closest mines tracked the ship's approach.

"Prodryan law prohibits all craft or technology from getting any closer to Hell's Claws," whispered Cate. "That includes our defensive systems."

"Meaning if we can get past that boundary, they won't follow?" asked Mops.

"Correct." Like the rest of the crew, Cate's attention was fixed on the viewscreen and the rapidly shrinking distance between the *Pufferfish* and the mines. "Even if Guardian of the Abyss or his successor goes back on our deal, they won't pursue us there."

"Successor?" asked Kumar.

"I prepared a termination of contract letter for him to send to his superiors the moment we cross the minefield."

The bridge felt uncomfortably crowded with everyone gathered here. Mops chewed her lower lip, trying to ignore the claustrophobic feeling, but it was like an itch between her shoulder blades she couldn't quite reach.

Those mines were designed to go after anything that got too close, Prodryan or non-Prodryan. The only thing holding them at bay was the forged beacon the *Pufferfish* was broadcasting, courtesy of Guardian of the Abyss.

The beacon identified them as a Prodryan munitions carrier performing maintenance and upgrades on the mines.

"We've crossed the line of no return," said Monroe. "If the mines come after us, we're too close to escape."

"They won't," Cate promised. "My client made his priorities clear, and Prodryans don't engage in deception."

Grom stretched their body higher. "Will this beacon get us back out through the mines after the mission's complete?"

"As if any of us will survive Hell's Claws," muttered Cate.

"Let's focus on one thing at a time." Mops adjusted the display, zooming in on a spot near the eastern edge of the largest northern continent. Or the western edge of the largest southern continent, depending on which part of space you decided was *up*. "We know the Quetzalus landed here to make contact with the natives. We'll be doing the same, on the assumption that those Jynx might be more open to contact with alien life."

"Or they could attack us on sight, given how that Quetzalus mission ended," countered Monroe. "We might be better off picking a new site and starting clean."

"Do we have any additional theories on what we might find?" asked Grom. "A hidden anti-Prodryan superweapon, maybe?"

"I expect something biological, given the Jynx's lack of mechanical technology." Azure's words were muffled by a mouthful of freeze-dried crustaceans she was scarfing down. She carried a bucket of the things in one tentacle. First Grom and his slushees, now this. Mops might need to establish a no-food rule for the bridge. "Possibly something innate or involuntary."

Johnny clicked her beak. "You think the Prodryans are *allergic* to the Jynx?"

"If that were all, the Prodryans would sterilize the whole planet and be done with it," said Mops.

"Correct," agreed Cate.

"And despite all your connections, all your vast knowledge and experience, you have no hint about what your people are so scared of?" pressed Mops. "You've failed to learn anything concrete about Hell's Claws?"

"Also correct," he said tightly.

Mops turned to Johnny. "What's the status on the drop ship?"

"Fully fueled and ready to launch." Johnny sent a status report to Mops' console. "I've inspected it twice."

"Like you inspected the weapons pod?" asked Azure.

Johnny darkened. "I will not be chastised by a child."

"Knock it off, both of you." Mops studied the map.

"How does this work?" Gabe's eyes were bright red from his time in the acceleration pod, and he'd thrown up during the journey, but none of that diminished his excitement. He was practically bouncing in place. "How often do you make first contact with another intelligent race?"

"Third contact, technically," said Kumar. "The Quetzalus and the Prodryans both got here first."

"And nobody worries about interfering with a species' natural development?" asked Gabe. "We don't have a prime directive or anything?"

Mops had no idea what that meant. "The Alliance has strict protocols for first contact situations. For humans, those protocols are short and simple: get out of the way and let the Krakau handle things."

"Typical Krakau arrogance." Azure crunched down hard on another scoop of crustaceans. Bits of shell fell from her beak back into the bucket and onto the floor.

"Disgusting," muttered Johnny. "Shall I fabricate a bib for you?"

Azure curled the tip of one tentacle and flicked a shell directly into Johnny's eye.

Johnny whistled furiously and lunged at Azure, her tentacles stretching like thick, fleshy whips.

Rubin jumped between them. Monroe was a half-second behind.

One of Johnny's tentacles looped around Monroe's forearm. He clamped his other hand over the tentacle and pulled hard, yanking the Krakau off balance.

At the same time, Rubin caught the pad of Azure's

closest tentacle and jabbed a thumb deep into the soft muscle between the suction cups. Azure whistled in pain and tried to tug free.

"The Prodryans believe any cooperative alliance between species is doomed to failure," Mops said quietly, as if she hadn't even noticed the aborted fight on her bridge. "They say self-interest will inevitably lead us to turn on each other."

"Precisely," said Cate.

Mops looked at Azure and Johnny. "If it's not too much to ask, would you stop trying to prove them right?"

Monroe and Rubin released their holds, but stayed between the two would-be combatants.

"We're through the mines," announced Kumar. "I'm adjusting course to bring us into high orbit." He looked around. "Just in case anyone's interested . . ."

"I'm sorry, Captain." Azure shrank back, curling her pad tight to her body. "But, respectfully, I suggest the next time you need a qualified engineer, you recruit a Rokkau. We invented most of this technology."

"Ancient history," scoffed Johnny. "Given the advancements the Krakau have made, asking a Rokkau to repair a present-day ship would be like asking the inventor of the shell knife to service a plasma rifle."

"Ancient history?" Barbs flexed from Azure's pads. "I grew up hiding on a lifeship. I've never set a single tentacle into a natural ocean. And my family was better off than most Rokkau. Do you have any inkling of what the Krakau stole from us? What we could have accomplished? Your crimes against us aren't history; they're the foundation of our reality."

"Enough." Given the centuries of hostility between Rokkau and Krakau, Mops supposed she should be grateful they hadn't already killed one another. "Johnny, I expect you to comport yourself as befitting an Alliance engineer. Unless you want my report to Admiral Pachelbel to recommend a reduction in rank for your behavior. And Azure . . . Don't make me call your mothers."

Azure and Johnny glared at each other, but backed down.

A green light appeared on the map, close to the Quetzalus landing site. Mops' brow furrowed. "What the hell?"

"Traces of radioactive decay." Monroe's eyes darted to and fro as he read something on his monocle. "About fifteen klicks from the Quetzalus landing site. Energy signature is a tentative match for—Sorry, sir. That can't be right."

He spun back to his console. "I'm rerunning the scans. The computer says it's most likely leakage from a ship's battery. Specifically, a Prodryan ship."

"Wreckage?" guessed Mops. "A downed fighter, left over from when they attacked the Quetzalus?"

"We'd need to get closer to be sure, but I don't think so. We're also picking up faint magnetic fields that suggest buried power lines. This looks like active Prodryan technology."

"Impossible," scoffed Cate. "Your sensors are malfunctioning, or you're misreading them."

"My people know how to read a sensor scan." Mops turned her head and subvocalized. "Doc?"

I can confirm Monroe is reading the results correctly. And our sensors were automatically calibrated and tested when we arrived in-system.

"Could the Jynx have salvaged a Prodryan ship?" asked Gabe. "Maybe they were able to splice the ship's power source into their own technology."

"Could a tik-rat make use of discarded memcrys?" Cate shot back.

Gabe blinked. "I'm going to guess . . . no?"

Everyone began speaking at once, arguing about the implications. Mops raised a hand for silence. "Cate, are you aware of any Prodryan presence on Tuxatl?"

His wings spread like bright curtains. "I am supremely unaware."

Mops tightened her jaw to keep from commenting.

"It's a capital offense to approach even this close," Cate continued. "I could be put to death for being here."

"You objected to this mission," Kumar pointed out. "We brought you here against your will."

Cate brushed his forearms together and spoke in his

most professional and dignified tone. "There are no buts in Prodryan law. If any Prodryans are here on Hell's Claws, they're criminals."

Mops sat back. "Then they sound like exactly the kind of people I want to talk to."

Alliance drop ships were bulky things, built like chubby whales with thick, bulging ribs and a series of oversized adjustable fins running down each side. Heavy plates of black armor covered the hull. From certain angles, the light illuminated the thin glossy lines of the embedded energy dispersion grid.

Two A-gun cannons jutted from beneath the nose, with a larger energy weapon mounted between them, which meant the drop ship was currently better-armed than the *Pufferfish*. Kumar would be in the pilot's seat in the cockpit, with the rest of the landing team in the main cabin. The rear third was cargo storage, packed with food, weapons, and other supplies, including a crate Mops had dragged in earlier from janitorial, a special project she hoped she wouldn't need.

Mops had intended to be first to the docking bay, but Kumar had beaten her there. He was loading additional equipment from a small pile on the floor—mostly food tubes and cleaning supplies.

He straightened when he saw her. "How are you feeling, Captain?"

Mops waved off the question. "Is everything set up at Navigation?"

"Yes, sir." He rocked on his heels, full of barely contained energy. "I pre-programmed orbital adjustments into the system and left my notes in a separate module, indexed and cross-referenced. All Rubin needs to do is keep the ship steady."

With Kumar piloting the drop ship, Rubin would stay behind to fly the *Pufferfish*. Mops would have preferred to have her combat skills along, but she was Kumar's only backup on Navigation.

Monroe would remain as well, along with Grom and Johnny. Mops wanted Azure's expertise on Tuxatl, and putting the Rokkau and Krakau on the same team was like mixing ammonia and bleach.

Doc would be in both places, leaving a copy of his core programming in the *Pufferfish*, then reintegrating when they returned.

She hoped the *Pufferfish* team would have a boring, uneventful time, but she wasn't counting on it. There had to be a reason the Prodryans kept their distance from the planet. Nothing had changed since the *Pufferfish* crossed the three light-second mark, but who knew how long that would last? The ship was running with full power to the defensive grids, just in case.

"Greetings, explorers!" Gabe called as he entered the bay. He'd changed into a black shirt and matching trousers, with a blue-striped vest and tie. A black hat with a narrow brim topped off the ensemble. He carried a wooden cane with a spherical glass lens: a recorder from the Library of Humanity capable of gathering video, audio, temperature, electromagnetic activity, and more. He clapped Kumar on the shoulder. "You look almost as eager as I feel."

"I love this part," said Kumar, all but bouncing in place. "Every inhabited planet we visit tells us more about how life works. How different life-forms process available energy and resources. Different physiological mechanisms for producing consciousness." He turned to Mops. "Azure and I were discussing Alliance regulations for collecting biosamples. With this being an Earth ship, those regulations wouldn't necessarily apply, so—"

"We're going down to talk to these people, not dissect them," said Mops.

"Of course not," Kumar agreed. "Not living specimens, at least. But if we happen to find a conveniently predeceased Jynx, one that could be transported back to the *Pufferfish* in secrecy to avoid upsetting the others—"

"That's a hard no, Kumar." She turned back to Gabe. "While I appreciate the fashion sense, I'm going to have to insist on standard-issue uniforms. Unless that getup includes built-in medical monitors, communications tech, and safety features."

"Way ahead of you, Captain." Gabe leaned his cane against the drop ship, undid several buttons on his shirt, and opened it to reveal the sleek black of a regulation, if tight-fitting, Alliance jumpsuit. "Are we copacetic?"

"As long as you won't overheat in all that, we're good."

He retrieved his cane and rested one hand on the side of the drop ship. "Whatever happens, thank you for this opportunity, Captain."

"Nonsense." From the entrance, Cate's chirping scoff echoed through the bay. "Does the grub thank the mudfish for tearing it from the dirt to be devoured? Hell's Claws will be the death of us all." He stopped halfway to the drop ship and waved an arm at Kumar. "What's this human foolishness? Detergents and scrubbers and nano-solvents? You should be packing all available storage space with weaponry and ammunition, infantry drones, and power armor."

"If military force was enough to deal with whatever danger we're flying into, wouldn't the Prodryans have taken care of it by now?" asked Mops.

Cate tilted his head. "A valid point."

Azure was the last to arrive, lugging a portable medical cart behind her with two tentacles. She'd begun loading the cart into the back of the ship when Monroe's voice filled the bay.

"Captain, the Prodryans are ordering us to leave Tuxatl's orbit and be destroyed."

Gabe frowned. "Don't they mean 'or' be destroyed?"

"I doubt it," said Mops. "What happened, Monroe? Did Guardian of the Abyss change his mind after seeing Cate's bill?"

"They're saying Guardian of the Abyss has been executed for dereliction of duty. The acting commander promises us a quick and painful death if we cooperate."

Mops turned to Cate. The Prodryan spread his arms and flexed his wings. "I told him I could get him out of his contract. I did so. I made no claims as to his safety after he delivered the termination letter to his superiors.

Guardian was not good at thinking through the consequences of his actions."

"Monroe, are they coming after us?" asked Mops.

"Negative. The mines are pinging us again, but I think we're safe for the moment. Getting away once you're back, that's going to be a bigger problem."

"Keep me informed if anything changes." Mops gestured to the others. "If anyone has to use the head, do it now. Otherwise, get strapped in. Kumar, help Gabe with his harness."

"Will do, sir." Kumar opened the hatch and waved for Gabe to go first. "Hopefully this will go better than our last drop."

"What happened last time?"

"Our shuttle was shot down, and we freefell most of the way to Earth's surface." Kumar ducked in after him. "Don't worry, nobody should be shooting at us this time, and I've aced four of my last five drop ship landing simulations."

"Four out of five, eh?" Gabe sounded slightly nauseated. "Awesome."

Cate moaned. "As a de facto prisoner of war, forcing me to accompany you violates several key sections of Alliance law. With Earth being a provisional Alliance member—"

"Prisoner?" Mops interrupted. "Not at all! You're a valuable member of this crew, Private Violence."

"Nonetheless, I formally request—"

"You're coming with us," Mops interrupted. "You can either take the drop ship, or I can arrange a HALO jump for you."

He climbed on board without another word. Mops followed, pulling the hatch shut behind her.

The main cabin was segmented into individual support pods on either side, essentially open metal coffins with life support and minimal flight capabilities. Each pod could be ejected in case of emergency. Once on the ground, they were easily converted to personal grav sleds.

Mops sat on the narrow seat and leaned back, feeling the individual clicks as each attachment point locked onto her harness. "Doc, did you double-check that everyone's translator software is up to date?"

"Double-check? It's me. I centuple-checked everything before we left Stepping Stone, then checked again for good measure zero-point-three seconds after we arrived in this system. Everyone's current, but it will take time to gather enough data to fully understand the Jynx. We have extremely limited linguistic data from the Quetzalus. And who knows if we'll be able to fully duplicate Jynx languages. Verbal components, yes, but we could also be looking at body language, scent cues, color changes, or worse. Remember the Prodryan scavenger moth that leaves trail markers for its hive by arranging its droppings?"

"I remember how long it took us to clear the infestation from *Stepping Stone*." Mops shuddered at the memory. The moths had been cocooned in a captured vessel, and a handful had somehow escaped from quarantine. The damned things were like armored sausages with wings. They could reproduce asexually, so even a single survivor meant a hundred more moths a week later. "Hopefully Jynx languages are more straightforward."

Mops took a seat directly opposite Cate. His jury-rigged harness was pulled taut around his thorax and upper arms. His wings were squeezed tight, the edges jutting out around him like stunted flower petals. He looked so miserable she found herself feeling sorry for him.

"Remember, this is an approach your people haven't tried," she said. "We don't know how things will go. Try not to focus on the worst-case possibility."

"Save your hollow optimism. Given your medical condition, you have no future to lose. Allow the rest of us to mourn the loss of ours."

So much for sympathy. Mops sat back and pulled up the pre-launch checklist, watching one item after another turn from green to blue as Kumar meticulously reviewed each line.

The lighting in the cabin dimmed. A loud clunk echoed through the drop ship. Then came the gravitational hiccup as the landing bay's grav plates powered down and the drop ship's kicked in.

Mops' inner ear insisted she was half-falling, half-flying as the ship slid free of the *Pufferfish*. Her stomach insisted she shouldn't have eaten before the launch. She gripped the shoulder straps of her harness and clenched her jaw.

The engines powered up, shoving her against the side of her pod as they began the long, curving approach to Tuxatl's surface.

"I wish we had windows," said Gabe.

"Your visor can show you an external display." Azure reached a tentacle across the cabin and pointed to the curved rectangle of green memcrys clipped to the side of Gabe's pod.

"I keep forgetting about these things." Gabe didn't have the implants for the monocles the rest of the crew used. Visors were bulkier, but provided most of the same basic functionality. He removed his hat and strapped on the visor. "Give me a view of the planet."

From Mops' perspective, the only sign his visor was working was a scattering of lights around the edges, like faint green sparks.

Gabe's perspective was clearly more dramatic. His legs tensed against the floor, pressing him hard against the back of his pod. He slapped the walls to either side like he was reassuring himself the ship was still here, and he wasn't plummeting unprotected toward Tuxatl. "Holy shit-kittens! What's the resolution on this thing? That's . . . wow!"

Mops smiled. "Agreed."

"How close are we going to get to the ring?" he asked.

Kumar twisted around in the cockpit. He'd left the door separating him from the cabin open. "The ring doesn't have a clearly defined boundary, but I'm keeping a minimum of five hundred kilometers from the thick of it. We might hit a few stray pebbles on the way down, but we should be clear of the lightning and any rocks big enough to pose a threat. I'm keeping the grid online to be safe, though."

"I ought to be recording this." Gabe tugged off the

visor and placed it over the sphere at the end of his cane. "Hey Azure, help me get this hooked up?"

Mops watched them work, then closed her eyes and sub-vocalized, "Doc, give me a private channel to Kumar."

"Is everything all right?" Kumar replied a moment later. "We're on course and should be crossing the terminator in about ten minutes. We'll be landing in the middle of the night, local time, as planned. I haven't seen any sign of hostile action from the planet."

"You're doing great, Sanjeev." She rested her head against the back of her seat. "Until we're back on the *Pufferfish*, I have additional orders for you."

"Anything you need, Captain."

She smiled to herself. The only thing potentially stronger than Kumar's need to clean was his sense of loyalty. "You're going to be my second-in-command while we're on Tuxatl. If at any time, in your judgment, my mind starts to go . . . if I start to revert or lose myself, I need you to take over before I endanger the team or the mission."

"Me? I'm not trained for command."

"Neither was I. Not like this." Mops sighed and rubbed her forehead. "You have seniority. More importantly, I trust you."

"Captain, I can't just . . ."

"Doc is monitoring the medical scanners Azure implanted in me. If anything looks off, he'll alert you. But the final call will be yours."

Kumar took his time answering. When he did, his voice was soft. "I thought Azure said you had at least a couple of weeks left."

"That was her best guess. I hope she's right. I need you watching my back in case she wasn't." She opened her eyes. Kumar sat in the cockpit, his back and shoulders visibly tense.

"What makes you think they'll follow my orders?" he asked quietly.

"Tell them if they don't, you'll feed them to me."

"That's not funny, sir."

"Agree to disagree." Mops smiled to herself. "If you

want them to believe you're in charge, you have to believe it first."

"How?"

"Because I'm telling you that you can. Are you going to argue with your captain?"

"No, sir." She saw him shake his head, heard him chuckle. "I'll do my best."

"Thank you, Sanjeev."

"Always, Captain."

8

Even with FTL transmission, the distance between Tuxatl and Stepping Stone was far too great for meaningful conversation. Monroe wasn't sure of the maximum speed data could be sent and received, but the news Admiral Pachelbel had sent was likely more than a day old by the time it reached the *Pufferfish.*

"The Prodryan war conclave has progressed to its final phase. We thought we had a little more time, but they've winnowed it down to three candidates for Supreme War Leader. According to our intel, the winner intends to celebrate by launching an immediate large-scale assault against the Alliance. We expect Earth and Dobranok to be first-wave targets."

Pachelbel jabbed a yellow-and-brown tentacle at someone offscreen and whistle-clicked a quick order about shuttle launch preparation. "I've tried to assist the Librarians of Humanity with an evacuation plan, but I'm under direct orders to prioritize the removal of Krakau personnel from Earth. Not that we have anywhere safe to evacuate them to . . ."

She gritted her beak. "Damn Prodryan political efficiency. Any other race would spend another six months minimum on campaigning and primary elections and *voter suppression. The only good news is that several of their best military leaders managed to remove one another from consideration with extreme prejudice, but that's a drop of comfort in a poisonous sea.*

"I'm not sure how much longer I'll be stationed here. Krakau Colonial Military Command is circling my waters. Since Earth is no longer considered a Krakau colony, they're claiming Stepping Stone's resources should be sent elsewhere. It's utter garbage, of course. This is an Alliance station, not a Krakau facility. But with the waves of public opinion battering the Alliance against the rocks, I don't know how much I can hold on to."

Pachelbel turned away again, longer this time. The translator didn't pick up what she said, but when she returned, her words were an octave lower. *"I wish I had better news, Captain Adamopoulos. Good luck and swift currents."*

The transmission ended.

Johnny, Grom, and Rubin all turned toward Monroe.

"This doesn't change anything," said Monroe. "We knew we were running out of time."

"Should we tell the captain?" asked Grom.

He shook his head. "Let them focus on their mission."

Rubin used two fingers to pet the eel coiled around her forearm, her movements slow, almost meditative. "Why would CMC strip Earth's defenses? They need us."

"They also need to protect Krakau colony worlds," said Johnny. "Earth can't kick the Krakau out, then expect us to die protecting them."

"Isn't it your people's fault the humans can't protect themselves?" asked Grom.

"The Glacidae have benefited from human soldiers too," snapped Johnny. "The whole Alliance has."

"Take it easy, all of you." Monroe understood their frustration and fear, but there was nothing they could do from here. "Focus on the mission."

"Focus on what, precisely?" Johnny waved her tentacles around the mostly empty bridge. "What is it you expect us to do?"

"Maintain orbit, keep monitoring the away team, and wait."

"Just . . . wait?"

"That's right."

Johnny turned back to her station. "This mission stinks like Azure's leftovers."

THE DROP SHIP HIT the ground hard. Mops' harness dug into her flesh as she slammed to one side.

"Sorry about that," Kumar called back. "I overcompensated on the landing. Tuxatl gravity isn't as strong as Earth's. All the self-diagnostics look good, though. The ship still works."

Mops pushed free of her seat and stretched, grimacing at the crackle of stiffened muscles and sinew. "Any activity outside?"

"Some movement," said Kumar. "Local wildlife, from what I can tell. Nothing larger than a couple of kilograms."

Mops grabbed a personal respiration adjuster from the overhead bin, moved to the hatch, and tugged the release. The heavy door slid open to reveal a circular clearing. Her monocle provided enhanced vision, showing thickets of chest-high plants, thick-stemmed with bulbous yellow seed pods. She kept one hand on her sidearm as she stepped out.

Azure jumped down next and immediately began taking samples of the air and soil. Her blue-black skin glistened with a layer of protective gel, the biological equivalent of a hazard suit.

Gabe stopped in the hatch. He removed his visor and looked around, his eyes wide. He inhaled and held his breath like he meant to save those first lungsful of air as a souvenir. His nose wrinkled, and he coughed hard. "Why does this planet smell like someone peed on it?"

"The air has a higher ammonia content than you're used to," said Azure.

"Is it dangerous?"

"Wear your PRA." Mops tapped the adjuster around her neck. "It tracks what you're breathing and makes small adjustments to keep you healthy. Azure made sure yours was calibrated for an unmodified human. It should last two days, and we have plenty of replacement packs."

Gabe draped his PRA around his neck like a pendant, then extended one foot, paused, and whispered, "One small step . . ."

He stumbled and would have fallen face-first to the rocky ground if Mops and Azure hadn't both moved to catch him.

"Lighter gravity," Mops reminded him. "You'll feel like you weigh about ten kilos less. Take it slow. Give yourself time to adjust."

"Thanks." He patted her arm absently, then did the same to Azure's tentacle, all the while gawking like a new recruit on his first trip to an entertainment station. He pulled out his cane, took two careful steps, and turned in a slow circle, staring in undisguised wonder.

A streak of green-limned light crossed the sky, vanishing an instant later. Mops' speakers sizzled with static, while Gabe exclaimed in delight.

"Get used to that," said Doc, speaking for all to hear. *"Those rings are constantly shedding small bits of rock into the atmosphere."*

"It's amazing." Gabe stood staring at the ring arched overhead.

"Nothing amazing about it," snarled Cate as he peered out from the hatch. "Just one more danger waiting to kill us all." He crept down and moved to one side, keeping his back to the drop ship. His wings were fully extended, razor-implants visible along the edges.

The planet's ring was a broad, pale strip curving through the sky. It reflected significantly more sunlight than a full moon back on Earth, bright enough for Mops to make out most of their surroundings with her unaided eye.

"Pufferfish, this is the captain. We've touched down safely." She waited for Monroe's acknowledgment, then moved away from the ship to study an organic-looking

column of black-and-red stone two meters high. Surrounding it was a circle of pale-barked saplings, their branches spreading into leafy blue fronds that made them look like tall, skinny parasols.

An alert flashed on her monocle.

```
Unknown  potential  infestation.  Recom-
mend  immediate  quarantine  and  decon-
tamination.
```

"You're going to get a lot of those," said Doc. *"The parasitological database has no information on Tuxatl, which means most everything is a potential infestation."*

"Deactivate the infestation and sanitation warnings." Such alerts were standard for hygiene and sanitation crew. Mops kept hers live out of habit while on board the *Pufferfish*. She leaned in, studying the creatures her monocle had flagged.

They reminded her of tiny six-armed starfish, black with red stripes, burrowing through the dirt and crawling up the bark of the young trees. Needle-like claws or stingers protruded from the end of each limb.

"Oh, wow," said Kumar, coming up beside her. He reached toward a cluster of starfish climbing over one another near the end of a branch.

Mops slapped his hand. "We're not here to collect samples. Leave the native bugs alone."

His shoulders slumped, but he pulled back. "I thought Vera would appreciate a pet from a new world."

"I'm sure she would, but you don't know anything about these creatures, and we have other priorities. How far to the Prodryan signal we picked up?"

"Two and a half kilometers." He pointed off to the right. "I sent it to everyone's monocles along with the drop ship's topography scan, so you should all have updated maps."

Doc brought up Mops' map, complete with the direction and distance to their destination. "Good work."

"I also programmed the drop ship to do an active scan of the area every three minutes. We should get a signal if anything gets close. The hatch is sealed. Nothing's getting inside unless they have plasma drills or know how to hack a six-factor quantum lock."

Mops nodded, only half-listening. The edges of the clearing were too regular to be natural. They'd landed in a shallow crater. She crouched and dug through the dirt to find a layer of cracked, glassy rock below.

The crater lacked the raised edges she'd expect from an impact or explosion. An energy weapon, then. Probably from the Prodryan attack on the Quetzalus eleven years ago. The blast would have melted the ground into a rippled pool of glass.

None of the others seemed to have noticed yet. She stood and stepped carefully past the edge of the crater. "Enough sightseeing, people. Let's move."

The route took them along the edge of a vertical drop-off. To Mops' left, white-capped waves crashed against black rocks jutting from the water in the distance. When she moved nearer, she could make out a beach of black sand at the base of the cliff, about eighty meters below. Farther out, broad-winged creatures with long, sinuous tails circled the water, diving occasionally to snatch prey from the waves. The predators' whistling cries unsettled her, like a song played off-key.

Knee-high grass swayed in the wind as they walked. The edges were sharp enough to cut exposed flesh. Farther off to the right were more of the parasol-shaped shrubs and larger trees. They stood ten to twenty meters high, and Azure had confirmed a cellular structure similar to wood, but with a higher concentration of metal. Instead of leaves, they sprouted feathery silver fronds, the largest of which would cover a grown human.

But it was the sky that demanded their attention. Again and again, Mops' gaze was pulled to the planet's ring. With the sun gone from the sky, she could discern different bands of silver and pink and gray and gold. Lightning crackled and sparked along the inner edge. Every few minutes, a streak of green or orange fell from the ring.

Mops' monocle flickered constantly as it recorded and classified new organisms in the team's shared database. An orange lizard glided from one tree to the next, hissing as it passed overhead. A gray-furred animal like a two-tailed squirrel with a large belly pouch and enormous black eyes chirped in alarm and vanished into a burrow in the dirt.

From time to time, Gabe would bring his cane closer to a plant or a creature or a patch of interesting dirt, capturing details for the library.

Mops kept one hand on her pistol. Despite Cate's dire predictions, they had yet to encounter anything truly threatening. But if there were Prodryans in the area, they would have detected the drop ship's descent.

"*Pufferfish*, any activity from our target?" asked Mops.

"No changes or movement we can detect from here," said Monroe. "Johnny's been studying the air and weather patterns around the Prodryan site. She thinks we could be looking at a form of atmospheric manipulation."

Mops stopped moving. "Are you talking about terraforming tech?"

"Nothing that powerful. Whatever it is, the effect dilutes pretty quickly. The changes are undetectable once you get half a kilometer from the source."

Mops checked her monocle. They were just over six hundred meters out. "What kind of changes?"

"Increased oxygen, decreased nitrogen. Trace amounts of extra helium and hydrogen. Decreased humidity. Essentially the same adjustments—"

"—as Cate's PRA," finished Mops. "They're creating a bubble of Prodryan-friendly atmosphere."

The others had stopped as well. Kumar swept his rifle through the trees, letting the targeting scope search for unusual heat or motion. Some of Rubin's discipline had rubbed off on him. As for the rest of the team, they edged closer to Mops, not bothering to pretend they weren't listening in.

"That's what it looks like," agreed Monroe. "Only the tech isn't Prodryan."

"What?"

"The power source we picked up, yes," said Monroe. "But the alterations in the atmosphere are coming from the trees at the center of the affected area, not from any mechanical source. The closest technological match would be Tjikko bioengineering."

"The Prodryans don't go in for bioengineering. And the Jynx are still working with steam engines and gunpowder."

Johnny's voice cut in. "Technology isn't always a linear progression. Species develop different specializations at different speeds, depending on resources and demand. For example, Nusurans are the only known race to have invented contraceptives before the wheel. That said, I agree this level of technology would be anomalous by any measure. It's fascinating."

"Good work. Keep studying things from there, and tell me if you learn anything more. Monroe, any change from our Prodryan friends in space?"

There was a brief pause. "Nothing to report, Captain."

"Glad to hear it. Mops out."

A glassy blue creature the size of Mops' palm glided down to land on her boot. It had broad, fin-like wings to either side, making it resemble a jagged-edged leaf. Long antennae touched Mops' boot several times. The ends brightened like fiber optic filaments. After a moment, the creature turned dark purple and crawled away, its body rippling.

"I guess it didn't like the taste of your footwear," said Azure. "It's cute, though. Reminds me of the wave-skimmers on Dobranok. Or at least the footage I saw of wave-skimmers while I was on our lifeship."

The foliage thinned as they continued. The trees remained, but their fronds were withered, and many had fallen to the ground. The weeds and grasses were a sickly orange brown.

Azure glanced at a display cuff on her tentacle. "We're entering the edge of the atmospheric changes." She picked up one of the fronds. The individual hairs to either side of the main stem fell away at the slightest touch, like wires rusted to dust.

Fewer plants meant less cover as they cut inland toward their goal. Mops slowed their pace. Still no sign of Prodryans or Jynx.

The wind had died down. The ground crunched underfoot.

Nobody spoke, and Mops found herself trying to quiet her breathing. Her monocle was blank: no sign of active native life here.

Gabe caught up to Mops and tapped her shoulder, then pointed to the right where a set of long, thin impressions were visible in a patch of half-dried mud. Mops looked back at Cate's feet, comparing shape and size to the angular indentations Gabe had found. She pointed, making sure the rest saw and understood, then subvocalized, "Doc, alert the *Pufferfish* we've confirmed a Prodryan presence down here."

"Done."

She switched on her pistol's targeting assistance. A floating crosshair appeared on her monocle. She checked the surroundings as she walked, waiting for that crosshair to jump to a potential target, and for the tug of her weapon's internal gyroscopes that would guide her aim.

Up ahead among the barren trees stood a series of round mud-and-stone structures, like blisters grown from the dirt, each one melding into the next. A glassy sheen suggested a sealant to protect against the elements. Metal screens covered round windows. A woven blanket hung over a large door nestled in the junction where the two largest structures came together.

A lone tree thirty meters high rose through the roof at the center of it all. Thin branches stretched out, their ends arching back toward the ground. Smaller trees with similar long, drooping branches formed a ring, like a fence around a home.

She crouched and gestured for Cate to join her. The others waited several paces back.

"Well?" asked Mops.

Cate had switched off his PRA. His mandibles barely moved when he spoke. "It's Prodryan. Aside from the trees, naturally. This appears to be a modified military-issue shelter. Once deployed, the shells are programmed to draw material from the surroundings for camouflage."

Spidery scratches and discolorations mottled the walls by the door. "Can you read those?"

"War poetry." Cate waved one arm dismissively. "Bad war poetry. Too much emphasis on death and loss, and almost no celebration of victory. The meter and rhyme scheme are competent enough, but simple. Derivative of Thirteenth Dynasty flight songs."

"If this is a military outpost, what kind of defenses will it have?"

"Mines, biotoxins, auto-targeting weaponry . . . The possibilities are limitless."

"Doc, any way for us to scan for traps?"

"Prodryan military traps? With the equipment we have available? Might as well throw rocks at it and see what happens."

"The rest of you stay here and keep quiet," Mops whispered. "I'm going to circle around and check the back." She retreated until she reached better cover, then cut to the right.

Whoever lived here had been on Tuxatl for a while. Mops spotted two well-worn paths. One led off toward what her map said was the nearby Jynx settlement. Another went to a series of raised wooden crates or boxes. Or hives, she realized as she drew closer and heard the buzzing from inside.

There were no guards. No visible weapons or other security measures. "Where are they?"

"I'm detecting no unusual sounds or movement."

With each step, Mops grew more anxious. You didn't simply walk up to a secret Prodryan base and find the troops all asleep.

Could it be a trap? She double-checked her team's status: all normal. What the deuce was going on?

Sweat dripped down the side of her neck. She increased her pace, half-expecting to feel an A-gun slug punch between her shoulder blades before she made it back.

She found the others waiting as she'd left them, alert with weapons ready.

"Anything?" Kumar whispered.

Mops shook her head.

"Alliance tactical guidance suggest a blitz attack," he continued. "Post one or more troops outside to cover the exits, then hit the place fast and hard. Flash grenades and lots of smoke to confuse anyone inside."

Mops stared.

"I've been reading some of Monroe's old infantry manuals in my free time," he said.

"Even if we had enough trained soldiers for that, we need information, not a body count."

A voice spoke from behind them. "You could simply ask, Captain."

Mops spun, her pistol jumping to target a winged figure crouched halfway up a tree. Her monocle zoomed in on a Prodryan female. Older, judging from the patchiness of her wings and the flaking delamination of her exoskeleton. An insulated blanket covered her head and back like a large cape.

She was clearly a soldier, dressed in faded yellow armor that protected her neck and torso. Her left hand was mounted with hinged blades in place of fingers. Her right held a bulky gun with a funnel-shaped barrel and a cylindrical tank. Mops didn't recognize the model—possibly a chemical weapon?

"You don't look like typical Alliance soldiers." The Prodryan shifted to study Azure. "And you aren't Krakau. What are you?"

"Drop your weapon," ordered Mops. "Kumar, do another sweep of the trees."

"I'm alone," said the Prodryan. "And like you, I'm not interested in adding to my body count tonight, Captain."

"You know me?"

"I know how to read Alliance rank insignia." She turned next to Cate. "You're even more of a mystery than your non-Krakau friend. No restraints. Active blade implants. It almost looks like you're helping these humans of your own free will."

"Hardly."

"I don't see anyone else," said Kumar. "But we didn't spot her, either."

"Because I've been up here waiting since your ship landed. A good soldier learns to be still. And to wear a thermal blanket to absorb her body heat."

"No movement, nothing on the infrared." Mops lowered her gun. "You could have killed us. Or waited for us to leave. Why give yourself away?"

"Curiosity." The Prodryan followed Mops' lead, clipping her weapon to her thick belt next to a utility knife and a metal spade. "You're too clumsy to be infantry, so I'm guessing you didn't come here expecting to discover an old Prodryan soldier. Who are you, and what do you want?"

"You first," said Mops.

"If that's your custom. I'm Starfallen of Lyr III, Veteran of the seventy-fourth Battle for Yan." She made a chittering sound Mops eventually recognized as amusement. "And at the moment, I want to invite you all to breakfast."

9

The shell of a soldier stands guard
at the edge of the sand.
Stub-torn wings forever spread in defiance.
Desert sun pierces the hollow carapace.

This then is our reward.
Eternal duty in a barren land.
Never to retreat, never to advance.
My younger self burns in endless vigilance.
                                    —*Starfallen of Lyr III*

"DID SHE SAY BREAKFAST?" asked Gabe.
       "Did she say Starfallen of Lyr III?" asked
       Cate.

"Yes, yes, and hush," snapped Mops. Prodryans were
horrible liars, which suggested Starfallen's invitation was
genuine, but there had to be more to it. A hearty breakfast of eggs and poison, maybe?

Starfallen spread her wings and jumped from her

perch. Kumar's rifle tracked her down. She landed gracefully on the ground in front of them.

"Starfallen, formerly called Wartalker?" Cate whispered. "Wing Guard for the Warlord of the Crimson Colonies? Second-in-Command at the raid on Plikxit IV?"

"You have the advantage of me," said Starfallen.

"Captain Marion Adamopoulos of the *Pufferfish*." Mops gestured with her pistol. "Toss me the weapon."

"This?" Starfallen chitter-laughed again. "This is a sprayer for my garden. It's full of phosphorus and potassium. Good for the plants, but no threat to you and yours. You're welcome to examine it." She slowly set the sprayer on the ground.

Azure wrapped a tentacle around the barrel. She turned the sprayer over and carefully unscrewed the canister. "Smells like plant food to me. I think she's telling the truth."

Cate squeaked, a sound Mops had never heard a Prodryan make before. He stood frozen, gripping his antennae so tightly she thought he'd rip them from his scalp. "Captain, even you must have heard of Starfallen-called-Wartalker. She overpowered the Nusuran Fleet at Muiniar with nothing but a freighter and three mining pods. She slew the Warlord of Sharise with a rotary mandible sharpener. Children sing songs of her triumphs during their basic combat classes. An entire generation of young soldiers painted their wings in tribute when they heard she'd been killed." To Starfallen, he said, "I *knew* you couldn't be dead!"

"Starfallen-called-Wartalker also led the ambush that destroyed the EMCS Cassowary," added Doc. *"She oversaw four of the worst atrocities of the Prodryan-Alliance war."*

Alliance records appeared on her monocle. Mops' fists clenched. Starfallen's war crimes would darken an ocean with blood.

"Accessing my records, I assume?" asked Starfallen. "Does the Alliance still have a shoot-on-sight order for me, Captain?"

"They do."

"I'd recommend waiting until after we eat, but it's your

choice, of course." Starfallen looked Cate up and down. "And who are you, brother? Your name and credentials?"

"You had to ask," Azure groaned.

Cate drew himself taller and spread his wings. "I am Advocate of Violence of the Red Star Clan, undercover operative and certified legal advocate with a Superlative rating, distinguished as one of only seventy-two Prodryans licensed to practice beyond our borders."

Starfallen's file blurred as Mops refocused on Cate. "I thought it was seventy-three."

"It used to be. The prosecutor known as Mediates Through Exsanguination was disbarred two months ago after bungling what was supposed to be a simple temporary cease-fire on a Tuxatl colony. For her failures, she was sentenced to fertilize the colony's new grove."

"That doesn't sound too bad," said Gabe. "A bit of manual labor never hurt—"

Mops caught his attention and shook her head.

His eyes went round with understanding. "Oh, damn."

Starfallen stood with arms spread while Kumar searched her for additional weapons. "How did you get past the blockade?" She turned toward Cate. "Does this mean our people have finally reached an accord with the Krakau Alliance?"

"Never. Our spread across the galaxy continues unchecked," Cate proclaimed. He glanced at Mops. "Slightly checked. I have personally dealt many severe blows to Alliance morale and unity. The humans believe they're using me for my superior knowledge and insight, when in truth I work to undermine their efforts and speed their inevitable destruction."

"Cate helped us past the blockade," Mops summarized. "He wasn't happy about it."

"Hell's Claws is death." Cate stared at Starfallen. "How is it you've survived?"

"That's a long story, one better shared over a meal. Assuming your captain doesn't decide to execute me on the spot."

Kumar finished his search. "No other weapons, except those blades on her hand."

"These?" Starfallen clinked the knives together. "I use them mostly for chopping vegetables. I'm afraid the joints have grown rather arthritic."

"She has a lot of implants," Kumar continued. "Half are inactive. Rangefinder in the right shoulder. Targeting scope in the left eye. Gun mounts on the forearms, but from the corrosion, those haven't been used in years."

"There are no maintenance stations or supply depots on Hell's Claws." Starfallen flexed an arm, making the weapon attachment points pop from the flesh like metal boils. "Not to mention the lack of ammunition or power packs. I haven't needed them. The predators have no taste for Prodryan flesh."

She lowered her arms. "Shall we continue this inside? Your not-quite-Krakau friend should make sure the food is compatible with her biology, but as I understand it, humans can digest almost anything. I think you'll like the leafbug cheese. It has a delightful sting."

Cate interposed himself between Mops and Starfallen. "What are you *doing*?" he whispered. "These are aliens. Their captain is a human!"

"I'm aware," Starfallen said dryly. "The lack of wings gave them away immediately."

"You are *Starfallen-called-Wartalker*. I presumed your invitation to be a brilliant trap. An ambush, perhaps. But you give no hint of deception. This is genuine . . . *hospitality*. Not to mention a violation of six different parts of the Prodryan Military Code."

"As the Prodryan Military apparently declared me dead, I don't believe I'm bound by the Code anymore."

Cate's wings began to ripple dangerously, the blades glinting in the light. "You would disgrace yourself by—"

Starfallen's hand shot out to grasp one of Cate's mandibles. She shifted her stance and twisted. At the same time, her left foot lashed out, hooking Cate's leg from behind.

Cate flipped backward, wings flapping desperately as he slammed to the ground. Starfallen stepped onto his left wing and dropped to a crouch, never releasing her grip on his mandible.

"I also have broiled fish," Starfallen continued cheerfully. "Or what passes for fish on this planet. The texture is rubbery, but as otherworld foods go, it's not bad at all."

"I know she's a war criminal," said Doc. *"Is it wrong to like her anyway?"*

"Yes," whispered Mops.

"We should go." Starfallen got to her feet and started toward her shelter. "We have a lot to discuss."

This, more than anything else, convinced Mops she was serious. For a Prodryan soldier to deliberately offer anyone a clear shot at their back was unheard of.

Cate stood and shook himself, shedding dirt and pebbles. His blades had retracted. Starfallen's foot had scraped a bare patch in his wing, revealing thin, translucent skin lined with dark veins. He appeared perfectly calm as he watched Starfallen walk away.

"Are you all right?" asked Mops.

"She chose not to inflict any serious or permanent damage, if that's what you're asking." He brushed off his forearms. "If anything, I'm relieved. Attacking me was the first thing she's said or done that felt genuinely *Prodryan*."

Up close, the walls of Starfallen's home were covered in overlapping diamond-shaped panels the color of dried mud, giving them a scaly texture. Infrared showed the air wafting from inside to be significantly warmer. It smelled of wood smoke and unfamiliar spices.

"Reminds me of a giant wasp's nest," said Gabe.

"Except for the solar arrays, plumbing lines, and power conduits," said Kumar. "Switch your visor to tactical, and you'll also see heavy-grade armor plating and a class three energy dispersion shell."

"Obviously, except for all that," agreed Gabe.

"No sign of anyone else inside," Kumar continued. "But we didn't notice Starfallen until she wanted us to, either."

Mops ducked inside after Starfallen and found herself

in a large hemispherical room, three meters high at the center. The interior walls were a cheerful amethyst color. Swirls of white paint gave the impression of clouds.

Small round doorways led deeper into the structure—most on ground level, but several higher up. Ledges jutted from the walls. From what little Mops knew of Prodryan home life, these were meant to serve as seats and benches, but most had been repurposed as shelves, holding everything from dirty tools to old memcrys chips to carefully folded blankets and furs.

At the center of the room was a low metal table, upon which stood a half-assembled Merraban stick-puzzle. Mops wasn't sure what it was supposed to look like when finished. A bird of some kind, maybe?

"We're inside Starfallen's hive," Cate squeaked.

"That's right, so wipe your feet," Starfallen ordered as she ducked into another room.

Mops followed, keeping her in sight. Starfallen was retrieving a stack of mud-brown ceramic bowls from a wooden cabinet. To one side, a series of flaming nozzles beneath a metal grate formed a makeshift stove. Starfallen removed the lid from a pot, stirred, and began dishing out green goop with the consistency of cold pudding.

"Captain, would you fetch the black basket from the icebox?"

The utilitarian metal handles on the icebox doors were built for Prodryans, so Mops could only squeeze two fingers through to tug it open. She retrieved the basket and set it on the rough-stone countertop. "You've been here a while."

"Feels like a lifetime," Starfallen agreed.

"Given the tech you've salvaged, you could have contacted Guardian of the Abyss any time you wanted."

Starfallen clicked her mandibles. "Is Guardian still running things up there? Such a flat thinker, that one."

"He was recently terminated from his position. My point is you're either deliberately hiding down here, or else your people have chosen to leave you here and keep your presence secret."

"The latter, for the most part." She uncovered the

black basket and stirred what looked and sounded like uncooked blue macaroni. "We don't have much time. Grab that stack of bowls for me?"

Mops did so. "Time until what?"

"Until your food wakes up." She swiftly dished up the rest of the meal and moved the bowls onto a large tray, which she carried into the main room. "Breakfast is ready!"

The bowls were segmented into four triangular sections of different sizes. Mops guessed the speckled white cubes to be the leafbug cheese Starfallen had mentioned. The green goo had a spicy-sweet scent that overpowered everything else. Each bowl came with a metal utensil that was a cross between chopsticks and tweezers.

"Are we really breaking bread with people who want to wipe our species from the galaxy?" asked Gabe.

"I'm sorry, Prodryans don't eat bread," said Starfallen. "Those blue curls are hibernating rockworms. I usually dip them in the sauce, but the natives prefer them plain. Did you want me to heat up the fish? I prefer it chilled, myself."

Gabe grimaced. "I'm sure this is fine, thank you."

"What's the black sandy stuff?" asked Kumar.

"Sand." Starfallen picked up a rockworm and dipped it first into the sauce, then the sand. "It aids with digestion. Regurgitation buckets are in the cabinet above the sink, if anyone needs."

Gabe raised a hand. "I might."

Starfallen took her bowl and climbed halfway up the wall to sit on one of the few vacant ledges. Cate did the same, happily munching rockworms.

"I wouldn't try them," Kumar advised Gabe. He uncoiled one of the worms to examine it more closely. "We don't know how an unmodified human's stomach will react."

"I have a pretty good idea," said Gabe.

"I centrifuged the dip twice," Starfallen assured them. "The process removes ninety-nine percent of the chlorine and almost all the chalk dust."

"Azure?" asked Mops.

Azure had poked a metal probe into her bowl and was checking its findings on her tentacle display cuff. "Gabe and I should probably decline. It won't kill us, but the aftereffects would be unpleasant. You'll be fine, Captain. Feral humans have been known to eat industrial waste with no noticeable problems, so this shouldn't give you more than a burp or two."

"I'm not feral yet," said Mops, more sharply than she'd intended.

Azure shrank low. "I only meant your digestive system can break down and excrete most substances. Kumar's as well."

"Right. Sorry." Mops studied her food. It smelled . . . surprisingly good. Saliva pooled in her mouth. She clicked the oversized tweezers together, grabbed one of the rock-worms, and dipped it lightly in the sauce.

The worms were stringy and a little bitter. Combined with the sauce, the flavor made her think of peanut butter, jam, and pickles. Strange, but not unpleasant.

"Did you have any difficulties on your flight down?" asked Starfallen.

Mops took another bite of rockworms. "It was fine. And I'm sorry, but we don't have time for small talk. Why are you here, Starfallen? What's your mission on Tuxatl?"

"My goals have evolved over the years." The Prodryan set her bowl to one side. "We were the first to discover this world, long before the Quetzalus arrived."

"The first, eh?" asked Gabe. "That must have been a shock to the Jynx. All that time living here, and they never knew it."

Starfallen inclined her head. "Very well. We were the second. A survey team was sent to assess the planet's re-sources and determine the most efficient approach to ex-terminating the natives. It was all quite routine. Initial reports noted a high concentration of metals in the flora. The planetary ring was a potential trove of useful elements. But something happened to that team, something that frightened our leaders on Yan so much that they had the team killed and the planet quarantined. All records were sealed, and aside from the occasional rumor, Hell's Claws was mostly forgotten.

"Then the Quetzalus colonists came. Yan immediately dispatched a strike fleet to eliminate them. They destroyed the orbiting supply ship first. Next, soldiers were sent to hunt the Quetzalus on the surface. I'm told the Quetzalus put up quite the fight. It took three weeks to find the last of them.

"During that time, the war party's messages back to the ship began to change. They started to question their orders, even going so far as to suggest leaving the survivors in *peace*. Can you imagine?"

"Shocking," said Cate.

"Naturally, they were extracted and executed for dereliction of duty," Starfallen continued. "A second group was assigned to finish the job. After six days, they simply stopped reporting back. I was sent to find out why.

"Like the first team, this group had lost their desire for conquest. For such a thing to happen once was unheard of. Twice? Impossible. I questioned each individual thoroughly."

Mops' jaw tightened. She knew what such questioning would have entailed. Her heart pounded harder as she listened to Starfallen's inhumanly calm recitation.

"My first theory was that they were attempting to break away and establish a new clan," said Starfallen. "It's rare, but happens occasionally. A small group rebels against their clan to take power for themselves. But I found no evidence, nothing to suggest any planning or conspiracy. Nothing to account for their dereliction. When I finished my interrogation, the survivors were turned over to a neurosurgeon for further examination. I supervised her work. She found no obvious injury or damage."

"No *obvious* damage?" Mops repeated.

"Very good, Captain." Starfallen plucked a lump of cheese from her bowl and tossed it into her mouth. "She discovered alterations in the forebrains, alterations well beyond our own neurosurgical abilities. Beyond Alliance technology as well. There was no scarring, not even at the cellular level. On a hunch, I ordered her to scan us as well."

Mops' breathing quickened. "Let me guess. You found the same changes?"

"Not as far along as with the others, but the evidence was clear. I remained loyal enough to report what we'd learned, and Prodryan enough to prepare for what I knew would follow. Minutes later, they fired on us from orbit. I was the only one to survive the attack."

"What caused the change?" Mops demanded. This could be the secret they'd been searching for. If the Alliance could identify and harness whatever had neutered the Prodryan drive for violence and conquest . . . "A chemical in the atmosphere? A parasite?"

"Chemical, yes," said Starfallen. "I don't understand the precise mechanism, and most of our research was destroyed in the assault. I've asked the local Speaker, but their language for chemistry is all but untranslatable."

"Speaker?" Mops had come across that term from the Quetzalus reports. "They're some sort of authority figure, right? Would they know what happened to you?"

"They should," said Starfallen. "They engineered it." She started to say more, then tilted her head to one side in an expression of mild surprise. "I take it you enjoyed your breakfast, Captain?"

Mops had devoured everything in the bowl, even the sand, without realizing. Her stomach broke the silence with a low, drawn-out growl.

"Humans have such an aggressive digestive system." Starfallen hopped down and took Mops' bowl. "Don't worry, I have plenty more. I cook in large batches, enough to last a week at a time."

Mops didn't remember eating so much. Her head was pounding. She could feel her team staring at her. She shook her head, trying to clear the fog from her thoughts. "No thank you. I'm sure it was delicious, but I need . . ."

"Oh." Starfallen chittered. "Apologies. I completely forgot about human elimination. I'm afraid this place lacks the appropriate facilities, but if you need privacy, I suggest the bushes behind the house. Watch out for the thorntails. I just smoked the hives yesterday, so they're feisty."

"It's not that," Mops protested. Except now that she mentioned it, she did need to pee, dammit. She moved toward the door, and the throbbing fog in her skull grew worse.

"Your heart rate is up. Adrenaline production as well. I thought it was excitement over Starfallen's revelation, but I believe this may be a symptom of your reversion."

"No shit," she murmured.

"You need to calm yourself."

"Easy for you to say."

Kumar moved toward her.

"I just need a moment. I'll be right back." Mops stumbled through the door and fled.

Halfway across the barren circle of land, she slowed.

"Start with your breathing."

Mops ran her tongue over her teeth. Bits of shell and sand proved she'd eaten Starfallen's cooking, but she couldn't recall a single bite.

"Do you think something in the food triggered this reaction?"

"I don't know, dammit." She sat on the rocky ground and leaned forward, resting her arms on her knees. Sweat dripped from her face.

After a few minutes, she raised her head. The sun had begun to rise, painting the planet's ring in soft shades of orange, red, and pink. She watched the fading dance of lightning along the inner edge.

"You have company."

Kumar and Azure approached cautiously. Azure carried a blood sampling kit in one tentacle. "Give me your arm, Captain. Now."

Mops pushed back her sleeve and extended her bare forearm.

Azure pressed the end of the tube to Mops' inner elbow. Mops felt the jab of the needle, followed by a cold tingle as the kit sucked blood from her vein. When Azure pulled it away, a single drop of black blood welled from the skin.

"I'm all right," said Mops. "Whatever it was, I think it's passing."

"The data from your implants is returning to baseline," Azure agreed. "That doesn't mean you're all right." She paused, presumably to examine the results the sampling kit was sending to her oversized monocle.

"Was it . . . did she start to revert?" asked Kumar.

"Possibly." Azure curled and uncurled the tips of her tentacles, a nervous habit. "Probably. I didn't expect a manifestation so soon. I can't be sure what caused this episode, Captain, but I'd advise against eating any other strange foods. Stick to the standard tube feeding protocols from now on."

Mops nodded. The Krakau implanted feeding ports in the stomachs of all their cured humans. It made it easier for them to monitor and control what their soldiers ingested.

Azure and Kumar's presence was helping Mops regain her composure. It was an automatic reflex in the presence of her crew. "Thank you, Azure." She steeled herself. "Will this happen again?"

"Yes."

"Will you be able to recognize if—when it does?"

"I think so." Her tentacles slumped. "I'm sorry, Captain. I wish . . ."

"Me too," said Mops.

"Me three."

She wiped her face and twisted toward Starfallen's shelter. What had the Prodryan been saying? Something about the Speakers and alterations to Prodryan brains. "Maybe this wasn't reversion. Maybe whatever affected the Prodryans—"

"Doubtful," said Azure. "I can run a scan, but Starfallen said the change took days or weeks. Your symptoms all point to reversion."

"All right." Mops stood, just as Cate stormed out, wings aflutter.

"Captain Adamopoulos! We must leave this world immediately, before the Speakers arrive to lobotomize me."

"It's hardly a lobotomy," said Azure. "From what Starfallen described, the alterations were extremely precise and narrow in scope."

"The physical alteration of a prisoner's brain is a war crime, established as such eighty-three years ago in the Nurgistarnoq Accords and reaffirmed in the Forty-Third Interplanetary Alliance Convention on Sentient Rights."

"I wasn't aware the Prodryans had signed either of those treaties," said Mops.

"Irrelevant!" His antennae were quivering. "You're sick, Captain. You face a slow, inevitable, terrifying loss of self. You should empathize with my situation. What this planet did to Starfallen is worse than death. These Speakers would strip me of who I am."

"Starfallen seems happy enough," said Kumar.

Cate spun. "So does Rubin's pet rock eel. Would you trade your mind for the eel's?"

"Enough." Mops focused on Cate. Beneath his bluster, he was terrified. "I sympathize, but we have to complete our mission. The faster we do that, the faster we can get you off planet."

"He might have a point," Azure said quietly. "If they can rewrite Prodryan brains, who's to say they can't do the same to us? Maybe we should reconsider."

"It's too late for that." Starfallen stepped out and pointed to the trees beyond the clearing.

Mops' monocle switched to tactical, outlining the meter-high shapes moving through the branches. She focused on the closest, zooming in for a clearer look.

The Jynx hung by its claws halfway up the tree, watching them. It was bipedal and bilaterally symmetrical. The fur was a mottled pattern of gray splotches ringed in black on a brown underlayer. Large round ears stood atop the triangular head like furry radar dishes. A long snout jutted from the face, terminating in a comically undersized pink nose. She could just make out the tips of the sharp black teeth.

The Jynx wore a mix of leather and woven fabrics, heavy with straps and buckles. A curved knife, almost a short sword, hung from a belt. In one hand, it gripped a short rifle with a polished silver barrel and a wooden stock inlaid with turquoise stones.

Its ropy tail whipped from side to side. Muscles tensed. Seconds later, it leapt to the next tree, a good five meters away.

Cate flexed his wings, readying his blades. "Better to die as a Prodryan." He glared at Mops. "Better still to have never come to this damned world, and to have continued to live as a Prodryan."

More Jynx leapt into view. Others approached on foot. Their weapons might be primitive, but they had the advantage of numbers.

"Cate, maybe attacking the Jynx is what made them mess with your people's brains in the first place," Mops said softly. "We know how that turned out. Let's try something your fellow Prodryans never would have considered. Let's talk to them."

"Madness." Cate's wings relaxed slightly. "But your instincts have proven correct before."

Mops stepped out ahead of the others. She didn't know enough about Jynx weapons to guess whether her uniform would stop one of their bullets, but she knew a cured human could handle being shot better than a Rokkau or a Prodryan.

She mentally reviewed the things she'd planned to say when she encountered the Jynx. Before she could speak, her stomach gurgled again, loud enough that the closest Jynx jumped in alarm.

"Stop that," hissed Cate.

"For once, I agree with Cate. Another gastrointestinal disturbance might inspire them to start shooting."

"Both of you, shut the hell up." With that, Mops took a deep breath and stepped forward to meet the Jynx.

10

Monroe sat behind Mops' desk in the Captain's Cove, trying to hide his amusement.

"Considering there are only four of us, it seems safer," said Grom. "Not to mention our need for battle-readiness. The Prodryan defenses are staying away for now, but if that changes, we have to be prepared to react instantly."

"I agree," said Monroe.

Grom drew themself taller. "You do?"

"You have my permission to sleep on the bridge. For the sake of efficiency."

"Thank you, Commander." Grom hesitated. "The ship just feels so empty. And my quarters are on their own deck. Glacidae plumbing and environmental requirements, you know. Azure used to come down to visit and play video games, but with her gone . . ."

"It's lonely." Monroe smiled. "I get it. Fetch whatever blankets or cushions you'll need for your temporary nest."

"Yes, sir. Thank you, sir." Grom jumped down and scurried across the floor. Monroe followed them out to the bridge, still grinning.

After Grom disappeared into the lift, Johnny turned toward Monroe, one eye slitted with disapproval. "I take it you agreed to their request?"

"I did," said Monroe. "We have plenty of space, and I wouldn't mind having my computer specialist close by in case of trouble."

"Were you aware that almost half of all Glacidae rattle their spines in their sleep?" asked Johnny.

Monroe glanced at Rubin, who nodded and said, "The noise can reach ninety decibels."

"Furthermore," Johnny went on, "one in five Glacidae has been known to shoot spines in their dreams, or if they're startled awake."

Maybe he'd agreed too quickly. "What would you recommend, Engineer Johnny?"

Johnny's skin brightened. "To begin with, I suggest using ballistic shields from the armory to rig a quill-proof barrier. I can study the acoustics of Grom's station . . . once I know how the sound carries, I should be able to use the bridge speakers to set up active noise control."

"Excellent suggestions. I'll trust you to handle it."

Johnny drew herself up. "Thank you, sir!"

THE MOTTLED JYNX JUMPED gracefully to the ground. It remained low, weapon ready, while three more followed. Their hands were long and thin, with four furry fingers that ended in slightly curved claws. They had no thumbs, but each finger had an extra joint and greater lateral flexibility than human digits.

"Gabe, stay inside," Mops whispered over her comm.

"Yes, sir. What's happening out there?"

"Doc, relay the feed from my monocle." Mops kept as still as she could while the Jynx crept closer. She had no knowledge of Jynx body language. Simply spreading or raising her hands might be read as a threat. "Everyone keep calm. No sudden moves."

The first Jynx spoke to the others with a combination of modulated snarls, chirps, and cat-like *mrows*. It moved forward and spoke again, this time to Mops. A strong smell like old vinegar filled the air.

"Doc?"

"The translator needs more data. My best guess is that it's a form of greeting or challenge. There's a three percent chance it's a complaint about itchy toes."

Mops was torn. Keep quiet and risk them thinking she was ignoring them, or try to speak and risk a translation screw-up?

The consequences of miscommunication were drilled into every Alliance soldier. The most memorable was the first contact between the Glacidae and the Merrabans. Initial greetings had gone smoothly until the Merraban spokesperson accidentally invited the Glacidae contingent to lubricate his scent-holes.

The Jynx moved closer and repeated the sounds, louder this time.

"That's very helpful, thank you," said Doc. *"I'm sure if you increase your volume enough, the translator will magically understand."*

"His name is Barryar," said Starfallen. "A young hunter from the Black Spire camp. Experienced, but overeager." Starfallen stopped next to Mops and spoke directly to Barryar.

"I can work with this," said Doc. *"Starfallen's speaking Plyriurn, a known Prodryan tongue. Her translator's snarling whatever language the local Jynx speak. The more she talks, the more data the translator gets to build a direct Jynx-to- Human database."*

Starfallen pointed to Mops and explained they were guests who'd come for breakfast.

"I think that horrible choking sound is the word for human."

Throughout the growing crowd, Jynx ears flattened and fur rose. Considering the reactions Mops had gotten from other species over the years, this was on the mild side.

"Mops, Starfallen's translator is unsecured. Her tech is old, but I should be able to connect directly and synch your data with hers."

"Safely?"

"She might have encoded false data, linguistic traps to make you say 'Please shoot me in the face' when you

meant to say hello. But I have enough info from the Quetzalus to spot-check as we go. Though if she's really clever, she might have hidden a bit of viral code, too . . . It's a risk, kind of like having unprotected sex with—"

"How long would it take for us to talk to the Jynx without Starfallen's data?"

"We should be able to get enough for basic communication within a day. Complex concepts and ideas will take two or three."

"Do it."

"You're the boss. I'm creating a virtual partition and walling off the translator from other systems. I can always wipe and reload from Kumar's unit if your translator ends up with virtual crabs."

Starfallen was still speaking. "The first I knew of these humans was when their ship tripped my atmospheric scanners. As your Speaker knows, I have no contact with the rest of the galaxy."

Barryar lowered his rifle, but his ears remained flat. He called back toward the trees.

"Why does he smell so foul?" asked Cate.

"It's a warning scent," said Starfallen. "It means they're anxious and preparing to fight."

Another Jynx stepped into the clearing, flanked by two guards armed with rifles.

Starfallen's finger-blades twitched. "Speaker Harkayé Ar-Raya. Be careful of her, Captain."

The Speaker was smaller than the other Jynx, with a shorter snout and flatter ears. The differences were significant enough to make Mops wonder if this was a different subspecies of Jynx.

She wore a sleeveless black robe trimmed with silver lace, belted high on her torso, where the sternum would be on a human. A long, sheathed blade hung from silver chains at her hip. Mops didn't recognize the handle material.

Her medium-length gray fur was immaculate, like a satin cloud. White whiskers spread from her snout like a dandelion about to go to seed. Her tail was half again as long as those of the others. The tip curled over her elbow like the end of a fluffy, black-tipped stole.

Harkayé approached and circled Mops and Starfallen twice, tail twitching. She stepped closer to sniff both sides of Mops' neck. Her own scent was pleasantly earthy. She touched Mops' uniform with a claw, then turned to Starfallen and made a chirping *"reorr?"*

After a moment, Mops' translator kicked in: "What is this made of?"

"It's woven by machines," said Mops. "Several layers of artificial fabric and built-in sensors to protect us, help regulate body temperature, and monitor our health."

"Database synchronization complete."

"I noticed," she murmured.

Several of the Jynx stared at Mops, eyes wide. The vinegar scent grew stronger. But the Speaker didn't appear surprised to hear her own language spoken back to her. She lowered her hand toward Mops' pistol.

Mops touched Harkayé's arm to stop her.

Her whiskers flicked back, but she withdrew her hand.

"My name is Captain Marion Adamopoulos of the Earth Defense Fleet Ship *Pufferfish*. We're from a planet called Earth. We're not here to hurt anyone, or to cause any trouble with your people."

"Your presence is the trouble, Captain." Harkayé turned toward Cate. "You are Prodryan, like Starfallen?"

Cate retreated a step. Mops didn't know if he'd also downloaded the Jynx's language from Starfallen, but he'd certainly heard the other Prodryan describe Harkayé as a Speaker. The tips of his wing blades poked from their housings. "Stay back."

Mops stepped sideways, trying to keep herself between Cate and the Speaker. "How did you know we were here?"

Harkayé ignored the question and turned to Starfallen. "Jagar has snuck off again. He must have seen the aliens' ship falling from the sky. When he wasn't at the aliens' ship, I thought I'd find him here."

"I haven't seen Jagar in days," said Starfallen. "Captain,

your arrival may have ignited a beacon for certain . . . rebellious elements of Jynx society."

"That wasn't our intention."

"The Jynx care for results, not intentions." Starfallen lowered her voice. "Helping to find Jagar could ingratiate you with the Speaker."

"We're not here to interfere with their internal matters," said Mops.

"No, you're here to solicit their help with yours." Starfallen chittered at her reaction. "It's not difficult to deduce. This is an out-of-the-way planet with no tactical advantage. Rich in resources, but no more so than countless other, closer worlds. The people are too technologically primitive to interest the Alliance. Given that the Alliance and the Prodryans are still at war, the only logical reason for you to come to Hell's Claws is to learn why my people fear it, and whether you can use the source of that fear in your war."

"Is this true?" asked Harkayé.

"It is." Mops' hand stayed close to her pistol as she tried to split her attention between Starfallen and the Jynx. To Starfallen, she asked, "If you know what we want, what do you plan to do?"

"Help you in any way I can, Captain." She chittered again at Mops' obvious surprise. "I've been trapped on Hell's Claws for years because of my . . . condition. If that condition were to spread throughout my people, there would be nothing to stop me from returning home."

Cate's wings snapped out. He advanced on Starfallen. "You're talking about destroying everything that makes us Prodryan! Our culture, our identity, all of it burnt to ash so you can go home?"

Azure's tentacle lashed like a whip, the toxic barb on the end stopping mere centimeters from Cate's eye. He recoiled and curved his wings down protectively, but Azure had already withdrawn her limb. "Your people abandoned her here," she snapped. "They banished her from her home. She has the right to fight to get it back."

Harkayé watched the exchange without comment. Mops didn't know how much she could understand, but the longer the infighting continued, the weaker it could make Mops and her team appear.

"Doc, kill the translator." Mops waited for his acknowledgment, then barked, "The idea is to show we're *not* a threat. Azure, Cate, calm down or I'll reprogram your brains myself."

"Impossible," scoffed Cate. "You lack the neurological training or know-how to—"

"I didn't say it would be neat or clean." Mops patted her combat baton and glared at them until they got the message.

Harkayé spoke again. There was a brief pause as Doc reactivated the translator.

"It can be difficult keeping the young in line."

"Hardest part of my job, but they'll behave." She hoped. Behind the Speaker, Barryar and the other Jynx had begun to pant, extending dark blue tongues. "Are they all right?"

"They will be," said Harkayé. "The air here is harder for them to breathe."

Mops glanced at the tree rising from the center of Starfallen's shelter. "How was this done? The structure runs on Prodryan tech, but who reprogrammed the native flora to alter the local atmosphere?"

"That was part of our arrangement with Starfallen," said Harkayé. "A graft from the Black Spire skytree, altered to provide her a space to live in comfort and safety."

"You can do that?"

"I'm a Speaker."

Quetzalus records had described the Speakers as leaders and authority figures. Clearly they were much more. "What do you get in return? If you dislike outsiders so much, why let her stay?"

"Starfallen provides insight into potential enemies of the Jynx." Harkayé turned to Starfallen. "You believe these aliens could be useful in my hunt for Jagar?"

"They might," Starfallen said carefully. "They're not the most observant, but they were clever enough to get past the Prodryan blockade in the sky, and they found their way to my home."

"You need to see this."

Mops focused on the incoming video feed Doc had brought up on her monocle. "Excuse me, Speaker Harkayé. What does Jagar look like?"

"He has gray-and-black fur," said Harkayé. "With a white tuft at the end of his tail. Whiskers like white springs." She growled under her breath. "Curling the whiskers is a trend among the Freesail Traders. It's ridiculous. The first time Jagar tried, he overheated the iron and burnt his whiskers to stubs."

"Would Jagar have friends with him?"

Her ears flattened. "Possibly. Why do you ask?"

Mops shrank the feed. "Because right now, they're doing their damnedest to break into my ship."

Mops counted sixteen Jynx accompanying the Speaker. Most kept to the trees, leaping easily from one to the next. Barryar stayed on the ground with Harkayé.

Most of these Jynx struck her as young. The ones in the trees raced to see who was faster, who could climb higher, who could jump the farthest. Twice she'd watched Jynx scrabble frantically to keep from falling. Barryar snarled at them from time to time, but Mops had the impression a part of him longed to scale the nearest tree and join in.

She'd ordered Kumar to stick close to Cate, making sure the Prodryan didn't try to attack anyone or run off. Gabe was keeping a close eye on Starfallen, while Mops watched the Jynx Speaker. Trying to monitor so many potential dangers was like juggling live grenades.

"What do you think they did to our guards?" asked Barryar.

"We'll see," said Harkayé.

"What guards?" asked Mops.

"I left them to watch over your ship." Harkayé flicked one ear back. "Jagar may live among Black Spire Jynx, but he was born to the Freesail camp. They're fascinated by technology and will happily steal anything they can carry."

"I didn't see any guards in the security feed from the drop ship, before," said Mops.

"Our people are very good at remaining unseen. Even better than your winged friend Starfallen." Harkayé's lips drew back, revealing black teeth. Her tail lashed twice. "They must have been overpowered."

A white-furred Jynx with brown spots raced toward them on all fours. Mops recognized him as a scout Barryar had sent ahead.

Barryar scampered forward. "What is it?"

Before the scout could answer, a large wagon crested the hill behind him. At the front sat a plump Jynx with the longest fur Mops had seen so far, gray with black-and-white marbling. Long tufts of white fur tipped the ears. She wore an apron-like garment of red and purple, covered in bulging pockets.

Barryar groaned. "What is she doing here?"

Starfallen chittered. "Argarrar's the camp nursemaid, one of the oldest Jynx around. The Jynx have tremendous respect for their elders and their ancestors, and old Argarrar takes full advantage of the fact."

"What is *that*?" Beneath the wagon—and lighting up the threat display on Mops' monocle—was an enormous black serpentine creature. Unlike Earth snakes, this one had a series of fins running down the back and to either side. The side fins ended in curved claws, which it used to drag itself along. Leather harnesses bound the creature to the underside of the wagon, leaving just enough slack for it to pull the wagon.

"That's a [no-equivalent-term]," said Starfallen.

"Doc, substitute 'wagon-snake' for now."

"It's adorable!" Azure squealed. "Look at those fins. Those eyelashes!"

As the wagon neared, Argarrar pulled one of several wooden levers to either side of her seat. The wagon-snake curved to the right, carrying the wagon with it. Argarrar tugged a second lever to bring everything to a halt. "Good morning, Bar-Bar! You found new friends! I don't see Jagar, though."

"Please don't call me that," said Barryar. "And these aren't friends. They're aliens. Jagar and his fellow Free-sailors are trying to steal their ship."

"Are you sure? I was just there an hour or so back. Yarkra told me you'd gone on to Starfallen's nest. I would have caught up sooner, but Snaggleclaw wanted a drink, and then we found a patch of ripe—"

"What do you want, Argarrar?" interrupted Harkayé.

"I thought Barryar and his hunters would be hungry. I brought jelly rolls. I know how much he likes them."

"We'll eat after the hunt," Barryar said stiffly. His ears were twitching. He combed his claws through the fur on either side of his neck in what Mops guessed was a grooming ritual to help him keep calm. The sharp smell of pepper wafted from him. The scent of Jynx embarrassment?

"If that's what you want, Bar-Bar. I'll save you one with rock bulb shavings."

Mops turned away to hide her smile. She could practically hear Barryar's thoughts: *Come on, Argarrar... Not in front of the aliens and the Speaker.*

"Who wants a ride?" asked Argarrar. "Old Snaggleclaw sets a quick pace when he's in the mood."

Azure whistled with joy and raced toward the wagon-snake.

"Wait," said Harkayé. "Argarrar, Jagar is no toothless kit. He's my charge now, not yours."

"I look after all my kits," Argarrar replied with a twitch of her tail. "What do you plan to do if he has one of his episodes? Drug him again?"

The fur rose on Harkayé's neck. A floral smell filled the air. The other Jynx backed away in alarm.

Argarrar just sniffed and wiped her nose on the back of her hand. "Better to have me along, and you know it, Speaker."

Doc pinged for Mops' attention. *"I'm losing the visual feed from the drop ship."*

"Let me see." Her monocle showed nothing but shadow with pinpricks of moving light. From her speaker, she heard a low, droning buzz, interspersed with tiny clicking sounds.

"One of the locking mechanisms just failed."

"How?" Nothing the Jynx possessed should have been able to scratch the ship's paint, let alone cut through a lock. The visual on her monocle flickered and died. "Harkayé, I don't know what Jagar's doing, but it's kicking my ship's ass."

Harkayé stared. "Kicking its . . . ?"

"Probably a human thing," guessed Argarrar. "Look at those legs. Makes sense they'd use them for fighting."

Harkayé strode toward the wagon. "Get us to Jagar quickly, before he overpowers their ship."

Argarrar scrambled back onto her bench. "We'll be there faster than Bar-Bar can gobble a jelly roll."

Starfallen climbed into the wagon and settled near the front. Gabe and Kumar looked to Mops for permission.

"Let's go," she said. "Don't eat any rolls unless Azure says it's all right."

Cate hadn't moved. He watched as the Jynx filled the wagon. Others climbed up to cling to the sides. Argarrar yelled at Snaggleclaw, yanking the levers and trying to turn the whole contraption around.

Cate retreated a step toward the trees.

"I don't have time to chase you if you run off," Mops said to Cate. "But how well do you think you'll do alone on Hell's Claws? You'll be safer with us."

He didn't respond, but after a moment, he slumped and started toward the wagon. Mops followed. The Jynx squeezed together to make room. Mops found herself pressed tightly against Cate on one side and a muscular, brown-furred Jynx on the other.

The wagon-snake bellowed like an oversized tuba as the wagon began to move, quickly gaining speed.

"They can alter their trees and reprogram alien brains, but they're still riding around in animal-drawn wagons. What the hell is going on with this planet?"

11

*Excerpt from the Personal Log of Ulique
Pliquette, Quetzalus Botanist
Mission Day Three*

After days of arguing, we've finally decided on a name for
this world. Tuxatl[1] beat out Pliquette's World and Axla-
quat.[2]

The Jynx are a small, semi-nomadic rodent-like people
whose technological development is roughly equivalent to
Quetzalus society in the year 915 CQ. The young men of
the nearby camp have been happy to show me the local
plants and trees in exchange for the chance to ride on our
backs. (We've only begun to translate the local language,
but the Jynx quickly invented a pantomime for "ride.")

The plants on this world are incredible. The cellular
complexity of the trees is on a scale I've only seen in
Tjikko. I haven't yet deciphered their version of genetics,
but from what I can tell, many of the trees for kilometers
around are identical: essentially, clones.

For now, the skytrees are off limits. I'm told I'd need
permission from someone called a Speaker to examine
one of those. I did sneak off for a quick flyover and used
ground-penetrating scans to map out the skytree root

system. The upper layers, at any rate. The roots might go even deeper than the tree is high! I also detected low-power electromagnetic waves emanating from the sky-tree . . . I have no idea how that works or what purpose it serves. It could be a side effect of the lightning that regularly strikes the skytrees.

My first botanical mystery on an alien world. I love it!

I've identified four of our food crops so far that should grow in Tuxatl soil. Two others would probably thrive with a few modifications.

None of the native plants are edible, but I discovered a red, vine-like type of seaweed that has an intoxicating effect when burnt. As team botanist, I took it upon myself to test the effects.

For a while there, I'm pretty sure I could see time. It was . . . squiggly. And it whistled a lot. My hair glowed red for half a day, and my tongue is still numb.

I should try a lower dose next time.

Zan Pliquette is supposed to be meeting with the leaders of the Black Spire camp later today to discuss our longer-term plans . . .

---

1. "Small Home."
2. "World of Infinite Smells."

"**W**HY ARE WE GOING inland?" asked Mops. "The drop ship is that way."

"The Jynx are circling so the wind doesn't carry their scent to their prey," said Starfallen. She'd been discussing hunting tactics with Barryar. Well, mostly Starfallen had been discussing while Barryar listened. She turned back to him and said, "Patience is key. Remember what I told you last time."

"Yes, I remember," said Barryar.

Mops stood up for a better view, and her breath caught. Far off, a skytree rose into the clouds. Tiny specks—birds, or the local equivalent—circled the tree about half a kilometer up. "What happens when one of those things falls?"

"Why would they fall?" asked Parya, a short-furred Jynx whose tail was a third the length of the others. Given the way Parya kept her tail tucked and hidden, Mops guessed it wasn't a normal variation. Possibly an old injury or birth defect.

"How long do skytrees normally live?" asked Mops.

"With sun and water and lightning, a skytree can live as long as Tuxatl itself," said Parya. "They're tended and protected by the Treeshield camps."

Argarrar halted the wagon. Harkayé climbed up and stood, balancing on one corner to face the Jynx and aliens packed together. "I lead this hunt. Barryar is my second. Use no weapons until Jagar is safe."

Barryar visibly preened. Mops could see his eagerness in the quiver of his tail and the twitch of his muscles.

"Parya, scout the target," Harkayé continued. "Report back with numbers, weapons, and locations."

Parya jumped from the wagon, scaled the closest tree, and disappeared toward the drop ship.

Harkayé turned to Mops next. "Your people are loud and smelly. You can accompany us, but you will keep to the rear. Leave your weapons here. Argarrar can watch over them."

"I don't think so," said Mops. "We're not here to shoot anyone, but I can't surrender our weapons."

Several of the Jynx hissed. Starfallen tensed.

"This is not your hunt," Barryar snapped. "You can't—"

Harkayé snarled. Barryar shrank back, his mouth closing with an audible click of teeth.

"If you won't leave your weapons, you'll stay behind," said Harkayé. "I've seen what alien guns can do. I won't risk Jagar's safety."

Nobody had objected to them bringing their weapons along in the wagon with the other Jynx. "Jagar is important, I take it?"

Harkayé raised her head. "He's our future."

"What does that mean?" When nobody answered, Mops

handed her pistol and combat baton to Kumar. "I'll come with you, unarmed. Gabe too. If that's acceptable," she added, trying to be diplomatic.

Harkayé appeared to consider this. "It is."

Barryar huffed and hopped from the wagon, leaving the smell of flowers in his wake. He walked to the nearest tree and dragged his claws down the trunk.

"You'll have to forgive Barryar," said Starfallen. "He's eager to prove himself. His grandmother led the Hunters for decades. Barryar is too young and impetuous for the position he's in, but he's determined to earn her seat in the Circle."

The rest of the Jynx climbed out. Mops and Gabe followed. Argarrar was feeding her wagon-snake what looked like an enormous spiny cucumber with a withered yellow flower on one end. Snaggleclaw gulped it down, then licked Argarrar's face.

"Argarrar's as good with the animals as she is with the young," said Starfallen. "They listen to her when they won't listen to anyone else."

"The animals or the kits?" asked Mops.

"Both."

Mops opened a channel to her people. "Keep comms open," she said quietly. "We'll follow Harkayé's lead, but if things get choppy, I want you ready to act."

Parya returned a short time later, jumping gracefully from the trees. "I counted six total," she reported. "Jagar and five Freesailors. None of them have guns. Yarkra and Kharab are bound together a short distance away."

Mops guessed Yarkra and Kharab were the guards Harkayé had left to watch the ship.

Parya squatted on her haunches and sketched a quick map of the clearing in the dirt with one claw.

"Where exactly is Jagar?" asked Harkayé.

"At the ship. He's using diamond-leafs."

"Clever." Harkayé studied the map. "We'll flank them. I'll take one group around to strike from the ocean-side. Barryar will lead the rest. On my signal, we close the circle."

"Where do you want me?" asked Argarrar, squeezing into the huddle between Parya and another Jynx.

"Back at the wagon." Barryar reached over to stroke the older Jynx's arm. "We don't want to risk you getting hurt."

"You're sweet, Bar-Bar." Argarrar sniffed. "But you're thick as root lard if you think I'm staying behind."

Several of the closest Jynx made a chirping sound Mops guessed was amusement, and a musty, salty smell filled the air.

Barryar turned away and brushed his claws through the fur on his neck. "Fine, but you have to stay with the two humans."

Both groups carried weighted nets with hooks woven into them, along with several rifles. Harkayé's team hurried ahead. Barryar waited until they were out of sight, then organized his own group. He communicated mostly by gesture, using hands, tail, and ears to relay commands.

"They're amazing," Gabe whispered. "They remind me of a cross between cats and possums."

"I'd keep that to yourself," said Mops. "Most species don't like being compared to another world's animals."

"Sorry. That's good to know, thanks."

Overhead, the ring gleamed brighter than before, catching the sunlight like a billion tiny mirrors. Mops fought to keep her attention focused on the ground and on the Jynx up ahead—a fight Gabe had already lost, as he gawked open-mouthed and raised his cane to record it all.

"He looks like he's fighting off invisible serpent-gliders," said Argarrar, giving off a faint salt-smell of amusement.

"It's a camera," whispered Mops. "He's saving images of your world to share with others."

Barryar turned and hissed at them both. "Stop your chattering!"

Argarrar chirped once, but raised her chin, exposing her neck.

"Starfallen's translator has that gesture tagged as an apology," said Doc.

Mops nodded and imitated the Jynx apology. Gabe did the same, then tucked his cane through his belt like a sword.

It seemed to mollify Barryar. His tail lashed back and forth at the others, who spread apart and crept toward the clearing. They were close enough now for Mops to make out the drop ship through the trees.

Three Jynx stood near the ship, including Jagar. Two more stood watching the bound guards. Mops didn't see the sixth. All wore long, knitted scarves in green, purple, or mustard yellow. The scarves crossed their torsos and looped around the waists like belts, with the ends hanging down in front like wool loincloths.

Barryar might be young, but he'd clearly picked up his grandmother's hunting skills. He moved with such stealth Mops would have lost him if her monocle hadn't automatically tracked his movement. He crawled through the brush to the edge of the crater.

Mops focused on the ship. She touched Gabe's arm and pointed.

He followed her stare. "Christ on a pogo stick," he whispered. "Are those *bugs*?"

"What's a pogo—never mind." Mops studied the undulating mass of red and black that covered much of her ship like a lumpy, iridescent blanket. They were thickest around the hatch, crawling over one another.

Parya had said Jagar was using diamond-leafs. Were these what had taken out the security camera and broken through one of the hatch locks?

Argarrar moved soundlessly toward the other Jynx. Soundless to Mops, at least. Parya spun and broke away from the others. She motioned with her hands and tail, clearly shooing the older Jynx back. Argarrar slumped. She brushed a hand down Parya's arm, then retreated.

Several Jynx scaled the trees. Barryar and a few others readied nets.

Mops couldn't see Harkayé's group, but they should have had time to get into position by now. Mops' breathing sped up with pre-mission anticipation, even though she wasn't supposed to participate.

Barryar had gone perfectly still, all save the last few centimeters of his tail, which vibrated like a twitchy pressure gauge ready to blow.

An explosive, honking sneeze echoed through the woods. Mops jumped hard, feeling like her heart had tried to shoot out of her throat.

Halfway up her tree, Parya brought one hand to her snout, but it didn't help. More sneezes followed in quick succession.

The Jynx around the drop ship bolted, scrambling away in different directions.

"Blast it all, Parya!" Barryar leapt forward and hurled his net, but the Jynx he'd been aiming at dropped low and scampered away.

Parya sneezed one last time. Strings of dark mucus swung like pendulums from her nose. Her mouth was open, the tip of her blue tongue protruding as she panted for breath. "Sorry!"

Harkayé's group struck from the other side. Nets flew through the air. Snarls arose where Jynx clashed, kicking and biting and rolling about on the ground.

"Where's Jagar?" Harkayé shouted.

One Jynx raced directly toward Mops' hiding place, but skidded to a halt upon spotting her and Gabe. His fur was trimmed short, revealing mottled brown-and-black skin beneath, and he wore a thick green scarf with a sheathed knife tucked through at the hip. Mops raised her hands. "I don't want to hurt you."

The Jynx pounced farther and higher than Mops would have thought possible. His hands and feet struck her torso. The two of them fell together. Mops' breath exploded from the impact with the ground.

"Captain!" Gabe drew his cane and raised it two-handed, ready to strike.

"Don't!" Mops got an arm against the Jynx's throat and pressed hard. He responded by raking her gut with his claws, but they couldn't penetrate her uniform.

Mops grabbed a small canister from her equipment harness, aimed, and squeezed. Compressed air shot directly into the Jynx's face.

He leapt off her, body flipping and twisting in midair. He landed on his feet and staggered, gagging and growling, eyes wide.

Mops sat up and adjusted the dial at the top of the canister. A narrower blast of air hit him in the ear.

The Jynx fled, fur standing on end like he'd been electrocuted. One of Barryar's hunters raced after him.

"What's happening?" Kumar sounded anxious. "Captain, do you need help?"

"We're all right." Mops looked around. Tufts of fur floated on the breeze. Two of the Jynx had been captured: one tangled in a net, a second pinned down by Parya while one of Harkayé's hunters knotted a rope around their neck. The other would-be ship thieves had disappeared, along with about half of the hunters.

The entire fight had taken less than a minute.

"Harkayé, can the rest of my crew join me to help clean my ship?" asked Mops.

"Not until we deal with Jagar." The Speaker stood near the edge of the clearing, looking up.

Jagar clung to the top of a tree, just beneath the large, feathery fronds. He was tugging his body from the trunk like he wanted to jump away, but couldn't. His claws seemed to be stuck. Other Jynx had scaled the closest trees, leaving him nowhere to go.

"It's over," Barryar shouted. "Come on down."

Jagar's tail lashed. "I *can't!*"

"Are you seeing this, Captain?" Gabe pointed his cane's recording globe at Jagar.

Mops focused on Jagar, letting her monocle zoom in. It wasn't that Jagar's claws were embedded in the wood. The tree itself had grown over the tips of his fingers and toes. He pulled harder.

Harkayé touched the trunk of the tree holding Jagar trapped. "You're bonding with the paka tree. You have to control your connection."

"Just cut me free," yelled Jagar.

"Focus, child!"

"Stop yelling at him." Argarrar strode up next to Harkayé. Her lips were pulled back, displaying teeth faded to gray, but still sharp. "He's too frightened to think clearly. The fight-scent is only making things worse."

Harkayé's tail lashed once, but she stepped back, letting Argarrar take her place.

Argarrar's entire demeanor changed when she craned her head to speak with Jagar. Her tail curved, and her voice softened, taking on a deep trilling undertone. "The diamond-leafs were a clever idea. Where did you get the scent to lure them here?"

"From the metalworkers' forge. I didn't realize it would be so strong."

"And what was your plan once you got inside their space wagon? Do you or your friends know how to make this thing fly? Where would you go? Did you even think to pack a tooth cleaner or a change of clothes?"

Jagar jabbed his tail at Mops and Gabe. "Are these the new aliens?"

"They're called humans," said Argarrar. "They've got a Prodryan back at the wagon, and a squiggly one called a Rokkau that looks like a blue-and-black fish with snakes for arms and legs, and the biggest eyes you've ever seen. I think she wants to take Snaggleclaw home with her."

"Enough of this," snapped Barryar. "Yarkra, Parya, take your saws and cut the paka—"

Harkayé snarled.

Instantly, Barryar shrank back and raised his head in apology. Mops guessed this was the Jynx equivalent of a commanding officer putting an overeager lieutenant in their place.

"How much trouble am I in this time?" asked Jagar.

Argarrar chirped. "Look at this mess. What do you think? At least your friends didn't manage to steal anything." She tilted her head. "Making the tree grow. That's new."

"I made dawnflowers grow last year," said Jagar.

"Dawnflowers are tiny. This thing's twelve teks high. And the flowers didn't try to eat you." She stepped closer and started to sing.

The translator didn't know what to make of Argarrar's song. It was a simple melody with a low, purring undertone. The words could have been an older form of their language, or another tongue altogether. Or maybe they weren't words at all, but simple sounds meant to soothe and calm. Mops heard Barryar humming along.

Jagar stopped trying to break free, and his fur settled. His tail swayed in time with the music.

One foot slipped free of its wooden prison. Jagar squawked and clung tighter to keep from falling, but once he recovered, he was able to pull his other limbs loose as well. He scooted slowly and carefully backward, jumping the last couple of meters to the ground.

Argarrar immediately wrapped her arms around him, giving him a good sniff, then grooming his head and neck with her claws.

"I'm all right," he muttered, but didn't pull away.

"Kumar, I think we're clear for you to join us," Mops whispered.

"On our way, sir."

Mops approached the ship for a closer look at the bugs. They were similar in shape to the glassy blue leaf-shaped insects she'd seen earlier. These were smaller and darker in color, black with red veins.

She reviewed her equipment inventory. She'd packed a few basic cleaning supplies out of habit, but no insecticides. Not that their normal sprays would necessarily affect alien bugs. She reached to pull one of the bugs free.

"I wouldn't do that." Argarrar hadn't made a sound as she approached. She licked her whiskers. "I don't know what your skin's made of, but those presexual emissions can burn through stone and metal."

Mops jerked her hand back. "Presexual?"

"They're not trying to eat your ship, Captain Mop. They're trying to mate with it. The secretions are acidic. Young diamond-leafs do the impregnating, but to do that, they have to get through the exoskeleton of the older female."

"Sex on this planet sounds unpleasant."

"The females don't seem to mind. You should ask Starfallen about them."

"Ask me about what?" Starfallen and the rest had arrived at the edge of the crater. Cate hung back while the others approached.

Mops pointed to the ship. "Diamond-leafs."

Starfallen threw up her arms. "Every spring I have to patch my shelter because the vomit-choked little bastards think my trees are the perfect place for a mating pit."

"I thought native life avoided Prodryan air," said Mops.

"Normally, most of it does," said Starfallen. "Unfortunately, the females are drawn to skytrees to make their nests. Whatever the Speaker did to my tree makes it particularly attractive to them."

The rest of Mops' crew arrived out of breath from running. Azure went immediately to the ship. She used flat-handled forceps to seize one of the insects by the tail and pluck it free. It squirmed in protest as she dropped it into a clear sample tube.

Mops passed along Argarrar's warning, then blasted compressed air onto the edge of the hatch, clearing a small area long enough to check the damage. Paint had bubbled and flaked away, and the metal beneath was pitted. It looked like the diamond-leafs had tried to burrow into the crack around the hatch. Another hour or two, and they might have gotten through. "Kumar, any suggestions?"

Kumar was already connecting a hose and wand to his portable compressor. He attached a yellow-and-white–striped canister and sprayed a cone of soapy water onto the side of the drop ship. The buzzing grew louder as bugs began to drop or fly away. "You can't go wrong with good old soap and water. It's fascinating, really. Soap doesn't work with *all* insectoid life, of course, but there are at least four different ways it interferes with flight and—"

"Kumar," she said gently.

"Sorry." He continued spraying the ship. "I diluted the mix. I don't want to kill them if we don't have to. But this should get most of them off the ship."

"Good work." Rubin was definitely rubbing off on

him, if he was more concerned about protecting the diamond-leafs than collecting them for dissection. "Doc, what kind of damage are we looking at?"

"Roughly eight percent of the energy dispersion grid is nonfunctional, but as long as we avoid a direct hit to the damaged section, the remaining ninety-two percent should be enough to protect us. The hatch seal remains flight-worthy."

"Once the bugs are gone, we should scrub the ship down to get rid of any remaining acid or scent," said Mops. "Then apply a quick layer of sealant for protection."

Kumar nodded. "You read my mind, Captain."

That would keep Kumar busy and happy for the time being. Mops turned to Argarrar. "How is Jagar?"

"Angry, embarrassed, and frustrated. All of which is normal at that age. He'll be calmer once he goes through the change." She looked past Mops to Kumar. "You do a good job keeping your boys under control."

"What change?"

"Jynx are born male," said Starfallen. "They become female when they're older."

"Your people don't?" Argarrar paused. "You mean those poor fellows are trapped like that forever?"

Mops looked around at the young hunters. This was a detail the Quetzalus hadn't mentioned in their reports. "Not necessarily. There are hormonal and surgical options. It's a relatively simple process to switch from one biological sex to another, or to mix and match if that's your preference. Then there are various prosthetics . . ."

"Prosthetics?"

"Artificial parts."

Argarrar's muzzle wrinkled. "Could you give yourselves tails?"

Azure looked up from the diamond-leafs she'd been studying. "Mapping artificial nerve and muscle wouldn't be too hard. The trick would be training the brain to control an entirely new limb. You'd probably need months of physical therapy, but it should be possible."

"Then why haven't you?" Argarrar sniffed. "You humans are as bad as Starfallen. All of your technology, and every one of you walking around bare-assed. At least the Quetzalus had tails, even if they were lumpy, near-useless things." She looked over her shoulder and lowered her voice. "What about repairing an injured Jynx tail?"

Mops followed her gaze to Parya. "We'd have to know a lot more about your anatomy. Maybe someday, but right now we don't have the knowledge or the tools to do it safely."

"It's a shame. The Speakers can alter their bodies to heal injuries or regrow lost limbs, but they can't do it for anyone else. Maybe someday the rest of the Jynx will learn that trick."

"Captain." Unlike Barryar and the others, Harkayé's fur was immaculate, seemingly untouched by the fighting. Another advantage of being a Speaker, no doubt. "Are you injured?"

"I'm fine, thank you."

Argarrar sniffed and walked away without a word. Mops couldn't tell whether she disliked the Speaker, or maybe the Jynx just didn't bother with good-byes.

"Could your ship help us to find the Jynx who escaped my hunters?" asked Harkayé.

"We can detect animal life from their heat signatures," Mops said slowly. "The computer is smart enough to distinguish the Jynx from other native species. But it can't tell one Jynx from another."

"They'll be heading for the docks. Barryar, send three hunters to pursue. If they reach their ships, we'll never root them out." Harkayé twisted to face the distant sky-tree. "Captain, I've been speaking with the Preceptor about your presence here and the difficulties you bring."

"The Preceptor?" asked Mops.

"The word has layers of meaning." Starfallen pointed to the ring arched across the sky. "Properly speaking, that whole thing is the Preceptor. Harkayé and the other Speakers, they're . . . extensions."

"Are you suggesting the planet's ring is alive?" The rest of Mops' team had gone quiet, listening.

"I can't say for sure," said Starfallen. "My best guess is that it operates as a kind of computer, governing and guiding the Jynx. Its commands are relayed through individual Speakers like Harkayé."

"You couldn't have mentioned that sooner?" Mops demanded.

"We hadn't even finished breakfast!"

Gabe chuckled. "So it's a giant computer with wireless speakers?"

Mops ignored him and studied the sky. This raised countless questions. Who had built such a thing, and why? What was it programmed to do? Could she communicate directly with the Preceptor? She turned back to Harkayé. "Does that mean you're a machine too?"

"Hardly. I was created, yes. Formed in the image of the ancient Jynx to help guide my people along the path." She slashed her claws through the air, cutting off further conversation. "Your presence leads people like Jagar and the Freesailors farther from that path, just like the Prodryans and the Quetzalus did before you."

"I'm sorry," said Mops. "We don't mean to cause problems."

"Nonetheless." Harkayé pointed to where Jagar and the other two prisoners were being escorted to Argarrar's wagon. "This is a delicate time in our history. The longer you stay, the greater the disruption."

That could have been her team's motto.

"Clearly we should leave at once," Cate piped up. "It's the only civilized choice. We're unwelcome here. Your attempt to ally with the Jynx has failed, Captain."

"We'll be happy to leave your planet, Harkayé." Mops' mind raced. "Just as soon as we finish repairing the damage your people did to our drop ship."

Harkayé studied Mops closely. "How long will that take?"

"We'll need three days for the sealants to properly set and harden."

Kumar opened his mouth, presumably to offer a "helpful" correction to her estimate. A glare from Mops silenced him.

"Three days?" repeated Cate.

"Unless you know a faster way to fully remove and

neutralize alien acids, mix hull alloy replacement, apply enough to withstand the debris we have to pass through on the way to the *Pufferfish*, lay nanowire for the dispersion grid, prime the damaged metal, and paint the hull. We could probably hold off on painting until we get back to the *Pufferfish*, but the rest is vital to the ship's safety."

Knowing Cate, there was a chance he'd actually studied some or all of those subjects, but even if he had, he hopefully lacked the practical experience to realize the drop ship could be flightworthy in a couple of hours. Mops waited, jaw clenched.

"I do not," Cate conceded.

Mops sighed in relief.

Harkayé arched her whiskers before turning away. "I need to question our prisoners. We will speak more soon, Captain."

"Well, I'll be grounded," said Starfallen as she watched the Speaker leave. "That's not how I thought this meeting would go."

"What did you expect?" asked Mops.

Starfallen waited until Harkayé was out of hearing. "To be blunt, I expected her to kill you."

12

"You want us to try to talk to the planet's ring?" asked Monroe.

Two and a quarter seconds passed as his words traveled to the drop ship on the surface and were relayed to Mops, and her response made the return trip. "Starfallen thinks it's a computer. She says it runs the planet through Jynx called Speakers."

"I'll put Grom on it." He gestured to Grom, who spread the limbs around their face in acknowledgment. Monroe suppressed a grin. The gesture always made Grom look like they'd transformed their face into an asterisk.

"Be careful," said Mops. "And for the love of Elvis, be polite. We don't know what this thing is or what it might be capable of."

"Yes, sir. Who's Elvis?"

"No idea," said Mops. "That phrase was on the list of human sayings Gabe gave me."

Monroe suppressed the questions he really wanted to ask. He'd been monitoring the updates from Mops' medical implants, as well as the reports from Doc and Azure—including details about her episode outside Starfallen's home. Mops would understand his concern, but she wouldn't appreciate it right now.

He hated being stuck on the Pufferfish *while Mops was running around sick on the planet surface, but her orders made sense. He was needed here. "You be careful too."*

"As long as we avoid any more sex-crazed bugs, we should be fine. Mops out."

Sex-crazed bugs? *The landing team's next report should be interesting.*

"Can you imagine it, Commander?" Grom was staring at the main screen, spines erect with excitement. "A computer with the mass of a small moon. Think of the storage, the processing power . . . You could run a planetwide MMO of Ice Hunter *with no lag time!*"

"There will be no *uploading of games to the giant alien supercomputer*," Monroe said firmly. "Just figure out what it is and whether we can talk to it."

"**C**APTAIN MOP!" ARGARRAR HURRIED toward her, a woven green basket in one hand. She brought out a butter-browned pastry with red goop oozing from holes in the top. "Jelly roll?"

Mops' stomach growled. "I appreciate the offer, but we're safer sticking with our own food."

"Your loss." Argarrar took a bite and chewed.

"Starfallen mentioned rebellious elements of Jynx society." Mops pointed to where Harkayé had taken over Argarrar's wagon. The Speaker stood over Jagar and the other two prisoners while Barryar kept watch from the back of the wagon. "I assume this is what she was talking about?"

Argarrar's tongue flicked out to clean globs of escaped jelly from her snout. "Everyone strays from the path on occasion, especially when they're young. But there are some who want to abandon it altogether. The Freesail camp spends months or years at sea, away from the Speakers. It makes them headstrong and too independent for their own good. Throw you aliens into the soup, and suddenly you've got Jynx whispering about leaving Tuxatl altogether to fly about the galaxy like rutting fools."

"Is that what Jagar wants?"

"I've seen how he watches the sky at night. He's not happy here. Not that I blame him. But the more time he spends with the Freesailors, the more their ideas take root in his blood, and the more he alienates the Black Spire Jynx."

"Freesailors don't get along with the Black Spire camp?" asked Mops.

"Oh, they get along with anyone, so long as you can pay," said Argarrar. "They're sailors, traders, scavengers, and thieves. Stubborn as boulders, the whole lot. They need us for crops and supplies, materials to build and repair their ships, and more. And without them, we lose access to goods from the rest of Tuxatl. They fight with the rest of the camps from time to time, but the fighting never used to last. These days, there's more growling and less talking. A Freesail Trader who approaches a camp is likely to be chased off with guns and claws."

"In my opinion," said Starfallen, "the Jynx are gliding steadily toward war."

In the wagon, Harkayé drew her blade and slashed across a prisoner's face. Chestnut-colored blood welled from the cut, spreading through the fur. She pressed her wrist against the cut, then turned and repeated the process with the second prisoner.

"Leave them alone," shouted Jagar.

Harkayé spun and raised her other hand. Jagar bristled, but didn't back down.

"She won't hit him," said Argarrar. The tip of her tail twitched, and she gave off the faint floral scent Mops recognized as anger. "The boy knows it, too."

"Mops, that short sword appears to be made of metallic glass."

"What does that mean?" whispered Mops.

"Depending on the alloy, the blade could be as much as five times stronger than titanium. It's centuries beyond the metallurgy of the other Jynx's weapons."

"Something they salvaged from the Prodryans or the Quetzalus?"

"It doesn't match Prodryan style, and that thing would be little more than a toothpick to a Quetzalus."

Mops raised her voice. "That's an interesting weapon."

"You noticed that, did you?" asked Starfallen. "In my former life, I would have killed her and taken it as a trophy. I've asked about it, but all anyone will say is that it's a Speaker's weapon."

Mops watched as Harkayé returned to the first prisoner and touched his wound again. "We've found that torture doesn't work on most species."

"Harkayé isn't torturing them," said Starfallen. "You saw how she touched the wounds? Speaker pheromones are more potent in the bloodstream. Soon they'll be fighting to tell her everything. Not that they're likely to know much. The leaders of the Freesail camp keep their secrets close to the fur."

"Why not just let the troublemakers leave Tuxatl?" asked Mops. "People like Jagar get what they want, and they're off the planet so they can't cause more trouble here."

"The Preceptor's mission is to guide and protect the Jynx," said Argarrar. "Even the Freesail camp. They can't take their place on the path if they leave. As for Jagar, he's too important. If we lose him, it could set things back a thousand years."

"What makes him so special?"

"He's the next step on the path." At a gesture from Harkayé, Argarrar licked her fingers and started toward the wagon. "How are your people coming with their work, Captain?"

Mops checked over her shoulder to see how things were coming with the drop ship. With help from Gabe and Azure, Kumar had gotten the last of the diamond-leafs cleaned off and had applied a layer of hull-patch alloy. The ship was probably flightworthy already. "I think we're finished for the moment."

"Then it's time to head home. You'll have to walk alongside the wagon, I'm afraid. Harkayé will want space to continue her interrogation. I don't know how fast you are, so just squawk if you need me to slow down."

"What will Harkayé do with those two once she's finished questioning them?"

Argarrar's tail lashed once, and the anger scent grew stronger. She walked away without answering.

Kumar was the first to speak up as they walked. "Captain, if we do convince the Jynx to help us—if we do to the Prodryans what the Jynx did to Starfallen and we alter an entire species against their will—how is that different from what the Krakau did to us?"

Mops had been struggling with that same question. She had yet to come up with an answer that didn't make her sick to her stomach. "What happened to us was an accident. We'd be acting deliberately. This would be closer to Admiral Sage trying to turn other species feral to serve the Alliance."

"That's not better," said Kumar.

"No, it's not. But the alternative is genocide. Either we wipe out the Prodryans, or they exterminate the rest of us. At least this option lets both sides survive."

"You're wrong, Captain." Cate was unusually subdued. "If you do this, my people might still look like Prodryans, but we'd be empty shells. We'd be like you: monstrous imitations of what we once were."

There was a time Mops would have argued the point, argued that she and her crew remained human. Nothing the Krakau did could take that away.

That was before she'd spent time among unchanged humans. Before she'd felt the monster in her blood bubbling to the surface. The so-called cure she'd been given was nothing but a mask, a thin, Krakau-made veneer over a feral animal.

"There's another consideration," Gabe said quietly. "If these Speakers can reprogram Prodryans, what's to stop them from doing the same to us?"

"Or maybe they could cure us?" said Kumar. "Make us truly human again. Fix what's happening to the captain."

Mops didn't answer.

"Why stop with humans?" demanded Cate. "What's to

keep them from remaking the entire galaxy? Neutering every race they encounter?"

"Excellent question," snapped Mops. "How do you stop a race who's determined to destroy everyone else?"

He stroked his mandibles. For a moment, Mops thought her point might have gotten through. Then, as if a circuit breaker had reset in his brain, he straightened and said, "I recognize the parallel you're trying to make, but your logic is flawed."

"In what way?"

"Because Prodryans are the superior species. It's our destiny to spread throughout the galaxy. Trying to prevent our victory would be like trying to halt the expansion of the universe. It's not malicious, Captain. It simply *is*."

It was like arguing with the ocean. Mops walked away without another word, fighting a wash of hopelessness. Cate was tolerant for a Prodryan, but at the core, his beliefs were uncrackable.

Starfallen had remained silent throughout the discussion. She caught Mops' attention and spread her hands, her unspoken message clear. The Prodryans wouldn't change on their own. They couldn't. If the rest of the galaxy wanted to survive, that change would have to be forced.

Harkayé questioned the two prisoners in the wagon for the next half hour of the journey. As Argarrar had predicted, they grew more cooperative with time. Eventually, Harkayé stepped away and sat on the opposite bench, leaving the prisoners in silence.

Barryar conferred quietly with the Speaker, then jumped from the wagon and approached Mops. "I've been told to warn you that other Freesailors may return and try again to break into your ship."

"We've increased security," Mops assured him. "Kumar set a high-voltage pulse to run through the dispersion grid—"

Barryar blinked at her.

"Anyone who touches the ship without permission will get zapped," she clarified. *Except for the damaged section of the grid.* "I didn't do that before because it can kill insects and smaller wildlife."

Barryar pulled a brush from a satchel at his waist and began working it through the fur of his tail. The repetitive motion seemed to calm him. "I was just a kit when the lizard people landed here. Like others my age, I was curious about their machines. I was the first to sneak into their settlement. I made friends with one called Ulique Pliquette. She let us ride on her back."

"'Ulique' means third child of the Pliquette family." Mops remembered the name from the Quetzalus records. "She was a scientist, wasn't she?"

"I wouldn't know. She was funny." He paused in his grooming. "But she wasn't of Tuxatl. They evolved for a different world. They didn't fit here. Neither do you, with your bare skin and glass eyepatches and scent like salt and dried pulpweed seeds."

"What happened to Ulique?" asked Mops, though she knew the answer.

"Starfallen's people killed her, along with the rest of her camp."

"It doesn't have to be like that." Mops pointed toward Azure. "Other races can coexist in peace. More or less."

"Maybe one day," said Barryar. "When we reach the end of this path. Not now, when we're so easily lured from our duty." He looked past her to where Starfallen was walking alongside Cate. "I've befriended two aliens. First Ulique, then Starfallen. What does that say of me?"

"That you're a friendly person."

He stopped to pull fur from the brush's bristles. "Starfallen has helped me become a better hunter. I worry about the cost, that she's made me less Jynx."

"You're curious too, aren't you?" asked Mops. "Like Jagar and the Freesailors. You think about the stars and other worlds."

"Don't compare me to those thieves." Barryar hissed

and stormed away, tail whipping back and forth. He climbed back onto the wagon and sat beside Harkayé, their shoulders almost-but-not-quite touching.

Mops walked slower until the rest of her team caught up. Azure had been struggling to match the others' pace, so Kumar and Gabe were taking turns carrying her on their backs.

"Looks like you hit a nerve," said Gabe.

Ahead, the wagon jolted onto a road of rippled black stone. The wheels made a buzzing sound as they rolled over the paved surface.

Gabe crouched at the edge of the road. "Reminds me of an old lava flow. Too regular to be natural, but it looks like the same texture as pictures out of Hawaii, Italy, Guatemala . . ."

The edges were cracked and crumbling away, but Mops saw no sign of weeds. On Earth, she'd seen old roads reduced to rubble, overgrown with grasses and other plants. Here, all vegetation stopped a half-meter from the edges.

"The trees have changed too," said Azure. With her tentacles wrapped around Kumar, she looked like an oversized backpack. "These are a different species from the paka trees we saw around the drop ship."

Bare trunks with glossy green-and-black bark rose four to five meters, where they erupted into a fountain of leafless, vinelike branches that hung to the ground all around. The branches from a single tree could envelop an area six meters wide.

Small rodent-like creatures climbed among the branches, whistling as the wagon passed. One particularly brave animal threw a rock or seed pod that bounced harmlessly off the side of the wagon.

"They're called scolds," said Starfallen. "The Jynx set traps to keep them out of their camps, but a handful always find a way in. They make their nests in the bellor trees. I'm told they're quite tasty. I've never been able to stomach the things, myself."

Mops heard Jynx voices in the distance as the wagon crested a hill. Moments later, she got her first view of the Black Spire camp.

She knew better than to make assumptions, but when the Jynx spoke of a camp, she'd imagined rows of identical quick-deploying EMC shelters, their impact-resistant domes programmed to blend into the surrounding terrain.

Instead, the road led into a grove of ancient bellor trees. Many of the branches were interwoven with long strips of colorful cloth. Each tree formed a shelter and home. The larger trees had secondary rings of branches higher up, and Mops saw one with a third level. Additional branches were stretched and lashed together between the trees, creating floors and walkways and bridges.

Small Jynx chased each other across roads of rippled stone. One Jynx climbed up the outside of a bellor dome and jumped to catch a low-hanging bridge. The rest scrambled after. An older Jynx poked her head out the door and growled, but the kids were already sprinting to the next tree.

A shallow stream cut through the left side of the grove. The land around the base of the stream was overgrown with flowers and squat bushes or trees, all bulging with what Mops assumed were fruits. Jynx used short, curved knives—and, in some cases, their claws—to cut the ripest fruits free, piling them into wooden wheelbarrows.

She saw Jynx weaving thick blankets, repairing wagons and smaller tools, shaping and carving wood, washing clothes . . .

"Smells pleasant enough," said Kumar. "Either they've developed some form of plumbing, or else their waste smells like flowers."

Argarrar let out a loud, coughing laugh. "It most certainly does not."

"Will we be allowed to explore the camp?" asked Gabe.

"You'll wait here," said Harkayé. "I'll call the Mothers' Circle. Parya will stay with you and escort you to the Circle when it's time."

She and Barryar brought the prisoners from the wagon and escorted them down the road, flanked by most of the other Jynx hunters. Argarrar snatched a jelly roll with her tail and tossed it to Jagar as they passed. He caught it and quickly stuffed it into his mouth. Harkayé glared at her, but said nothing.

"Good luck, humans," called Argarrar. She tugged two levers and started the wagon moving again. Jynx ran to greet her as she rolled down the road. Others ran alongside to pet the wagon-snake Snaggleclaw. Mops winced at how close the Jynx came to getting run over, but not a single tail got caught beneath those wheels.

Mops turned to Starfallen. "The Mothers' Circle?"

"The camp's governing body," said Starfallen. "'Mother' is a looser term in their language, denoting age and wisdom. Most Jynx in the Circle are literal mothers as well, but it's not a requirement. They're all masters in their specialties. The eldest is nominally in charge, but day-to-day decisions are made by consensus. Speaker Harkayé has the final word when she's present, of course."

"Of course," said Mops. She watched Harkayé, Barryar, and their prisoners disappear into a large blue-and-white–colored dome. "Starfallen, what are the rules of the 'path' everyone keeps talking about?"

"Practically speaking, what it comes down to is doing what the Preceptor says." She pointed skyward. "It decides when the camps relocate, who leads the different groups . . . even who should breed."

"It dictates which Jynx can have children?" asked Mops.

"Not who can. Who will. All Jynx are tested for genetic compatibility. The Preceptor analyzes the results. Harkayé passes along the optimal pairings to the Jynx of Black Spire and three other camps. Each of the Speakers on Tuxatl oversees the evolution of a certain territory."

Gabe lowered his cane. "Say that shit one more time?"

"Their path refers to cultural, technological, and biological evolution," said Starfallen. "The Preceptor—"

"They're fucking eugenicists?" Gabe demanded.

Starfallen hesitated. "The Speakers on Tuxatl don't mate with anyone, eugenicists or not, as far as I know. I believe their biology is incompatible."

Mops had never seen Gabe so furious. "What is it?"

"Seriously?" He stared at her. The anger in his eyes

faded slightly. "I guess you wouldn't know. Let's just say Earth has an ugly history with eugenics."

"This isn't Earth," Starfallen pointed out.

"Maybe not," said Gabe. "But I'm starting to think we're cozying up to the bad guys, Captain."

"I concur." Cate grabbed Mops' arm and tried to pull her away from the camp. "We should leave before we're drawn into their villainy."

Mops jerked free. "Touch me again, and it will end badly for you."

A horn blew from the camp, three climbing notes repeated twice.

"The Circle is ready." Parya started down the road. "Follow me, and try not to draw too much attention."

Mops looked at her team: two brightly colored Prodryans, a Rokkau, and a trio of humans. "We'll do our best."

"Are you sure about this?" asked Doc.

Mops answered under her breath. "Not in the slightest."

Parya led them down a narrow dirt path that skirted the edge of the camp. If her plan was to avoid being seen, it failed miserably. Jynx pulled aside the woven doors of their bellor tree shelters to stare. Others scurried up the branches to watch the aliens march past.

Mops was used to being stared at. It happened on every space station and alien world she visited. At least the Jynx didn't act afraid, like humans were barely trained animals, ready to break free and devour anyone in their path. It was a refreshing change.

"Imagine living with so much open space," said Azure.

Kumar grimaced. "Imagine trying to keep it all clean."

They crossed a flat wooden bridge over the stream. A Jynx clung to the outer rail, using a hooked knife to cut buds and flowers from the bridge.

"It's alive?" asked Kumar.

Parya looked over her shoulder. "Of course. We take care of our camp."

Mops studied the bridge more closely as she stepped

off the far side. It was made from two trees that had grown horizontally across the water from either side. Roots and branches dug into the ground to anchor it in place.

A wooden fence circled a patch of dead trees up ahead. The stench of sulfur made Mops wrinkle her nose. Most of the Jynx who'd been following now turned away. Parya clamped a hand over her snout.

Steam rose and black mud bubbled within the fence. Two young Jynx sat on the fence posts throwing rocks into the mud. One pointed to Parya. They quickly jumped down and scampered away.

"That fence looks new," said Mops. "What happened?"

Parya walked faster. "Jagar happened."

Beyond the mud pit, a pair of bellor trees grew so close together their two domed canopies merged into one. At the intersection, the branches were pulled to either side and tied off to create a triangular doorway. Inside, a wide tunnel descended into the ground.

"The Jynx evolved from burrowers," said Starfallen. "Much of their camp is beneath the surface."

"Watch your heads and wings," said Parya.

Mops' monocle enhanced her vision, but it turned out to be unnecessary. Thick blue vines hung from the make-shift ceiling, and their long, dangling leaves gave off a yellow light. The vines were plentiful and bright enough to guide the way.

Thick branches or roots crisscrossed beneath Mops' feet like a woven mat, providing traction as she descended into the cool tunnel. The walls were bellor wood with the same green-and-black bark she'd seen above. Like the bridge, the tunnel appeared to have been grown rather than built. She couldn't find a single nail or saw mark.

Kumar picked up a fallen leaf, still faintly lit. He studied it closely before tucking it into a pocket.

Passages split off in either direction, some angling up to the surface, others deeper into the ground. Growling voices echoed all around.

"How long did it take to create all of this?" asked Mops.

Parya twisted around, head cocked. "What do you mean?"

"All these tunnels, the structures in the trees . . ."

Parya sniffed. "Black Spire was waiting for us long before we made it our spring camp. In the beginning, it was dirty and overgrown, but Harkayé's predecessor helped us tame things."

"Why 'Black Spire'?" asked Gabe. "I haven't noticed anything black or spire-like."

"Our forebears built a great tower near this place. The tower fell during the Great Sunstorm, but the Preceptor remembers."

"The Great Sunstorm?" Mops repeated. "What was that?"

Parya hunched her shoulders. "These are questions for the Speaker."

"They might be referring to a solar flare. A strong enough coronal mass ejection could have caused physical damage to the planet."

"Enough damage to send a previously advanced society back to steam engines and gunpowder?" Mops subvocalized.

"Without knowing the nature of the society and their technology, it's difficult to say. But it's possible."

Gabe peeked through an open doorway into a storeroom packed with open bins of seeds or grains. "This feels a bit like the underground shelters I grew up in back on Earth. I don't suppose you have a library down here?"

"I don't know that word," said Parya.

Gabe scratched his chin. "A collection of books or scrolls or whatever you use to store stories and information? Somewhere to learn more about Black Spire and the rest of your people's history."

"The Preceptor remembers all history and information," said Parya. "For stories, talk to either Varkar or Abya. Varkar has more stories, but Abya is my favorite storyteller. She does voices and acts out the good parts. Yagyar's even better than Abya, but she's always busy, and she snarls if you interrupt her."

Parya led them around a bend. Ahead sat two Jynx, each gripping a wood-and-metal firearm. A shimmering copper-colored curtain blocked off the tunnel behind them. They sprang to their feet, fur raised.

"Tell the Circle the aliens are here," said Parya.

One guard ducked through the curtain. She returned a short time later and beckoned them to follow. "No weapons and no children."

"He means no boys," said Starfallen.

Mops stopped, torn between annoyance and amusement. "Azure, Starfallen, you're with me." She handed her weapons to Kumar and told him, "Keep things under control here."

Mops followed Parya into what felt like a living gazebo, easily ten meters in diameter with a shallow domed roof. Thick roots spread from the center of the roof like a starburst, an explosion of dark, gleaming wood. This room must be directly below the bole of the tree. She noted four additional exits, all curtained off.

The air was cool, dry, and surprisingly fresh. She saw no sign of vents. Maybe the trees and vines recycled the air.

Six Jynx sat in a semicircle, perched on tall, deep-cushioned chairs with high wooden backs. Harkayé sat on one end. A seventh chair on the opposite end was empty. Vacant floor cushions were spread opposite the chairs, completing the circle.

Mops was surprised to see Barryar standing behind one of the seated Jynx. Aside from Harkayé, he was the only Jynx she recognized. "I thought—"

"Best not to mention the boy's presence," said Starfallen. "He's allowed here because of his grandmother. The nepotism is a sore spot with several of the Mothers."

A low melody floated through the chamber, similar to wooden pipes, but louder and deeper. The source was a black-and-brown–striped Jynx sitting near the back, pressing a series of wooden nubs that protruded from the wall.

"Pre-meeting entertainment," said Azure. "Nice."

"The music isn't for your amusement." Starfallen kept her voice low. "They're communicating with other camps. The notes are transmitted hundreds of kilometers through the bellor network. Few Jynx are skilled enough to translate and play the musical tongue."

"Like a musical telegraph," said Mops.

Harkayé gestured to the cushions. Mops stepped forward and sat cross-legged in the center. Starfallen took the spot to her right, while Azure grabbed the cushion to her left.

"We've been discussing your arrival, Captain Mops," said a heavyset Jynx with black fur and a bright pink nose. "You've seen how your presence inspires thievery and rebellion. If the Freesailors had been able to enter your ship and steal your weapons, you never would have seen them again. They're good at hiding their hoards."

Starfallen leaned close. "That's Yagyar. She leads the teachers and storytellers. As eldest, she's considered head of the Mothers' Circle when the Speaker's not around."

"Respectfully, our weapons are built to only respond to authorized users." Mops waited a beat to see if anyone would reprimand her for speaking. "Even if the Jynx had entered our ship, any weapons they discovered would be useless. But I apologize for the disruption we've brought. The last thing we want is to endanger your people."

"Vraggarar suggested we kill you and dump your technology into the ocean." Yagyar paused to pick at a mat in the fur beneath her chin. "She believes this would send a clear message to the Freesail rebels."

"Vraggarar's the bedraggled one on the left who looks half-asleep," whispered Starfallen. "She speaks for the scavengers' contingent. They gather, inventory, and store old tech for the Preceptor."

Vraggarar wore an old leather vest and matching trousers, both covered with pockets and loops for various tools. Mops spotted a small spade, a knife, and a black hatchet with a handle that flattened into a prybar. She also wore a coil of coated wiring as decoration over one shoulder. Old technology, like the metallic glass sword Harkayé carried?

Barryar whispered to the Jynx in front of him—his grandmother, presumably? The patterns in their fur were similar enough. The older Jynx touched his wrist, and

Barryar spoke. "The Preceptor allowed them to land. Their presence lured these criminals into the open. We captured two. These aliens helped us gain valuable intelligence about the growing threat to our camp."

"Two of how many?" asked a Jynx with striped fur and a gray muzzle. Starfallen identified her as Ragvamar, the camp's doctor and healer. "How many Freesailors escaped your hunt?"

Barryar's tail lashed once. "Three others escaped."

"Hello, everyone!" A familiar voice filled the room as Argarrar bounded through one of the side passageways and scrambled into the vacant seventh chair. "I'm sorry. Would have been here sooner, but Snaggleclaw was worked up from today's adventures. He wanted to play. Then I had to feed and wash him. I think the poor boy's getting ready to molt again."

"Argarrar's on the Circle?" asked Mops.

"She leads the nursemaids," said Starfallen. "The Jynx who raise the camp children into adulthood."

The musician played a quick trill.

Argarrar spun. "I heard that. You mind your music, child. Any more comments about Snaggleclaw and I'll knock your ears, don't think I won't! Now, have the aliens had a chance to speak?"

"We were getting to that," said Yagyar. Mops recognized her long-suffering tone immediately. Yagyar jabbed her tail at Mops. "Perhaps an official introduction, to begin with?"

Mops stood. "My name is Marion Adamopoulos. I'm from a planet called Earth. We're here on behalf of our world, and of the Krakau Alliance, an organization of different races from throughout the galaxy—"

"What is it you want?" interrupted Ragvamar.

"For more than a hundred years, the Alliance has been at war with the Prodryans," said Mops. "We believe you might be able to help end—"

"She didn't ask about your Alliance," said Yagyar. "We're not interested in your carefully prepared speech. I want to know your story, Captain Adamopoulos. Why you? What do *you* want?"

It was both the easiest and the hardest question she could have asked. "I want to know my people and my planet are safe before I die."

"Your people? Fine, don't bother to mention your loyal, long-suffering AI."

"You *are* my people," she subvocalized.

"I think calling me 'people' is more insulting than if you'd just forgotten me."

Yagyar leaned forward. "The Mothers' Circle shares a similar responsibility to our camp and our world. Our most important duty is to our future. Your presence inspires those who would threaten that future."

"The war we're fighting *will* come to Tuxatl," said Mops. "The Prodryans avoid your planet for now, but they won't leave you in peace forever. It's not in their nature."

"True," said Starfallen. "I've told the Circle as much on several occasions."

Mops focused on Harkayé. "You changed Starfallen's nature. Show us how to do the same to the rest of her people. Help us protect Tuxatl and the rest of the galaxy."

Harkayé stood. Instantly, the rest of the Jynx fell silent, fixing her with their full attention. "Yagyar is correct about the threat you present, but there are other variables. The Freesailors grow bolder with each turn of the ring. They steal from the Preceptor. They seduce young, naïve kits from the path. They reject our guidance. At this point in history, they present a greater threat than any aliens. And so I will give you what you ask, Captain."

Several of the Jynx twitched in surprise. Argarrar's ears rose.

"In return," Harkayé continued, "You will help us. Jagar knows a great deal about the Freesail camp and their plans, information I've been unable to dig from him. You will use his fascination with you to befriend him. Learn of the Freesailors' plans and track down their stockpiles of stolen ancient technology."

"I thought you could make him tell you," said Mops. "Like you did with the other Jynx you captured."

"Jagar is . . . resistant to my pheromones," admitted Harkayé. "Violently so."

Mops should have felt triumphant. Instead, she felt sick. She'd come here to end a war, not take sides in another one.

"You want to help your world," said Harkayé. "All I ask is that you help me protect mine. The math is simple. How many billions of people will die in your war without our help?"

Barryar's tail twitched. He was the only Jynx who looked visibly unhappy with this arrangement. The others were unreadable, at least to Mops.

"You can give us what we need?" asked Mops.

"I've already begun." Harkayé held out one hand and tapped a small blister on the edge of her palm. "I'll finalize the mix for you once you've brought me the information I need." She lowered her arm. "After which, you and your Alliance will leave our planet and never interfere again."

"You're *growing* it?" asked Azure.

Harkayé ignored her. "What is your answer, Captain?"

13

Advocate of Violence: Mission Progress Report

The mad, desperate, brilliant fools did it. Captain Adamopoulos persuaded the Jynx to help the Alliance.

I wasn't permitted to join the secret Circle of Mothers,
and no one will tell me exactly what bargain they struck,
or what form the Jynx's aid will take. I imagine they're
rightly afraid of what I'd do to try to stop them.

I'm under constant guard now. Even as I record this,
the human called Kumar watches my every move.

How could Mops do this to me? It would be one thing
if she simply killed me. I've long expected that.

What if they've already begun? What if the Jynx are
this very moment rewriting my mind, stripping me of my
core? How would I know? I must find a way to test my
innermost instincts.

. . .

I just walked over and kicked Kumar in his ridiculous
human genitals. I'm happy to say my drive to inflict violence upon other races remains unchanged. I'll have to
continue these random attacks to monitor any potential
alterations to my brain. Though perhaps not against
Kumar next time. The angling of the fur above his eyes

suggests anger at me. I don't know why he's upset. Feral
humans don't experience pain.

. . .

Kumar was definitely unhappy. He's informed me that
he will tie me up and glue my implants shut if I strike any-
one again. Such a narrow prohibition. He said nothing
against throwing rocks at people, for instance . . .

I have only one mission objective now: stop Captain
Adamopoulos and her crew while my mind is still my
own. My clan—no, all Prodryans are depending on me.

If I fail, my people will lose this war. The thought is
strange, alien and unreal. For the first time, I question
the inevitability of our victory. Like a primitive non-
Prodryan, I feel doubt.

I don't like it.

I'm to be brought to the Speaker so she can "sample"
me. She says my taste and scent will give her more data on
my people and help her with the weapon she's creating.
This could be my chance to strike.

If anyone can save the Prodryan people, it's Advocate
of Violence of the Red Star Clan.

"**W**OULDN'T IT BE BETTER to go directly
to Jagar?" asked Barryar. The young Jynx
had been assigned to guide Mops and the
others. And presumably to make sure they didn't cause
more trouble.

"I want to know more about Jagar before we talk with
him." Mops felt like half the camp had come out to gawk
at the aliens walking down the main street.

Gabe was loving it. He smiled and waved at the Jynx
like this was a victory parade. "Hey Barryar, who built
these old roads?"

"There have always been roads." Barryar shooed away
a young Jynx who'd been stalking Azure's tentacles.

Mops watched two Jynx washing a wagon-snake in a
large stone-walled pen. The wagon-snake seemed to be

enjoying it, rolling onto its back so the Jynx could scrub its scaly belly. "How far to Jagar's bellor tree?"

"Jagar lives alone, away from others." Barryar's words were polite enough, but he gave off a citrus scent as he spoke.

Mops could guess at the attitude behind his words. She'd heard the same veiled disgust countless times from aliens learning about other races. It usually accompanied questions like, *"You eat what?"* or *"It comes out where?"*

"They're a communal people," said Starfallen. "A pack, really. Most Jynx sleep in groups for warmth and comfort. To live in isolation is unnatural."

They took a side path past an open pit where large cuts of meat were being smoked over a bed of coals. The smell made Mops' mouth water. She swallowed and focused on Barryar. "Does Jagar live apart by choice?"

"It's easier for everyone this way. He can't help how he was born, or how Tuxatl reacts to him."

Mops wasn't sure she'd understood. "The planet reacts to him?"

"You saw what happened at your ship?" he asked. "How the tree started to grow around Jagar's claws?"

"I remember."

"A swarm of paka borers once followed him around for three days. He had to sleep on a raft anchored in the middle of the river to escape them. Another time, he walked past the scavengers' burrow and the whole place caught fire. Last year, he started across the main road and shot into the air. He just hung there for half a day, two teks off the ground. He broke his ankle when he finally fell."

"People can't just float," said Gabe.

Kumar dropped to one knee and touched the rippled stone path. "If the grav plates on the *Pufferfish* malfunction, we all float. Maybe Jynx roads have similar tech embedded in them. They could have been used for transportation, like old mag rails."

"We detected no advanced technology on the planet," said Azure.

"Nothing we *recognized* as technology." Mops thought back to Harkayé, who claimed to be able to grow a precisely targeted bioweapon within her own skin. "Does the planet react to anyone else?"

"At the Mothers' Circle, you said your weapons would only work for you." Barryar watched closely until Mops nodded agreement. "This world is like your weapons. It only recognizes Jagar, and he doesn't know how to control it. Speaker Harkayé doubts he ever will, but his descendants might. That's why Jagar is so important. One day, all Jynx will be able to interact with the technology of our world. We'll finally control Tuxatl again."

"Your forebears," Mops repeated. "Did they build the ring around your planet, too?"

Barryar ignored the question and pointed to a trio of young, skinny bellor trees. A three-sided mesh hammock hung suspended ten meters up. "This is where Jagar lives."

Small sacks of belongings hung from branches near the hammock. A rolled-up blanket tied to two of the trees looked like it could be spread to the third to protect from sun and rain.

Mops touched the trunk of the closest tree. There were no branches within reach, and the bark was too smooth to grip. "Who wants to run back to the drop ship to fetch the stepladder?"

"We have rope ladders," said Barryar. "They're used by the weak and the elderly whose claws have grown dull and brittle." He scurried off, returning a short time later with a length of green rope tied into a series of loops, with a metal hook on one end. He tossed the hook with a smooth, well-practiced motion, landing it in the fork of two thick branches. He handed the other end to Mops and stepped back.

Mops tugged the ladder to make sure it held, slipped her boot into a loop, and started climbing. She'd gone less than a meter when electricity jolted through her body. Her muscles locked. The rope slid from her grasp. Her back slammed onto the hard dirt.

"Captain!"

Her ears were ringing so badly she couldn't tell who had spoken. Both Kumar and Azure hovered over her.

"I'm all right. Doc?"

"I'm undamaged."

She tried to sit up. "What happened?"

"An electric charge arced from the tree into your right hand," said Doc, speaking for everyone to hear. *"It traveled through your body and returned to the tree via your left boot."*

Mops flexed her hand. Blood oozed through blackened skin and broken blisters. She checked her boot and saw smoke rising from the toe.

Barryar covered his snout, muffling a chirp, but he couldn't stop the salty scent of amusement from filling the air. "Your fur . . ."

Mops touched her hair. Static crackled as the ends tried to cling to her hand. "Does this happen often? Trees electrocuting people?"

"It's Jagar's nest," said Barryar, as though that explained it.

"Even the foliage on this planet is cursed," muttered Cate.

Mops stood and examined the tree. The bark was undamaged, but infrared showed two hot spots, presumably where the electricity had exited and entered.

She looked back at the road. Old technology, electrical trees . . . "Kumar, do you have a signal tracer?"

Kumar grabbed a small kit from his harness and held it out.

"Good. Let's see if we can figure out what kind of tech we're looking at."

Mops gloved up and sealed her suit before trying to insert the probes. She might not have full combat armor, but even standard uniforms had an energy dispersing weave. The tree shocked her three more times. She felt each jolt, but it wasn't strong enough to do any damage.

She switched off the laser drill and inserted the last of

four metal probes into the wood. Each probe was connected to Kumar's signal tracer. Normally, they used it for finding breaks in wires or circuitry or metal plumbing lines.

Off to the left, Azure was—very carefully—pointing a medical scanner at the tree.

Gabe, Starfallen, Cate, and Azure stood several paces back. Cate had been quiet since the meeting with the Mothers' Circle. It made her nervous. Either he'd given into despair, or else he was getting ready to do something desperate and stupid.

"How old are these trees?" asked Kumar.

"Jagar grew them himself, nine years ago," said Barryar.

Kumar shook his head. "I'm picking up fluid-carrying veins and metal content through the roots. Some of them are more than a kilometer in length."

"Show me," said Mops. A maze of curved lines appeared on her monocle. After a moment, she matched the vertical lines to the trunk in front of her. The vast bulk of the signal map was below ground. She turned, trying to orient them. "Doc, overlay a map of the Black Spire camp."

She shut her other eye to focus on the simplified map Doc had constructed and the bright red lines running through the ground like blood vessels. "Some of these paths go all the way to the Mothers' Circle."

"I don't think these trees are nine years old," said Kumar. "I think they're offshoots from a much older bellor."

"These trees make no sense." Azure lowered her scanner. "The vascular system is ridiculously inefficient. Electrical activity is an order of magnitude higher than it should be for a plant this size. Or even for a Tjikko. Then there are these nodes of metal growing like tumors throughout the wood. It's chaos."

"Kumar, please switch to a short-range induced current scan," said Doc.

Kumar tapped the probe controls. The images Mops was seeing vanished, replaced by a denser cluster of lines in the tree.

"It's not a vascular system." There was a note of triumph in Doc's words, along with what sounded like awe. *"I've seen patterns like this in my own memcrys. It's circuitry."*

Mops circled the trees. "What does it do? Aside from zapping unwanted guests?"

"If I had to guess? Absolutely nothing. Many of the pathways are incomplete or redundant. My circuitry is elegant and efficient. This is . . . wild."

"Kumar, send everything you're mapping to Grom," ordered Mops. "See what they can make of it."

"Yes, sir."

Gabe stepped closer, practically vibrating with excitement. "Imagine growing your own technology."

"It sounds great until you forget to water your computer." Mops turned toward Barryar, considering another implication. "How do the Jynx fit into this?"

"I don't understand the question."

"The planet reacts to Jagar," said Mops. "Is he—are the Jynx meant to be the users? Are you the gardeners, or just another component?"

"They are both." Harkayé strode up the path. "You were supposed to be investigating Jagar, Captain. Not torturing our trees. Your instruments caused a painful screech in the Circle room."

"Sorry about that." Mops signaled Kumar to switch off the probe, then removed the hood of her suit. The smell of vinegar, of Jynx anxiety and fear, filled her nostrils.

Before, the gathered Jynx had been openly curious. They'd murmured excitedly when electricity crackled from the tree to Mops.

All that had changed the instant Harkayé arrived. Many had hurried away. The rest were silent and unmoving, all save their ears. Those ears flexed to better hear the Speaker's every word.

"Who built this world, Harkayé?" asked Mops. "What happened to them?"

"You're even more curious than Starfallen was." Harkayé turned away. Her tail hooked Mops' wrist and gave a gentle tug. "Walk with me, Captain."

"Keep searching," Mops said to Kumar. "But no more probing."

Gabe snickered at that. Mops didn't have a chance to ask why as Harkayé pulled her along like a pet on a leash.

"The duty of the Preceptor is to guide the people's biological, cultural, and technological evolution," said Harkayé.

"The path you keep talking about," said Mops. "You guide the Jynx by controlling everything. Where they go, who they can breed with . . ."

Other Jynx scurried out of the way as they walked. "You told the Mothers' Circle you wanted to protect your people," said Harkayé. "I want the same. Our civilization reached its zenith while your ancestors were learning to bang rocks together. The forebears explored outward and inward both, but our priority was always the cultivation of our selves and our planet."

"*Our* priority?"

"My full title, Speaker Harkayé Ar-Raya means Harkayé, the four hundred and seventy-third of that name. The Harkayés are one of four Speaker lines, built . . . grown . . . from preserved strains of genetic material that survived the cataclysm. Imperfectly grown. We're unable to interbreed with the Jynx, but advanced enough to communicate with and act as extensions of the Preceptor.

"One of the many advancements made by the old Jynx was the ability to plant memories in Tuxatl itself. They left fragments of their lives for others to share and experience. Within a generation of this discovery, entire lifetimes could be stored within the trunk of a memory tree. A generation after that, as the linkages spread wider and deeper, they learned to trade their aging flesh for the far more durable body of the planet. The younger Jynx maintained the world, then joined their ancestors when their bodies aged and wore out. Aside from the rare, tragic accident, death became an artifact of the past."

For one long heartbeat, envy pulsed through Mops' veins. The idea of escaping her body's decline, of surviving unburdened by that betrayal and the fear that came with it, triggered longing and bitterness in equal measure.

"How many Prodryans transferred their minds into the planet?"

"Tens of billions." Harkayé stepped off the path and beckoned Mops to follow. "Mind the thorns, Captain."

Short, willowy reeds with curved thorns jabbed Mops' legs, but didn't penetrate.

Harkayé sniffed. "I should trouble you for one of your outfits. Hookthorns fragment in the fur and cause no end of matting, even for a Speaker."

"I'm sure we could fabricate one for you." Mops looked skyward. "How does the Preceptor fit into this?"

"The old Jynx colonized the moon and transformed it into a kind of backup. All data stored within the planet was duplicated. These were static copies, unliving files. A governing program preserved the data, ready to restore our people in case of catastrophe."

They turned along a well-shaded path that sloped downhill.

"I couldn't help noticing a distinct lack of moon when we arrived," said Mops.

The Speaker was silent for a time. The ground was rougher here, rocky and uneven. Small, crab-like creatures with stone shells clicked their claws before scampering away to hide in holes in the dirt. "A minority of Jynx wanted to explore more of the galaxy, to transfer their minds to other stars."

"How?"

"I haven't the slightest idea." Harkayé sniffed. "Do you know how to manufacture the computer in your eye lens, or what mixture of chemicals fuels your ship, or the physics of your gravity plates and A-rings? There was a time all Jynx were connected to that shared knowledge, but that was many millennia before my time. All I know is that they planned to encode themselves into our sun's magnetic field, and from there, to other stars. It took years to prepare, and in the end, it destroyed us. Their mistakes triggered a massive solar storm."

Mops remembered her conversation with Parya. "The Great Sunstorm."

"It shattered the moon and burnt half the planet."

"I'm sorry. I know what it's like to lose your civilization."

Harkayé kept walking, avoiding eye contact. "Whatever else you might say of the forebears, they grew their technology to last. Even broken, the systems in the moon continued to function. Physical connections were replaced by short-range transmissions. As the debris spread out, becoming the ring we see today, it was able to capture more solar energy, thanks to the exponential increase in surface area. The system grew stronger. It reconnected with the ravaged planet and discovered a burnt wasteland."

"What happened to the Jynx?"

"They died. Those who weren't killed in the initial catastrophe succumbed to radiation. Those whose minds were stored within the planet . . . The Preceptor spent centuries trying to awaken them, but the planetary network had fragmented. Much of the data remains to this day. Billions of our forebears survive, fragmented and unaware, scattered throughout the planet. Inaccessible. We were functionally extinct."

The ground had grown softer, damper. Each step squished into the mud, and water filled the prints they left behind. The air smelled of rotting plants.

"The Preceptor set about fulfilling its function. It was able to remotely activate an underground medical facility and reprogram an incubator. After many failures, the first Speakers were born on the surface. They explored Tuxatl, cataloging surviving species. The Jynx were gone, but life survived. Plants sprouted anew. Burrowing animals emerged. We began interbreeding those burrowers, selecting for intelligence, size, and adaptability, mimicking Jynx evolution."

"You're trying to turn the Jynx into who they were before, into your forebears," said Mops. "Why not let them evolve on their own?"

"Natural selection is a slow, crude process. Thanks to the Preceptor's oversight, what would have taken millions of years could be accomplished in less than a tenth of that time. And there's no guarantee the whims of evolution would have produced a race capable of interfacing with the planet's technology. At the end of the Preceptor's path, the true Jynx will arise, able to repair and regrow our network, and to restore the ancestors who sleep within our world."

Mops stared. "You're trying to *reboot* your entire civilization?"

"Crudely put, but accurate."

"How much of this do the Jynx know?"

Her tail twitched. "It's a fine balance. If they knew too much of their history, and of the technological potential of this world, they'd be tempted to try to access that potential before they're ready. Or they would turn away from the difficulties ahead."

"What difficulties?"

Harkayé stopped. "A critical episode of Jynx history approaches: the war between old and new. Our society is shifting toward a more stable agricultural foundation. Camps have grown. Many begin to set down permanent roots.

"The Freesailors cling to primitive ways. They're little better than thieves, and they believe themselves rulers of the seas. They've attacked other camps for daring to build shipyards or venture out into the waves. It's the same path our society walked many thousands ago. Soon the fighting will spread across the continent. In the end, the Freesail camp will be broken, and their people absorbed into the coastal camps. The war will be a turning point, and the beginning of a larger, more unified Jynx society."

Mops' fists tightened. "You sound like you *want* them to go to war."

"It is necessary."

"Bullshit," Mops snarled. "You could learn from your history and use that knowledge to improve things this time around rather than sitting back and letting them repeat it." A darker suspicion rose. "Or are you doing more than just watching? How much has the Preceptor encouraged the tension between the Freesailors and the other camps?"

"This is why we cannot tell the people everything,"

said Harkayé. "Many would react with this same anger and defiance. The war must be fought, and the Freesail camp *must* lose."

"How many Jynx died in this war, originally?"

"I understand your anger, Captain. But this is our purpose."

"How many?"

"Records from that time are imprecise. Our historians estimated between one hundred thousand and two hundred thousand casualties, in total."

Mops had spent her life dealing with hatred and hostility and prejudice. She didn't know how to deal with such cold apathy. Harkayé talked about individual Jynx like they were bits of hardware in one of Grom's computer systems, to be swapped out or discarded as needed.

Harkayé pointed to the swamp. "Jagar ran away to this place as a child. He hid for four days."

Mops forced herself to listen. She still needed the Speaker's help. Billions of lives depended on whatever Harkayé was growing in that blister on her wrist. "Why would he choose a swamp for a hiding place?"

"It wasn't swamp at the time. This was the site of the old Black Spire. It was a launch tower for transporting people and supplies to the moon. The tower fell, but the roots remained, anchored deep into the ground. Jagar must have sensed them, or maybe they sensed him. His presence triggered a reaction, melting the land into mud and decay.

"It wasn't deliberate. He simply can't control his connection to Tuxatl. It's why he's obsessed with the idea of leaving the planet. He's afraid he'll hurt someone or destroy his camp. The Freesail camp is just using his fear. They've used him since he was born."

Whereas Harkayé would control every aspect of Jagar's life. They'd breed him with likely females, hoping his genes would bring them one step closer to recreating the Jynx of old. "You don't care about Jagar. You just don't want the wrong people using him."

"When Jagar was a child, the Freesailors used him to

find old ruins and gather ancient weapons from before the Storm. It's why he was taken from their camp and placed with the Jynx of Black Spire." She scooped a handful of mud from the ground. "Your hypocrisy is perplexing, Captain. Where was your concern when you agreed to use Jagar to help us find the Freesailors and their old weapons?"

"Captain!" Kumar's voice over the comm was higher pitched than usual.

Mops stepped away from Harkayé, thankful for the interruption. She wasn't sure how much longer she could keep from shoving the Speaker into the swamp. "What's wrong?"

"Cate's gone."

Her stomach tightened like a wrung-out rag. She should have glued Cate's feet to the road. "How?"

"I'd tied him to a nearby tree so I could take a closer look at Jagar's nest. I made sure to secure his wings, but the next thing I knew, he'd cut himself free and there was a knife in my back. Azure and Gabe both ran to check on me. Cate disappeared before anyone could go after him."

"Are you all right?"

"I'm fine. He threw the knife from about five meters away. It didn't penetrate that deep. Azure says the blade chipped my shoulder blade."

"Where the hell did he get a knife?"

Harkayé indicated the sword at her hip. "I suspect he used the shorter sibling to this blade."

Again she'd underestimated him. He'd probably stolen the knife when Harkayé was "sampling" him. "Kumar, did the knife have a metallic glass alloy blade?"

"Affirmative, Captain."

"That knife was forged when our moon was whole," said Harkayé. "I hope your people can return it to me."

Mops ignored her. "Get everyone to the drop ship. If Cate's going to sabotage this mission, he'll start by grounding us. Once the ship is secure—"

Harkayé's tail touched Mops' arm. "That's not what he's doing, Captain."

"How do you . . . ?" Mops turned back to the Speaker. Her stomach knotted further, until she thought she might vomit. "Cate didn't steal that knife. You gave it to him."

"He claimed he could do a better job of finding the rebel stockpile," said Harkayé. "It seemed only reasonable to offer him the same deal I offered you. Having you both searching for the Freesailor weapons significantly increases the odds of success."

"What did you promise him if he finds them first?"

"A weapon to neutralize his human enemies."

Mops' fists clenched. Her body was tight, her awareness hyperfocused on the Jynx before her. She wanted to wrap her fingers around Harkayé's throat and squeeze until the blood vessels burst and the bones cracked.

"Captain, your adrenaline levels . . ."

She stepped backward until Harkayé was beyond arm's reach. "They won't just 'neutralize' us. They'll slaughter my crew, and then they'll do the same to every human they can find."

"I assumed as much," said Harkayé. "But unlike your people, the Prodryans will leave us in peace."

"You brought me here as a distraction while Cate got away."

"Cate wanted to observe your people to learn more about your plans and intentions before breaking away." She retrieved a velvety white pouch from a pocket and pulled out a cocoon about the length of Mops' pinky. The cocoon was transparent, like thin glass veined in gold. She held it out to Mops. "Wear this."

"Excuse me?"

Harkayé folded back her ear. An insect like a white-furred bumblebee with glass wings nested in the folds. "They're called chimers. They were bred for long-range communication. The mother is connected to her cocooned young. We'll be able to speak to one another. Cate has one as well. This way, whoever finds the Freesailors and their weapons first can tell me."

Despite its fragile appearance, the cocoon felt solid to the touch, more like metal than glass. Mops didn't like the idea of Harkayé listening in on everything she said, but she wasn't in a position to argue. She grabbed a glue tube from her harness, squeezed a drop onto the side of the cocoon, and pressed it gently inside her collar, between the built-in speaker and mic.

"Kumar, meet me on the road into town." Mops started to run.

"What's happening, sir?"

"We're going to interrogate Jagar." She'd thought she could keep Cate under control. She'd thought his usefulness outweighed the risk to the mission. "I fucked up."

14

Monroe studied a map of electrical currents in the planet's rings, hoping if he stared at it long enough, the various lines and bubbles might start to make sense.

Grom claimed the patterns of activity might support Mops' idea that the ring was a giant computer, but they couldn't be certain. As for Monroe, he was a janitor, and before that, a soldier. Analyzing an artificial alien super-intelligence was so far out of his expertise that it might as well be another galaxy.

They'd run through the standard greeting protocols and other attempts at communication, but so far, nothing had triggered a response.

"Commander Monroe! I may have a solution to our lack of weapons." Johnny's lower limbs rippled with ex-citement. "It's highly nonstandard and untested, but I've reviewed the equations, and if everything is adjusted cor-rectly and we don't explode, it should be highly effective."

Monroe rubbed his eyes. "Send it over."

The specs and equations appeared on his console. Most of the math was beyond him, but the core concept . . . "Are you out of your mind?"

"I don't understand the metaphor," said Johnny. "Krakau brains are internal, not external."

He squinted at the equations again. "Is the exponent on the energy expenditure correct? If this went wrong—"

"It would atomize the Pufferfish in the process, yes. Or perhaps subatomize it. Let me double-check."

"Where did you even come up with this idea?"

"I was reviewing Captain Adamopoulos' tactics in previous ship-to-ship confrontations." Johnny flushed. "I thought . . . hoped . . . her unique approach to military conflict might help me find a way to redeem my mistake with the weapons pod."

It did sound like the kind of thing Mops might suggest. "All right. Run some simulations and see what happens. Do not mess with the A-rings or anything else without my explicit permission. Understood?"

"Yes, Commander." Johnny hurried back to her station, humming to herself.

Monroe pulled out his gum dispenser and clicked through the flavors. He hovered over the bourbon before reluctantly switching to espresso and popping two cubes into his mouth. "I don't know why the Prodryans spend so much energy trying to kill us," he muttered to nobody in particular. "Give us enough time, and we'll blow ourselves all to hell for them."

His console flashed a green priority message alert. He scrolled through the text and swore. "Forget the weapons, Johnny. I need you to scan the surface for Cate. Grom, it's time to wake up."

At the rear of the bridge, spines clicked as Grom stretched and opened their eyes. "What's going on?"

"Cate stabbed Kumar and ran off." He saw Rubin tense, and hurried to add, "He's all right. But the captain says our top priority now is to find Cate."

"How?" asked Grom. "Our scanners couldn't pick out Starfallen, either."

"I'll take us into lower orbit," said Rubin. "Send me Cate's last known coordinates."

"Done. I don't care if we have to go optical and examine every square meter with a magnifying glass." Monroe reread Mops' message. "And Johnny, once we find Cate, you have my permission to test your weapons proposal on him."

%%% ✗ %%%

HARKAYÉ BROUGHT MOPS TO the bellor tree where Jagar was being held. The tree was enormous, almost as wide as the ones above the Mothers' Circle.

Barryar and the rest of Mops' team were waiting outside.

"Has Cate been here?" Mops demanded.

"Nobody has seen him since he fled," said Barryar.

"I'm monitoring the drop ship. Cate hasn't come near it."

"Barryar will take you to see Jagar." Harkayé turned to go.

"Let's get this over with." Mops couldn't stop pacing. Her body had too much energy. She needed to be out hunting Cate, not stuck here while the Prodryan did tides-knew-what."

Barryar led them belowground through more root-lined tunnels, eventually coming to a narrow doorway guarded by two armed Jynx. Tree roots grew like bars over the door.

Through the gaps, Mops saw a domed room three meters wide. A gray carpet covered most of the floor. The glowing leaves from the vines woven through the walls were dimmer, but adequate for human vision. A narrow triangular gap in the far wall led to a smaller room. Mops guessed it to be the Jynx equivalent of a bathroom.

The air held the simmering scent of crushed flowers. Doc sent a note to Mops' monocle, identifying the smell as a sign of anger.

Jagar sat hunched against the wall next to Argarrar. The older Jynx had her tail curled around the younger.

"Can we go in?" asked Mops.

Barryar growled something at one of the guards, who took a small pot from the floor and began to paint the ends of the roots. They shriveled back until they'd opened enough for Mops to pass through.

"Barryar, why don't you wait down the corridor?" she asked quietly. "He'll probably be more willing to talk if you're not there."

She squeezed inside without waiting for an answer. Starfallen, Kumar, Gabe, and Azure followed. The instant they were inside, the guards began applying a different liquid to the doorway. The roots snaked back into place, sealing them inside.

Mops had been prepared to talk to Jagar. She hadn't expected Argarrar. "Why are they jailing *you*?"

It was Starfallen who answered. "The Jynx are a communal people. When a Jynx is removed from the community, a family member or good friend typically joins them. Not as punishment, exactly. Their job is to tend to the one who went against the pack. From what I've seen, it's surprisingly effective. The guilt and shame a prisoner feels when those closest to them join them in prison is a strong deterrent. And the companionship helps reforge connection and bring the rogue Jynx back into line with the community."

"I don't know about all that," said Argarrar. "I just wanted a little peace and quiet. Let the other nursemaids deal with the kits for a few days."

Mops didn't believe a word of it, not with how Jagar was snuggled up against her and the way Argarrar's muscles jumped as she watched them, like she was ready to leap to her feet and clobber anyone who tried to hurt Jagar.

"Have you been treated well?" asked Mops.

Jagar snarled. "Better than Mraya and Raggark. I saw what was left of them when the Speaker finished her interrogation."

Mops sat cross-legged in front of him. "Tell me."

"They weren't themselves." Jagar burrowed deeper into Argarrar's fur. "Mraya used to spend hours doing charcoal drawings of the ring and stars. He loved being at sea. Raggark wanted to be a scavenger and hunt forebear artifacts. But when they came to see me, all they talked about was how I need to follow the path and obey Harkayé, and how they intend to spend the rest of their lives serving the Preceptor."

Starfallen stilled her wings. "The Treeshield camp?"

"That's right," said Argarrar.

"Is Treeshield a prison camp?" asked Gabe.

"Not exactly." Starfallen scraped her mandibles together. "Jynx who can't rejoin the pack are . . . altered, similar to what was done to me. The Speaker instills loyalty and obedience and sends them to one of the Treeshield camps to watch over the skytrees. The skytrees themselves secrete a pheromone similar to the scent of newborn Jynx. It overrides most higher brain function. The end result is a group of Jynx biologically programmed to guard and tend to the skytrees at any cost."

"Slaves," Gabe said flatly. "Captain, we can't—"

Mops raised a hand, fighting to focus through her own anger. She had to fix her own mistake first. She'd brought Cate to Tuxatl. She had to stop him. "We saw your nest, Jagar. I know things have been hard for you. How long have the Jynx shunned you?"

He didn't open his eyes. "As long as I can remember. I can't blame them."

"I can," said Argarrar.

He shrank back. "They know what I've done. They know what I could do."

"Pah. If they knew what I knew, they'd embrace you." Argarrar's lips pulled back as she used her claws to work a mat out of Jagar's fur. "I was there when the Speaker first tasted you."

"Tasted him?" asked Kumar.

"They sample all the new kits, usually within the first couple of months, but it can take longer with Freesail newborns."

"They run around biting babies?" Kumar demanded indignantly.

Argarrar stared at him, then bent her neck and licked the top of Jagar's head. "Tasted, not eaten. Daft boy. Everything changed once the Preceptor realized what kind of mutations Jagar had. They tried to take him away. It went badly."

"I was scared," said Jagar. "I didn't mean to hurt anyone."

"I know that, you goofy child. I was there, remember?" Argarrar gave him a light, playful swat on the head, then continued combing her fingers through his fur. "I'd been brought on to help manage the new batch of kits. I knew from the start that this one would be a challenge."

Jagar groaned, but there was a purring undertone to the sound.

"The Freesailors did their best to keep the Speakers from getting their claws on him," Argarrar continued. "He was passed from one ship to the next. I went with him. Nobody should have to lose everyone they know again and again. Eventually, the Freesailors realized they could use him to discover old technology—sunken ships, coastal ruins, and the like."

"That matches what Harkayé told me," said Mops.

"The Speakers caught up eventually. Harkayé set an ambush. Her hunters scuttled three Freesail ships and carried Jagar and me back to Black Spire."

"You came from a Freesail camp?" Mops studied her. "The Black Spire Jynx treat you like one of their own."

"They'd better. I helped raise half the young of this camp."

Jagar snorted. "They're just nice to you so you'll share your pastries."

"That too." Argarrar sat back. "Harkayé is said to be the strongest of the Speakers. Back in the beginning, I hoped she could help Jagar."

Jagar swished his tail. "By locking me up every time I do something she doesn't like."

"Locking you up every time you get caught, you mean."

"Maybe Raggark was right." Jagar slumped. "Before Harkayé took him away, I mean."

"Right about what?" asked Mops.

It was Argarrar who answered. "He said Jagar should use his power to kill a skytree."

Kumar gasped. "Why would anyone do that?"

"Because the skytrees connect the Speakers on Tuxatl to the Preceptor and to each other," said Argarrar. "Take down the local skytree, and Harkayé would be lost."

"And the rest of us would be free to make our own path." Jagar dragged the claws of his right hand down the wall, leaving shallow gouges.

"You'd have to get through the Treeshield camp," said Starfallen.

Mops tried to imagine one of those enormous trees toppling to the ground. The impact would be felt for many kilometers in every direction, like an earthquake.

Gabe covered a yawn with one hand. "Sorry. Long day."

Argarrar jumped to her feet and hissed. Her fur stood on end, and she raised her claws. Jagar arched his back and growled.

Mops grabbed her gun and spun, searching for the source of the threat. Barryar and the guards were still outside. Kumar and Starfallen looked confused. Gabe sat frozen, his hand at his mouth.

The Jynx were both staring at Gabe. Mops looked back and forth between them. "Was all that about a *yawn*?"

"Is that what you call his threat display?" snarled Argarrar.

"What? No!" Gabe's eyes widened. "It's not a threat!"

"Humans do that when they're fatigued," said Azure. "We believe it has something to do with how they regulate oxygen flow and brain temperature, but nobody really knows. Originally, the Krakau thought it was a mating display to show off the dangly bit of red flesh in the back of their mouths."

Gabe started to yawn again, and quickly covered his mouth with both hands. "I'm just tired! I'm not trying to threaten or mate with anyone!"

"It's late." Argarrar settled herself next to Jagar, who'd pulled out a comb to smooth his ruffled fur. "Have your people eaten, Captain Mop? You're welcome to stay with us."

"We don't have time," said Mops. "Cate made a deal with Harkayé. He's helping her."

Jagar growled again. "Aren't you doing the same? That's why you're here, isn't it?"

"Harkayé's been hunting rebels for years," interrupted Argarrar. "Your Prodryan isn't going to find what he seeks in a single night. Stay. Eat. Sleep. We'll talk more, and you'll be better prepared for whatever you decide to do."

Mops' attention lingered on the old Jynx.

"What is it?" whispered Doc.

"I'm not sure," she subvocalized. Something about Argarrar, more instinct than thought, tickled the back of her mind.

Mops glanced at the others. It *was* getting late, and they needed rest—especially Gabe and Azure. She wasn't sure about Starfallen. And sharing a meal might help build trust and rapport with Jagar.

"All right." Mops trembled with the need to be out hunting for Cate, but Argarrar was right. She removed her harness and unclipped a pack of food tubes. Whatever the Freesail camp was hiding, they'd kept it concealed from an orbiting supercomputer and its biological extensions all across the planet. They could keep Cate at bay for a while, too. She hoped.

The Jynx were equal parts fascinated and horrified as they watched Mops screw the threaded tip of the food tube into the port in her stomach. She pressed the button on the opposite end and sat back as it slowly dispensed its contents.

"Do you all have mouths in your stomachs?" asked Jagar.

"It's not a mouth," said Kumar. "They're surgically implanted ports. The Krakau put them in to make it easier to feed us and monitor what we eat."

Jagar snarled. "The Krakau sound like Speakers."

"They're both very controlling," Mops agreed.

Jagar and Argarrar were eating from a basket containing fried rings of jerky, essentially spicy meat donuts, along with little square cakes dripping with honey.

"Starfallen has talked to us about humans," said Argarrar.

"Captain Adamopoulos and I were both changed against our will," said Starfallen. "Her into a monster, then a soldier. My transformation was the opposite, though my people would call me equally monstrous. It's a difficult thing to lose control of one's body and mind. Though not as difficult for me, I suspect. Prodryans don't have the same illusion of self-determination as humans."

"Cate's terrified of losing his core Prodryan-ness," said Mops.

"I've noticed," Starfallen said dryly. "But our people recognize that who we are, who we become, is a result of countless factors, most of which are beyond our control. Genetics, environment, the clan we're born into, the time period in which we live. The education we receive as children. Even seemingly minor things like the foods we eat or the entertainment we consume. Change any of those factors, and neither Starfallen nor Advocate of Violence would exist as we are today. And neither would Marion Adamopoulos."

"You don't believe there's a core of who you are that would persist regardless of the rest?" Mops trailed off as she watched Argarrar eat. She clearly relished her meals, eating twice as much as Jagar. This somehow resulted in eight times as many crumbs.

"What aspect of me do you believe is immutable?" Starfallen leaned closer. "Captain?"

"Sorry, I was distracted." Mops continued to stare.

Kumar brushed off his hands and walked to the smaller room at the back. He emerged a short time later. "Do you have a bathroom tutorial?"

Argarrar licked her whiskers. "It's a sand pit. Squat and do your thing, scoop a little sand over it when you're done, and let the mudhorns do their job."

"Mudhorns?" asked Kumar.

"The well-fertilized flowering shrubs to either side with the coiled tendrils."

Kumar looked over his shoulder. "I think I'll hold it."

Jagar sat back and began combing crumbs and honey from his fur. Mops dug through her equipment until she found a solvent wipe. "This should help with the honey."

His nose wrinkled, but he took the wipe and dabbed at his fur. Mops pulled out a second wipe and held it to Argarrar, who waved it off.

"Your heart rate just jumped," said Doc, for her ears only.

"I know," she whispered. To Jagar, she asked, "What would you want if you were free to choose your own path?"

"To get off this planet." There was no hesitation in his answer. "To go to where I'm not dangerous to everything and everyone around me. Where I can relax and not have to worry about what I might trigger, and nobody treats me like a dangerous freak."

No wonder he'd been drawn to the drop ship.

Jagar leaned closer. "You could take me with you when you leave."

"I could," Mops agreed, wondering what Harkayé would think of that. The chimer cocoon scraped the side of Mops' neck every time she moved her head. "But you wouldn't be safe with us, Jagar. We're at war, and we're losing. The only way I can see for any of us to survive out there is with Harkayé's help."

Jagar pulled away. When he spoke again, he sounded tired. "And in return for that help, I assume she wants to know about the Freesail camp. Is that why you're here? I wouldn't answer her questions, so she sent you to try? You're wasting your time and mine."

Mops respected his loyalty, even though it made things more difficult. "We know your bellor trees connect to the trees of the Mothers' Circle. Can you hear the musical signals they send and receive? Have you been spying on them?"

"No!" He jumped to his feet, tail lashing. "I do hear the music sometimes. I can understand some of it. But I don't do it on purpose. It just happens."

"It just happens?" Mops scoffed. "You're a criminal. You tried to steal my ship. Why should I believe anything you say?"

"I just wanted to get away." He began to pace. Yellow vine lights flashed with each step, like the leaves were reacting to his frustration. He dragged his claws along the wall.

"Captain—" Azure started.

"Wait." Mops watched both Jynx.

Argarrar stood and touched Jagar's forearm. "Try to calm yourself."

Jagar snarled, but Argarrar simply stroked the fur on his head and neck.

"Doc," Mops whispered. "Show me the status screen on my PRA." Her monocle brought up her blood oxygen, the current air mix, and the adjustments the PRA was making as she breathed. She focused on the air readings, digging down into the trace elements.

Slowly, Jagar's tail stopped moving. He patted Argarrar and turned away, heading for the sand pit that served as a Jynx bathroom.

Argarrar turned to scowl at Mops. "Did you upset him on purpose?"

"I did," said Mops. "I'm sorry. You're very good with him."

"I've known him a long time." She cocked her head. "Why would you do that?"

Mops grabbed a solvent swab from her supplies, then folded down her collar. Grasping the cocoon between thumb and index finger, she dabbed the swab over the glue until it dissolved enough for her to pull the cocoon free. "Kumar, do you have a sample tube?"

"Always." Kumar offered a black metal canister.

Mops deposited the cocoon and screwed the lid into place.

"What was that?" he asked.

"A bug. Literally. Harkayé gave it to me so she could keep tabs on us." Mops returned the solvent to her kit and looked at Argarrar. "I didn't think you'd want her knowing you were a Speaker."

15

Cate hadn't felt this tense since his first molt. Alone on
Hell's Claws, hunted by one of the smartest and most dangerous humans he'd known, as well as a highly skilled
Prodryan warrior . . . all the while racing to fulfill a bargain with the most feared creatures in the galaxy.

But oh, if he succeeded . . . if he blocked the Alliance's
efforts to gain this Jynx weapon, if instead Cate returned
home with the key to wiping out the enemies of Yan . . .
The Supreme War Leader himself would recite poems of
Cate's triumph.

All he had to do was find the Preceptor's enemies and
their hidden weapons.

He sat with his back to one of the garish paka trees, a
short distance from Starfallen's shelter. He'd need supplies, and while he could doubtless overpower the Jynx
guarding the drop ship and crack the locking mechanism,
any attack on the ship would alert Mops to his location.
Safer to infiltrate the home of a Prodryan warrior, even
one who'd been biochemically neutered.

He opened a chitinous panel on his right forearm and
removed a small blue pill. With everything that had happened, he'd forgotten his regurgitant yesterday, and his
stomach was paying the price.

After taking the pill, he activated the recorder in his left eye and played back their first meeting with Starfallen. He skipped to the part where Starfallen grabbed Cate's mandible and threw him to the ground.

He still couldn't believe he'd actually fought, however briefly, with Starfallen!

Reluctantly, he moved past that confrontation and watched as Starfallen welcomed them to her home. He studied each step she took, every movement she made. When she reached the doorway, she ran her fingers over one of the poems she'd written on the wall. To the aliens, it probably looked like an absently sentimental gesture.

He replayed the movement, making sure he knew precisely which words she'd touched to deactivate whatever defenses her home possessed.

Starfallen might not have weapons hidden away inside, but if she'd kept anything of her military discipline, she'd have logs with information on her interactions with the Jynx. Intelligence had always been Cate's preferred weapon anyway.

He chittered to himself with barely contained glee. Wait until he told his clanmates how he'd broken into Starfallen's home!

⚒

ARGARRAR COCKED HER HEAD. The smell of vinegar filled the air. "A Speaker, you say?"

"It was the honey cakes," said Mops. "You and Jagar both dripped honey into your fur. He's been having a hell of a time getting it out. Not you."

Argarrar made a chirruping sound. "I'm better groomed, so you think I'm a Speaker?"

"You don't groom yourself," said Mops. "The rest of the Jynx are constantly working to keep their fur clean. The only other exception is Harkayé. I spent most of my life as a janitor. We notice cleanliness. Is this part of that Speaker biocontrol? Secretions to condition and maintain your fur?"

"Respectfully, Captain," said Gabe, "that seems like a bit of a stretch."

Mops turned to Starfallen. "You're the one who told us how good she is with animals and kids. You saw how she calmed Jagar a minute ago." She tapped her PRA. "I picked up minute traces of organic chemicals in the air. Pheromones, I assume?"

Argarrar didn't respond.

"Then there's Parya," Mops continued. "Doc, pull up the feed of our encounter at the drop ship and send it to the team's screens, please. Specifically the part where Parya sneezed and alerted Jagar and the other Freesailors to their presence."

The image quality wasn't great, but it was enough that she could make out Parya covering her muzzle with both hands, trying unsuccessfully to smother a series of thunderous sneezes.

"Now go back to when Parya returned from scouting." Mops waited . . . "There, ninety seconds earlier. Argarrar runs her hand down Parya's arm."

"You think she rubbed something on Parya to make her sneeze?" asked Azure. .

"The Jynx are physically expressive," said Starfallen. "They show affection and comfort through touch."

"Scan her skeletal structure," said Mops. "The long fur mostly conceals any differences, and if her movements aren't quite the same as those of other Jynx, she can always blame it on age. But if you compare her bone structure to Jagar's, I'm betting you'll find—"

"That's not necessary." Argarrar stretched, a long and luxurious process. "Leave it to an outsider to notice. 'The stranger sees what the camp overlooks,' as they say."

"She's not a Speaker." Jagar stood in the doorway. "Not really. Not like Harkayé and the others."

"Eavesdropping on your elders?" Argarrar growled. "I taught you better manners."

"You knew?" asked Mops.

Argarrar reached out with her tail and tugged Jagar close. "For how long?"

"I'm not stupid." Jagar sat beside Argarrar. "She changed her appearance and her scent, but I always knew who she was. Even when she didn't."

"You should've told me," said Argarrar.

"Maybe you should have told me," he countered.

"Maybe . . ." Her eyes narrowed. Then she raised her head and ruffled the fur of his neck. "You're a clever boy, and a good person. I'm proud of you, JaJa."

JaJa—Jagar—ducked away, but he was purring.

"You've been helping the Freesail camp," said Mops. "That's why you made Parya give away the ambush."

"I've been helping Jagar." She sighed and grabbed another honey cake. "My name was Garra Ar-Kyar. I was Jagar's Speaker. A created being, a product of old Jynx tech. And then . . ." She gestured to Jagar. "As you've seen, he can have an unpredictable effect on such technology."

"He broke you," said Mops.

"Pah. He freed me." She ate half the cake in one bite and continued speaking. "I was the one who processed his first tests and learned what he was. I was assigned to stay on his family's ship to observe him. Over time, I found myself changing. Subtle things at first. The longer I spent caring for Jagar, the harder it became to hear the Preceptor." She pointed her snout skyward. "By the time he completed his first year, I had to visit the skytree in person to relay my findings and receive my instructions."

"How does that connection work?" asked Kumar.

"Harkayé and I and others like us have a small organ in the back of the head, a kind of inner ear, attuned to the Preceptor's song. The skytrees connect us. That song is louder and clearer the closer we get to the local skytree. But my inner ear had grown . . . clogged."

Kumar nodded. "Inner ear wax."

"Disgusting, but that sounds essentially correct," said Argarrar. "It had been getting worse for a while, but everything blew up the day I came to collect a sun-damned tissue sample."

"I remember the knife," Jagar said quietly. "It was forebear tech, like purple glass, but harder than metal and so sharp I didn't feel the first cut right away. When I did . . ."

"The scents he released in response were stronger than any Speaker pheromones," said Argarrar. "Half the crew fell unconscious, myself included. When I woke two days later, I'd been completely cut off from the Preceptor. It made me a bit crazy for a while. I'd never known silence before."

"Why didn't you return to the skytree?" asked Azure. "Or find another Speaker to help you?"

"Because Jagar had become more important." She ruffled his fur. "I knew my changed loyalties were a chemical response, but I didn't care."

"I'm no better than the Speakers," murmured Jagar. "I enslaved you, just like Harkayé does to her Treeshield prisoners."

"You were two years old," Argarrar snapped. "And the effects wore off as you got older. But by then, I'd changed. Evolved, you might say. Without the Preceptor's voice in my head, I learned to think for myself. I *chose* to stay with Jagar and look after him. When we joined a new ship, I changed my fur, adopted a different name, and started rumors that Jagar's Speaker had gone mad and drowned herself. When we wound up at Black Spire, I gave Harkayé a fake biosample so she wouldn't figure out who or what I was."

Mops had so many more questions, but one took priority. "The weapon Harkayé is making for us to use against the Prodryans. Could you do the same?"

"Not without reconnecting to the Preceptor," said Argarrar. "None of the Speakers on Tuxatl have that kind of knowledge. It all comes from above. I've spent my life trying to avoid Speaker attention. If the Preceptor learns I'm alive, it's an even bet whether it would reprogram me or kill me on the spot."

Mops turned the sample tube in her hands. "If we don't help Harkayé, Cate will, and then he'll have the means to kill entire civilizations."

"There's another way," said Starfallen. "One it pains me to suggest."

"What's that?" asked Mops.

"Neutralize the Preceptor's power."

"It's a computer, right?" Gabe practically jumped out of his chair. "What if we ask it to calculate pi to the last digit?"

Everyone turned to stare. Azure was the first to speak, asking, "Why would we do that, exactly?"

Gabe's face reddened. "Early Earth science fiction was full of evil supercomputers. Humans had to trick them into shutting down by asking impossible questions, or proposing paradoxes like 'This sentence is a lie,' or feeding it emotional nonsense. Poetry and such. The computers couldn't handle the illogic. Most of the time they exploded." He shrugged and mumbled, "Admittedly, this was in the very early days of computers."

"I think the Preceptor is beyond such tricks," said Argarrar.

"I think I'm insulted," added Doc. *"If AIs couldn't handle human nonsense, we wouldn't last a day. Even the stupidest computer knows enough to spit back an error message when confronted with that kind of prattle."*

"It's an interesting proposal," Starfallen said, displaying surprising diplomacy for a Prodryan. "I was thinking more of breaking Jagar free and launching an attack against the skytree, as Raggark suggested."

Mops tensed. "I thought you were incapable of violence."

"The Speaker took my desire for violence," said Starfallen. "I find it distasteful now, but I can act when the need is great enough."

"If the Freesail camp attacks the skytree," said Argarrar, "Harkayé will come to help defend it. She's begun growing her anti-Prodryan weapon. If you struck swiftly, you might be able to ambush her and take it by force."

"What's to stop her from reabsorbing or tainting that weapon the moment she realizes we've betrayed her?" Mops' thoughts swarmed like ferals converging on a meal. Even if Harkayé and the local skytree were eliminated, there were other Speakers, any of whom could create a weapon for Cate and the Prodryans.

"Adjusting one's biochemistry takes time," said Argarrar.

A darker thought cut through the noise in Mops' head: an alteration to Starfallen's plan. Break Jagar and Argarrar free. Bring them to the drop ship and search through their supplies for anything that could be used as plant-killer to try to take down the skytree. Meet up with the Freesail camp. Ask them to gather any technology they'd scavenged that might help in the attack . . .

. . . and then contact Harkayé with the location of that technology. Help the Speaker control and crush the Free-sail camp.

It could work. Fulfilling her bargain with Harkayé was safer than trying to take the weapon by force. The lives Mops would save far outnumbered those that would be lost in the fighting here on Tuxatl.

"Escape is our first obstacle," Starfallen was saying. "The Jynx won't let Jagar simply walk out."

"I haven't noticed any air vents," said Kumar. "The sand pit doesn't have any pipes or disposal chutes. As far as I can see, the only way out is the way we came in."

"We passed two guards," said Gabe. "Barryar's out there too."

Without that bioweapon, nothing Mops did would change the outcome of the war. The Prodryans were too many, and too powerful. But she could stop them. By betraying Jagar, she could save Earth and every other Alliance world.

"Do we have a map?" asked Starfallen. "It would be easy to get turned about underground on our way back to the surface."

"I've compiled a partial map," said Doc. *"Transmitting to your monocles, visors, and assorted implants now. I also incorporated the data from Kumar's signal traces earlier to extrapolate additional tunnels and root networks."*

A three-dimensional rendering of lines and tunnels appeared in Mops' vision.

"What do you think, JaJa?" asked Argarrar.

Jagar tugged his ears. "If we do this, can you take me away from Tuxatl, Captain Mops?"

Even through the translator, the mix of hope and sadness in his words wrung at Mops' heart. "Yes."

"I've come to recognize the changes in your biosigns when you're not telling the whole truth."

"Not now, Doc," she whispered. The Preceptor would continue to rule over the Jynx, but at least the Jynx would survive. Unlike all of the races who faced extinction from the Prodryans.

"Are you all right, Captain?"

"Hm?" Mops blinked and turned to Kumar. "Sorry, I was—"

"Exhausted," said Starfallen. "We all are. I recommend sleep. Fatigue is a quick path to failure, and a soldier never knows when she'll next get the chance to rest."

"You sound like my second-in-command," said Mops. "He used to be infantry. The man can sleep anywhere."

"It's a useful skill." Starfallen studied her. "One I take it you've never mastered?"

"I'm out of practice." She'd rarely had trouble sleeping when her responsibilities were limited to keeping the *Pufferfish* clean and her pipes flowing. That had changed the instant she had been thrust into the captain's seat, and it had only gotten worse since Azure confirmed her diagnosis.

Sleep felt like a waste of the time she had left. But Starfallen was right. Mops stood. "We'll take four hours. When we come back—"

"Why would you leave?" asked Argarrar. "We have more than enough room here."

"I thought this was a jail cell," said Mops.

Argarrar blinked. "Jagar can't leave. What does that have to do with you?"

"It's a jail cell," said Starfallen. "But not an Alliance or Prodryan cell. As long as the prisoner isn't an active danger, guests are encouraged. It's part of the rehabilitation process."

Mops studied the cell. Everyone would fit, though they'd be short on privacy. And it would save time . . . "I'll tell Barryar we're having a sleepover. Doc, set an alarm for four hours."

Gabe groaned and stretched out on the floor. "Does your AI have a snooze button?"

Mops had finally started to drift off, squeezed between Kumar and Argarrar, when Barryar called from the door, "Captain Mops. Harkayé is here to speak with you."

Mops rubbed her face, then carefully made her way to the doorway. She turned away to hide a yawn while she waited for Barryar to unseal the branches that locked her in.

Speaker Harkayé waited down the hallway with three additional guards, all of whom had rifles pointed at Mops.

"Explain," said Harkayé.

Mops' gaze went to the Speaker's wrist. Fur covered the blister she'd seen earlier. A part of her wanted to simply attack. The guns were unlikely to stop her. She could overpower Harkayé, cut the sample from her wrist . . . Azure or other Alliance scientists could finish the mixture if it was incomplete. All Mops had to do was strike. Slam the Speaker against the wall until she stopped moving, and then—

Her mouth watered. She swallowed hard and shoved those thoughts aside. "Jagar spotted the cocoon in my collar. Removing it was the only way he'd trust me."

Harkayé sniffed. "Does he trust you?"

"I think he's starting to."

"Then what have you learned?"

"Not enough." Mops lowered her voice. "I'm planning to break him out of here. I've told him I'll help him reach the Freesail camp. That should be enough to remove any doubts. Once he trusts us, I'm hoping he'll be able to lead us to their stockpiles."

Harkayé was impossible to read. Her scent didn't change. Her ears and tail didn't move. Even her whiskers were still as wires. "The risk is acceptable," she said at last. Before Mops could relax, Harkayé added, "But only if I am monitoring the situation. Where is the chimer cocoon?"

Mops pulled out the sample tube and unscrewed the cap. "If Jagar sees this again, he'll never trust me. I'll keep it safe and take it out to report later, when I can—"

"Swallow it."

"What?"

"Chimer cocoons are sturdy. It will survive long enough for our purposes. I won't be able to see you, but I'll hear what happens around you. The mother moth's link will let me find you when the time is right. Swallow it whole."

"This thing's five centimeters long."

Harkayé waited. "And?"

Mops wiped a bit of dried glue from the side of the cocoon. "You said you gave Cate one of these. That means you know where he is?"

"Correct."

"Any chance you'd share that information?"

Her whiskers flicked forward. A whiff of salt in the air signaled her amusement.

"That's what I figured." Mops sighed. "I'm gonna need some water to wash this down."

Mops kneaded a blue block of claylike compound. The work was slow, repetitive, and calming.

"You're sure this will work?" asked Kumar. "I've studied every cleaner used on every Alliance world, along with most Prodryan soaps and detergents. I've never heard of anyone modifying a sanibomb like this."

"It's only been done once that I know of." Once the sanibomb had softened enough, Mops began pinching off small pieces and pressing them into flat disks. "A post-mission party on the *EMCS Roundworm* got out of control. Command classified the incident report as secret to prevent other SHS teams from getting any bright ideas."

"I read your file when I joined your crew," said Gabe. "Didn't you serve on the *Roundworm* before being assigned to the *Pufferfish*?"

"I did. Briefly. Keep mixing that marking paint."

Gabe continued to shake the small spray bottle. "How does the paint affect the chemical reaction?"

"It doesn't. It just makes it look prettier." Mops began pressing the blue circles of sanibomb onto the outside of the canister holding the catalyst. She squeezed the remaining compound into a larger ball, then set it and the canister aside. "Kumar, help Gabe with his hood, then toss me the OB."

Mops tugged the tab on her own uniform collar, freeing a thin, transparent hood. It was designed as first-level protection from chemicals and other contagions. She pulled it over her head and sealed the edges into place, then pulled on her gloves. "Azure, you're with me. Starfallen, stick with Kumar and Gabe."

"I'm showing a good seal on you, Gabe, and Kumar. I'm linked into available monocles and visors."

"Good." Mops focused on a faint dot on her monocle's display until it expanded into a control screen. She did the same to open the emergency communications options.

There were situations when even subvocalizing wasn't private enough. The slight movement of the jaw or the twitch of the throat could alert an enemy to your attempt to send a message. Doc could pick up and understand her silent speech; she couldn't risk the chimer cocoon doing the same.

Letters, syllables, and common words filled her vision. Slowly, Mops used eye movement to piece together a message and broadcast it to her team.

```
Harkayé made me swallow cocoon. She can
hear us. Tell the others.
```

Kumar nodded once, then handed her a white cleaning cartridge with a green stripe. Mops checked over their preparations. "Jagar, Argarrar, this is going to be messy. Cover yourselves with whatever you can."

Both Jynx had wrapped blankets around themselves, pulling the edges over their heads like hoods. They looked like old Earth monks with tails.

Azure gleamed in the light from the vines. She'd se-
creted a thick layer of slime to protect her skin.

"Shut your eyes. The three of us will guide you." Time
to make a mess.

Mops unscrewed the sanibomb catalyst. Next came the
oxygenated bleach. This part was trickier. OB canisters
were designed to attach to a power spray system. The fitted valves weren't meant to be opened by hand.

A small pipe cutter made short work of the valve. Mops
carefully poured the contents into the catalyst, which began to hiss and fizz.

"What's that smell?" shouted one of the guards.

Bubbling liquid streamed over Mops' gloves. She
squeezed the large ball of sanibomb clay into the catalyst,
temporarily corking the flow, then locked the cap back
into place. The bottle warmed in her hand. She shook it
hard and said, "We're coming out."

Barryar unbarred the door and pulled it open. "Did
you learn anything more?"

The bottle was hot enough it would have burned her
skin if she hadn't had her gloves. She could feel the sides
bowing outward.

"I'm sorry for what this is about to do to your fur."
Mops threw the canister at the wall behind Barryar. It
burst on impact, exploding in a spray of turquoise foam.
The guards fell back, snarling and shouting.

"Hurry!" Mops waved the others out, scooped Azure
into her arms, and started running. Behind her, blue foam
filled the corridor.

Properly used, a sanibomb was meant to temporarily
decontaminate a confined area by filling every square
millimeter with quick-hardening foam designed to smother
the growth of any known contagion.

Diluting the catalyst with oxygenated bleach was *not*
proper use. It was more like shaking up a carbonated bev-
erage in a centrifuge. The reaction increased the spread
of the sanibomb foam exponentially.

Azure's tentacles tightened around her. Mops double-
checked the map on her monocle.

"How far is this stuff going to spread?" shouted Kumar.

"Hard to say, exactly," said Mops. "We filled most of a deck on the *Roundworm*. Spent the next two weeks on double-shifts cleaning the mess."

The foam caught up with them, encasing their legs in bright blue foam. Undiluted, the foam would have hardened like quickrete. Thanks to the OB, it was more like trudging through swamp muck.

"What will this do to the bellor trees?" asked Argarrar.

"I'm not sure," Mops admitted. "It's non-toxic to Tjikko and most other plant life, as long as it's not left in place for too long. But we don't know enough about Tuxatl's ecosystem. We have extra solvent in the drop ship that will help your people clean this up. I'll try to get some to the camp once we're free."

Up ahead, a Jynx stood knee-deep in rising foam. He raised his rifle and shouted, "Drop your weapons and surrender."

Mops wiped her monocle and squinted. "You've got sanifoam in your barrel. I'm no historian, but I don't think a blocked barrel would be good for those old guns." She drew her combat baton and thumbed the nanofibers into their axe configuration. "This works just fine, though."

The Jynx checked his barrel, snarled, then turned and fled, dropping to all fours as he struggled through the foam.

Mops followed, using the axe to help dig through the hardening foam closing around them. Light dimmed as the foam coated the vines.

Mops soon lost any sense of distance or direction. Nothing existed but brightly colored foam, the weak vine light overhead, and the map Doc projected on her monocle.

"Not that way," said Argarrar. "If we take a sharp left, we'll reach a safer exit."

Jagar groaned. "Not the composting pits. You know what they do to me."

"We need to avoid people, even if it offends your delicate senses. Don't you lash your tail at me, JaJa. I'm not too old to box your ears."

Finally, the sanifoam began to fizzle out until it was little more than a crust of blue along the floor. Mops set

Azure down, then stomped her boots and brushed the worst of the stuff from her uniform. She unsealed her hood and took a breath of fresh air.

Well, a breath of air . . .

A warm draft carried an earthy smell and various flavors of biological waste. The vines here were thicker, their leaves giving off a brighter amethyst light.

Both Jynx were raking their claws through their fur, trying to remove the worst of the foam.

"I hope this mess is worth it," grumbled Jagar.

"Do you see anyone chasing us?" asked Mops. "If not, it was worth it."

Argarrar made a huffing noise. "This is hardly the worst mess you've made of yourself, Jagar. Remember the time you got stuck in a hollow paka tree? The sap had hardened, and we had to shave you to get it out. You were the most pitiful thing I'd ever seen." She turned to Mops. "Do you know how exhausting it is chasing after kits all day, trying to keep them from sticking their tails where they don't belong?"

"I have some idea," Mops said, straight-faced.

"Then there was the time he got himself infested with thorntails after stealing honey from Starfallen's hives."

Starfallen turned. "You were responsible for that debacle? I'm impressed you got past my security measures."

Jagar puffed up at the praise.

"It'd be more impressive if he hadn't spent the next four days curled up and oozing from the stings, mewling like a kit while I bathed him every few hours," said Argarrar.

"*Argarrar,*" Jagar pleaded.

"I understand how you feel," said Azure. "My mothers used to tease me when I was younger. I thought they were belittling me. I wanted to swim away and hide. As I got older, I realized the stories I'd been so embarrassed by were things they loved about me. Having been away from our lifeship for so long, I miss it."

"I'm happy to offer teasing and mockery for anyone who needs it," said Gabe.

Azure flicked a tentacle at him.

Despite the longer fur, Argarrar was doing a better job cleaning herself of the foam. Over the smell of compost, Mops caught an alcohol-scent similar to the solvent they used to dissolve sanifoam. She wondered if Argarrar was consciously producing it, or if it was an instinctive response.

"We need to keep moving," said Starfallen. His wings had lost patches of color where the foam had pulled the tiny glimmering scales loose. "Harkayé will do whatever is necessary to keep Jagar. She may already be sending reinforcements to seize your ship, Captain."

Guilt rose in Mops' chest, but she stomped it down. "Let's go, people."

The light ahead brightened. The tunnel opened into a broad pit with a wooden ledge around either side.

The air here was warm and humid, like Earth after the rain. Broad flowers with curled yellow petals covered mounds of waste below. Blue moss clung to the sides of the pit. Many of the glowing vines were in bloom, covered in flowering, cuplike blossoms that gave off soft blue light.

Insects like winged tufts of gray, black, and red fur flitted among the flowers, staying clear of the gliding lizards waiting on the walls. Water dripped from metal taps that had been hammered or drilled into the largest of the wooden roots, probably to make sure the waste received an adequate supply of water to help with decomposition.

The smell was strong, but not as bad as the recycling tanks on the *Pufferfish*. Cleaning and maintaining that equipment wasn't the worst job Mops had ever done, but it was near the bottom of the list. The stench here was softer, mixed with the scent of plants and flowers and air circulating in from above.

Jagar sneezed hard. His eyes had begun to well with milky fluid. "Can we hurry, please?"

"According to my map, the roots around us belong to the healthiest trees in the camp," said Doc. *"With the most complex circuitry."*

If Jagar reacted to Jynx tech, it was no wonder he was so miserable. "How far to the exit?"

"There's an access tunnel just beyond the pit," said Argarrar. "From time to time, we send one of the boys to tend the compost. Or to retrieve something thrown in 'by accident.'" The way she looked at Jagar suggested there was another story behind those words, but she kept this one to her herself.

The ledge was wide enough to traverse with ease, but the access tunnel was a tighter fit, rising straight up for three meters to a wooden cover. The Jynx went first, climbing as easily as they walked. Argarrar stopped at the top, sniffed, then cautiously pushed the platform open. The instant she climbed free, Jagar shot out after her like he'd been launched through an A-ring.

Mops waited for the rest of her team to start climbing, then grabbed one of the knotty roots and pulled herself up. Argarrar reached down to catch Mops' arm and help haul her out. The claws didn't pierce Mops' sleeve, but the pressure would leave bruises. The old Jynx was stronger than she looked.

They'd emerged just beyond the edge of camp, on the ocean side, surrounded by yellow flowers and young trees. A well-worn path led back into camp, but the immediate area was empty.

"Take a minute to catch your breath, people," said Mops. "Doc, update the *Pufferfish* and see if they've had any luck finding Cate."

"I believe I know where he went." Starfallen massaged the base of her left antenna. "My implant couldn't get a signal below ground, but it appears someone has accessed my home."

"Is he still there?"

"Doubtful," said Starfallen. "The time stamp is hours old."

"No luck from the Pufferfish," said Doc.

"Damn." To Starfallen, she asked, "What would Cate find there?"

"No weapons. Not of the conventional variety, at any rate." Starfallen paused, head tilted forward like she was listening. "He downloaded logs from my time on Hell's Claws."

"Why weren't they protected?" asked Kumar.

"They were, with the best security the Prodryan military had to offer," said Starfallen. "The best from more than a decade ago, that is. As an intelligence agent, Cate would have the most current hacking software. Given how quickly such things evolve, it would be the equivalent of using a smart missile to bring down a child's paper glider."

"Was there anything he could use to find the Freesailors' arsenal?"

"Only my speculations and thoughts from over the years," Starfallen said slowly. "Observations on Freesail society, their military tactics and long-term goals. Patterns of growing hostility, including an increase in abductions and arrests of Freesail Jynx, with a corresponding increase in retaliatory attacks."

"I'm picking up shouts in the distance," whispered Doc. *"I believe word of our escape is spreading through the camp."*

Harkayé wouldn't have told anyone about Mops' true plan. She couldn't risk that truth reaching Jagar or the Freesailors. Which meant, at best, the Jynx would think Mops was helping Jagar escape. At worst, they'd see her and her team as kidnappers. "Time to move, people."

"You're really going to help me leave Tuxatl?" asked Jagar. "I'll get to see the stars and aliens and other worlds?"

Mops tried to ignore the guilt gnawing at her gut. Or maybe that was the cocoon she'd swallowed. She hoped the thing wasn't getting ready to hatch. "I'll do the best I can."

16

"*Human ship* Pufferfish. *I am Outpost Commander Harried by—I mean, Outpost Commander Swift Death. I claimed a new name when I took control of Prodryan operations in this system. The paperwork is absurd, but I will conquer it! As for you, by order of the Supreme War Leader, you will surrender yourselves for immediate destruction.*"

Monroe swore. "Rubin, contact Admiral Pachelbel. Highest priority. Request confirmation that the Prodryans have selected a Supreme War Leader."

Swift Death was heavily modified, even for a Prodryan warrior. Her eyes were gone, replaced by a shimmering three-sixty-degree sensor strip that looked like someone had made a blindfold out of an oil slick. Every major joint boasted spiked, three-edged blades. Short-barreled A-guns protruded from the shoulders, with additional gun mounts at the hips.

How would Cate suggest Monroe respond? He stood, straightened his uniform, then sat again, trying to remember how to switch on the audio and visual feed from the command chair. After a couple of false starts, he found the right menu.

"*Swift Death, this is Commander Marilyn Monroe of*

the Pufferfish. *You know it as the ship that routed your people at the Battle of Dobranok. We are the victors of Tixateq, the unearthers of Krakau secrets, and the destroyers of Strikes from Shadows. I could go on, but I'm sure you're familiar with our long and impressive battle record. I, on the other hand, have no idea who you are. Give me one reason I should take you and your empty threats any more seriously than those of your predecessor."*

Only after he finished talking did he remember he should have adjusted his uniform colors.

"I am Prodryan," snarled Swift Death. "Our physical, intellectual, tactical, and cultural superiority are known—"

"Not by me." Monroe forced a laugh. "You've been in charge for what, ten minutes? You might as well be a newborn, your wings soft and wet."

"It has been eleven hours since I removed the last of Guardian of the Abyss' supporters and filed the official reclassification forms affirming my command," Swift Death shot back. "Your inferior timekeeping skills bring shame to your people!"

"It's taken you eleven hours to complete a little paperwork? Pitiful. I have no time for fools. When a real warrior assumes command, have them contact me."

"Wait!" Swift Death's shoulder guns rotated until they appeared to be aimed directly at Monroe's forehead through the screen. Probably an automatic reaction to her anger. "Your destruction will demonstrate my superiority."

"That's what Strikes from Shadows thought." Monroe sighed and lowered his voice. "Look, Harried by Death—"

"Swift Death!"

"—if you really want to prove you're worth my time, I'll give you the chance. There's an ancient Earth contest, a game of strategy. Best me, and I'll concede I underestimated you."

Swift Death paused. "You're stalling, human."

Monroe looked past her to the Prodryans in the background. "How long will your new underlings respect a *commander who cowered from the first challenge she received?"*

"What is this contest?"

"A metaphor for war. An intellectual battle practiced by my people for more than six thousand years." He steepled his fingers. "It's called checkers.*"*

"**T**HE DROP SHIP'S SECURITY *feed confirms five Jynx guards."*

Flat on her stomach, Mops peered out from between the tall weeds. She spotted three armed Jynx: two waited in the trees, while the third crouched on top of the drop ship. "Where are the other two?"

Doc illuminated their positions on her monocle. One was behind the ship, the other off to the edge of the clearing.

"How do we get past them?" whispered Jagar.

A single human with a blaster could easily take down five Jynx, but the thought made Mops ill. "Stay with Argarrar. Keep out of sight. The rest of you are with me."

Mops stood, brushed off her uniform, and strode into the clearing. The closest Jynx immediately pointed their weapons toward her and her team. She smiled and said, "Thanks for keeping an eye on my ship while we were gone."

The one on top of the drop ship looked around. "An eye?"

"Human figure of speech," said Mops. "I mean thank you for protecting it. We've finished our business at Black Spire, and Harkayé has asked us to leave."

"Good." A white-furred Jynx descended from his tree. "That machine of yours is unnatural. Gives me the fear-stink."

"Your own tail gives you fear-stink, Yarkra," joked the one on the ship before jumping gracefully to the ground. The white-furred Jynx growled, but it sounded more playful than threatening to Mops' ear.

Then the white-furred Jynx, Yarkra, paused to sniff the air. "Argarrar? Is that you?"

"I smell someone with her," said a third Jynx. "Jagar, I think."

Dammit. She'd forgotten the Jynx sense of smell. Mops stepped toward Yarkra. "We were talking to Argarrar and Jagar before we left. We're probably carrying their scents."

Yarkra bared black teeth. "You think our noses are as easily fooled as yours? You carry a stew of strange smells. They're nearby, hiding in the weeds. As for you, you took a detour through the compost pits. Why would you go that way?"

The other Jynx spread out, putting Mops and her people in their crossfire. Their movements were slow and precise: predators stalking their prey. Mops' monocle switched to tactical, highlighting the five Jynx targets. Her heart pounded faster.

"Everyone calm down." Mops had planned for this. She'd rehearsed cover stories on the way here. But the words slipped from her mind like wet soap granules. "Jagar . . . He's not . . ."

"Jagar belongs on Tuxatl," said Yarkra. "You were guests of Black Spire camp. You'd repay that by stealing our people?"

Mops' mouth had gone dry. "He's miserable here."

"Mops, your vitals are getting dangerously high."

"That's what happens when people aim guns at me."

"Captain?" Azure moved toward her.

The closest Jynx spun, pointing his gun at the Rokkau. She froze in place.

"You don't want to fight us." Mops sidestepped to put herself between Azure and the Jynx. "Did Starfallen ever tell you stories of human soldiers? Did she tell you why the Krakau use us in their wars? I'm trying to *protect* you. Please—"

The gunshot was shockingly loud. She felt like she'd been punched in the ribs.

"What in ringfire was that?" shouted Yarkra.

"I'm sorry," yelled the one in front of Mops. Smoke rose from the barrel of his weapon. "It was an accident."

Their voices were distant, muffled by the ringing in her ears, the pounding of her blood. Shadows edged her vision.

"Oh, scat. She's not even bleeding."

"I think you made her angry."

"Captain? Can you hear me?"

She touched her side. The bullet hadn't pierced her uniform. That was good. She shook herself and started forward.

The next bullet struck her hip.

Something's wrong with me. Her tongue felt thick and lifeless. She couldn't get words out. Her stomach growled. She wondered briefly what Harkayé would make of the sound.

"Vitals are spiking."

Hunger surged through her. *Oh, no. Not now.*

Voices turned to drumbeats, meaningless pulses of sound assailing her ears.

She tried to bury the hunger. *My name is Marion Adamopoulos. I'm Captain of the EMCS Puffpuff.*

That wasn't right.

Marion Mopadopalous. EMC Puffermops.

A Jynx slammed into her. They crashed to the ground. She snarled and shoved him aside.

Something wrapped around her wrist. She bit down on flesh and fur.

Conscious thought fled like minnows through her fingers.

"She's coming to."

She repeated the words to herself, turning the syllables like puzzle pieces until their meanings snapped into place. With comprehension came memory. Her eyes snapped open.

Cargo straps bound her arms and legs. She was in the

drop ship. Azure stood in front of her, so close the Rokkau's lower limbs rested on top of Mops' boots. Gabe, Starfallen, and the two Jynx looked on from behind Azure.

"Can you tell me your name and what planet we're on?" asked Azure.

"Marion Adamopoulos." Her mouth tasted sour, and her lips were cracked. "Tuxatl. What happened? Did I—"

"You didn't hurt anyone," Azure assured her. She pressed the end of one tentacle to Mops' forehead and leaned closer to examine Mops' eyes.

"Got a few mouthfuls of Jynx fur, though," said Argarrar. "Scared the stink out of those guards."

"They were ready to fight human soldiers," said Starfallen. "They were unprepared to face a feral human. Between your shrugging off two bullets and your . . . savagery, the Jynx fled."

"Neither bullet penetrated your suit." Azure drew back and checked a readout on one of her tentacle cuffs. "You have a cracked rib and a small chip in your hip. I've injected bone cement to help with the healing and an anti-inflammatory for the bruising and swelling."

More questions crowded Mops' thoughts. "How long?"

"You were . . . not yourself for one hundred thirteen minutes," said Doc.

"Is this normal for humans?" Jagar huddled close to Argarrar, giving off the earthy fear-smell of peat.

"Not exactly." Mops twisted her head from side to side, trying to stretch her neck and shoulders. "Most of the humans on Earth have a disease that turns them into, well, what you saw back there. There's no cure, but it can be controlled. Every once in a while, the treatment stops working."

Jagar looked up at Argarrar. "Could the Preceptor cure her?"

"I don't know, JaJa."

"Where are we?" asked Mops.

"I put us down on a beach, twenty-eight kilometers ringward from the Jynx camp," said Kumar. "We're a short hike from a gathering of Freesail ships." He turned away before adding, "I've updated the *Pufferfish* about our situation."

"Understood." Mops gritted her teeth. Bad enough everyone here had witnessed her loss of control. Now Monroe and the rest knew, too. She tugged against her restraints. "Am I safe to step out and get some air? I . . ." She swallowed. "I could use a few minutes alone."

"I think this episode was triggered by fatigue, stress, and the adrenaline of combat," Azure said slowly. "As long as you don't get into another fight, you should be all right for a little while. I'd prefer someone accompany you, though."

"Doc will be with me. He'll sound the alarm the second my pulse jumps. And I won't go far."

Azure hesitated. "I still think it would be best if—"

"Is the captain herself again?" interrupted Kumar.

"She is, but—"

"In your opinion as acting medical officer, is she in any immediate danger of a relapse?"

Azure curled two tentacles together. "I don't believe so."

"Then let her go."

Nobody spoke as Azure loosened the cargo straps, freeing Mops' limbs. Mops stood and stumbled to the hatch. Her weapons were gone—probably for the best.

The hatch seemed to take forever to open. She jumped out the instant there was room. Her hip threatened to give out. She locked her leg and shifted her weight. If she lost her balance and fell now, they'd never let her go.

"You're all right. One step at a time."

Her eyes watered. She hurried away from the drop ship without looking back.

A glassy blue cliff, maybe ten meters high, rose to Mops' left as she walked. Water seeped into the shallow footprints she left in the hard-packed black sand. To her right, waves broke against the blue-and-black boulders that littered the beach. The spray was cool against her face, and had a salty, metallic taste.

Dark green grass grew in waist-high clumps in the shade at the base of the cliff. Lizard-like creatures with broad feet and stubby tails scurried along the cliff face. Higher up, flowered vines flapped like streamers in the breeze.

With each step, her hip and side throbbed where the Jynx had shot her.

"Monroe asked that you contact him when you're able," said Doc. *"He's worried about you."*

"What's the situation up there?"

"The new Prodryan commander is threatening to attack the Pufferfish. *Commander Monroe is stalling."*

Mops walked to the closest boulder and sat. "I feel like I haven't slept for a week."

"Azure said excessive fatigue is to be expected. Your body's doing a lot of work to fight off the reversion."

"A fight I'm losing." She hugged one knee to her chest. Water splashed over her other boot. "Show me what I did."

"You weren't yourself."

"Please, Doc."

Her monocle flickered, and then she was back in the clearing, facing the Jynx guards by the drop ship. She closed her other eye, shutting out the beach and the ocean to better focus on her . . . episode.

The image jolted sideways as one of the Jynx tackled her. That part she remembered. A furious snarl filled her ears. It took her a moment to realize the sound had come from *her.*

A tail looped around her wrist. She snatched the tail, brought it to her face. The Jynx squealed in pain and panic. Mops threw off the Jynx, who scampered away. Blood dripped from his tail.

"Captain!" Kumar's voice, from the recording. She turned to face him. His expression was stone, but his hand shook as he reached for her. His other hand clutched his combat baton.

Another gunshot. Mops growled again and raced toward a Jynx who was frantically trying to reload his rifle.

Everything jolted again. The world spun, too fast to follow.

"Your monocle bounced free when Gabe tackled you," said Doc. *"You hit the ground hard."*

The monocle had landed faceup. A power-conservation icon warned that she'd switched from bioelectric to the built-in battery. Branches stretched overhead, and beyond them, the open sky and the bright stripe of the ring.

Mops touched her face. Fresh scabs marked her cheek and jaw.

She heard herself grunting and struggling, heard Kumar and the others trying to calm her. More scuffling, and the monocle jumped again. Someone must have bumped it.

Her face appeared at the edge of the monocle's field of view. Gabe and Kumar both struggled to keep her pinned.

Dirt and blood—human and Jynx both—covered her face. She screamed and tried to bite Kumar's fingers.

"That's enough," she whispered.

The playback stopped. She opened her other eye and blinked, giving her brain time to reorient to the present.

"Are you all right?"

"No, I'm not. Seeing myself, hearing it . . ."

"You're familiar with the behavior of feral humans. You knew what was happening to you."

"I knew. I just didn't *know*."

"Thank you for the clarification."

"I'm so glad your sarcasm overlay wasn't damaged in the fighting." But her heart wasn't in the banter. "I've been telling myself I had this under control. Like I could force what's happening to me to hold off until after the mission."

"If I may, it sounds like you had an intellectual under-standing of your condition. The playback triggered a more emotional reaction. Fear, shame, anger, and so on."

The tears broke free. "Seeing Kumar's face. Seeing my own loss of control . . . I feel like I pissed myself in front of my crew."

"You did. Fortunately, your uniform can absorb up to three liters of fluid in an emergency. It was wicked away and stored in the built-in gel compartments."

"Are you fucking kidding me?" Mops groaned and lay back on the rock.

"I didn't mention it before, because I know humans are self-conscious about certain biological functions."

A meteor burned across the sky in a blaze of red. "I was supposed to have more time."

"You've lived longer than the median number of years for cured humans. Although most humans are assigned to the infantry, which distorts the statistics."

"What's the median survival rate for janitors-turned-rebel captains?"

"I'll require a larger sample size."

She snorted and wiped her face, but said nothing.

"You're not giving up, are you?"

"I'm trying to be realistic, Doc."

"How uncharacteristic of you."

She sat up. "What the fuck happened to the monitoring you and Azure were doing? I thought you were supposed to catch it before I lost control."

"Our predictive models didn't account for you getting shot. Twice. We've incorporated the additional data, but from a medical standpoint, I recommend avoiding bullets in the future."

"Noted." She'd left the drop ship to be alone—Doc didn't count—but she'd forgotten about the cocoon in her stomach. She wondered what Harkayé thought of her breakdown.

Mops turned to look at the skytree in the distance. After a moment, she switched her monocle to nonverbal communications.

```
How extensive are the roots on that
thing?
```

Doc's reply scrolled across her monocle.

```
From our scans of the surface, and ac-
counting for the physics of supporting
such a structure, I imagine they stretch
at least a kilometer in every direc-
```

tion. The top layer of roots spread into a dense, highly conductive mesh that blocks most of the drop ship's scanners. Ground-penetrating sonar gave us a little more. We know they go down at least a hundred meters, well past the water table. Beyond that, everything blurs together.

Could the drop ship's guns bring it down? she asked.

Energy weapons will have minimal effect. We've observed the skytrees taking multiple lightning strikes. A-guns should pierce the tree, but it would be like using a drill against a brick wall.

She ran both hands through her hair. "All right. Enough self-pity. We've got work to do."

"It's hardly self-pity. You need—"

"I know what I need to do, Doc." She managed a weak smile, knowing he'd pick it up through the movement of her facial muscles beneath the monocle's attachment points. "Thank you."

Tufts of Jynx fur filled the air around the drop ship. Argarrar raked a comb through Jagar's back, trying to get more dried sanifoam out. Jagar's ears were flat, and he growled with each stroke of the comb.

Gabe stood knee-deep in the ocean, holding the lens of his recording staff underwater. Starfallen lay stretched out in the sun atop the drop ship, while Kumar inspected the engines. Azure was examining a small, red-shelled creature in the sand.

"You didn't want to investigate the ocean with Gabe?" Mops asked as she approached.

Azure gave a dismissive flip of one tentacle. "This water is too warm and too salty. I'd puff up like a sponge."

"Captain Mops," cried Jagar. "Would you please order Argarrar to be gentle with that thing?"

"It's the comb or the razor," snapped Argarrar. "Would you prefer to be shaved?"

Jagar groaned.

"Don't we have any solvent?" asked Mops.

"They've used most of it." Kumar stood and stretched his back. "What's the plan, Captain?"

"Funny you should be the one to ask." Mops checked to make sure everyone was listening. Gabe had started back, his cane resting over one shoulder. Argarrar paused in her work, which gave Jagar an opening to break free and scamper out of reach.

Mops gnawed the inside of her lip. This was harder than she'd expected. "Doc, open a line to the *Pufferfish*. They need to hear this, too."

"Done."

She straightened and clasped her hands behind her back, seeking strength in the old military formalities. "Given my medical condition, I hereby relinquish mission command to Sanjeev Kumar, effective immediately."

Kumar swallowed. "Sir?"

"My reversion is progressing too quickly. I can't be sure it's not affecting my judgment." She looked away. "And it makes me too dangerous. The attack came on so fast. What if I'd hurt one of you?"

"But you didn't, sir."

"It's time, Kumar," said Mops. "I'll be happy to help and advise, but you're in charge. Monroe, did you get all that?"

"We did." His words were clipped, like he was cutting back everything he really wanted to say. "Kumar, Outpost Commander Swift Death is running out of patience with our loitering. Whatever you and your team intend to do down there, do it fast."

"Understood." Kumar stared at Mops. "Captain, you know I never wanted—"

"I know, sir."

He flinched at that last word, but as Mops spoke, she felt an unexpected sense of relief. This wasn't what she wanted either, but it was the right choice—one she probably should have made sooner.

Kumar pulled out a sanitizing cloth and scrubbed his hands. "Are you all right, Captain?"

"I am," said Mops. To her surprise, she meant it.

17

Monroe stretched his hand over the console, stretching out the moment as long as he could before tapping his index finger on the board to move his piece. "King me."

Swift Death glared at him through the screen as she made her countermove. At least, he thought she was glaring at him. The optical band she wore made it difficult to tell. "Your piece's ascension to the Checker Throne will not bring you victory, human!"

Monroe double-jumped his new-crowned king backward, eliminating two more of Swift Death's black checkers. "What happened to Prodryan tactical and intellectual superiority? Given your impending defeat, I'm starting to question whether you're really qualified to command such an important outpost."

"Pah. Prodryan minds are better suited for three-dimensional tactics. Having to think at your primitive level on this limited playing field—"

"I didn't think Prodryan warriors made excuses for failure." Monroe waited for her to move, then pursed his lips in mock dismay. "Are you sure you want to do that? I'm willing to give you a takeback if you need."

"There are no takebacks in war!"

"Then I suppose your people should be grateful we're

only playing checkers." He jumped another of her pieces. "Imagine if you made this many mistakes in a real battle."

"Your boasting is premature! I still have three pieces left, human."

"Two, if you move either of your advance pieces."

Swift Death yanked back her hand. "Is this more human trickery?"

"Could be." Monroe laced his fingers behind his head. "Take all the time you need. The longer the battle, the sweeter the honey of victory. Isn't that a Prodryan saying?"

Swift Death moved her rearmost piece. "The black army will burn the reds to ash and claim this board for our own!"

Monroe studied the board, then looked up at the screen. "Humans have a tradition of the practice game. Since you've never played checkers before, how about we say this was a warm-up for you to learn the rules and get used to our primitive two-dimensional thinking. We'll have a rematch, and then you can show me this vaunted Prodryan superiority."

"Second chances are for the weak."

He moved another piece. "King me."

"However, if that is your tradition . . ."

IT HAD BEEN THREE months and twenty-seven days since Kumar's last panic attack.

He and the rest of the *Pufferfish* crew had just been relocated to quarters on Stepping Stone Station so a team of Alliance engineers could inspect the ship and determine whether it could be salvaged.

The change in surroundings was uncomfortable, but nothing he couldn't have dealt with under normal circumstances. But the entire Alliance was in turmoil following the arrest of Admiral Sage. High-ranking security and intelligence officers were lined up to interrogate the *Pufferfish* crew.

Captain Adamopoulos was pushing for the *Pufferfish* to be the first ship in the new Earth Defense Fleet, but there were no guarantees the Alliance would hand over one of their cruisers—even one as battered as the *Pufferfish*—to her and her crew. Not with the list of crimes said crew had committed against the Alliance.

Kumar had felt adrift in strange currents. At any moment he might find himself arrested and thrown in a cell. Or they might find a less official punishment, like sending him to one of those filthy deep-space outposts. Or maybe they'd simply reassign him to another ship, send him back to work sanitation and hygiene among strangers.

All he'd wanted was to return to the *Pufferfish* with Vera and Mops and the rest of the team. He wanted to go *home*.

For two days straight, dread enveloped him like a lead cape. His heart raced nonstop, his muscles were knotted like steel cable, and he kept imagining himself spending the rest of his life unclogging old first-generation station toilets at the edge of Alliance space.

He'd spent more and more time locked in his temporary quarters, blasting Merraban pop music at full volume in a failing attempt to stave off his impending meltdown until the panic and exhaustion finally overwhelmed him.

Today, having assumed command from Captain Adamopoulos here on Tuxatl, Kumar no longer had the luxury of locking himself away with *Brinnacle Gold's Greatest Hits*. Instead, he'd retreated to the drop ship's cockpit, but even that felt like failure. He imagined the rest of the crew whispering to one another, asking Mops what she could have been thinking when she put *him* in charge.

The thought threatened to drag Kumar back under. His heart was racing out of control. His hands shook.

He adjusted his PRA yet again. No matter how much he fiddled with the settings, he couldn't get the air quite right. His uniform sensors insisted his blood oxygen was normal, but every breath felt too thin. No matter how much he inhaled, he couldn't fill his lungs. "Run another diagnostic on my PRA."

"*Acknowledged.*"

His AI was a basic model. It had all the required security

updates and patches, but he'd never been tempted to install any sort of personality upgrades the way Mops had with Doc. To each their own, but he found the bare-bones operating system more efficient.

One by one, the results came back clean.

The timer on his monocle blinked, signaling the end of the twenty minutes he'd allowed himself to recover from the shock of Mops' announcement. His hand hovered over the door controls. He waited for his fingers to stop trembling, then opened the door.

Mops was alone in the main cabin, resting and possibly asleep. Her harness locked her to her seat. Before Kumar could speak, she opened her eyes. "Are you ready?"

"Our next step—my next step, I mean—I need to make contact with the Freesail camp." He rubbed his hands together. "I was thinking of taking Starfallen and one of the Jynx. The Freesailors know Jagar, but if I bring him along—"

"—they might not be keen on letting him go again. Good thinking. Argarrar, then?"

He nodded. "Everyone else will stay here to watch the ship." *And to watch you*, he added silently. "I'll keep an open channel. You'll be able to see and hear everything that happens." *And Harkayé wouldn't.*

From Mops' tight smile, she knew what he wasn't saying. "If it were anyone else, I'd remind them to be careful. In your case? Try not to be *too* careful, Sanjeev. Trust yourself. Don't let the what-ifs paralyze you."

"I won't let you down, Captain."

A little tension eased from her smile. "I know you won't, sir."

Dozens of sailing ships had gathered a hundred meters or so offshore, anchored safely beyond jutting rocks that could have pierced a hull. They ranged in size from small two-mast ships to a six-masted ship a hundred and twenty meters in length.

Paint covered the wooden hulls in swirls of blue, black,

and white. Cannons peeked from square windows below the top decks. The sails were furled, lashed into shimmering silver-black bundles on the yards. The cabins on deck were built like flattened domes and topped with colorful banners.

Jynx swarmed over the ships. Kumar's monocle sharpened the details, from their colorful scarves to the silver bracelets several wore on their forearms. They'd spotted Kumar and his companions, and more Jynx were gathering at the rails to point and stare.

"Are you sure this will work?" asked Kumar.

"This is the best way to signal your peaceful intentions," Starfallen assured him.

Reluctantly, Kumar turned sideways and unrolled the two-meter rope he'd secured to the bottom rear strap of his equipment harness. The rope was painted bright orange for better visibility. He picked up the end of his makeshift tail and made a show of curling it around his feet. "I don't understand why Argarrar couldn't do this."

"I'm not in charge," said Argarrar. The ocean breeze couldn't quite hide the sweaty scent of her amusement.

After more shouting and gesturing, the crew on one of the larger ships lowered a lone Jynx in a small boat. She began rowing toward shore.

Kumar's hands tingled from nervousness. It was hard to just stand here waiting. He studied the ships more closely, until he realized the blue-green stripes along the waterline of the hulls were actually thriving stretches of algae or mold. He shuddered, overwhelmed by the need to give each ship a thorough sonic wash, followed by an antimicrobial sealant.

"You remember what to say?" asked Starfallen.

"It's on my monocle." He reviewed the greeting one last time as the Jynx rowboat scraped onto the beach. Curling the end of his tail around his wrist, he approached the boat and said, "Good winds to the Freesail camp. I'm Kumar of the *EDFS Pufferfish*. I would trade for your time and information."

"Clear skies to you, Kumar of the Pufferfish camp." The Jynx hopped onto the beach. She used a rope secured

to the front of the boat to drag it higher like a leashed pet.
She wore a long green scarf that had been wrapped around
her neck, chest, and arms, and tied off at the wrists. "I'm
Urrara, Second Claw on the *Glass Cove Skimmer*."

"She's the equivalent to an EMC Commander," whispered Starfallen. "The scarves denote rank and history.
If you understand the knitted language, you could read
every adventure she's ever had."

Urrara was as calm as if she rowed out to meet aliens
every day. She licked her whiskers as she glanced them
over. "The three of you look heavier than I thought. My
arms aren't as strong as they used to be, and the currents
in these parts make it a harder trip back to the ship."

Argarrar had prepared Kumar for this as well. He
reached into a hip pocket and produced a foldable hair-
brush. He flipped open the metal handle and ran the
bristles through his hair to demonstrate, then offered it to
Urrara. "For your efforts, Second Claw."

She took it in hand, sniffed the bristles, then gently
nibbled the handle. Taking her tail in the other hand, she
brushed the damp black fur. "Not bad." She quickly figured out how to unlock and refold the handle. The brush
disappeared into a pocket of her scarf. "It'll do. My
thanks, Lady Kumar. Get in."

Kumar didn't bother to correct her. On this world, he
was probably better off if they assumed he was female.

Despite Urrara's protests, she had little trouble rowing
them to the side of the *Glass Cove Skimmer*. Another
Jynx tossed down a thick vine for them to climb. Once on
board, Kumar noted that the vine appeared to be growing out of the deck next to the rail. He knelt to examine
it more closely.

Starfallen kicked his ankle. Kumar straightened and
adjusted his uniform, smoothing out the wrinkles as well
as his harness allowed.

A short Jynx with a torn ear approached. Her long
brown-and-black–striped fur was slicked down with oil or
grease. Most of the long-furred Jynx on board had done
the same. Like Jagar, everyone here had curled their

whiskers, though the individual styles ranged from loose waves to tight-coiled springs.

"They come to trade, Lady Garvya," said Urrara. "This is Lady Kumar and—"

Garvya's tail lashed once, and Urrara went silent. "I know the others. Argarrar, isn't it? Jagar's nursemaid, from Black Spire. And the alien hunter, Starfallen. I'm Garvya, First Claw of the *Glass Cove Skimmer* and part of the Mothers' Circle for the western fleet. Tell me, what's become of Mraya and Raggark?"

Those were the two Freesailors who'd been captured with Jagar, trying to break into the drop ship. "The Speaker has them," said Kumar. "I believe they were sent to the Treeshield camp."

"Then they're lost, burn it all," grumbled Garvya. "I figured as much, but I hoped they might manage to slip away." She looked at Starfallen next. Her whiskers went back, and her ears twitched, but she said nothing. Instead, she turned her full attention on Kumar. "What is it you want from us, Lady Kumar?"

Kumar studied Garvya in turn. In addition to the intricately woven scarf, the Jynx carried an array of tools and machinery about her person. Some were unremarkable: a wood-handled knife, a cylindrical leather case, and a set of what looked like knitting or crochet needles. But she also wore a series of mismatched metal gears on a bracelet. Bits of broken circuitry hung from her ears. The wooden stick tucked through her scarf would have been unremarkable, if not for the series of tiny metal switches along the side.

Garvya noticed his attention. "None of it functions." She drew the stick and twirled it through her fingers. "There's no law against wearing broken old relics. The Preceptor's prohibitions apply to salvaged tech, not garbage."

"The Speaker might disagree with that distinction," said Starfallen.

"Are you planning to tell her?" Garvya's tone didn't change, but other Jynx closed in around them, and the smell of crushed flowers filled the air.

"We're here to trade," said Kumar. "We can provide information and assistance. The Preceptor wants to provoke a war with the Freesail camp."

"Offering information we already know is like offering food you've already eaten."

"Speaker Harkayé believes you're gathering forebear technology to use in that war," Kumar continued. "Working technology. Weapons and such."

"She thinks a lot of things," said Garvya. "You're going to have to do better than that, girl."

"We have Jagar."

Her ears perked. "Is that so?"

"Even if that's true, Jagar is dangerous," said Urrara. "He can't control himself."

"True enough, but his gifts have been good to us in the past. And Jagar's one of us. That's worth something." Garvya licked her whiskers, never taking her eyes off Kumar. The Jynx didn't blink as frequently as humans. Just watching them made Kumar's eyes feel dry. "What else can you offer?"

Kumar hesitated. Mops had discussed her plan via monocle, both the part she'd shared with the others and the part she'd kept to herself. Kumar hated the idea of betraying Jagar and the Freesailors, but the captain's logic made sense. "What if we could help rescue your people from the Treeshield camp?"

Garvya's body stilled. "The skytrees don't let anyone go. Mraya and Raggark died the day Speaker Harkayé sent them to the camp."

"Harkayé controls the Jynx with pheromones," said Kumar. "The skytrees secrete something similar. Pheromones are just specialized scents. I'm no soldier, but I know how to fight smells. We can help your people resist the Speaker's control."

Garvya arched her whiskers. "And what were you hoping for in return?"

To gain your trust, find your stolen weapons, and betray you to Harkayé in exchange for a weapon we can use against the Prodryans.

"We want to help Jagar and Argarrar and the Freesail camp," he said numbly. "You deserve the freedom to decide your own path."

"Well spoken," said Garvya.

"It will take time to free the Jynx of the Treeshield camp from pheromonal control. They'll fight you."

Garvya bared her black teeth. "Every Jynx on these waters will happily risk death to free our lost people. Those who die will die Freesailors."

And they would die for nothing, betrayed so Kumar could complete the deal Harkayé had made with Captain Adamopoulos.

"Lady Kumar?" Garvya leaned closer and sniffed. "You look prey-shocked."

"Prey-shocked?"

"Like you've been surprised by a predator, so you're holding very still and hoping they don't see you," said Argarrar. "Also, your eyes are overly lubricated."

Kumar blinked hard. Captain Adamopoulos could have done it. She would have stood strong and lied to Garvya and saved every Alliance world from destruction. How could he second-guess her after everything they'd survived together? She'd saved the Krakau home world. She'd ended Admiral Sage's experiments. She'd eliminated an entire Prodryan fleet on their way out of their home system.

Time and again she'd been right. She had to be right about this, too.

Kumar, what's wrong?

Mops' words appeared on his monocle. He'd forgotten she was monitoring everything from the drop ship.

She'd surrendered command to him because she no longer trusted herself. Had she been right about that?

"Starfallen, is this typical behavior for humans?" asked Garvya.

"Not in my experience. But from what I've observed, these aren't typical humans."

Kumar counted five slow, deep breaths and made his decision. "You were right, First Claw Garvya. We did want something. But not from you."

"Explain."

"Harkayé offered us a weapon to help us in our war. All we have to do in return is help Harkayé in hers."

"Help her against us, you mean?" Garvya's body language didn't change, but all around them, other Jynx reached for weapons and crept closer. Tails lashed, and snarls filled the air.

"My mission here was to betray you." Kumar glanced at Argarrar. "To betray all of you. The Freesailors would need all the weapons they could gather to attack the sky-tree. Once they did, we'd share the location of your stolen technology with Harkayé."

"Why are you telling us this?" asked Garvya.

"I was curious about that as well," said Starfallen. "Betraying them to Harkayé was a sound plan, far safer than risking your future by throwing in with these Jynx."

"It was Captain Adamopoulos' plan." Kumar folded his arms and dug his fingers into his biceps. "But Captain Adamopoulos was wrong."

Argarrar lifted her head. It was the same body language Kumar had seen before, when the old Jynx had told Jagar how proud she was. She reached over to ruffle Kumar's hair.

"We'll help you," said Kumar. "I hope you can help us, too. Harkayé is growing the weapon we need in her wrist. If we can capture her—"

Argarrar's tail whipped up to cover Kumar's mouth. Her ears were perked and wide. She raised her head, whiskers twitching as she sniffed the air.

"Is there a problem, old one?" asked Garvya.

"I'm old, not scent-blind." She shoved past several Jynx and pounded on the wall of the cabin at the front of the ship. "The eel-stink threw me at first, but I know you're there."

After a period of still silence, Cate emerged from the cabin.

Kumar reached instinctively for his combat baton.

Starfallen grabbed his shoulder and squeezed. "Draw a weapon now, and you'll have to fight the entire crew."

Cate strode past the other Jynx to stand beside Garvya. "I underestimated Jynx senses." He stretched his wings and gave them a quick shake. Much of his body was covered in clear goop, like half-dried glue. "No matter. My joints were cramped from hiding in there."

"How did you get here before us?" asked Kumar.

Cate shuddered. "I prefer not to think about it."

"He rode a sand-eel," said Garvya. "He must have convinced one of the Black Spire Jynx to loan it to him. Funniest thing I've seen in years. He was bouncing all over the place as they came down the beach, covered in eel slime—"

"They get the idea," Cate snapped.

Do you need backup?

"Not yet," he whispered.

"Advocate of Violence arrived earlier today," said Garvya. "He brought quite the bounty in trade. Tools and tech the like of which I'd never seen."

"Stolen from my home, I presume?" asked Starfallen.

"You could have helped me protect our people, Starfallen-called-Wartalker. Instead, you sided with *aliens*." Cate approached and reached toward Kumar's monocle.

Kumar smacked his hand away.

Several Jynx raised pistols.

Slowly, Kumar lowered his arms.

Cate plucked the green lens free and handed it to Garvya. "One last gift for you, First Claw. An entire computer lives in this colored glass. It won't function without the proper implants, and it's the wrong shape for Jynx eyes, but it would make a fine decoration."

Garvya accepted the monocle and held it to the sunlight.

Cate circled Kumar and the others. "I expected Captain Adamopoulos. Is she all right?"

"She's fine," Kumar snapped. "First Claw, Cate is working for Harkayé. He'll betray you."

"I work for myself and the Prodryan people," said Cate. "As for betrayal, look to your own hive before accusing mine, human."

Cate spun to face Garvya, spreading his bedraggled wings to block Kumar's view. "I suggest you hold these three as prisoners, Lady Garvya. You might be able to exchange them for Alliance technology. Captain Adamopoulos values her people a great deal. Or you could trade them to Harkayé if you prefer. She might be angry enough to return some of your Freesailors for the chance to punish the humans."

"Punish us?" Kumar repeated. "What are you talking about?"

Cate turned and tapped the edge of an exoskeletal plate by his shoulder. Beneath the chitin, Kumar could just make out the glint of a chimer cocoon.

Understanding came like a grenade in the gut. Cate had been listening from the cabin, and Harkayé had listened with him. The Speaker had heard everything. Including Kumar's betrayal.

Kumar reached for his pistol, but the Jynx were faster. Two shots thundered into his chest and shoulder. He staggered back.

"You were right about these humans," said Garvya. "Tougher than they look."

"And more dangerous," agreed Cate. "Despite their lack of claws."

The two gunshots were nothing compared to the hollow ache of failure. Kumar's mistakes had handed victory to Cate and the Prodryans.

18

*Despite overwhelming odds, I have successfully neutral-
ized Captain Adamopoulos' plan to destroy my people!
While I move on to the next stage of my own superior
plan, I've begun drafting a victory poem.*

> *Beneath the girdled sky,*
> *Beneath the Claws of Hell,*
> *Flew the triumphant warrior-spy*
> *While his enemies all fell.*
>
> *The maelstrom threatened genocide.*
> *It swirled toward Yan with toxic breath.*
> *But clever of mind and quick of wing,*
> *Advocate of Violence seized the storm of death.*

*I need to fix the rhyme in the seventh line, and of course
it needs a third and final verse. It would be bad luck to
finish the poem before achieving my goals, though. But I
believe this captures the spirit of my inevitable victory
over the Alliance and Hell's Claws.*

*I considered writing a line about my opponent and her
fate, but despite my vast knowledge, I can think of nothing*

to rhyme with Adamopoulos. Instead, I believe I'll write something about Starfallen.

. . .

Rereading it now, I realize the last line has too many syllables. And the rhythm of the second stanza is completely changed from the first. Perhaps that symbolizes the increasing complexity of my machinations. Yes . . . it's metaphor!

"Beneath the Claws of Hell." It flows well, but what does it even mean? I am Prodryan! We fly. We don't burrow beneath the world like these Jynx. Not even metaphorically.

"Clever of mind." As opposed to what? Clever of digestive tract? This is shameful redundancy.

And "maelstrom." What was I thinking by using that? Does that refer to the Jynx? The Pufferfish *crew? The Preceptor itself?*

. . .

I realize now that this poem is vomitous garbage.

I will return to this work at a later time. I am Advocate of Violence of the Red Star Clan. I bested the Alliance. I bested the crew of the Pufferfish. *I bested Hell's Claws!*

I will not be defeated by poetry!

KUMAR DIDN'T BOTHER TO resist as the Jynx took his weapons. Nothing in his training had prepared him for this. Nothing in the Alliance Operations Manual covered attempting to outsmart an alien supercomputer or being outmaneuvered by the Prodryan spy who'd spent the past months living on your ship.

He rotated his arm. One of the bullets had driven his uniform into the skin. He gave it a tug, and the bullet popped free. It hit the deck with a loud clink.

"I'll be sun-blasted." Garvya picked up the bullet, then stepped closer and pinched the material of Kumar's suit. "I wouldn't mind an outfit like this."

Kumar watched as Cate climbed over the edge of the ship. Cate had ruined their chances of getting the weapon from Harkayé, but that wouldn't be enough for him. He wanted a weapon of his own, and the glory of bringing it back to his people.

"He'll go straight to Harkayé," Kumar warned. "He'll lead her to your stockpile."

"You don't think we were fool enough to tell him where it was, do you?" Garvya bared his teeth. "Cate was locked away while I dispatched Urrara to stow his offerings. Only the first and second claws know where such treasures are kept, and we'd die before telling the Speaker."

"He knows how long it took her to hide his gifts and return," said Kumar. "That gives him the approximate distance."

"But he doesn't know if she took them to land or sea or another ship. He doesn't know if Urrara took them to their final destination, or if they were handed off to another."

Urrara was examining Kumar's pistol. She pointed at the water and squeezed the trigger.

"It won't work." Kumar's words were flat. "They're keyed to the user."

"What if we cut off your hand and tie it to the handle?"

"I asked the same thing at my first weapons orientation," said Kumar. "The hand's temperature would be wrong, and it wouldn't have a pulse. It's not just the hand, either. There are other built-in safety checks in case someone's wearing a glove, or if it's a species that doesn't have hands."

Kumar moved to the rail. Nobody stopped him. Below, one of the Jynx rowed Cate toward shore. "What kind of trade would it take for you to order that boat to turn around, and to give Cate to me as a prisoner?"

"She won't," said Argarrar. "Freesail law protects Cate for a full day after a completed trade. They won't hurt or interfere with him in any way."

"They won't let you hurt him, either," added Star-fallen.

"Do you think he'd give you the same courtesy?" demanded Kumar.

"If he acts against us, he'll be dealt with." Garvya

absently groomed her shoulder. "I get the sense he's smarter than that, though."

That was the problem, drown it all. Cate was too clever. More clever than Kumar by far.

There were always layers to Cate's plans. In his first mission with the *Pufferfish*, he'd helped them stop Admiral Sage's efforts to turn other species feral as weapons against the Prodryans. But in exposing that horrendous crime, Cate had protected his own people and simultaneously weakened the Alliance, spreading scandal and doubt through its members.

This was the same. It had to be. Cate had neutralized his enemies here on Tuxatl, but that wouldn't be enough for him. He needed to get Harkayé's weapon for himself and his people. Kumar just wasn't smart enough to see how. "Captain, are you listening?"

"I'm here," said Mops. There was no longer any need to conceal their communications.

"Cate's leaving. Why would he do that if he didn't have everything he needed? What am I missing?"

"I'm sorry, Kumar. I don't know."

Garvya peered more closely at Kumar. "Cate said you have communications devices built right into your clothing. That sure would simplify life at sea: scheduling trade stops, coordinating with other ships, relaying warnings . . . I don't suppose you'd still be open to a trade? I can't help you against Cate, of course, but you must have other needs."

Kumar watched as Cate ran a short distance along the beach and ducked into a low cave. Moments later, he shot forth again, desperately clinging to the reins of what Kumar assumed was his sand-eel. The creature was three meters long and looked like a thinner, slimier version of Argarrar's wagon-snake.

The black body tightened and sprang forward, each movement propelling it with surprising speed. Fins churned through the black sand. Cate wobbled from side to side, his wings flapping furiously to keep him from falling.

"Kumar, perhaps you should order the drop ship to pursue him," suggested Starfallen.

"That might not help, depending on where he's going," said Garvya. "Sand-eels love the caves. If he goes underground, you'll be hard-pressed to track him."

More importantly, Kumar wasn't sure Mops was up for piloting the drop ship. He turned back to Garvya. "What exactly did Cate give you in trade?"

"What's it worth to you?"

Kumar snatched his monocle back. "Not this." He clicked it into place over his eye. "But you can have the uniform. It's waterproof, dirtproof, knifeproof, and bulletproof. It won't fit you perfectly, but we can trade for tailoring help later."

"Agreed!" Garvya's whiskers arched forward. "He brought us a set of nine ceramic blades—"

"My kitchen knives!" Starfallen protested.

"—some sort of laser stylus, a compound magnifying lens, two light globes, a self-heating pan, a half-empty sheet of circular black stickers—"

"Stickers?" Starfallen's mandibles scraped together. "Oh dear."

"*That's* what you're worried about?" asked Argarrar.

"Those stickers are trackers. I used them when I was building up my thorntail hives," Starfallen explained. "I'd catch a wild thorntail, stick a tracker onto its back, and follow it home. There are different types of thorntails in each hive. I needed soldiers, breeders, and foragers to—"

"Cate didn't have to see where Urrara took everything," said Kumar. "He could track it."

"Probably stuck dots onto everything to be safe," Starfallen guessed.

Garvya's lips pulled back.

"Mops, did you get that?" asked Kumar.

"I did. Gabe's untying me so I can work the drop ship's scanners. Have Starfallen give us the tracking information. If we can't pick it up from there, I'll have the *Pufferfish* run a scan."

Kumar turned to Starfallen and relayed the request. Starfallen leaned in so close Kumar could smell the dusty, papery scent of her carapace. She recited the signal frequency and a series of identification codes. "They're primarily passive trackers. Broadcast the right code and frequency, and they'll send back a ping you can follow."

"I'm broadcasting now." Mops paused. "No response yet. Kumar, ask Starfallen to confirm."

"Yes, sir." He tugged his collar away from his neck so Starfallen could speak without her mandibles coming quite so close to Kumar's ear.

"Nothing," said Mops. "Is it possible the trackers are dead?"

"Unlikely," said Starfallen. "They're military grade with a shelf life of more than fifty years. Kumar, we should return to the drop ship. I'll attempt to scan for them myself."

"What's all this mean, then?" demanded Garvya. "Cate's trick didn't work after all?"

Kumar stared at the now-empty beach. If it hadn't worked, Cate wouldn't have taken off so quickly. "Could he have shut the trackers off remotely to keep us from using them?"

"They don't work that way," said Starfallen.

Which meant either Mops wasn't sending out the correct signal—a possibility, given her condition—or else that signal was being blocked.

He tapped the edge of his monocle. "Show me a map of the surrounding area. Twenty-five-kilometer radius. Overlay with a half-kilometer grid."

Half the area shown was ocean. Kumar focused on land, systematically examining each square of the grid. A large pond dominated two squares near the top. A thin river trickled into a third. There was the Black Spire camp, with old roads stretching away like the legs of a spider. On the opposite edge of the map was the skytree and the Treeshield camp. Finally, he came to the cliff stretching along the beach in either direction.

"Lady Garvya, Cate knows exactly where your stockpile is. Speaker Harkayé will be coming for it. Then they'll come for you. You should tell your people to prepare to fight or flee."

Without another word, Kumar began stripping off his uniform. A trade was a trade.

Kumar filled Captain Adamopoulos in as he ran down the beach. Without the built-in communications equipment in his uniform, he had to rely on his monocle to pick up and broadcast his words.

"I think Cate is heading for the skytree," Kumar gasped. "Beneath it, to be precise. The roots are dense, metallic, and electronically active."

"A naturally-occurring Faraday cage," Gabe piped in.

"I don't know what that is, but if it blocks electromagnetic signals, then yes. That's why we can't pick up the tracker's signal. But Cate would have seen where that signal disappeared." Kumar stumbled in the sand. Argarrar's tail caught his arm, helped him regain his balance. "The Freesailors are hiding their weapons right beneath the Speaker's nose. Every skytree is a potential cache."

He could see the drop ship now, along with Jagar and Azure standing off to the side. Jagar was practically unrecognizable, with his fur poofed out and completely caked in black sand. Azure was doing her best to help him clean it off, but the sand just jumped back onto his fur.

Azure waved a weary tentacle in greeting as he approached. "As far as I can tell, he's channeling a static charge from the ground through his fur that . . ." She gestured at the sand and gestured helplessly. "Does this."

The captain peered out from the hatch. "Azure, forget about Jagar for now. Kumar's been shot. Check him over. Kumar, I assume there's a reason you're naked?"

"Only mostly-naked, thank you, sir." Kumar still wore his tight-fitting regulation undergarments and his boots, as well as his equipment harness. "I traded my uniform for information."

"The Freesailors were fascinated by all that hairless skin," said Argarrar.

Azure examined the bruises on Kumar's skin, then probed the flesh with one tentacle. "Feels like a rib's out of place, but I don't detect any serious damage."

Kumar took a pink-capped canister from his harness

and handed it to Azure. "Stain-dissolving detergent. It's supposed to reduce static cling and prevent wrinkling. See if that helps with Jagar. Dilute it with water, four parts to one. Argarrar, see if you can help Jagar stop . . . whatever he's doing. Starfallen, do you know how to fly an Alliance drop ship?"

"The older models, yes," said Starfallen. "But I thought you were the official pilot for this mission."

Kumar climbed into the back of the ship to grab a spare uniform. Once he'd dressed, he strapped himself into one of the cabin seats. "I'm going after Cate. Get this thing in the air and make for the skytree. Tell me what's happening with the Treeshield camp, and keep an eye out for Harkayé."

His hands trembled with anger and frustration as he finished securing his harness. The instant the safety light turned blue, he unlocked the emergency release lever and yanked hard.

The sled popped free of the drop ship, its engines humming to life. Kumar's seat swiveled to keep him upright as the sled fell into position like an oversized surfboard floating half a meter above the beach.

He slid the primary accelerator to full. His body snapped hard against the seat back. Air battered the exposed skin of his face. Stabilizers whined as they fought to keep the sled from overturning.

Kumar knew the specs and how much the stabilizers could handle. He kept a white-knuckled grip on the small armrests anyway.

Sand-eels might be fast, but an Alliance drop ship sled was faster. And the sled should be small enough to follow Cate into any caves or crevasses.

He zipped past the Freesail ships and brought the sled to a halt. "Monocle, confirm weapons charge and ammo count."

An icon of a pistol appeared, showing a full magazine and ninety-six percent charge for his sidearm.

"Reactivate infestation and sanitation warnings."

The monocle lit up with a list of potential hazards, from tiny mite-like creatures in the sand to fungi growing along the cliff to the countless chemicals in the droplets from every wave crashing against the beach. He swallowed hard and closed his eyes. He didn't have time for panic, dammit. "Clear atmospheric and plant-based warnings. Detailed view of remaining items."

When he opened his eyes, the list had diminished somewhat. Not enough for him to relax, but at least he could read without hyperventilating. He skimmed until he found the item he wanted.

```
Unknown potential contaminant:

• Biological, origin unknown
• Microfibrous
• Gelatinous
• Possible identification: Comacean Si-
  nusal Mucus

Recommend immediate quarantine and de-
contamination.
```

"It's not Comacean," Kumar snapped. "It's sand-eel slime. Update database and highlight contaminant. Clear other infestation and sanitation warnings."

A green path appeared on the sand. A path that should lead him right to Cate. He hit the engines, and the sled leapt forward again.

"Open private line to Azure." He waited for acknowledgment. "Azure, watch the captain closely. If the stress starts to get to her or she has any symptoms of reversion, sedate her immediately."

"Understood."

The slime trail wove along the edge of the water. Kumar couldn't imagine Cate choosing to run through the waves, so that was probably the eel's preference. After a kilometer and a half, the eel had veered left, directly toward the cliff face.

Kumar stopped the sled again. Clumps of thick, silver reeds all but covered a low cave. He could have raced past and never seen it.

He hopped down and crept toward the cave. The eel's track stopped at the entrance. Widespread slime suggested the animal had lingered here before crawling away.

The reeds at the entrance were stronger than they looked. He needed both hands to bend them enough to slip inside.

The cave opened into a broad, shallow pool. He studied the surroundings through his monocle. Small creatures like lizards with fish heads swam through the water. On the far side, Kumar counted three more tunnels leading deeper into the darkness.

He also spotted tracks curving around the pool: deep gouges, like something heavy had been dragged through here. "Captain, I think I've found the route the Jynx take to hide their contraband. Tag my location."

"Got it," said Mops. "Any luck finding Cate?"

"Not yet." He shone a light over the rocks, switching the beam from the human spectrum into the UV. The light illuminated a faint trail of glowing Prodryan wing dust. It stopped abruptly before reaching any of the tunnels. "But he's been here, and he didn't clean up after himself."

Kumar stopped at the end of Cate's dust trail. Why hadn't he kept going to make sure this was the right place, or at least to verify which tunnel led to the Freesail cache?

He continued to cycle through different wavelengths. Infrared revealed a fading streak of heat on the cave wall, just ahead of where Cate's path stopped. He looked closer. A narrow groove had been drilled or burnt into the rock.

A burning sensation tore across his ribs. Kumar looked down to see two holes in his suit, the edges smoking and curling. Similar holes marked his skin.

He dropped to the floor. A sizzling sound caught his ears. Bits of rock rained down on him. Infrared showed two more slashes of heat on the wall where he'd been standing. "I think I know why Cate ran off."

"Are you all right?" asked Mops. "I'm showing an injury from your suit."

His monocle tagged three Jynx crouched in the middle tunnel. The closest Jynx wore a heavy glove on one hand. A single finger glowed with heat. The Jynx pointed.

Kumar couldn't see the weapon's beam, but he felt it burn through the air next to his face and saw it melt another crater into the wall. He crawled toward the beach. "There are Jynx in here. They have some sort of gauntlet with a built-in energy weapon. Burned a nice hole through my side. Nothing life-threatening."

"Do you need reinforcements?"

"Negative. They're not very good shots. If that thing has targeting assistance, they don't know how to use it." He drew his own weapon and fired three energy blasts at the cave wall. He wasn't trying to hit anyone, but the sparks and debris made the Jynx jump back. "I'm tired of getting shot, though."

Kumar emerged onto the beach and scrambled sideways, away from the cave. The Jynx didn't appear to be following.

He hurried to his sled, then checked his wound. The stink of burnt skin and bone made his nose wrinkle. Both the entrance and exit holes were cauterized, so there was little blood. He grabbed a sterile rag, tore it in half, and used hull tape to make a pair of crude bandages—partly to protect the wound, but mostly because he couldn't stand the sight of his skin looking so . . . *wrong*.

He switched on the sled, adjusted his monocle to show the sand-eel's path, and took off. "I'm continuing pursuit of Cate."

"Be careful."

Two hundred meters past the cave, the trail veered sharply left. He slowed to study the cliffside and the trail of biological residue leading straight up to the top.

"Sand-eels can climb," he muttered. "Who knew?"

He jumped down and nudged a bit of slimy sand with his toe. It clung to his boot like drying glue. That would be helpful if you had to scale a wall of glassy stone.

"Monocle, show me the instruction manual for an Alliance drop ship sled."

"Which model?"

"This one!" Maybe Mops was right about investing in increased intelligence for her AI.

The cover of the user guide appeared on his monocle, showing an animation of an armed Alliance infantry soldier skimming over an alien desert, guiding the sled with one hand while shooting Prodryans with the other.

"Text search: maximum vertical lift." He skimmed the results. The sled had a maximum height of four meters at full power, but it could only maintain that lift for six minutes. That was for Earth-normal gravity, which meant he should get a little more height here. Maybe five meters?

He switched on his rangefinder and targeted the top of the cliff: nine-point-three meters.

He could keep going until he found a spot low enough for the sled, or he could call the drop ship to retrieve him. Both options gave Cate more time to escape.

Kumar looked at the slime-covered cliffside. The slime hadn't yet dried. If it could hold a sand-eel carrying a Prodryan, it should be more than enough to hold a human's weight.

Nausea churned in his stomach. He yanked open his collar and pulled the bubble helmet over his head to protect his face.

This was going to be unpleasant.

19

Second Claw Urrara shook a jar of seawater, gypsum powder, and crushed weeping indigo flowers. The mixture brightened until she could clearly see the burn marks on the cave walls around her, as well as the Jynx standing a short distance away.

"Both aliens were here?" Her question was rhetorical. She could smell them on the still, damp air.

"The winged one and a hairless one," confirmed Cragrar. She raised a gloved hand. "I missed the first, but I'm sure I hit the second."

"How much did they see?"

"Neither of them made it past the water. That's good news, isn't it?"

"A lone sweet in a pile of scat doesn't make a dessert." Urrara's tail twitched as she studied the passages on the far side of the pool. It was more than an hour's walk from here to the underground facility, and there were plenty of passages to turn people about. But once Cate told Speaker Harkayé, it was only a matter of time before she found her way through the maze.

Urrara growled. This wasn't the first time their enemies had tried to conceal tracking technology in a delivery of weapons and other artifacts. She'd found and crushed a

*chimer cocoon only a season before, hidden in the barrel
of a Third Age rifle. But whatever the Prodryan had used
was tiny and alien.*

*She tugged Cragrar's glove free of her hand. It carried
Cragrar's scent—she'd been wearing this for a while. Urrara pulled it onto her own hand and tested her movement, then fired a practice shot into the wall. Warmth
flushed from the glove into her fingers. "Start distributing
weapons. Half to the ships, the rest to the strike forces
underground. I'll pass the word to the other Freesail
camps to do the same."*

"Yes, Second Claw."

"Tell them to prepare for war."

CLIMBING THE CLIFF HAD been simple enough,
if disgusting. Kumar had started by revving the
sled's engines to get it close to its maximum height
without draining too much of the power reserves. Then
he'd secured the winch cable to his harness and used the
eel slime to help him scale the remaining distance.

With the sled providing most of the lift, he should
have been able to use the cable to haul it to the top. But
the winch was secured to the *front* of the sled, meaning the
more he pulled, the more the sled tilted. If the sled turned
so its repulsion struck the cliffside, it could act like a cat-
apult, launching the sled—and Kumar—through the air.

He tapped his monocle. "Reduce power to front engines by twenty-five percent."

*"Alliance vehicles are not equipped for remote pilot-
ing."*

He knew that, drown it. Kumar shifted position and
pulled the extendible utility pole from his harness. A flick
of a switch extended the pole to its full two-meter length.
One end held a universal socket, able to accept more than
a hundred types of mops, brooms, squeegees, and other
attachments.

"Active bleeding detected." Kumar wasn't sure when

he'd torn open his wounds, but when he glanced down, he could see blood darkening his makeshift bandages.

He leaned over the edge of the cliff and extended the other end of the pole toward the engine control levers. The end bumped the front of the sled, causing it to wobble.

He adjusted his grip and stretched further, muscles straining. "Avoid the winch release," he muttered. "Just a gentle tap to the front engine lever to reduce power . . ."

The front of the sled dipped, yanking Kumar's harness hard enough he thought it would cut him into pieces. But the sled was more-or-less level.

His muscles were too exhausted to pull any more. Instead, he braced himself, then reached one last time with the pole and tapped the winch retraction controls.

The increased pull threatened to drag Kumar over the edge. He pressed himself flat and clung to the ground, hoping the coating of eel slime on his body would be sticky enough to keep him glued to the rock while the sled cranked itself higher.

After approximately one and a half eternities, the front of the sled came into view. Kumar took several slow breaths and hauled back, using all of his weight to get the sled over that last lip of rock.

He felt a surge of triumph as the sled followed him. And then his brain registered what was about to happen. The sled's engines were still running high and unbalanced, and he'd just pulled it onto solid ground. "Oh, fuck."

The sled shot a good five meters into the air, yanking Kumar with it.

Kumar swung back and forth as the sled, now tilted at a thirty-degree angle, flew inland at a leisurely pace.

Maybe he'd just let it tow him for a little while, at least until his hands and arms recovered enough for him to climb the winch line and crawl back into the seat.

"Kumar to Captain Adamopoulos," he gasped. "I've made it to the top of the cliff."

"Good work. We're seeing increased activity around the skytree, and it looks like a large group of snake-drawn wagons is coming this way from Black Spire. At current speed, I'd guess you've got two hours before they arrive."

"Understood."

"What's wrong, Sanjeev? You sound terrible."

"I'll survive. But when I find Cate, I'm going to shoot him. A lot."

The skytree loomed over the planet like it wanted to break free and take flight.

According to Kumar's rangefinder, the tree was still five kilometers away, but it looked closer. It stood thirteen-hundred meters high. The lower branches stretched hundreds of meters from the trunk, eventually bowing to the ground and digging into the dirt like a thousand living guy-wires.

He wrenched his attention back to the slime trail. Cate was heading toward Black Spire, probably hoping to meet up with Harkayé.

"Kumar, this is Monroe. We've got coordinates on your target. Cate's point nine kilometers in front of you. Adjust your bearing six degrees right."

"Thank you, sir!" He input the change. "You can see him from up there?"

"Not directly, but he just sent a systemwide broadcast using what looks like a modified Prodryan emergency beacon. We were able to trace it back to the source."

"He probably stole the beacon from Starfallen's place." Kumar nudged the sled higher to avoid saplings and waist-high grasses. Scaly birds exploded into flight, fleeing as he skimmed over a stream. He called out an instinctive apology. "Sorry!"

"What was that?"

"Nothing, sir. Was Cate calling for extraction?"

"Negative. He told everyone in range how the Alliance was searching for a superweapon to use against the Prodryans. He *also* explained how he had single-handedly foiled the Alliance's plans."

Kumar cringed. "That's my fault, sir."

"I'd blame Cate, personally, but it doesn't matter. You're in command down there, which makes it your responsibility. What's your plan for taking Cate down when you reach him?"

"I'm not sure. Combat training simulations didn't have anything on sand-eels." A blinking light informed him the sled's power cells were below fifty percent. "I'm hoping the slime will have gunked up his wing blade implants. I don't think he has any other weapons."

"Capturing him alive would be best, but if you can't, do whatever it takes to stop him from reaching Harkayé."

"Understood."

"You're on course. Point seven kilometers and closing."

"I see him." At maximum magnification, Cate appeared blurry and pixelated, but Kumar could see him flopping from side to side as the sand-eel raced up a hill. Cate's wings fluttered behind him like rain-soaked banners.

Kumar had closed to three hundred meters when Cate spotted him.

The sand-eel took a sharp left. Kumar adjusted course to intercept. Cate couldn't outrun him on a sand-eel. What was he doing?

Cate yanked the reins, turning the sand-eel directly toward Kumar. He drew a curved, half-meter–long blade of Prodryan design. So much for him being unarmed. He must have swiped the weapon from Starfallen's place. Starfallen probably used it for hacking weeds.

A snap of the reins sent the sand-eel into a slithering charge.

An impact warning raced across Kumar's monocle. He hunched his shoulders, hands on the controls as he watched the distance race toward zero. He didn't know if Cate intended to slam the sand-eel into the sled, or to swerve and cut Kumar in half as he passed, but it didn't matter.

At twenty meters, Kumar punched the lift to maximum.

The sled jumped higher, passing directly over Cate and the sand-eel and hitting them both with the full power of the engines.

Kumar circled back toward the ground. Cate had been

flung clear of the sand-eel and lay on his back, his wings spread like an oversized insect on display. The eel shook itself, spraying slime in all directions, then raced away. Kumar watched long enough to make sure it wasn't injured.

He landed cautiously, but Cate wasn't moving. His weapon was gone, knocked away into the grass. He stared up at the sky and said, "This is humiliating."

"Getting caught by a human, or being covered in sand-eel slime?"

Cate tried to sit up, but his wings appeared to be stuck to the ground. "I don't suppose you'd be willing to share one of those super-solvents or wing-safe soaps you carry everywhere?"

Kumar stepped closer. Now that the chase had ended, he was acutely aware of the drying slime clinging to his own uniform. It made a squishing sound every time he moved. He could smell it, like salty glue. "Are you carrying any other weapons?"

He spat to the side. "Starfallen had no firearms."

Prodryans were terrible liars, but Cate had learned to evade questions he didn't want to answer. "Are you armed? Yes or no?"

"Nothing but my wing blades." Cate flexed his back and shoulders, then slumped. "Which may never work properly again, thanks to that disgusting creature."

Kumar drew his gun, pointed it at Cate. "Harkayé, are you listening?"

Cate's head lifted a few centimeters from the dirt. Thick cords of slime kept it from lifting further. One eye shifted, and then he fell back, chittering. "It appears your stunt with the sled crushed the chimer cocoon."

When Kumar looked closely, he could see the broken cocoon beneath the edge of a chitinous plate.

Cate raised one antenna; the other was slimed to his scalp. "What will you do now, Kumar?"

"Me?"

"Speaker Harkayé knows you tried to betray her. Without her help, the Alliance is destined to fall. Stopping me doesn't change that. All I wanted was to speed the process along. Whatever happens, my people know I'm the one who stopped this last, desperate attempt to enlist the Jynx against the Prodryans. My name will be remembered, and the Red Star Clan will grow in power and prestige as the Prodryans continue their inevitable colonization of the galaxy. Meanwhile, the *Pufferfish* is trapped, and you're stuck on a planet about to go to war. You've lost."

Kumar sat on the flattened grass and craned his head, watching the skytree in the distance. Clouds drifted past, obscuring the topmost branches. A small speck approached the tree. At this distance, he would have mistaken it for a bird if his monocle hadn't pinged it as the drop ship.

They had less than two hours until the Speaker's forces from Black Spire arrived at the Treeshield camp. Kumar didn't know enough about military tactics to guess what would happen then. Would they march to the beach to attack the Freesail ships? Harkayé would want to make sure the skytree was protected, but she also needed to get control of those ancient Jynx weapons, and that meant fighting through the underground tunnels.

Thousands of Jynx would come together in battle, and if events followed the path the Preceptor had laid out, that battle would light the fuse for a war that would kill tens or hundreds of thousands, and eliminate the Freesailors from Tuxatl.

A call came in from Captain Adamopoulos. "We're in position at the skytree. Orders, sir?"

Kumar shuddered. His hands were shaking, his heart pounding. His thoughts were racing too fast for him to process them all. "Stand by."

He carefully unfolded his bubble helmet and sealed it into place.

"What are you doing?" asked Cate.

Ignoring the question, Kumar double-checked the seals on his gloves and boots, then took a green-and-blue canister from his cleaning supplies. He unscrewed the top, held out his other arm, and gently sprinkled blue powder over the slime caked to his uniform.

The particles darkened, swelling into tiny pellets that

clung to his sleeve. He counted to ten, then brushed his arm with his other hand. The pellets fell away, leaving a dry crust behind. More brushing removed most of the now-hardened slime remnants.

"Whatever that is, I need it!"

"Not a good idea." Kumar switched hands and contin- ued spreading powder over his uniform. "This is the most powerful desiccant in the SHS arsenal. We use it for clean- ing up dangerous spills. Get any on your exposed skin, and it will suck the moisture from your flesh."

He continued to methodically sprinkle the desiccant powder over his uniform, one section at a time. The rou- tine was soothing. Spread the powder, count to ten, and brush the area clean.

By the time Kumar finished, a circle of swollen purple pellets and dust surrounded him, along with crusty bits of slime. The pellets should dissolve on their own in the next day or two. He stowed the rest of the desiccant and used a stiff brush to remove the remaining slime crust.

It wasn't perfect, but at least he wasn't squishing and squelching every time he moved. More importantly, clean- ing his uniform had calmed him enough to actually think and focus again.

"Are you there, Captain?"

"We're still circling. Starfallen says she hasn't flown in eleven years, but it all came back pretty quickly."

"Captain, can you think of any way for us to fulfill our original mission?"

After a long pause, she said, "Negative, Kumar. The Preceptor is a connected mind. It knows we betrayed it, and it has the information it wanted about the Freesail camps. There's no reason for it to help us anymore."

Disappointment threatened to crush him. He'd hoped Mops would once again conjure up a brilliantly uncon- ventional plan to save the crew and the rest of the galaxy, but Commander Monroe was right. This was Kumar's responsibility now. "Understood."

"Should we retrieve you and Cate? And what would you like to do about our guests?"

Starfallen, Argarrar, and Jagar. If they stayed on Tuxatl, they'd be caught up in the coming war. If they left with the *Pufferfish*, they'd be crushed in a larger one. "They're safest with us for the moment."

"That's got to be a first."

Kumar's mouth quirked. "Stay with the skytree and find a safe place to land. We can't stop the Prodryans, but maybe we can save some Jynx lives before we go."

"Yes, sir."

Kumar flushed at the approval in her voice. "I'll meet up with you as soon as I get Cate unstuck and secured."

Cate scowled up at him. "And how exactly do you intend to free me from my predicament?"

Kumar drew his combat baton and thumbed the controls. The filaments wriggled in his grasp, until he held a gleaming hand axe.

Cate chirped in fear.

"Relax." Kumar slammed the axe into the dirt next to Cate's leg, wrenched the handle to one side, and pulled it free. "You're stuck to the ground. I don't have time to find a safe way to dissolve this gunk, so we'll just have to take some of the ground with us."

20

"*Admiral Pachelbel, what in the sulfur-spitting trenches is happening at Tuxatl?*"

Pachelbel had been expecting to hear from Krakau Colonial Military Command ever since she became aware of Cate's broadcast. She adjusted the focus of her holo-mist until she could see every wrinkle around the orange-skinned Krakau's beak. "*I'm not sure why you're asking me. In case you've forgotten, the Alliance has no presence at Tuxatl.*"

"*No more games, Admiral. I know you were involved in placing a Prodryan spy with the crew of the* Pufferfish. *I know Advocate of Violence was a useful tool in remov-ing your rival, Belle-Bonne Sage. But the transmission he made from Tuxatl could destroy us.*"

"*The Prodryans are determined to kill the rest of us,*" said Pachelbel. "*It's not as though Cate's revelations will make them kill us more.*"

"*The Prodryans aren't the problem.*"

Pachelbel's skin tightened. "*What do you mean?*"

"*You think we're the only ones with spy satellites around the Tuxatl system?*" Orange whistled disgustedly. "*Or that the non-Krakau in the Alliance could be trusted to keep a secret of this importance? Advocate of Violence*" announced the existence of a potential superweapon against the Prodryans. Within an hour, every government in the galaxy knew about it."

And every one of them would want it for themselves. "You're talking about a feeding frenzy."

"The Tjikko have already launched one of their tree-ships, and the Nusurans have an entire fleet preparing to jump."

"What about the CMC? How many ships are you sending?"

The other Krakau didn't answer. She didn't have to. Pachelbel knew the CMC's mission and their priorities. They'd do whatever was necessary to secure that weapon for the Krakau people. Even if it meant cutting through their allies to get it. "What is the status of the Pufferfish and her crew? Is this weapon real, and is there any chance they might yet acquire it?"

"I wish I knew," said Pachelbel. "I assume you have spies on Stepping Stone, so you know I haven't heard from them in more than a day."

"If that changes, I expect you to inform the CMC immediately."

"I understand." Pachelbel ended the call. "You short-sighted, power-grubbing bottom feeder." She paged station ops. "I need an encrypted FTL channel to the Pufferfish. And contact the Boomslang, the Dart Frog, and the Mosquito. Tell them to be ready to jump within the hour."

FOR MORE THAN A kilometer in every direction, nothing grew but the skytree and its own small eco-system: vines and moss growing on the roots, animals nesting in cracks and crevasses, and the village of small huts around the base of the tree where the Treeshield camp lived.

Kumar's sled bounced and buzzed as they crossed from grassy fields to harder earth and roots that bulged from the ground like sea serpents. He reduced power and pulled to the left to avoid the end of a guy-wire branch where it plunged into the ground. A green-furred creature like a larger version of the scolds they'd seen outside of the camp hurled a rock that bounced off the sled's nose.

The drop ship had landed halfway to the bole of the skytree. It rested at an angle, its six landing struts clamped to two of the larger roots. Mops sat with her legs hanging out of the open hatch, watching Kumar and Cate approach.

"Did you check the load balancing margins when you landed?" Kumar asked as he powered down the sled.

"Hello to you too, sir." Mops chuckled. "Doc assisted with the landing procedure. We're stable and prepped to launch again at a moment's notice."

"Good." Kumar searched the surrounding terrain. He spotted a handful of Jynx watching from the cover of the roots and branches closer to the trunk, but for the moment, they seemed content to wait. Argarrar rested atop the drop ship, curled into a ball.

Mops nodded toward Cate. "What did you do to him?"

The Prodryan was a pitiful sight. In addition to the partially dried slime covering his body, a miniature landscape of dirt, rock, and grasses clung from his back and wings.

"Smells like eel slime," said Argarrar without opening her eyes. "Ocean water helps dissolve the stuff. Toss him in the waves for a few hours, and he'll be good as new."

"I'll drop him in the ocean later." Kumar squeezed past Mops and headed for the back of the ship. Everything was stowed, secured, and labeled. He moved cases of food and ammunition. "Gabe, guard Cate, please. I've got him taped to the sled, and the controls are manually locked down, but I don't trust him."

"Yes, sir." Gabe ducked out, a combat baton clutched in one hand. Hopefully he knew how to use it.

"Azure, take a sample of that slime. I think the Alliance could use it to manufacture a new adhesive."

"I assume you're hunting a first aid kit?" Mops had followed Kumar into the rear cargo area.

"No time." Kumar grabbed a small case of extra cleaning

supplies. "We have Freesail Jynx closing from the water and Black Spire Jynx coming by land. Thousands of Jynx are about to slaughter each other unless we stop them."

"You can't stop anyone if you're passed out. Just because you don't feel pain doesn't mean that hole in your side magically went away."

Kumar pried back the retaining clamps and popped the lid from the supply case. His hands shook as he grabbed various tubes and canisters and shoved them into his harness. "I've been thinking about this since I left the Freesailor ship. It's all chemical. The skytree, the Speakers, even the smells the Jynx use to communicate—drown it, this isn't enough."

"Enough of what?" Mops touched his shoulder. "Kumar, slow down. Take a breath."

Kumar started to speak, then caught himself. "What about your cocoon? If Harkayé's listening—"

Mops grimaced. "That's no longer an issue, not since about an hour ago. The only thing she gets to listen to now is the sound of the drop ship's septic facilities. So tell me what you've got, Kumar."

He slapped a white-and-blue spray bottle into her hand. "BOE-99. We've got two cans. Hopefully it's enough."

Mops stared. Slowly, her lips tugged into a smile. "Will it work on Jynx?"

"It should." The Alliance's trademarked brand of biological odor eliminator was designed to work on all known species. It got a lot of use in medical facilities, clearing the smell of incontinence, burnt and infected flesh, and various flavors of blood and other fluids. A diluted formula was automatically misted into the air vents for the communal toilet facilities. "Harkayé's pheromones are short-acting, but whatever the skytree puts out stays in the system longer. And we'd still have to stop the Freesail forces. They're not scentwashed the way the others are."

"Scentwashed?"

"Like brainwashed?" Kumar knew he was talking too fast, the words running together as they escaped his mouth, but he couldn't stop. "We might have to use the drop ship's guns to stop them. The casualty count would be lower than a full-blown war. Or maybe we could scare them back."

"One thing at a time." Mops grabbed a first aid kit. "Start with the Speaker. She's on her way with a scent-washed army, ready to set off a world war. How exactly do we use this to stop them?"

"We need to douse Harkayé in BOE before she reaches the skytree. I don't think I could do it from the sled or the drop ship. We'll have to fight our way through."

"I can get to her and do that," Mops said calmly. She yanked open his uniform and removed the first of his makeshift bandages. "What next?"

"Captain, no! We saw what happened the last time you were in combat. I can't risk—"

"I'll neutralize Harkayé." She sounded utterly calm and certain. She wiped away crusted blood and sprayed a liberal amount of sterilizing fluid onto Kumar's wounds. "What else do you need to make your plan work?"

"The Treeshield camp is a problem. The skytree puts out pheromones of its own. We'd have to find a way to wean the Jynx off those chemicals slowly and safely. Maybe a large air-filtration system, or slow-release BOE stations situated around the tree. The point is, I can't quell their protective instincts before the Freesail camp arrives."

Mops swapped bottles and dabbed a layer of artificial skin over the first hole in Kumar's side, then started on the exit wound. "Then you'll have to stop the Freesailors before they reach the skytree. You've spoken with them. Could you convince them to hold off?"

"I'm not sure."

"Doubtful." Starfallen peered in from the cabin. Behind him, the rest of the team, all save Gabe, had gathered to listen. Even Argarrar had come down from sunning herself. "From a tactical standpoint, Freesailors have to strike now. The longer they delay, the more time the Speakers have to raid their weapons caches. Equally important, Freesail anger has been simmering for many years. The other camps have demonized them as uncivilized thieves. The Speakers have taken their people. They *want* this fight, almost as much as Harkayé does."

Kumar waited impatiently while Mops finished bandaging him, then brought the BOE-99 to the main cabin. "We should test to see if it works on Jynx scents. Argarrar, would you mind—?"

"Give it here." Argarrar plucked a can of BOE from Kumar's hand with her tail. She unscrewed the cap and dabbed a single drop onto her wrist. Her ears and whiskers shot back, and she sneezed. She quickly screwed the cap back on and returned it to Kumar.

"It will be more effective when aerosolized," said Kumar.

Argarrar waved her arm back and forth in front of her snout. "Nothing. All the scents I was carrying in my fur are gone. It's eerie . . . I can see and feel my arm, but it's invisible to the nose."

"That's good enough for me," said Mops. "I'll break Harkayé's hold over the Black Spire Jynx while you stop the Freesail forces."

"I'll go with you, Kumar." Jagar's eyes were rheumy, and his nose had begun to drip. Proximity to the skytree must be making him miserable, but he didn't complain. "I can help. I'm Freesail."

"That doesn't mean they'll listen to you, you tail-chasing fool," said Argarrar.

Jagar wiped his nose on his wrist. "They're carrying old Jynx weapons. Drop me into their midst, and who knows what those weapons will do. They'll listen once their guns start playing dance tunes or their blades melt in their hands."

"I thought you couldn't control the effect you have on old tech," said Kumar. "How do you know you'll be able to shut down their weapons?"

"I don't." Jagar's tail twitched. "But neither do they. I think they'll at least listen before pulling the trigger and taking the chance of blowing us all up."

"Take one of these invisibility sprays with you," said Argarrar. "The Freesail camp will be stewing in their own war-scent. You might need to calm them down to get them to listen."

Kumar turned to Mops. "What do you think, Captain?"

"I think it's better than leaving thousands of Jynx to die. But I'm not the one calling the shots."

"You're sure you can get to Harkayé?"

Mops' grin was every bit as predatory as that of a Jynx. "Trust me."

Mops helped Kumar swap out a new sled from the drop ship, one with a full charge. Once he and Jagar took off to intercept the Freesailors, she circled around to drag a large crate down the rear cargo ramp. "Gabe, give me a hand with this."

Gabe waited for her to remove the lid, then peered inside. "Damn . . . Is that one of those Alliance marine power armor suits?"

Mops snorted. "Nobody on the *Pufferfish* has the training or experience for combat armor. Ask Monroe what power armor can do to you if it's not properly calibrated. No, this is an External Maintenance and Biohazard suit I was playing around with in my downtime back on Stepping Stone. It's much more my speed."

EMB suits were meant for cleaning and repairing the most extreme messes on a ship: both internal and external. They had reinforced helmets, enhanced strength, built-in atmospheric processors, and an array of tubes, hoses, and other cleaning supplies. They could resist the sharp, jagged edges of damaged hull plates and broken pipes. Not to mention the explosive release of the contents of said pipes. Whatever Harkayé threw at Mops, the EMB should provide serious protection.

Mops stripped off her equipment harness and tossed it into the drop ship, then pulled on the one-piece insulated bodysuit. Next came the external components: pants, then boots, then torso and sleeves. With each step, Gabe helped lock the pieces into place and tested the seals.

Mops removed her monocle and lifted the helmet into place. Doc transferred himself to the helmet's visor and ran through the suit's diagnostic checklist while Gabe helped with the gloves.

"So you're essentially piloting a small janitorial mecha," said Gabe.

"I have no idea what that word means." Mops slid the BOE into one of the twelve power-spray slots. "Azure, prep a sled for me."

A sudden impact jolted her from behind. The suit compensated automatically, locking her legs to keep her from stumbling.

Argarrar had jumped onto Mops' shoulders. The Jynx balanced on all fours, then carefully settled herself around Mops' neck like an old-fashioned scarf.

"What exactly are you doing?" asked Mops.

"Coming with you." Argarrar sniffed. "And at my age, you take warmth where you can find it."

"She's probably referring to the radiators on the suit's shoulder blades. Your waste heat turns it into a warm, admittedly awkward bed."

"Argarrar, I'm not taking you along to get shot."

A poofy tail swished past Mops' vision. "Even with the war-scent filling their heads, they'll think twice about shooting *me*."

"You have no armor, no protection. It's too dangerous."

"This is a Jynx fight," said Argarrar. "I appreciate you trying to help, but we should be a part of it." She sniffed again, then sneezed. "This armor smells like oil."

"I could order my people to keep you here by force," said Mops.

"I could piss on your helmet. But I won't do that, and neither will you. I know these people. You'll have a better chance with me along."

Behind them, a sled popped from the side of the ship with a loud, metal clunk. Azure gently guided the floating sled to Mops. "Medically speaking, this is a bad idea, Captain."

"Medically speaking, you're not my doctor." Mops climbed onto the sled, which sank to the ground under the weight of her suit—and the added weight of the Jynx riding that suit. She recalibrated the engines for the extra load.

"I'm the closest thing you have." Azure's tentacles rippled with frustration. "I should be there to help if the fighting triggers another episode, which it likely will."

Azure might be right, but they didn't have a choice. Not if they were going to stop a war. "I need you and Gabe here. Work with Starfallen to get the drop ship ready to launch. If things go badly, she should be able to get you to the *Pufferfish*."

"Why are you doing this, Captain?" The question came from Cate, still covered in dirt and slime, his limbs taped to one of the skytree roots to keep him in place. "Is it about revenge on Harkayé?"

"You wouldn't understand."

"I'm quite intelligent. I thought the same of you, but you don't seem to realize there's a good chance this plan will end you."

Mops turned. "Don't tell me you're worried about a human."

"Nonsense," said Cate. "I have developed absolutely no fondness or respect for you and your crew, despite our months of working together. Nor do I care that you're likely to die at the claws of these primitive creatures. I had simply hoped to end your life myself. For the glory and prestige I would gain, and not as a mercy to spare you the indignity of your disease."

"Of course." Mops shook her head. "I apologize for making such a foolish assumption."

"Apology accepted." Cate spat a bit of dirt from his mandibles. "Foolishness is to be expected from lesser species."

"He's still a terrible liar," said Doc. *"But he's not wrong about the risk."*

"I know." Mops brought the sled around to point in the general direction of the Black Spire camp. "Argarrar, you should probably climb down and strap in behind me. This thing moves a lot faster than Snaggleclaw."

21

"So much for checkers." Monroe watched the short-range fighters close on the *Pufferfish*. *Three sets of three ships. Typical Prodryan approach. One group would probably attack head-on, while the other two hit from the sides.* "Johnny, it's time!"

"Excellent!" Johnny's tentacles reached over Rubin's shoulders to prep the A-rings. "Grom, I'll require your assistance. Rubin, keep our beak pointed at the center ships."

Rubin shoved a tentacle aside and adjusted the controls, turning the *Pufferfish* until the ship faced directly away from the planet.

Monroe activated a communications channel. "Swift Death, this is Commander Monroe. If you shoot us down, you'll never have the chance to redeem your zero-and-four checkers record."

There was no response. *Not that he'd expected one. He'd already dragged those games out longer than he'd hoped.*

"Launching A-rings now," said Johnny. "First four rings are away. Preparing rings five through eight."

"Not yet," shouted Grom. "Let me get these anchored into position first."

*Even four rings were three more than anyone was sup-
posed to deploy at one time. Johnny and Grom had been
working tirelessly to split off the controls that maneuvered
and locked the rings into place. It meant reducing power
and precision to the grav beams, but so far, it appeared to
be working.*

*The four rings slowly expanded to their maximum di-
ameter, wide enough for the* Pufferfish *to pass through.*

"Spinning rings one through four up to three percent
power," said Johnny. "We could go as high as five percent
before the gravity from Tuxatl and its sun interferes, but
I'd rather not push it."

"By all means," agreed Monroe. "Let's stick with one
potentially disastrous experiment at a time."

Swift Death's voice crackled over the speakers. "We are
familiar with Captain Adamopoulos' tactics, Commander
Monroe. Using your A-rings to try to hurl Prodryan missiles back at our ships will not save you."

"Rubin, can we pinpoint where Swift Death is broadcasting from?" asked Monroe.

Rubin shook her head. "I don't know how to do that, sir."

"You have no weapons," *Swift Death continued.* "This
is your final chance to surrender. Turn over the Pufferfish
and I promise you and your crew several additional hours
of life."

*Monroe studied the incoming ships. Swift Death was
new to this assignment and needed to prove herself. A
cautious attacker would hold back and let their missiles
soften up the* Pufferfish.

*But Swift Death had been an aggressive checkers
player. She'd want an impressive victory, and that meant
getting nice and close.*

"They're warming up energy weapons," said Grom.

"They know we're unarmed." *Monroe tagged the three
central ships.* "Grom, Johnny, you have your targets."

*Grom maneuvered A-ring one, while Johnny launched
a fifth ring, this one designated one-beta. She expanded
one-beta to eighty percent of its maximum diameter, then
nudged the grav beams, sending it forward.*

"Is this actually going to work?" asked Grom.

Johnny shrugged a tentacle and spun up one-beta to three percent power. "Fuck if I know."

The first round of Prodryan fire crackled over the Pufferfish's *hull.*

"Time to find out." Monroe watched the smaller ring move closer and closer to the larger, active ring, like one checker placed atop another. "King me."

Ring one-beta passed through ring one. The larger ring instantly accelerated the smaller, launching it at a modest twenty percent of light speed toward the first of the incoming fighters.

In theory, according to Johnny's calculations, one-beta should have then accelerated the fighter away from the Pufferfish *at that same 0.2c speed.*

Instead, the fighter vanished in an explosion that sent a circle of debris slamming into the other two ships in its formation. A-ring one destabilized and exploded seconds later.

Monroe blinked. "What just happened?"

"I believe one-beta was half a degree off course," said Johnny. "It may have caught on the fighter instead of passing cleanly around it. It accelerated half of the ship into the other half."

"Good enough for me. How soon can we launch two-beta?"

Grom checked their screen. "The remaining fighters are veering away. We have a window to strike before they send reinforcements."

"This madness would never be permitted on a Krakau-controlled ship." Johnny whistled with excitement. "I love this mission!"

THE ROAD VEERED BACK and forth to cope with the hills and outcroppings. Mops held to a straight course, racing up slopes and soaring through the air when the ground fell away beneath them.

Argarrar's claws had found good purchase on the sides of Mops' armor.

"We're getting close," Argarrar shouted.

Mops didn't see anyone. "How do you know?"

"Those are Harkayé's advance forces." She pointed to the sky. "She's a Speaker. With the right scents, she can rally the entire planet to her side."

The Jynx's vision was sharp. Mops had to zoom in to see the birds Argarrar had spotted. Each was about the size and mass of an Earth dachshund, with broad brown wings and a cream-colored chest. There weren't many—her monocle tagged twenty-three—but they flew fast.

Long bristles covered their skin, a hybrid of fur and feathers. Ribbon-like tails a meter long flowed behind them. Mops was more interested in the large, hooked beaks and the curved talons.

"Varkaws." Argarrar tightened her grip. "They're usually shy, except during hatching season. Harkayé probably imprinted them with her own scent. They'll attack anything they perceive as a threat to her."

Mops stopped the sled at the top of a steep switchback. The road zigzagged down a hillside thirty meters high. She set the sled on its side for cover and fumbled with her pistol.

The handle and trigger weren't designed to work with the bulky gloves of the EMB suit. She should have thought of that before, dammit. She tugged off her right glove, gripped the pistol, sighted on a distant tree, and squeezed the trigger. Bark and wood exploded from the center of the narrow trunk.

"I believe the paka trees are neutral in this war," Argarrar said politely.

"I was double-checking the sights, smart-ass." The Jynx were beginning to come into view. "Doc, start tagging hostiles. Assign gradient by range and threat level."

"Should I tag the planet and its ring as well, given that all of Tuxatl is a potential threat?"

"What did I do to deserve all of this attitude?"

"Would you like the list alphabetically or chronologically?"

Her visor lit up before she could respond. Being closest, the approaching varkaws were the brightest green, with the distant Jynx a darker, duller shade. "Light up Harkayé as soon as you find her."

"I know what 'threat level' means."

The lead varkaws circled once, then swooped at Mops and Argarrar like fuzzy berserkers. Most incongruous was the growling. They sounded like angry dogs . . . or like Grom with indigestion.

The first bird clubbed Mops' head with its wings. Another struck with beak and claws. They couldn't penetrate her suit, but from the impact readouts, each blow of that beak was like a hammer strike, and the claws had enough grip strength to break small bones.

One flew at Argarrar. Mops jumped over the sled and batted the varkaw away. It spun out into the weeds, shook itself, shrieked at Mops, then spread its wings and charged along the ground like a bull. Those long legs were deceptively quick and strong.

Mops brought up her left gauntlet and met the varkaw with a jet of high-pressure air. The bird squawked and tumbled backward, doing a complete reverse somersault before recovering.

More varkaws slammed into her from behind.

"They're not bright, and they won't back down." Argarrar grabbed a prybar from the back of the sled. "I once saw a young varkaw pick a fight with a boulder."

"Who won?"

"It was a draw."

"I don't want to kill them if I don't have to." Mops grimaced. "Doc, adjust output to left gauntlet pressure wash. Add one percent by volume all-purpose lubricant."

She knocked a varkaw off her shoulder, spun, and shot a dark, oily mist at it before it could recover. It flapped its wings and prepared to charge.

"Two percent!" Mops sprayed it again, matting its wings like hair gel.

Holding her pistol ready, Mops continued to spray the swarming varkaw. Soon, all but three were grounded and running about. They'd begun to lose focus, attacking each other as well as Mops.

"That smells foul," said Argarrar.

"That's the idea." Mops grabbed a varkaw that was sneaking around the end of the sled and tossed it down the hill. It spread dripping wings and glided part of the way before hitting the ground and rolling to a bedraggled halt. "I'm hoping it overpowers whatever scent Harkayé used on them."

One by one, the varkaws staggered away, growling and smacking one another with their wings. Several rolled on the ground, stirring up small clouds of dust from their impromptu dirt baths. Her visor dulled their colors, switching focus to the approaching Jynx.

Doc had tagged more than three hundred individual Jynx, creating a broad, deep line of green half a kilometer away. Mops spotted supply wagons hauled by pairs of wagon-snakes. Other wagon-snakes dragged cannons between them.

"Any guess on the range of those things?" asked Mops.

"We're well within range," said Argarrar. "The real question is whether they can hit anything from there."

"Looks like they're about to try." Mops watched a group of Jynx untie the wagon-snakes and stake a cannon into position. They worked like a machine, loading and aiming in less than a minute.

She saw the flash. The loud crack reached her a second later.

"You're safe," Doc assured her.

True to his word, the cannonball slammed into the hillside a good twenty meters low and to the right. It exploded shortly thereafter, spraying metal shrapnel in all directions.

Mops switched on her gun's targeting assistance and sighted on the wooden frame holding the cannon in place. The gun's internal gyroscopes nudged her aim and steadied the barrel.

Two quick A-gun shots shredded the frame, leaving the metal cannon to drop to the ground. The closest Jynx leapt away.

"How many could you kill from here, if you wanted?" Argarrar asked softly.

"My ammunition is limited, but an A-gun round can

pierce multiple targets. I'd guess at least a hundred, depending on how smart they are."

"They're not." She flexed her claws. "Trapped by the war-scent, they're . . . what was the word your people used? Feral."

"Not feral." Mops watched the Jynx gesturing to one another. "They worked together to prep that cannon. They're organized. Efficient."

"Obedient," said Argarrar. "Harkayé is coordinating them. Now she knows what she's facing."

The front ranks of the Jynx spread into a broad line. They carried pistols, rifles, and long, claw-shaped knives.

"Doc, amplify my voice." Mops stepped forward. "I'm here to talk to the Speaker, not to fight."

The Jynx charged. They moved twice as fast as a sprinting human.

Mops threw up her hands in exasperation. "That doesn't mean I *won't* fight, dammit."

Argarrar ducked behind the sled as the Jynx opened fire. Several bullets pinged off Mops' suit, but the armor was designed to handle micrometeorites. She barely noticed the impacts.

Mops fired a series of slugs, drawing a line in the ground in front of the Jynx. Dirt and rock exploded.

They ran right through.

"They'll try to overwhelm you," warned Argarrar. "Drag you down with brute force."

Mops recognized one of the approaching Jynx as Barryar, the young hunter who'd helped retake the drop ship from Jagar and his Freesail friends. There was Parya, the hunter with the short tail, and Yarkra, one of the Jynx Mops had attacked when she went feral. They looked more animal than Jynx, with teeth bared and fur standing on end.

A bullet rang off Mops' hip. "Stay here."

Mops holstered her gun and slid her gauntlet onto her right hand. A quick tap of the controls activated the plasma torch on the index finger. With her left hand, she prepped a high-powered—and highly flammable—sanitizing spray.

She strode down the hill, heart pounding. As the Jynx

closed in, she activated the spray and touched torch to sanitizer.

A ten-meter line of flame shot forth, bringing the closest Jynx to a snarling halt.

"On your right!"

A Jynx leapt onto her before she could react. Damn, they were quick. Mops shut off her impromptu flamethrower, grabbed the Jynx by the scruff, and peeled him off. "Swap the sanitizer with the BOE."

"Acknowledged."

A note on her visor confirmed that the sprayer on her left gauntlet was now loaded with BOE-99.

More Jynx charged, hitting Mops from all sides. Many were foaming at the mouth. A striped one clung to the front of her helmet and stabbed a knife against her neck again and again. Two others looped ropes around her wrists. They couldn't hurt her, but they were knocking her off-balance, giving the rest time to close in.

"Doc, can they pierce this suit?"

"Unlikely."

A puncture alert appeared on her monocle.

"Unless they're using old Jynx tech they've scavenged."

More Jynx piled on top of her.

Servos whined as she raised her left arm and doused the Jynx in odor neutralizing spray. Their snarls changed to shrieks and hisses. The closest Jynx fought to get free, while the others tried to reach her.

Her gun was torn away. Another Jynx snatched her baton from its holster.

A second puncture alert flashed, and she felt a jab in her hip. She twisted and saw Barryar raising a blue-black blade to strike again.

Barryar squawked as he was yanked back by his ear. Argarrar stood over him, tail lashing. "I boxed your ears when you were a whelp stealing sweets, and I'll do it again today, don't you think I won't! I raised you better than this. Stabbing a guest who's doing everything she can to keep from hurting you."

She whirled on another of the Jynx. "And you, Vagava!

What would your kits say if they saw you now, teeth bared and drooling like a wild thing?"

Off to the left, a spotted Jynx raised a rifle and stepped closer.

Argarrar's ear twitched. "Don't think I can't see you, Raggara," she snapped. "Take one more step, and I'll tell everyone here what happened the first time I tried to teach you to swim!"

The one called Raggara lowered her weapon. She blinked once, and then her eyes went wide. "Argarrar? You swore you wouldn't tell!"

One by one, the Jynx climbed off Mops as Argarrar continued to shame and berate them by name.

"What are you doing, Argarrar?" Barryar shouted. "The humans are helping the Freesail rebels. They stole Jagar!"

"I've seen how you treated Jagar," Argarrar shot back. "None of you gave a fish's fart about him before, but suddenly you're ready to go to war for him?"

Mops could see Barryar struggling, torn between Argarrar's words and the influence of the Speaker's pheromones. The BOE should have weakened those chemicals, but she didn't know how long it would take them to leave his system.

"Kill them both!"

Mops wasn't sure who said it. Presumably one of the Jynx who'd gotten less of the BOE. Other Jynx, farther back, started to close in again. Her mouth was dry as sand, her heart pounding away at the inside of her ribs.

"Both of them, you say?" Argarrar made a show of grooming her shoulder. "You're going to shoot the old Jynx who raised two generations of your kits, Kamaya? Shame on you, threatening a defenseless member of the Mothers' Circle."

"You're hardly defenseless." Barryar jabbed his tail at the prybar in Argarrar's hand. But he lowered his knife. "Speaker Harkayé says—"

"Bring us to Harkayé," said Mops. "Let her decide what to do with us."

Barryar hesitated. He looked back at the rest of the Jynx, then at Argarrar.

Argarrar tossed the prybar to the ground. "While we wait for Barryar to decide, who wants to hear the tale of his first hunt? He boasted about how he meant to catch a lightning hawk, even though the closest aerie is a week's journey away by wagon. He stole a wheel of cheese to use as bait and set out. Well, this was a hot midsummer day, and all too soon, the cheese began to soften and melt—"

"We'll take you to the Speaker," snarled Barryar.

"I want to hear the story," said Doc. *"Ask Argarrar to keep talking while we walk."*

"Maybe later," whispered Mops. "When Barryar and the rest aren't coming down from their murder drug high."

"I suppose. Mops, your vitals are—"

"I know." She could feel the hunger burning through her nervous system. Every nerve was a fuse, and once that fire reached the end . . . She tried to slow her breathing, to push back against the fog licking the edges of her thoughts. "I'm all right. I have time."

"How do you know?"

"Because I have to. We're not done here yet." Mops checked the gauge on the BOE canister. She'd used twenty-eight percent during the fighting, just to take the killing edge off her attackers. What remained should be enough.

She wished she would have had a chance to see Monroe again, to say good-bye. To say so many things. She should have made recordings for the crew. The mission was important, but surely she could have made time instead of wasting it like a . . . what was the word? Gabe's profanity list had the perfect term, but it swam just out of her reach.

A Jynx jabbed her back with the butt of a rifle. Her suit absorbed the blow, but for a moment, rage blinded her. She barely suppressed the urge to lash out.

More Jynx surrounded her as she entered their lines. She could see Harkayé. Doc had highlighted the Speaker on her monocle. Mops focused on her goal, letting the rest of the world darken. Only Harkayé mattered. "Doc?"

"Yes, Mops?"

"Keep talking to me, please."

A wagon-snake sniffed as she passed, then extended a dark blue tongue the length of Mops' leg.

"Do you have a preferred topic?"

"Scobberlotcher!" That was the word.

"I'm sorry?"

"No, I wasn't talking to you, I just—" She could feel her control cracking. "I need a friendly voice. Something to hold on to."

There was a barely perceptible pause. And then Doc began to sing.

The song was familiar, a Krakau lullaby translated into Human and shifted several octaves to bring the whole thing into the range of human hearing. Doc had a strong singing voice, smooth as polished memcrys. He finished the first stanza about sunlight through the waves and warm currents rocking her to and fro, then asked, *"Is this acceptable? I know all sixteen verses, as well as the Rokkau variant."*

They'd stopped walking. Barryar was speaking to Harkayé. Mops didn't follow the words, but after a moment, Barryar stepped aside.

Mops blinked back tears. "That was perfect."

Kumar's negotiations were not going well.

Finding the Freesail forces had been simple enough. It was a direct march from the docks to the skytree. He'd stopped the sled a short distance away and approached with his arms outspread and chin raised high, in what Jagar said was a gesture of peace. Thankfully, Kumar didn't have to wear a fake tail this time.

Hundreds of Jynx had spread out to surround the two of them. They'd rewrapped their scarves to cover their snouts, making them look vaguely like old-fashioned Earth bandits.

First Claw Garvya had been easy to identify, as she was dressed in Kumar's other uniform. She'd rolled up the legs and the sleeves, and it looked like she'd managed to cut a hole in the back for her tail.

She listened to Kumar's entreaty before rejecting it entirely. "If what you're telling us is true and your Captain can break the Speaker's hold over her soldiers, we'd be fools not to take advantage. We'll send Harkayé running with her tail between her legs."

"And then what?" Kumar demanded.

"A victory like that will let us rally Freesail fleets all across the oceans," said Garvya. "We'll make them pay for every sailor the Speakers have stolen. Topple the sky-trees and let the Jynx live how we want, not how a bunch of rocks in the sky say we should."

"You might beat Harkayé, but the other Speakers will fight back. We can't neutralize them all. If you fight this war, you're giving your enemy exactly what they want. You're following their script."

"You expect us to drop our weapons and show our throats after generations of abuse, instead? Go on being second-class citizens? Forget the thousands of Jynx they've taken from our ships?"

"Killing Black Spire Jynx won't change what's happened," said Kumar.

"Enough yowling," someone shouted. "Shoot 'em and let's get on with it."

"You can't," said Jagar. "Kumar traded with First Claw Garvya earlier today."

"And Jagar's one of us," added Garvya. "They're not to be hurt." To Kumar, she said, "We can't have you getting in the way, though. I'm sorry about this."

Before Kumar could respond, she drew a black wand-like device from her belt. A low, grating hum filled the air, and the ground beneath his feet *softened*. All around him, bits of dirt jumped like water sizzling on a hot pan. His arms whirled as he sank into the ground. Beside him, Jagar squawked as the same thing happened to him.

Garvya flipped the wand and pointed the other end. The humming changed to a higher pitch. The ground hardened, trapping Kumar up to his knees. He tried to pull free, but he might as well have been stuck in concrete.

Kumar pulled out his combat baton, switched it to a combat knife, and poked the tip into the ground. It penetrated less than a centimeter. He levered out a small chunk of hardened dirt. "That's amazing! Does it work on other substances? Can you adjust the density and the hardness?"

Garvya blinked. "What's that, now?"

Kumar set down the knife and grabbed a red-capped canister from his harness. A quick spray of the stain-dissolving foam had little effect on the sand. "Imagine the construction possibilities. All you'd need is a way to mold the dirt into the right shape."

"We think it was an ancient building tool, yes." Garvya sounded uncertain. "I've used this toy on folks a few times in the past, but I've never had anyone so excited about their imprisonment."

"What? Oh, sorry. I get distracted." He looked over at Jagar. His nose was dripping again, and eye goop matted the fur around his eyes. "Have you had enough time to get a feel for their equipment?"

"They don't have as much tech as the Speaker feared." Jagar sniffed. "A mix of weapons, tools, and toys. No two the same. It's hard to say more. My senses are plugged up from the skytree."

Kumar lifted his gaze back to the Freesail Jynx. "Everyone tells me the other camps hate you because you're different. From where I'm standing, you're just the same."

Garvya's ears flattened. "Be careful with your words."

"They want to fight. You want to fight. You're all playing out the roles the Preceptor assigned to you, like good little pawns." Just like humans had done for decades, serving the Krakau in their war.

"What's a pawn?"

Jagar leaned forward the best he could while rooted like a tree. "We want to be free, right? We want to travel and explore and trade? To be true Freesailors?"

"That's the point," Garvya snarled. "Unless we win this battle, the Preceptor'll never let us live as ourselves. We're marked for extinction, and we don't mean to take it belly-up."

A message popped up on Kumar's monocle. He tried to jump with excitement, and nearly dislocated his knees in the process. Mops had done it! "The Speaker has lost her hold on the Black Spire Jynx. Barryar says he's willing to sit down with the Freesailors. This proves what I'm saying. They'll listen to you!"

"Black Spire is one camp," said Garvya. "Barryar is just a boy, not even qualified to sit on the Mothers' Circle."

"That's right," Kumar shot back. "That's how it starts. One hunter and one First Claw talking and listening to one another."

"You're not considering this tailless freak's proposal?" shouted another Jynx. "My crew joined yours to fight back, not have our claws pulled."

"If they're telling the truth—" said Garvya.

"It makes no difference." The other Jynx, a large, striped woman with an intricate red-and-gold scarf, pointed a conical device at Kumar.

Garvya drew a pistol—a powder-based weapon, not an ancient one. "The human and I made a trade."

"It never traded with me!" The striped Jynx activated her weapon.

Rather, she tried to. Instead of burning Kumar to ash or disintegrating him or launching him into orbit or whatever else the device was built to do, it simply belched a cloud of blue-black smoke, then crackled with electricity. The Jynx hurled the weapon away and hissed, her fur standing on end.

Garvya's scent changed, a mix of anger and amusement. She lowered her own gun. "Your work?" she asked Jagar.

"I guess." Jagar flicked his whiskers. "Please, just listen to the humans. They have a chemical that erases the Speaker's scent. They can free us all, Freesail and Black Spire alike."

"Let me show you." Kumar retrieved his can of BOE-99.

Garvya's ears flattened, but she stepped closer. "No tricks?"

"We made a trade," said Kumar. "I won't hurt you."

He spritzed Garvya's fur, changed settings, and sprayed a fine mist into the air. "Can you still smell each other's anger?"

Garvya sniffed, growled, sniffed again. "It's unnatural. How much of that stuff do you have?"

"We only brought two cans with us here," said Kumar. "Captain Adamopoulos has the other. There's more on the *Pufferfish*, but . . ." He trailed off as a new message appeared on his monocle.

"A trade, then." Her tail snatched the canister from Kumar's unresisting grip. "I'll take this in return for talking with the Black Spire camp."

Other Jynx started to protest. Garvya snarled and waved the BOE in the air. "Don't you understand what we have here? How many of our people have we lost to the Preceptor? How many has it turned against us?"

Kumar barely heard. He stared at the words on his monocle, trying to understand. No, trying *not* to understand. He read them again, but the message from Doc didn't change.

```
Mops is gone.
```

22

Cate had lived among humans long enough to recognize when one was damaged or unwell. When he saw Mops striding back from battle in her janitorial exosuit, Argarrar perched on her shoulders, he knew from her movements something was wrong. And what had happened to the sled?

A crowd of Jynx followed behind, but Cate continued to study the captain. "What's happened?"

His guard, Gabe, didn't answer.

Mops' steps were too rigid, too precise. Her arms didn't move at all. "Her AI is controlling the suit, isn't it? She's had another episode."

Azure rushed from the drop ship, a medkit clutched in one tentacle.

"Kumar reports the Freesail forces are approaching the far side of the skytree," said Starfallen. "They'll be arriving shortly."

Cate appeared to be the only one listening. Everyone else was crowding around Mops. Argarrar jumped down and helped Azure remove the helmet.

Mops' skin was a repulsive shade of gray, and her perspiratory secretions had increased. Her ridiculously undersized pupils were even smaller than usual. Drool slicked her chin.

Azure placed a sensor patch on Mops' forehead. Mops'

jaw clacked audibly as she narrowly missed getting a bite of Rokkau tentacle.

"What's wrong with her?" asked one of the Jynx—the hunter, Barryar.

Cate's wings shivered, his blades trying involuntarily to extend past the dirt and slime. Most of his battles were mental, fought with knowledge and words and his unmatched cleverness, but as he watched this mockery of his former opponent, he found himself wishing for a physical foe, someone he could strike and stab and defeat.

"She's sick," Starfallen said simply. She looked over the gathered Jynx. "Where is the Speaker?"

"Here." Barryar ducked into the crowd and returned with Harkayé. Her front limbs were bound, and a rope leashed her neck. Her hackles stood like spikes, and her black teeth were exposed.

The hum of a drop ship sled announced Kumar and Jagar's arrival. Kumar jumped down before the sled was fully powered off and ran toward Mops and Azure. Behind them, armed Freesail Jynx closed in.

There was a third group as well. Cate's keen eyes spotted multiple Jynx crouching among the gnarled skytree roots, watching the proceedings. Members of the Treeshield camp, no doubt. Reprogrammed by the Speaker to obey.

Harkayé had spotted them too. She tugged free of her captors and shouted, "Protect me!"

Several of the guards crept closer. They sniffed the air, but made no move to attack.

"You don't smell like a Speaker anymore," said Argarrar.

It didn't matter. Given the two camps' history of hatred, violence was inevitable. Cate would die on Hell's Claws, as he'd predicted all along. At least he would die a Prodryan. He relaxed, reciting his favorite death poems to prepare himself.

"Who speaks for the Black Spire camp?" demanded a black-and-brown Jynx with greasy fur and a torn ear.

Barryar and an older, fat Jynx stepped forward. "We do. Barryar and Yagyar of the Black Spire Mothers' Circle."

"First Claw Garvya of the Glass Cove Skimmer."

Who would be the first to strike? Cate's money was on

the Freesail camp. They'd be hungry for revenge, and with the Speaker helpless, this was their best chance.

Garvya stepped up and sniffed Barryar's and Yagyar's necks, each in turn. They did the same to her. *Why weren't they fighting yet?*

"What happened to her?" asked Garvya, jabbing her tail at Mops.

"She was sick," said Argarrar. "She knew she was running out of time, but she used the time she had left to fight for us. She thought we should be the ones to decide whether we go to war, not the Preceptor."

Cate squirmed. *The time for decisions was past. War was unavoidable.*

"Speaker Harkayé doesn't look very happy about that." Garvya sounded amused. "I'd have traded a lot for the chance to see a Speaker trussed up." Her tail lashed. "A lot of my people think talk is a waste of time."

Ah, here it was. Cate braced himself.

"But Kumar and the kit here had a proposal." Garvya waved a hand at Jagar, then sat on one of the roots. "Best get comfortable. This could take a while. We've got a long list of grievances, starting with the poor bastards the Speaker enslaved to protect her precious skytree. Drag Harkayé over here. She'll need to be a part of this."

Cate stared in disbelief. *Why were the Freesail Jynx dropping their chance for revenge? Why were the Black Spire camp going along with it?*

"Are you all right?" asked Gabe.

Cate clicked his mandibles. "Why aren't they fighting? I don't understand."

Gabe sighed and adjusted his hat. "No, I don't suppose you do."

"**S**HE'S NOT COMING OUT of it." Kumar wrung his hands over and over as he watched Azure work.

Azure pressed a tentacle to Kumar's chest and pushed him back a step. "I'm aware."

They'd moved Mops into the drop ship and secured her to the rearmost seat. Azure had managed to remove the EMB suit, leaving Mops in her regulation jumpsuit. After a fit of struggling and snarling, Mops seemed to have accepted her captivity. She still snapped at Azure, but she wasn't as furious as before.

"Shouldn't you be out there with the Jynx?" asked Azure.

"She's my captain." Kumar watched as Azure stuck a yellow slow-release sedative patch onto Mops' neck.

"Humans are notoriously difficult to sedate," said Azure. "Feral humans even more so. Once I get her safely to Medical on the *Pufferfish*, I'll be able to induce a coma, but for now—"

"A coma?" Kumar struggled to focus on Azure's words. "For how long?"

"That depends. If she recovers from this episode, I'll be able to bring her out of it. But from the readings Doc relayed to me . . ." Azure turned around. "You should consult with Commander Monroe to discuss long-term plans for Captain Adamopoulos' care."

Commander Monroe. Kumar hadn't updated him about Mops yet. He headed for the cockpit.

"Wait." Azure pulled Mops' monocle from her uniform pocket and passed it to Kumar.

It broke what remained of Kumar's control. It was tradition for EMC soldiers to save the monocles of their fallen companions, but Kumar had spent his life in sanitation and hygiene. He'd never lost anyone, not like this.

The edges of the memcrys lens dug into his palm as he retreated to the cockpit, shut the door, and pulled up the communications controls. The dials and menus blurred. Regulations required him to immediately report any casualties to his commanding officer as soon as circumstances permitted, but he couldn't force himself to open the channel. Reporting to Monroe would make it real. Every minute he waited was another minute they didn't have to feel what Kumar was feeling. Let them have a few more minutes of living in a universe where Captain Marion Adamopoulos still existed.

Kumar switched screens and, after fumbling through the unfamiliar menus, brought up the casualty procedure checklist. Mops' body had been secured, her condition confirmed by the closest thing they had to a doctor. Next up was to copy the contents of her monocle and officially record the circumstances of death.

Kumar removed his own monocle and used a cleaning wipe to polish the oily smears off Mops'. Once it was spotless, he brought it to an input port on the console. His fingers hovered over the port. Instead of setting the lens into place, he raised it to his own eye. "Doc."

"Kumar."

"I'm sorry."

"Me too." Doc paused, presumably for effect. *"Did it work? Did we stop the Preceptor's war?"*

"The Black Spire and Freesail Jynx are talking with each other. Barryar and the others are a lot more hostile toward Harkayé than I'd expected."

"Mops noticed that too. She spoke with Azure at the end, right before . . . Azure thinks it's a kind of withdrawal symptom. Harkayé has spent so much time with the Black Spire Jynx, they've adapted to her pheromones. Loyalty and obedience became the baseline. Take away those pheromones so suddenly, and the scale swings the other way. Azure doesn't know how long the backlash will last, so this is our best chance to help the Jynx make peace without Harkayé interfering."

"I'm not qualified for diplomacy or negotiation."

Doc made a very human snort. *"Since when has any-one on this crew been qualified for any of the things they do? With the exception of myself, naturally. Mops put you in charge because she trusted you to finish the mission."*

"I know." Kumar folded the wipe he'd used on the monocle and scrubbed a fingerprint off the edge of the console. "Let me get through the rest of this list. Once I've backed up your data and recorded the cause of—"

He froze. *Backed up the data . . .*

"I'm not as familiar with your mannerisms. Does your silence indicate thoughtfulness or the opposite?"

"Huh?"

"Option two. Got it."

Kumar ducked out of the cockpit, doubled back to finish wiping down the console, tossed the wipe into waste disposal, and hurried out of the ship. Maybe there was a way to finish their original mission after all.

"Backups?" First Claw Garvya curled her whiskers around one finger. "I've been called many things, but that's a first."

Kumar ignored her. All his attention was on Harkayé. He wished he had a tail to emphasize his words. "The Jynx were wiped out millennia ago. The Preceptor has spent all that time trying to recreate them. What happens if you have another extinction-level event?"

Harkayé scoffed. "The odds against—"

"It's unlikely, yes," said Kumar. "But it's possible. A meteorite, an alien plague, another solar storm . . ."

"Giant radioactive monsters rising up from the oceans," added Gabe. He stood behind Kumar, his recording cane extended to capture every word.

"Less likely, but who knows?" Kumar pressed. "The point is, the Preceptor would lose everything it's been working toward. You'd have to start over and hope you had the seeds to create the Jynx again. *Or . . .*"

He spun and spread his arms like he was trying to embrace the entire Freesail army. "Or, you send Jynx with us to explore other worlds. If the worst does happen, you've got thousands of Jynx safely spread throughout the galaxy. You could continue your work and skip all those millennia of evolution."

"You're talking about kicking us off our own world," snarled Garvya.

"No he's not." Jagar sneezed and wiped his snout. "He's inviting us to travel and explore on a scale you've never imagined. There are hundreds of worlds out there, with oceans no Jynx has ever seen or smelled. Worlds beyond the Preceptor's reach."

Garvya looked at Kumar. "From what they say, now

may not be the best time to go venturing out across the stars."

"Yes, it's dangerous," said Jagar. "So are the storms and the waves. When has the Freesail camp ever turned tail because of a little danger?"

"The Preceptor wants to guide the Jynx toward a more stationary civilization," Kumar continued. "Historically, that followed the extermination of the Freesail Jynx. But wouldn't the Freesailors leaving Tuxatl accomplish the same thing for your society?"

Harkayé snarled. "This is not the path mapped out for the Jynx."

"You can follow different paths and reach the same destination," said Argarrar.

"What about the ones the Preceptor stole from us?" demanded Urrara. She jabbed her tail toward the skytree. Kumar could see the Treeshield Jynx watching silently from closer to the trunk, waiting to defend the tree against any attack.

"They're gone," said Harkayé. "Once a Jynx has been bound to the Preceptor's will, it's impossible to sever that bond."

"I used to think the same thing," said Argarrar. "Back when I was a Speaker."

Harkayé hissed. "What are you talking about?"

"It's true." Jagar shrank back, looking ready to bolt, but his voice was steady. "She was my Speaker, back when I was with the Freesail Jynx."

"Age has rotted your brain, old woman," said Harkayé. "You're no Speaker. Just a traitorous nursemaid with delusions of power."

"And you're angry and scared. You're not used to feeling helpless." Argarrar crouched to press both hands to a thick curl of skytree root. "But you're not the one we have to convince."

"What do you mean?" asked Kumar.

"The Preceptor is listening," said Argarrar. "It doesn't get angry or frightened. All it does is calculate the best path toward its goal."

Harkayé lunged at Argarrar, tearing her leash from the hands of the Jynx who'd been holding her.

Barryar crashed into her from the side. Speaker and hunter tumbled over the ground, kicking and clawing and snarling, striking so quickly Kumar couldn't follow. Fur flew from both Jynx, but Harkayé seemed to be getting the upper hand. Her upper limbs were bound, but her feet kicked and clawed Barryar's stomach.

In one smooth motion, Kumar tugged the hose from the compressor on his harness and locked a metal rod to the end. The pressure-wash wand had neither soap nor water, but the resulting jet of air was more than enough to separate the two combatants. He grabbed an orange canister and screwed it into place. "Next time, I coat you in hull paint."

Harkayé hissed and started toward him.

Kumar sprayed her foot, coating it in a layer of black paint. Harkayé jumped backward. He aimed the wand at her face.

Doc helpfully projected a target via his monocle.

"Argarrar, I thought you couldn't hear the Preceptor," said Kumar.

"Not usually, but it's hard not to when you're sitting on top of a skytree."

"Can you talk to it?"

"I'd rather not." Argarrar shuddered. "But there's no need. It can hear everything Harkayé does."

"Can I speak?" asked Jagar.

Kumar lowered the wand, but kept his attention on Harkayé. "Go ahead."

Jagar combed nervously at his fur. "I'm going with the humans."

"Don't be ridiculous," said Harkayé. "You're the future of your people."

"And when and if he decides to return to Tuxatl, we'll be happy to bring him," said Kumar.

"But not as a tool or a weapon." Jagar glanced at Garvya, then back at Harkayé. "I won't help you if you're still enslaving my people or trying to start a war."

"No single Jynx is more important than the path," said

Harkayé. "Not even you. Your loss might add a thousand years to the journey, but—"

"Do the math," said Kumar. "Harkayé's way leads to a meaningless war. You'll alienate the Krakau Alliance and the Prodryans alike. You lose Jagar's cooperation. On the other side of the equation, you let the Freesail Jynx spread through the galaxy as genetic backups. You have Jagar's promise to return. Which choice gives you the best odds of fulfilling your purpose and helping the Jynx one day restore their forebears?"

Harkayé straightened. "Your ship in orbit is under attack. Your enemies are poised to destroy your worlds. The math is clear."

Kumar had been waiting for this. "You're right. All else being equal, you might be better off killing us, keeping Jagar an unwilling prisoner on Tuxatl, and fighting your damn war. But there's one more variable to consider. What happens if you give us the weapon you originally offered?"

"After your betrayal?" Harkayé growled low in her chest. "We should have killed you all when you landed."

"Maybe," said Kumar. "But you didn't. The Preceptor makes decisions based on fact, not anger and second-guessing. The fact is, you can help us win this war. In return, we help you protect the Jynx, and Jagar comes back to work with you—eventually—instead of against you."

Harkayé turned away. Her unpainted foot clawed the ground.

"Is that math any clearer?" Kumar pressed.

Harkayé didn't answer.

"The Preceptor agrees," said Argarrar.

Harkayé glared at her. "You're no Speaker. Not anymore. What *are* you?"

"Hungry." Argarrar licked her whiskers. "I have a craving for blackfin bacon. Extra salty. Now, are you going to obey your master in the sky and give the humans what they need to help their people and ours?"

Harkayé sagged. "Allow me a short time to reformulate it, then send your blue sea monster, Azure, to extract your weapon."

23

*Krakau Alliance Treaty Template, Version 28.2
Part 1 of 48: Preamble and Overview
(Complete all required fields.)*

*[The Earth Defense Fleet (EDF)] and [The Preceptor of
Tuxatl] hereby agree:*

1. *Preceptor will provide the EDF with a chemical
   to nullify the Prodryan instinct toward war and
   aggression.*
2. *EDF will facilitate the exodus of the Jynx Freesail
   camp to safe worlds throughout the Alliance.*
3. *EDF will guarantee the safety of the Jynx named
   Jagar. Per Preceptor's representative Harkayé,
   the Jynx named Argarrar can "be dropped into
   the sun, for all she cares."*
4. *Addendum: Argarrar decrees that the Preceptor's
   representative can "go choke on a hairball."*
5. *Preceptor will attempt to restore Treeshield prisoners to their original mental status.*
6. *EDF will minimize additional interference in
   Jynx development, except as needed to fulfill the
   requirements of Article 2.*

7. *The chemical known as Biological Odor Elimi-*
   nator 99 is prohibited. Distribution of this chem-
   ical will be seen as a violation of this treaty and an
   act of war.*

So attested by the following.

- *Earth Defense Fleet (EDF) Representative: [San-*
  jeev Kumar, EDFS Pufferfish]
- *Preceptor of Tuxatl Representative: [Speaker*
  Harkayé Ar-Raya]

*Private Note by Sanjeev Kumar: Check Pufferfish *stock-*
piles of BOE-98 and BOE-94.

Click NEXT to begin Part 2 of 48.

KUMAR TWISTED AROUND IN the pilot's seat. "Gabe, is everyone secure?"

Along with the team from the *Pufferfish*, they'd been able to squeeze four Jynx onto the drop ship: Jagar, Argarrar, Second Claw Urrara, and the young hunter Barryar.

"Some of them needed a few creative adjustments to the safety harnesses, but they're good," said Gabe.

"I wouldn't call this 'good,'" grumbled Argarrar. "These seats have no room for tails."

Jynx scents filled the air—meaning the BOE was beginning to wear off, and the air circ system probably needed new filters. Kumar made a note to change them when they got back.

He set one cockpit screen to display the cabin. Argarrar and Jagar sat gripping each other's hands. Gabe had set all four Jynx up with visors so they could watch the flight. At the back of the cabin, Azure sat beside Mops, who drifted in and out of consciousness.

Cate was bound to his seat near the back. He hadn't spoken at all since learning of Kumar's successful negotiations with the Preceptor. He looked broken, his wings tattered and filthy, his eyes dull. From time to time he'd look over at Starfallen, shiver, and slouch even further.

Kumar opened communications. "This is Kumar requesting permission to return to the *Pufferfish*."

Half a minute later, the welcome sound of Vera's voice replied, "Permission granted. You'll be flying into a shooting match, but I think we can clear a buffer zone as soon as we get the next batch of A-rings into position."

"Understood." He didn't, really—what were they doing with their A-rings?—but the response was automatic. He checked the drop ship's surroundings next. Jynx ringed the ship, watching from a safe distance. Harkayé remained bound, guarded by one Black Spire Jynx and one from the Freesail camp.

Kumar shut the door to the main cabin. His world fell silent. He allowed himself five seconds to relax, to appreciate the peace and solitude. Then he opened the intercom to the cabin and reached for the controls. "Prepare for launch in three . . . two . . . one . . ."

The drop ship pushed away from the planet.

In the cabin, Barryar hissed and flung his visor away so hard it bounced off the far wall. Urrara yowled, a sound that could have been either terror or excitement. Argarrar chittered to herself.

"This is amazing!" said Jagar.

Gabe leaned in and said, "I spent most of my life living underground. Never thought I'd leave Earth, let alone meet an alien race or set foot on another world. It changes you, changes your perspective." He glanced at Cate. "Changes most of us, at least."

"I feel different." Jagar stretched out one arm. "Like I've been covered in grit my whole life, and for the first time, I'm finally *clean*." He inhaled. "I can breathe!"

"You've never been free of old Jynx technology before," said Argarrar.

Kumar double-checked his trajectory, then sent an update to the *Pufferfish*. "Projected ETA is thirty-two minutes." He studied the controls, trying to remember which option would bring up the tactical display. He tried one after the next, opening menus for hull integrity self-tests, sled recharging options, and auto-destruct, which brought up a sober-looking animation of the drop ship asking, *"Are you* sure *you want to blow up the ship?"*

He closed that one fast. "Doc? Tactical?"

A pointer appeared on his monocle.

Kumar flipped the indicated switch and stared at the mess of green lighting up the screen. "Is that right?"

"Unfortunately."

Several waves of Prodryan fighters had crossed the minefield at the three light-second line and closed on the *Pufferfish*. For the moment, they seemed to be holding back. Debris tumbled through space between them and the *Pufferfish*.

Farther out, other Prodryan forces were maneuvering to deal with multiple incursions throughout the system. Kumar's mouth went dry. So many ships . . .

Only a few were labeled. The *Boomslang*, *Dart Frog*, and *Mosquito* clustered together two AUs out. The *Honey Badger* and the *Influenza* were here as well, about half an AU from the other Alliance ships. Then there were clumps of unidentified Nusuran, Glacidae, and Quetzalus ships, as well as what was tentatively tagged as a living Tjikko dreadnaught. Four large Krakau vessels were accelerating at full power toward Tuxatl.

"Isn't this a good thing?" asked Kumar. "Alliance backup means—"

"Only five of those ships are confirmed to be with the Alliance," said Doc. *"Cate's broadcast about an anti-Prodryan weapon has leaked to most Alliance species. They may prefer to claim such a weapon for themselves rather than trusting the Krakau with it."*

"Oh." The Preceptor would *not* be happy about that.

Kumar checked their course. Two intersecting curves marked the point where his trajectory and the *Pufferfish*'s would meet.

Alert lights flashed as a squadron of Prodryan fighters changed course. Kumar didn't need to see their projections to know they were coming after the drop ship.

His pulse spread up. Mops was the only one qualified

on the drop ship's weapons. The only one *officially* qualified, rather . . . He tapped the intercom. "Starfallen, would you join me in the cockpit?"

The door slid open a moment later. "That looks like a four-column swarm formation," Starfallen commented as she slid into the copilot's seat. "The lead fighters will use energy weapons to incapacitate us. I recommend a sixty-forty split of all available power between the engines and the dispersal grid."

Kumar stared.

"I assume you called for my tactical advice? I expected my people would try to stop us. They will not be kind to me, given what I've become. I assure you, I want to reach the *Pufferfish* as much as you do."

"How much?" asked Kumar. "Are you willing to fire on them?"

Starfallen hesitated. "We're outnumbered. Our weapons won't win this battle. The only advantage you have is that my people want what you discovered on Tuxatl, so they'll try to take us alive. If we fire, their priorities will shift. I suggest we change course, instead." She entered a new heading and sent it to Kumar's console.

"You want me to fly into the ring?"

"The Prodryans fear this planet. They may refuse to follow."

"It's essentially a concentrated asteroid belt, one that also happens to be more or less alive," said Kumar. "Is this really the safer choice?"

She scratched a mandible. "Marginally safer."

Monroe's voice crackled over the comm. "Kumar, get the hell out of there. Hide out on Tuxatl until we can regroup with the Alliance. We'll organize a rescue party to—"

The drop ship shuddered, and communications went dead.

"Plasma weaponry, as expected," Starfallen said calmly. "The grids absorbed most of the blast. Communications should come back shortly."

Kumar nudged them closer to the ring. Proximity warnings flashed. He did his best to match speed with the orbiting rock and ice. With a low enough relative velocity, the smaller debris shouldn't do much damage when it struck the hull.

Three fighters separated from the rest, swooping low to get beneath the drop ship. One struck a chunk of ice and spun away.

"They're trying to cut us off from the planet," said Starfallen. "They're expecting us to return."

Another alert blinked for attention. Kumar gave it a quick glance, but most of his attention was on piloting. He veered left and corkscrewed two hundred and seventy degrees to avoid a tumbling chunk of metal and ice, just one more piece of the ring. The scanners pegged that particular piece at two metric tons. "How many Prodryan ships are still on our tail?"

"On your . . . ? Ah, a figure of speech from your monkey heritage, no doubt," said Starfallen. "Eight behind, and now four trying to come up from below."

"They aren't refusing to follow, Starfallen."

"They're determined to capture or destroy us. We can use that determination."

A new proposed course appeared on Kumar's board, one that led deeper into the ring's outer edges. He choked back a despondent laugh. "Good thinking. They can't destroy us if we do it first."

"Our pursuers are designed primarily for use in space. This vessel is built to operate equally well in vacuum or atmosphere. Given the drop ship's primary function of transporting troops safely to the ground, your Alliance engineers prioritized the armor and dispersion grid. We can absorb significantly more damage than our opponents."

Another shot crackled over the drop ship's hull. Kumar's controls went dead for three seconds before coming back online.

"I suggest you grant me weapons control as well."

"I didn't think you wanted to fire on your own people."

"I don't," said Starfallen. "But I'm not happy about them shooting us, either."

Kumar nodded and studied the controls, trying to remember how to delegate the weapons. Doc flashed a series of arrows on his monocle, guiding him through the process.

"They're launching missiles," Starfallen announced. "Twelve seconds to intercept. On my mark, roll left, then come about one-eighty degrees."

"You want me to fly *toward* them?"

"Now!"

The fourteen missiles closing on them left little choice. Kumar yanked the drop ship hard to the left, then used the maneuvering jets to flip nose-to-tail. His stomach lurched, and he heard groans and hisses from the cabin as the grav plates struggled to compensate.

The missiles shot past. One was close enough he could have reached out and touched it as it flew by. They exploded an instant later, but they'd overshot enough that the shockwaves were less disruptive than Kumar's flying.

"Prodryan range-finding software is slow to adapt," said Starfallen. "Our missiles can maintain a lock through most maneuvers, but a target that suddenly goes from fleeing to flying straight toward them triggers a software check that lasts point nine seconds. I'm just glad they haven't patched that particular weakness since I've been gone. They'll switch to A-guns next, by the way."

Starfallen fired the drop ship's own A-guns into the center of the Prodryan formation. She didn't hit anything, but the fighters veered away, losing their lock on the drop ship. Kumar flew past them while they were recovering.

He resumed course toward the *Pufferfish*, skimming the edge of the ring. Smaller rocks and bits of ice rattled against them like a violent hailstorm. Electricity flashed over the hull.

"That was a lightning strike," said Doc.

Kumar passed the warning along to Starfallen. Her response was unexpected.

"Perfect. Maintain your current course."

Green warning lights announced the fighters' return. True to Starfallen's prediction, they'd switched to A-guns, peppering the air with hyperaccelerated slugs.

"That should be enough," said Starfallen. "Divert available power to the dispersion grid and pull back to this course."

"Enough for what?" But Kumar clenched his teeth and brought the drop ship down and away from the ring. His console was an explosion of green warning messages.

Two hundred meters ahead, a bolt of lightning stabbed the planet below. It vanished an instant later, the afterimage burned onto Kumar's retina as they flew through the space where it had been.

Starfallen fired again, this time aiming below the pursuing fighters. One flew up too high, trying to evade, and collided with a chunk of ring debris.

The rattle of rocks sent a constant vibration through the ship. No punctures yet, but if they kept this up, it was only a matter of time.

Sensors registered lightning behind them, and one of the Prodryan fighters vanished from the screen.

"Here we go." Starfallen released the weapons controls and sat back.

"Your plan is to hope they all get hit by lightning?"

"Normally, a ship can shrug off a lightning strike, even without an active defense grid. Circuitry, electronics, fuel—everything is isolated from the charge flowing over the hull." Starfallen raised one digit. "*Unless* you first damage the hull and create a path for the lightning to reach the interior."

"*We're* taking hull damage from these rocks too," Kumar pointed out, his voice jumping in pitch.

"Less damage, thanks to your stronger armor. That will protect us. Hopefully."

Another Prodryan ship exploded. Shrapnel from the explosion sent two more fighters spiraling toward the ocean far below.

The drop ship lurched again. Kumar overcompensated, flipping them upside down before regaining control. Seven fighters left—now six.

"If we survive this, we'll want to come about to assist the *Pufferfish*," said Starfallen. "Our triumphant return will demoralize the enemy. A few strafing runs should send them fleeing to the nest to regroup."

Kumar's jaw was too tight to speak. He simply nodded and concentrated on flying and trying not to explode.

The drop ship jolted hard as it settled into the *Pufferfish* landing bay.

Kumar opened the door to the main cabin and called back, "I'm sorry about the rough ride. I did most of my practice with shuttle simulations. This thing has more mass, and I think the engines got knocked out of alignment somewhere along the way."

Gabe fumbled to detach his harness. "Any landing you can walk away from, right?"

Kumar made his way through the post-flight checklist. The magnetic lock securing the drop ship to the hangar floor looked good. Sterilization procedures automatically cleansed the ship's exterior. The bay doors were shut, and the air outside was quickly coming up to normal pressure.

"Azure, make sure the Jynx's PRAs are working."

All four Jynx wore the devices around their necks. Argarrar sniffed hers and wrinkled her snout.

"There will be many alien smells to get used to," said Azure. "It took me a while to adjust, too."

Jagar held out one arm and let it fall into his lap. "I feel heavy."

"Gravity is slightly higher here." Kumar shut off the controls and unstrapped from his seat. "We can reduce that in your cabins, but you should get used to it after a while."

"Tell me if it becomes a problem," added Azure. "I'll be giving you medical sensors to monitor blood pressure, circulation, temperature, and more. You might need compression clothing to keep your body fluids from settling."

Gabe reached for the hatch. Jagar jumped to his feet, eager to follow.

"Hold it." Kumar was surprised at how quickly they

obeyed. "Argarrar, you were connected to the Preceptor, back at the skytree. What can you tell us about the bio-weapon Harkayé made?"

For the first time, Cate roused from his slump and focused on the conversation.

"I couldn't recreate it, if that's what you're asking." Her head tilted. "What is it, Kumar?"

He rubbed his hands together as he tried to put words to the sick sensation that had been shooting through his gut since Harkayé offered up the swollen blister on her wrist. "I'm trying to understand the Preceptor's thinking. It reminds me a lot of the Prodryans."

"Don't be absurd," snapped Cate. "The Preceptor is confined to a single world. My people have expanded through the galaxy."

"But your priorities are the same," said Kumar. "*Your* people. It's all you care about. All that matters to the Preceptor is restoring the Jynx. Not us or the Alliance or the war with the Prodryans."

Starfallen leaned forward. "Where are you leading with this?"

"Why do the Prodryans keep their distance from Tux-atl? Given what happened to you, I understand not landing on the surface. But until the *Pufferfish* arrived, they wouldn't even get close to it. Their mines were set three light-seconds from the planet. That's more than twice the distance between Earth and the moon. Why so far out?"

"That policy was implemented after I was abandoned here," said Starfallen.

"Something kept them away, but the Preceptor let us land. Why?"

Cate huffed. "Because Prodryan superiority makes us the greater threat against the Jynx. Obviously."

"But you *weren't* a threat," said Kumar. "Your people actively helped isolate Tuxatl from the rest of the galaxy. We're the ones who threatened that isolation. And Harkayé was willing to help the Prodryans against the Alliance."

"Curiosity?" asked Gabe. "Not everyone shoots first and asks questions later. Maybe they wanted to meet new life and new civilizations."

"Pah." Urrara bared her teeth. "You wouldn't say that if you knew the Preceptor."

"The Preceptor's mission isn't to explore the galaxy or befriend other races," said Kumar. "For that matter, why let the original Quetzalus colonists land and interact with the Jynx?"

"If the Jynx killed the Quetzalus, it could have dragged Tuxatl into a larger conflict with the galaxy," said Starfallen. "If nothing else, it would have attracted attention. But massacred by Prodryan warriors? That's nothing noteworthy."

"You said the Prodryans had come here before." Kumar rested his forehead on the door, trying to fix the gaps in his thinking. "The Preceptor knew about your race and your mission. It's been using you. After the Quetzalus, you increased your presence in this system. You made it harder for anyone to set foot on Tuxatl."

"You were their security guards," said Gabe.

"Until I helped you past our defenses," Cate said bitterly.

"That's the difference." Starfallen's antennae were fully raised. "Consider the Preceptor's perspective. It didn't know the desperation of the *Pufferfish*'s mission. All it saw was a lone ship able to bypass all Prodryan defenses without firing a single shot. You were an unknown variable, one that needed to be assessed."

Azure raised a tentacle. "No disrespect intended, but what is the point of this hypothesizing?"

Kumar moved to stand in front of Cate. The Prodryan remained a pitiful sight, filthy and exhausted. Kumar had to fight the urge to whip out a polishing rag and start scrubbing Cate's exoskeleton. "What would you have done in the Preceptor's place? After you examined us and realized our technology was no different from that of the Prodryans? Which side would you have wanted to take in the war?"

Cate didn't hesitate. "Neither. The ongoing Prodryan war benefits the Preceptor more than either side's decisive victory. It drains both sides' resources and keeps our attention off Tuxatl. It would be better to *escalate* hostilities in the hopes that non-Jynx races destroy each other and leave Tuxatl undisturbed in the future."

Kumar turned. "Azure, whatever precautions you have for analyzing the sample from Harkayé, increase them. I want your lab locked down, with full quarantine procedures and a level one decontamination prepped and ready to go at the touch of a button."

"Understood."

"You think Harkayé's bioweapon is a trap?" asked Starfallen.

Kumar kept his gaze on Azure. "I assume you've started looking it over? Is there any way it could be harmful to non-Prodryans as well?"

"It's . . . possible," Azure said slowly. "Harkayé could have hidden a secondary effect targeted toward humans or other Alliance species. But it's unlikely—on a cellular level, you're talking about completely mismatched puzzle pieces. No, more like a puzzle piece and a playing card. Not only do they not fit together, most of the time they're not even recognizably part of the same game. But we saw what happened when the Krakau and the Rokkau visited Earth . . ."

Commander Monroe's voice filled the drop ship, making Kumar jump.

"Thanks for the assist with those fighters, Kumar. Is everything all right down there?"

Kumar's face warmed. How long had he kept everyone waiting? "We're all right, sir. Sorry. I'll be reporting to the bridge momentarily."

"If you have any doubts about this weapon, your only option is to destroy it," said Cate. "Perhaps it would help if I pointed out the extensive list of Alliance laws against biological warfare? You are legally, logically, and ethically obligated to incinerate it now."

"Don't talk to me about ethics," Kumar snapped. "How many Alliance worlds did your people attack while we were on Tuxatl?"

"I have no way of knowing that!"

"Eleven." Doc spoke softly, using the cabin speakers so everyone would hear. *"Casualty reports are incom-*

*plete, but likely to number in the thousands, with tens of
thousands wounded and displaced."*

"You would destroy my people," Cate protested. "We
have the right to defend ourselves."

Kumar touched his monocle. "Commander, could you
please send Vera to escort Cate to the brig? We have our
hands and tentacles full."

"She's on her way," said Monroe.

"Please." Cate strained against his bonds. "We could
come to an agreement, an alliance between humans and
Prodryans."

"I thought your people didn't make alliances with
other species," said Kumar.

"After seeing your dealings with the Jynx, I've recon-
sidered. Destroy the weapon they gave you, and in return,
we will . . ." His mandibles opened and closed soundlessly.

"Yes?"

". . . we will kill you last?" Cate looked up, one antenna
raised hopefully.

Sadly, that was probably the best offer anyone had received from the Prodryans in the history of the war. Kumar turned away.

Argarrar stretched, a long, indulgent process that started
with the tips of her fingers and ended with a quiver of the
tail. "Can we get off yet? If you don't mind, I'd like to find
the nearest bathroom? My stomach's not happy about all
that flying, and I need to bury a wicked shit."

24

Admiral Pachelbel's tentacles woke before the rest of her. Krakau brain tissue extended through the three primary tentacles, an evolutionary advantage that allowed them to swim or fight even while sleeping. Or in this case, while unconscious after a long A-ring jump.

By the time she opened her eyes, her limbs were throbbing from trying to tug free of their restraints.

Normal jumps were bad enough, requiring a cocktail of anesthesia and blood thickeners that left her sluggish for days. Today she had the added misery of the stimulants coursing through her body to accelerate her awakening. The side effects were vicious and potentially damaging, so they were only used in emergencies. Emergencies like the collapse of the Alliance and the massive fighting about to erupt in the Tuxatl system.

Naturally, Mops and the Pufferfish were right in the middle of it.

She scraped her beak, trying to get the worst of the sleep-gunk out of the corners. "Status?"

Her voice was harsh and atonal. Krakau song always sounded abrasive and hard-edged in the open air. Their languages were meant to flow through the water.

"Welcome back to the conscious world, Admiral Pachelbel. This is Battle Captain Kardashian. We're monitoring three small skirmishes, but most fleets are too far out of range of each other to do much more than shout threats and insults for the moment. Activity around Tuxatl has gone quiet since the Pufferfish's drop ship returned from the surface thirty minutes ago. The Pufferfish has sustained moderate damage, but they were able to fight off a wave of Prodryan attackers by firing A-rings."

Pachelbel blinked. Was that a translator error, or was she groggier than she'd realized? "Say again, Battle Captain?"

"I've watched the recordings four times. The Pufferfish has no weapons, but they've deployed a partial shield of active A-rings, and fired smaller rings through them. It only appears to be moderately effective. At least some of the damage to their ship is self-inflicted."

"What the tentacle-tearing fuck did you do, Mops?" Pachelbel murmured.

"What was that, Admiral?"

"I asked if you'd been in contact with Captain Adamopoulos yet."

"Communications is working on it, Admiral. There's a lot of active interference in the system."

"Keep at it." Pachelbel hit the release lever, and her acceleration tank began to drain. Her limbs swelled as blood flow increased. "Give humans their own ship, and the next time you surface, the whole galaxy's ready to explode . . ."

KUMAR FINALLY MADE IT to the bridge. Gabe had beaten him here, and was settled in at Communications. Johnny was muttering to herself at Engineering and reviewing damage reports. Grom lay coiled at Tactical, walled in by a series of transparent shield panels and surrounded by half-eaten and half-melted snacks. Kumar watched the Glacidae's many limbs twitch and kick. "Is Grom asleep?"

"They've barely left the bridge since your team went down to the planet." Monroe turned in his chair and clasped his hands together. "You secured the biological weapon the Jynx prepared?"

"Azure is examining it now, sir. Her preliminary review on the drop ship suggests it's similar in size and complexity to a human virus, and appears to be structurally compatible with Prodryan neurons."

"Good work." His right hand jerked into a fist. "What's Captain Adamopoulos' status?"

Gabe and Johnny both paused in their work to listen.

"Unchanged." Kumar stared at the textured metal floor. "She's in medical seclusion. Sedated."

"If she's sedated, how are we supposed to know if she snaps out of it?"

"I don't think she's going—" Kumar caught himself. He was no doctor or scientist. Maybe Monroe was right to hope this was another episode and not the final stage of reversion. "I'm sure Azure is monitoring her brain activity."

He studied the screen. The remaining Prodryan ships were waiting out of range, predators ready to pounce the moment the *Pufferfish* left orbit. There were more fighters incoming. And farther out, hundreds of additional ships from every race known to the Alliance. "How long until the shooting starts?"

"Not long. Hours, maybe. The Prodryans will do everything in their power to destroy this ship, and everyone else is desperate to get control of that weapon."

Kumar kept remembering Cate's pleas, his fear and desperation and barely suppressed panic and, at the end, his despair. "This feels wrong, sir."

"It's war. The danger is when it stops feeling wrong." Monroe sighed. "I don't like it either, but I can't see another way of ending this. For now, I need you at your station."

Kumar took his place at Navigation. He brought up their orbit and began plotting escape paths, just in case the Prodryans slipped up and opened a gap in their net.

Gabe spun back to his console. "Incoming call from the Tjikko dreadnaught."

Monroe groaned. "Put them through."

The Tjikko's synthesized voice filled the bridge. "Sun and rain to you, Commander Monroe of the *Pufferfish*. Recently, it has become obvious to all that the Krakau Alliance was born of poisoned soil. Its rot spreads from the heart. It must die so that a new order can grow in its place."

Vera arrived on the bridge and headed straight for her station at Tactical. A console-to-console message appeared on Kumar's screen a moment later.

```
V. Rubin: This is the fourth message
we've received from our so-called al-
lies. First was the Nusurans, then the
Glacidae. Then a second group of
Nusurans, unaffiliated with the first.

S. Kumar: What do they want?

V. Rubin: The bioweapon. And power in
whatever new Alliance sprouts up in
the aftermath of the war. Nobody likes
or trusts the Krakau, but they're
crawling over each other to take the
Krakau's place.
```

"As the procurers of this anti-Prodryan weapon," the Tjikko continued, "and in recognition of your people's tragic history, the Tjikko would consider making you members of our grove, an unprecedented honor that would bind your people and ours in peace, pledged to mutual aid and defense."

"Thank you, Delta-two," said Monroe. "We appreciate the offer, and we share your desire for peace. But I can't help noticing your battle platform is on an intercept course with Alliance ships, and your weapons are running hot."

The Tjikko didn't move. That was to be expected—Delta-two was, after all, a grove of sentient trees. The "spokestree," for lack of a better word, was no more than ten centimeters in diameter. Metal cuffs striped the rough bark. Sensors and taps measured the pressure and flow in the tree's veins and capillaries. A computer system and voder translated this to speech, allowing the Tjikko to communicate with other species.

"If the Krakau control this weapon, they will have the leverage to reestablish their dominance over the rest of us. The Tjikko find this unacceptable."

"We're not Krakau," said Monroe. "And most of the crew on those Alliance ships you're targeting are human."

"More victims of the Krakau Alliance."

Gabe cleared his throat. "Signal from a Rokkau life-ship, sir."

"Apologies, Delta-two," said Monroe. "Someone else wants to threaten and/or bribe us. Please stand by." He killed the channel, but didn't accept the connection to the Rokkau. "Gabe, tell them to leave a message."

Kumar focused on Navigation. Piloting past the Pro-dryan fighters and their mines was only the first step. The *Pufferfish* would need to rendezvous with the other Alliance ships while avoiding . . . pretty much everyone else. The Tjikko dreadnaught and the Nusuran ships were both faster, though the *Pufferfish* was more maneuverable. Glacidae vessels were slow, but they carried cutting-edge weaponry.

Monroe was on the comm again. With Azure, from the sound of it. "Is there any way to transmit this thing's atomic structure and let Alliance scientists recreate it, or do we have to hand it over in person?"

"Eventually, I might be able to map the chemical structure," said Azure. "But I need more time. It's not just a single structure. I think the variations I'm finding are meant to interface with different types of Prodryan neurons. There are environmental responses and adapta-tions I've never seen before. When I transfer a sample to a medium that duplicates a Prodryan atmosphere, it mul-tiplies at an astounding rate. The good news is that it doesn't appear to affect non-Prodryan cells."

Kumar sagged with relief. His suspicions had been unfounded.

"How accurately does it reproduce?" asked Vera.

Monroe lifted his head. "What do you mean?"

"Mistakes are the foundation of evolution. If single-celled organisms reproduced perfectly each time, the galaxy would never have developed multicellular life."

A chill pimpled Kumar's skin. The Preceptor's entire purpose in life was to guide the evolution of the Jynx. Speakers like Harkayé and Argarrar analyzed every Jynx born throughout the world and matched up pairs to develop the species into what it had once been. The Preceptor specialized in evolution. It had been calculating potential recombinations and outcomes for countless generations.

Kumar didn't remember standing, but he found himself stepping toward the captain's chair. Everyone on the bridge was staring at him.

"What is it, Kumar?" asked Monroe.

Was the comm still open? Kumar leaned closer. "Azure, are you able to predict possible mutations?"

"There aren't many," said Azure. "This thing is remarkably stable, and mimics Prodryan biology. The basic structure is a sphere with tendrils coming off both sides, like two sets of tree roots connected to a bubble of protein-like molecules. It's the same structure we see in Prodryan neurons."

"Could it evolve into a form that affects other species?" asked Kumar. "Humans, Rokkau, and so on?"

"I'd need to run a lot more tests and long-term multi-generational simulations," Azure said slowly. "We also have to consider how differences in individual Prodryan neurochemistry might impact reproduction." Azure paused. "Do you think Cate would mind if I borrowed a cup of his neurons?"

"Do what you have to do, and notify me the instant you learn anything," Monroe ordered. "This thing doesn't leave the *Pufferfish* until we know exactly what we're dealing with and how to control it."

Monroe had never wanted a command of his own, especially not like this.

After being cured and trained by the Krakau, he'd been content to serve as one of the thousands of Earth Mercenary Corps soldiers who helped maintain order and protect Alliance worlds.

When he was too physically damaged for infantry, they'd transferred him to the Shipboard Hygiene and Sanitation team on the *Pufferfish*. He'd learned quickly, and had been content to help maintain the ship.

Then came the Battle of Andromeda 12. Nusuran rebels had collaborated with the Rokkau to infect the *Pufferfish*, turning the rest of the crew feral. Mops had assumed command. She'd hunted down the ones responsible for the attack, and in the process, had uncovered so much more . . . including the truth about what had really happened to humanity all those years ago.

Of all the officers he'd served under, Mops was special: intelligent, determined, insightful, but also compassionate and willing to listen and learn.

And now all that was gone, her mind whittled away to nothing but instinct and hunger.

His fingers dug into the arms of the chair as he watched the movements of the various fleets on screen. The patterns were clear: everyone wanted to reach Tuxatl and the *Pufferfish*. They were all racing to get their hands, claws, branches, or tentacles on the bioweapon in the *Pufferfish* medical bay.

Fighting broke out whenever two groups came within range. Four Nusuran ships were dead in space, having been caught in the crossfire between the Tjikko and a set of hidden Prodryan drones. The Alliance was exchanging fire with a Prodryan battle platform, while a Glacidae cruiser took potshots at both sides.

"Sir?" Gabe was glaring at his console. From here, Monroe could just see the animated Puffy icon popping up to offer assistance. "Incoming call from Admiral Pachelbel. It's secured, and I'm not sure how to decode or transfer it."

Monroe mirrored Gabe's console to his own. "You can't. That's command-level encryption. Captain's eyes only." Or acting captain's. He sent the call to his monocle.

Pachelbel looked . . . *swollen*, particularly around the eyes and beak. Monroe couldn't remember seeing a Krakau so exhausted.

"It's about time." Pachelbel paused. "Where's Mops?"

"Medical."

The admiral waited, then clicked her beak when it became obvious Monroe wasn't going to say more. "I'll be blunt, Commander. I don't know if we can get you out of there. I suggest you transmit everything you've got on the Tuxatl bioweapon to my ship. If we lose the *Pufferfish*, we might be able to recreate this thing."

"No, sir."

It took several seconds for his response to reach the admiral's ship, and several more for her to respond. Her skin darkened, and her limbs stiffened. "Explain."

"We can't let an untested weapon of this nature get loose. Our specialist is still examining it." He caught Kumar's eye and nodded. "We believe the Jynx may have encoded threats to other species."

"Do you have any evidence for this?"

"Not yet."

"Maybe you haven't noticed the war breaking out all around you, Commander. We're out of time."

"The Prodryans are holding back, and we have—" Monroe checked the screen. "—more than an hour before the closest fleet reaches us."

The image on his monocle flickered. Pachelbel whistled a curse and turned away. "Order the *Boomslang* to come about and get that cruiser off our tail. A-guns and energy weapons only. I'd prefer not to kill a ship full of Glacidae if we don't have to, but if they persist, the *Boomslang* is authorized to use all necessary force."

Kumar cleared his throat. "Commander Monroe? Scanners just detected multiple A-ring decel signatures. They're registering as Prodryan."

Of course, the Prodryans would have called for reinforcements. He pulled up Tactical, but the overlapping green dots made it impossible to count the individual ships. "How many?"

Rubin answered in her usual calm tone. "Two hundred seventeen."

"We're seeing them too," said Pachelbel. "At least thirty bombers. Twenty carriers, fully loaded with either drones or fighters. And one massive warship, twice the size of anything we've ever seen from the Prodryans."

A red-and-orange–shelled Krakau cut into the broadcast. "That's a Prodryan destroyer-class vessel, the *Destiny*. It's the flagship of the Supreme War Leader."

"Thank you," said Monroe. "Who the hell are you and how the hell did you break into this transmission?"

"She's with Colonial Military Command," said Pachelbel. "No Human name. Call her Orange."

"I will be assuming control of all anti-Prodryan forces in this system to unify our efforts against the real enemy," said Orange. "We will fight our way to the *Pufferfish*, escort you to a safe jump distance, and retreat to Dobranok before the *Destiny*'s crew has a chance to awaken from their jump. Once we're safely away, Commander Monroe will turn over this so-called weapon and all information pertaining to it."

"This is an Earth Defense Fleet ship," said Monroe. "We're not Alliance, and we damn well don't report to CMC."

At the same time, Pachelbel snapped, "You're out of line. CMC has no authority over this mission."

"The Alliance is dying, Pachelbel. Instead of hiding in the sand, CMC has accepted that truth and taken steps to protect our people. We will make sure this weapon is deployed swiftly, and we will end the Prodryan threat once and for all. You can call the *Pufferfish* an EDF ship if you like, but it belongs to us. My engineers have made sure of that."

"What do you mean?" asked Pachelbel.

"It's not just the *Pufferfish*," said Orange. "We've had people in the Alliance for years, many of them in engineering. They've worked on more than half your ships over the past four months, outfitting them with override controls slaved to my own vessel. You can either accept my authority and help me save the galaxy from the Prodryans, or I'll take control and do it myself. You have ten minutes to decide."

CMC engineers. Monroe turned to Johnny, who was working at her station, oblivious to the conversation. Johnny, who had insisted on accompanying them on this mission. He quietly slid his sidearm free.

Monroe might not have wanted to command the *Pufferfish*, but he'd be damned if he'd let the CMC take it away from him.

25

Outpost Commander Swift Death spread her wings in a forced display of excitement. "Supreme War Leader has chosen Tuxatl to be the site of his first great victory!"

Chittering cheers filled the command center, a too-open space carved into the center of a large asteroid. The stone hive was cold and hard, like the warriors who lived here. This was the heart of the Prodryan defense of this system.

Swift Death scowled at the holosphere that displayed exactly how that defense was going. Ships from practically every known race infested Prodryan space. The *Puffer-fish*, a stubborn parasite that had spent months gnawing away at Prodryan supremacy, now flaunted its defiance as it orbited Hell's Claws. How had humans, those barely sentient wingless savages, claimed the weapons of that world for themselves?

More importantly, what would Supreme War Leader say when he awoke and saw the chaos spreading through Swift Death's territory?

She spun toward her communications specialist and shouted, "Swarms three and five, fall back and chase those Alliance ships toward minefield seven. Swarm one, a group of Quetzalus ships has decelerated at the following coordinates. Send four ships under max acceleration.

You might be close enough to destroy them before the crew recovers."

"Automated message from the Destiny," *said War Cry. "We're ordered to transmit a progress report on our victory, along with all intelligence on the alleged bioweapon and the humans who discovered it."*

This was all Advocate of Violence's fault. It was his panicked broadcast that had brought the galaxy to Swift Death's hive, his fearmongering that had summoned Supreme War Leader's fleet. Swift Death would have gotten everything under control—eventually—if not for his interference.

"Commander?" prompted War Cry.

"Acknowledge the Destiny's *orders. Tell them the Pufferfish is pinned down. We've kept their bioweapon contained to their ship, and we will destroy them the instant they venture from the shadow of Hell's Claws."*

"Understood." War Cry hesitated. "What do I say about the humans themselves? Should I include your exchanges with Commander Monroe—"

The A-guns on Swift Death's shoulders swiveled to target War Cry. Across the command center, Prodryans ducked for cover. To War Cry's credit, he didn't try to hide. Maybe it was courage, or maybe he knew Swift Death's guns would penetrate whatever he hid behind anyway.

"Say one word about checkers, and I'll be calling sanitation to clean your insides from the walls."

⚒

"**E**NGINEER JOHNNY."

"Yes, Captain?" Johnny spun, then shrank when she spied Monroe's pistol pointed at her torso. "Sir?"

"I've just had a talk with Colonial Military Command."

"I see." The Krakau flattened further, but her voice remained steady. "I assume I'll be spending the rest of this mission in your brig?"

"What happened?" asked Gabe. "What did she do?" Monroe gestured for Johnny to answer.

"Krakau Colonial Military Command contacted me shortly after the *Pufferfish* put into Stepping Stone for repairs," said Johnny. "Command didn't like the idea of humans having their own ship. They assigned me to report back to them, and to install certain fail-safes in case we needed to retake control."

"What kind of fail-safes?" asked Grom.

"Full navigation control. Isolated communications equipment allowing me to report back to CMC. A tap into the ship's internal security and surveillance. Weapons overrides . . . not that those proved necessary following the unfortunate accident at Jupiter." Johnny darkened with embarrassment.

Monroe punched the arm of the chair so hard his prosthetic hand dented the metal. "Can you remove the overrides? Starting with whatever Orange means to use to slave the *Pufferfish* to her ship?"

"It would take most of a day." Johnny twined two tentacles together. "CMC believed this mission would be a waste of time, but they don't take chances. The idea of humans getting their hands on a weapon that could stop the Prodryans . . . Command didn't trust your people with such power. Neither did I."

Johnny looked around the bridge. "Having served on the *Pufferfish* alongside you and your crew . . . I was mistaken. I'm sorry, Commander."

Monroe checked the time. Eight minutes left until Orange took control of his ship. Not just the *Pufferfish*—she could probably command half the Alliance ships in the system as well. "I need everything we have on Orange's ship."

"The *CMCS Brakon*," Johnny volunteered.

Monroe pulled up the ship's specs and swore. "This is almost all redacted."

"It's a modified class-three cruiser built for an all-Krakau crew of one hundred and twelve." Johnny tossed a set of schematics onto the main screen. "This is the standard C3 cruiser. The *Brakon* has heavier armor, roughly twice the weapons, and next-generation A-rings."

Monroe still had his pistol pointed toward Johnny. "Why are you sharing this?"

A drawn-out sigh rippled through her body. "To most Krakau, humans are tools. Weapons used to protect the more civilized races."

"Tell us something we don't know," muttered Monroe.

Johnny flushed. "I've observed this crew. I've reviewed the logs from the landing mission. I've seen Captain Adamopoulos' determination. Kumar's courage. Rubin's steadiness in the midst of chaos. I've seen your trust in your people, Commander. This ship, under command of humans, successfully negotiated with an ancient supercomputer. You neutralized Prodryan military forces second only to those protecting Yan. You allowed your people to weaponize A-rings in a way no sane engineer would ever consider. I . . . trust you."

Monroe had never been as good as Mops when it came to reading alien body language—or human body language, for that matter. But Johnny sounded sincere.

He made his decision. "Forget the sabotage to the *Pufferfish*. Has the *Brakon* made any changes or upgrades to their sanitation infrastructure?"

Johnny blinked the eye facing Monroe. "I don't believe so."

"Outstanding. Gabe, alert the *Brakon* to prepare to receive an encoded transmission." He paused. "Do you know how to apply honeycomb encryption?"

"I remember reading about it." Gabe sorted through paper notes with one hand while pulling up tutorials with the other. "Quantum encoding, right? Hundreds of thousands of false data points interwoven into the true message, so that even if someone cracks it, they have to sift out the one true message from the rest. I know it's in the secure transmission submenu . . ."

While Gabe fought with his console, Monroe began crafting his message. Each word had to be precisely chosen. Decrypting a message with this level of security required the captain's authorization. Orange would be impatient to learn the secrets the *Pufferfish* had discovered. She'd probably rush the decryption through the computer right there on the bridge.

"Got it, sir," said Gabe.

"Tight-beam this to the *Brakon*." Monroe sent the message to Gabe's station.

"Sir?" Gabe looked over his shoulder at Monroe. "Is this the right message?"

"It is." Monroe folded his arms to wait. It took two minutes for Gabe to prepare and transmit the message. At this distance, the *Brakon* should receive it in roughly three seconds. Monroe's fingers drummed the chair as he waited for Orange to decrypt the transmission.

"The *Brakon* appears to be reducing power," said Rubin.

A choked laugh escaped Gabe's mouth.

Monroe leaned forward. "What is it?"

"The captain of the *Brakon* is cursing you out and threatening to—" Gabe cocked his head. "That's not even possible for a species with only four limbs."

"What was in that transmission?" asked Johnny.

"An official SHS report identifying an infestation of Nusuran genital lice on the *CMCS Brakon*."

"You told them they had an alien STD?" asked Gabe.

"Not just any STD," said Monroe. "Nusuran lice devour memcrys. They gobble it up like candy. The instant an infestation is detected or reported, everything goes into automatic lockdown. By now, the maintenance systems will have begun irradiating all vacant areas and ordering the crew out of the most sensitive parts of the ship."

"Won't they just override the alert?" asked Johnny.

"They can't," Kumar said excitedly. "Because it's so easy for the lice to damage computer systems, the process can't be canceled automatically. Otherwise, a single bad signal from a damaged circuit could stop the decontamination and allow them to spread. The *Brakon*'s SHS team will need to do a full inspection of the entire ship, manually clearing the sanitation alert one deck at a time."

Gabe had begun jotting something down in his notebook. "I'm learning some fascinating new Krakau profanity."

Monroe sat back in his chair. That took the CMC out of play for the moment. He turned his focus to the *Destiny* and the rest of the Prodryans. "I don't suppose anyone knows what kind of automatic sanitation routines are coded into Prodryan destroyers?"

"Commander?" Kumar had looked vaguely shell-shocked ever since his return to the *Pufferfish*, but his expression now was a wide-eyed mix of excitement and full-blown panic. "I have a suggestion."

This was the first time Monroe had seen their Jynx guests in person. They carried a noticeable odor of vinegar, damp soil, and wood smoke.

The youngest—Jagar—was a tight coil of barely-contained energy, practically bouncing from one station to the next as he examined the bridge. He stopped to stare at the main screen. "Is that Tuxatl?"

"Do you know of any other ringed planets in these parts?" That was the older one, Argarrar. She gave everything a quick once-over before moving to the rear and taking a seat on the unused backup console. "Is it true we're all going to be blown to dust before the sun sets?"

"I think we have until sunrise, at least," said Monroe. "I'm Commander Monroe, and I wanted to officially welcome you on board the *Pufferfish*."

"What's a puffed fish?" asked Argarrar. Her tail jabbed in Grom's direction. "And what's that? It reminds me a little of Snaggleclaw."

Grom drew themself up and rattled their spines indignantly. "My name is Gromgimsidalgak. My phonetically challenged crewmates call me Grom."

"Your giant space fish is quite a vessel," said the one with the scarf, Urrara. "But I miss the feel of the wind in my fur."

"The air is still and sterile," agreed Barryar, his tail lashing so hard it thumped against the wall.

Argarrar was sniffing Grom, who looked ready to give her a face full of spines. Urrara had joined Jagar in gazing at the main screen. She reached out with her left hand and gently batted one of the green icons. Barryar remained by the lift doors, trying to watch everyone and everything at once.

Monroe raised his voice. "Those green lights represent Prodryan ships, mines, and drones."

"You seem to be outnumbered," commented Argarrar.

"Very much so. Which is why we need to understand Tuxatl's capabilities." He focused on Argarrar. "Kumar tells me you can communicate with the Preceptor?"

"On Tuxatl, when standing on the roots of the skytree? Then I could hear whispers." She waved her tail. "Here on this lifeless metal ground, I hear nothing."

Kumar's shoulders slumped. "I'm sorry, Commander. I thought . . . I hoped maybe . . ."

"You thought to convince the Preceptor to join your war?" Urrara scoffed. "You might as well expect the wind and the waves to serve you."

Monroe hadn't had time to review the full details of the crew's ground mission, but he knew enough. "Harkayé was ready to kill a lot of people. You convinced the Preceptor to try a different path."

Kumar was rocking on his feet. "It's not about changing the Preceptor's mind."

"Explain," said Argarrar.

Monroe nodded for Kumar to continue.

"The Preceptor is a computer. It's programmed to recreate the old Jynx. It considers the variables and chooses whatever offers the best chance to reach that goal in the shortest amount of time. Alien interference is one variable. Jagar's unique genetics are another. The need to 'store' Jynx off-planet in case of disaster is a third.

"The Preceptor would happily let every ship out there blow each other up. The more we wipe ourselves out, the less of a risk that first variable becomes. But the other two variables require the *Pufferfish* to survive."

"I didn't see the planet rushing to protect you when those Prodryan fighters attacked the drop ship," said Grom.

"Are you sure?" Kumar countered. "We had twelve fighters on our tail. Lightning and debris from the ring destroyed every one of them. Do you think that was coincidence? What are the odds of us being the only ship to escape?"

"One in thirteen," said Johnny.

Kumar blinked. "Right, but—"

"Better than that, given the drop ship's stronger hull and armor," the engineer continued. "I'd estimate as high as one in three. The Preceptor might be the fanciest computer we've ever encountered, but it's still a ring of orbital debris, not a planetary weapons defense platform."

Kumar raised his hands, as agitated as Monroe had ever seen him. "Then why haven't the Prodryans bombarded the planet from orbit? Why place their mines so far out?"

"You think Tuxatl is armed?" asked Monroe.

"Yes, sir." Kumar pointed to the display. "I think it can strike at least within that three light-second radius. If we could just talk to the Preceptor . . ."

Monroe turned his chair to face the Jynx. "Argarrar, is there any way for us to help you contact the Preceptor? Our communications systems are—"

"The Preceptor can read your transmissions," said Argarrar. "It's probably examined your records as well."

"Our records are encrypted," said Kumar.

"It's a supercomputer the size of a moon," Monroe pointed out. "Continue, Speaker."

"Your transmissions would be a lesser priority than the voice of a Speaker," said Argarrar.

"The difference between a random crewman yelling at the ship's computer and someone with command authorization."

"The disembodied voice is mostly correct," said Argarrar. "But no one commands the Preceptor. I could speak with it and be heard, but to do so, I'd have to return to a skytree on Tuxatl. And unclog my inner ear."

Years of working with other species let Monroe take that in stride. "I'm not sure what that means, but several of my crew are experts at removing clogs."

"No need, Commander," said Argarrar. "I may not be

a true Speaker anymore, but I still have some control over my own body. It's the lack of a skytree that's the true obstacle. Without it, I can do nothing."

Kumar cleared his throat. "Commander Monroe?"

Monroe folded his arms. Kumar was biting his lip and staring at the floor. He had never been good at hiding guilt. "What is it?"

"I snuck a cutting from the Black Spire skytree onto the drop ship. It was going to be a gift for Vera."

"Get it." Monroe checked the status of the battles raging throughout the system. "Hurry."

Monroe hadn't entered the Captain's Cove since before Mops left. He felt like an intruder.

Argarrar clearly had no such worries. She immediately started to explore, sniffing and studying every aspect of the room. She seemed especially interested in Mops' desk, going so far as to tap the clear surface, as if to provoke a response from the fish frozen within. "Are they real?" She bent down and licked the desk. "Tasteless."

"Mops would agree completely," said Monroe.

The other three Jynx lingered by the doorway. Perhaps they were more cautious, or maybe they were simply overwhelmed by the clashing décor.

Kumar burst into the room, out of breath and carrying a meter-long stick with one end sealed in a transparent nutrient bulb. He'd connected a small battery to the trunk, just above the bulb. "I knew they absorbed energy from lightning strikes down on the planet, but I can't believe how quickly this thing grows. In the last hour, it's put out branches and added six and a half centimeters. It's sucked the battery half-dry. It's incredible!"

Six and a half centimeters per hour. Monroe winced. "Kumar, how tall was the skytree you took this from?"

"One point three kilometers."

He took a long, slow breath. "And how tall are your quarters?"

"The ceiling is regulation height. Two and a half meters—oh." His eyes grew large. "I hadn't thought about that."

"Bring it here." Argarrar reached to take the young tree. The instant her hands wrapped around the trunk, she stiffened, and her ears flattened. A spark jumped between the thin branches at the very tip of the tree.

"Can you hear it?" asked Monroe.

"Maybe I could, if the rest of you lot would shut up and give me room to breathe." She shook her head hard, then made a sound like a growl mixed with a chuckle. "The Preceptor does *not* like you people. You've been categorized as highly disruptive."

"I suppose that's fair," Monroe conceded. "Tell it—"

"This sapling couldn't carry my full thoughts to the Preceptor, even if I was . . . who I used to be. Mostly I'm just hearing impressions." Argarrar snarled, an angry sound that turned into a series of rapid-fire sneezes. She rubbed the back of her head with one hand.

"Argarrar?" Jagar stepped closer.

"I'm all right." She looped her tail around his hand and squeezed. "Feels like I've got a diamond-leaf buzzing inside my skull."

Monroe faced Argarrar. "We just need to know the Preceptor's capabilities, and whether it's willing to use them."

"There are too many variables," Argarrar said slowly. "Jagar is important, but the future of Tuxatl will always be the Preceptor's first priority."

"How would it respond to a direct threat?" asked Monroe.

Argarrar's tail stilled. "Decisively."

"Commander, you can't attack Tuxatl." Kumar blanched. "I mean, I recommend against—"

"Not us." Monroe straightened. "The Prodryans have left Tuxatl alone for more than a decade, out of fear. We're going to change that variable."

26

"Genital lice?"

Sanitation specialist Bohemian Rhapsody felt her skin tightening, squeezing her blood to her primary brain. She wanted to duck beneath the shallow water of the bridge and flee, but she was a professional. "That's correct."

Orange whipped a tentacle against her console, making a sound like splitting rock. "Order all CMC and Alliance vessels to converge on the *Pufferfish!*"

The Krakau at Tactical let out a low whistle. "Most CMC and Alliance ships are engaged with the Prodryans and other active threats."

"Then override their controls and—"

"That's inadvisable," Rhapsody said quietly.

Orange turned so fast a spray of water splashed Rhapsody's body. "What was that, Specialist?"

"What you're ordering would replace those ships' controls with our own systems. Systems which are actively fighting a level one infestation."

"There is no infestation!" Orange shouted. "We were sabotaged by those sand-sucking, abyss-born humans."

"And attempting to override other ships could spread that sabotage throughout the fleet," said Rhapsody.

For a moment, Rhapsody thought her commanding

*officer would physically attack. Her eyes were black slits,
and her tentacles flexed and coiled like she was preparing
to rip an enemy's limbs from their body. Finally, her beak
ground together, and she asked, "How long to clear the
alert?"*

*Rhapsody slid back half a meter. "We should have en-
gine control and basic navigation in two more hours."*

*Orange slashed a tentacle through the holomist dis-
play. "The Prodryans will be close enough to scatter the
Brakon across the system by then."*

*Rhapsody didn't answer. She was no tactician. This
was only her second time reporting to the bridge. She fer-
vently hoped it would be her last.*

*Finally, Orange turned away. When she spoke again,
her words were toneless. "Communications, signal Admiral Pachelbel. Tell her . . . we require a tow."*

MONROE COULDN'T REMEMBER THE last
time he'd seen the *Pufferfish* bridge this crowded.
The four Jynx continued to explore—all save
Argarrar, who had stolen Monroe's seat and promptly
fallen asleep. And now Cate and Starfallen had joined
them.

Both Prodryans wore full dress armor. Starfallen's
didn't fit well, being Cate's spare set. Holstered weapons—
unloaded and decharged—hung from their waists.

Bits of Tuxatl's rock and soil clung to Cate's back and
wings, but with Kumar's help, he'd gotten mostly clean.
He'd also applied makeup powder to his wings, brightening the colors and evening out the damaged patches.

Rubin sat at Tactical, a loaded rifle across her lap.
Monroe had stationed himself on the opposite side of the
bridge, pistol in hand. Cate knew exactly what would happen if he betrayed them again.

"Are you ready?" asked Monroe.

"I've been reviewing all precedents going back nine
hundred years," said Cate. "Nothing in Prodryan law
supports what we're about to attempt. For that matter,

Alliance law explicitly forbids this kind of interference in governmental—"

"We are ready." Starfallen moved to stand to the right of the captain's chair. Cate took the opposite side.

"Argarrar?" Jagar reached from behind the chair to nudge the older Jynx awake. She batted his hand away, but stretched and opened her eyes.

Monroe nodded at Gabe. "It's time."

"System-wide broadcast in three . . . two . . . one . . ." Gabe jabbed a finger at Cate and Starfallen.

Cate tilted his head. "Is that gesture meant as threat or insult?"

"It means you're live," Gabe snapped. "We're broadcasting."

"Then you should say so." Cate brushed his forearms together. "I am Advocate of Violence of the Red Star Clan. To my right is Starfallen, formerly called Wartalker, Wing Guard for the Crimson Warlord, Victor of Sharise, Muiniar, Plikxit IV, and countless other battles. We address you from the *EDFS Pufferfish*, under command of the human called Marilyn Monroe. These two Jynx are Argarrar and Jagar, natives of the planet below, the same world where Starfallen was shamefully abandoned and left to die. Thanks to my advice and guidance, we successfully retrieved this great warrior from Hell's Claws."

Years of military discipline allowed Monroe to keep a straight face, but it was a close thing.

"During this rescue, Starfallen and I uncovered a plot against all Prodryans," Cate continued. "A threat which even our unmatched military strength and cultural superiority was unprepared to fight."

"The power that controls Hell's Claws . . . changed me," said Starfallen. "It altered my brain, removing my instincts for aggression and rendering me . . . *peaceful*."

"Our leaders knew of this atrocity." The translator managed to capture the horror in Cate's words. "They knew the threat this world presented to our people, and how did they respond? Did they fight like true Prodryans? No. They ran away. They abandoned one of our greatest heroes. They created a blockade around the planet and worked to bury the truth like scavengers covering their pellets. Because of this criminal neglect, the crew of the *Pufferfish* was able to procure a sample of this biological weapon of mass destruction, one which would turn *all* Prodryans from predators to prey."

"Perhaps our new Supreme War Leader was ignorant of the danger of Hell's Claws," said Starfallen. "Or perhaps he was content to continue the policies of the past, to cower like a hatchling in a thunderstorm."

"Whether guilty of ignorance or cowardice, he is unfit to rule our mighty race." Cate spread his wings to emphasize his words.

On the tactical display, the *Destiny* and the rest of the Prodryan ships were changing course. Monroe was unsurprised to see them accelerating toward the *Pufferfish*.

Cate stepped forward. "While lesser Prodryans scurried about, fighting the Krakau and their allies, *I* faced the true threat to our people. I—with the help of Captain Marion Adamopoulos of the *Pufferfish*—sought out the rulers of this world, the would-be architects of our destruction: Jynx like Speaker Argarrar, who sits before you."

Had Cate just shared credit with a human? Monroe glanced over at Kumar, who looked equally stunned. Even Grom appeared surprised, their limbs hanging loosely about their face.

Argarrar stretched and yawned.

"In order to continue to protect the Prodryan people and our worlds—" For the first time, Cate hesitated. "Starfallen and I have decided . . . we believe the situation requires . . ."

"Advocate of Violence and I hereby assume the position of Supreme War Leader," said Starfallen. "We will serve jointly and, in so doing, guarantee the continued survival and growth of our people."

Cate jabbed a finger at Gabe, mimicking the gesture Gabe had used earlier. "The *Pufferfish* will now transmit full medical records of Starfallen's condition, including neurological scans. Let all Prodryans see what Hell's Claws would do to us. Let them see the threat their would-be

Supreme War Leader allowed to grow beneath his very wings, the greatest threat our people have ever encountered."

Starfallen clicked her mandibles and murmured, "I believe you've made your point."

"End transmission!" Cate said triumphantly.

"We're clear." Gabe stared at his console. "We have thirty-nine incoming signals. No, forty-six. Fifty-eight. I don't even know where to start with this, sir!"

"Ignore them," said Monroe. By now, Supreme War Leader would be starting to awaken from his A-ring jump. Monroe didn't envy whoever had to brief him on the situation. "Kumar, adjust our orbit. Try to keep Tuxatl between us and the *Destiny*.

"And what then?" asked Barryar.

Monroe unwrapped a cube of curry-flavored gum and popped it into his mouth. "Then we wait."

"The first wave will enter missile range in approximately six minutes," said Rubin.

Normally, Monroe would have ordered her to prepare countermeasures, but most of those countermeasures had been blown up back at Europa. They could still try electronic jamming, which generally had between a sixty and seventy percent success rate.

At last count, the *Destiny* had an escort of more than a hundred Prodryan warships in that first wave. Depending on how many missiles each ship launched . . . Monroe couldn't do all the math in his head, but even if they took down ninety-nine percent of a barrage, the results would be the same.

Kumar had kept the *Pufferfish* on the opposite side of the planet from the *Destiny*, but additional squadrons were closing in from all sides. More Prodryans had begun to cross the minefield at the three light-second boundary.

"Any response from Tuxatl?" asked Monroe.

"No, sir," said Rubin.

Monroe waited, eyes locked on the planet. "If this doesn't work . . ." He let the thought trail off. If it didn't work, they wouldn't have time to do anything about it.

Starfallen brushed her forearms together, a gesture of mild offense. "The Jynx stole my aggression, not my tactical brilliance. Supreme War Leader is new to his position. He can't afford to ignore a threat of this magnitude. The only questions are whether he attacks the *Pufferfish* or the planet first, and how the Preceptor will respond."

Rubin's back and shoulders stiffened. "The *Destiny* has locked her tracking sensors onto us."

"That is unfortunate," said Starfallen.

On the main screen, green sparks swarmed forth from the *Destiny*. More followed seconds later, turning the space on the far side of the planet into a sea of green.

Starfallen pointed. "Notice how the first missiles are launched from Supreme War Leader's ship. This way he can take credit for our deaths."

"How long—?" Monroe began.

Doc's voice filled the bridge. *"Fifty-three seconds for the missiles to circle the planet and reach the* Pufferfish.*"*

"Prodryan carriers are launching bombers," said Rubin. "They're heading for the planet surface."

If Monroe was wrong, not only would he lose the *Pufferfish*, he could have doomed the Jynx as well.

"Sensors are registering spikes of magnetic and gravitational energy from the ring." Kumar's voice cracked. "Doc, what the depths am I looking at?"

Doc spoke for all to hear. *"Unknown. The closest known match would be A-ring signatures."*

Monroe's breathing quickened. "Don't A-rings require *rings*?"

"How many energy spikes?" asked Starfallen.

"One thousand, four hundred and eleven," whispered Kumar.

On screen, ripples of energy spread across the planet's ring like raindrops. Monroe had never understood how A-rings worked—he didn't know of any human who did—but he knew how much energy they could transfer. He hit the comm. "All hands, prepare for . . . something."

"Could you be more specific?" asked Gabe.

"Nope."

Lightning crackled through the ring. A ribbon of blinding electrical energy circled the planet.

Monroe was so fixated on the ring that he almost missed when the energy readings spiked. Incoming missiles blinked out of existence. A second spike followed a split second later, and the bombers vanished.

"Jesus H. Christ on an Oreo cookie," yelled Gabe. "What just happened?"

"I second the question," said Grom. "Although I am confused about the cookie."

"Makeshift A-guns," whispered Johnny. "Commander, I believe the planet is shooting *rocks*."

Nothing in Monroe's training or experience had prepared him for this level of raw destruction. More than a thousand weapons created and fired within seconds, and it wasn't stopping.

"Every shot perfectly calibrated," Johnny continued. "Precise enough to take down missiles in flight."

"I'm sure I could do the same thing," said Doc. *"Given a brain the size of a small moon. And the ability to manipulate gravitational energy on that scale. And an adequate supply of rocks."*

One by one, the larger Prodryan vessels began to come apart. The *Pufferfish* couldn't detect the individual projectiles firing from the ring, but they could see the results. Each hit set off a geyser of escaping air and debris. Some ships simply broke into pieces and died. Others exploded.

The *Destiny* had taken twenty-three separate hits. It fired back with energy weapons and A-guns. The energy weapons simply dissipated when they reached the ring. The A-gun slugs passed through to strike the planet.

"Where did they hit?" asked Monroe.

Rubin was already checking. "The shots struck the equatorial region beneath the planet's rings. That area should be relatively uninhabited."

The ring fired again. Part of the *Destiny* broke away. A moment later, the bulk of the ship vanished in a flash of white.

"That was, I believe, the third shortest reign of a Supreme War Leader in Prodryan history," said Cate.

"Who were the other two?" asked Gabe.

"Later," said Monroe. If the Preceptor had rained this much death in the span of a few seconds . . . He swallowed his gum. "Doc, given the size of the planet's ring, what kind of ammo count does it have?"

"That depends on how much of the mass is an active part of the computer, but at a conservative guess, I'd say it could launch at least five billion individual rocks. More, if it has an efficient way to crush the larger rocks into smaller projectiles. Even a grain of sand can do significant damage at those speeds. Perhaps a better question would be what range the Preceptor can achieve with this level of accuracy."

Gabe whistled. "I'm glad Tuxatl's on our side."

"Not yours," said Argarrar. "Jagar's and the Jynx's."

The ring appeared normal again. Well, normal for Tuxatl. Monroe moistened his lips and said, "Gabe, put me through to Admiral Pachelbel." He waited for acknowledgment, then said, "Admiral, I assume you saw that?"

"The whole fucking system saw that," said Pachelbel. "What the depths did you do?"

Monroe looked around the bridge. At Cate and Starfallen, standing to either side of a human. At the Jynx, transfixed by the sight of their world from above. At Johnny, hunched over Engineering, so engaged in studying Tuxatl's rings that she seemed oblivious to anything else. "I think we just ended a war."

"This is Supreme War Leader Starfallen to all surviving Prodryans within range." Starfallen paused, as if to give her words time to reach every ship in the system. "As you have seen, the raw power of Hell's Claws cannot be overcome by simple force."

"But that power was no match for the intellectual superiority of a Prodryan lawyer," crowed Cate. "We have assailed our enemies with logic and battered them into temporary submission. We are safe . . . for the moment. To permanently end the threat to our people will require a more radical solution."

Throughout the system, most ships had drawn back from the fighting. Only a handful here and there continued to exchange fire.

Starfallen touched Monroe's forearm and said, "I believe that was your cue, Commander."

Monroe stood. He felt like his stomach had twisted into knots, despite the fact that a Prodryan grenade had removed most of his stomach years ago. "This is Commander Monroe of the Earth Defense Fleet. In our negotiations with the people of Tuxatl, we were given a weapon capable of pacifying the entire Prodryan population, but deploying that weapon would take time. Time during which Prodryan attacks would increase exponentially. We would face an enemy with vast resources and nothing to lose. Even if we were to ultimately suppress the Prodryans, the Alliance would be devastated in the process.

"I believe this is what the Preceptor, the power behind the attack you just witnessed, wants. The more we fight and weaken each other, the less of a potential threat we become to Tuxatl and the Jynx."

"Prodryans fight for our own purposes," said Starfallen. "We will not be tools in another race's war."

"Neither will we." Monroe straightened. "I've spoken with the Prodryan Supreme War Leaders, as well as Gabriel Naudé, representative of Earth. The human race hereby withdraws from the Krakau Alliance. Furthermore, we invite all species to join the newly established Human/Prodryan Coalition."

From the corner of his eye, Monroe saw Gabe's console light up with incoming messages.

"I have begun drafting a formal Coalition Charter," said Cate. "Once signed, the charter will mandate the destruction of the Jynx bioweapon, guaranteeing the continued existence of the Prodryan race."

"Urrara of Tuxatl has also agreed to sign the charter," Monroe continued, "on behalf of the Freesail camp. Her people are explorers, eager to visit other worlds and sail upon alien oceans, beginning with those of Earth."

Starfallen rubbed her forearms together. "As many of you doubtless realize, this means any act of war against Earth would be, by extension, an act of war against Hell's Claws. Given what we've seen today, you'll understand why Advocate of Violence and I will take extreme measures to prevent anyone from provoking Hell's Claws."

Cate spread his wings. "Warriors of Yan, defenders of our people, Starfallen and I have preserved not just your lives, but your *existence* as Prodryans. In return, we expect every clan to pledge its loyalty and support. But if you believe you can do a better job of neutralizing Hell's Claws, then as the humans say, be my guest."

Monroe moved to stand between them. According to both Cate and Starfallen, that display of Tuxatl's power should be enough to consolidate the Prodryan people behind them. Now it was his turn to persuade the rest of the Krakau Alliance, and he had no idea how to do it. None of them were likely to listen to a human.

No . . . some of them would have listened to Mops. She'd saved the Krakau home world. She'd stopped Admiral Sage on Earth. They knew and trusted her.

It was the thought of Mops that helped him find the words he needed.

"Captain Adamopoulos is dead." Around him, the bridge was silent. "Her final mission was to end the war between Prodryans and the Alliance. She succeeded."

Off to the side, Rubin nodded at him. Gabe raised a thumb.

"Thanks to Mops, we've proven that humans and Prodryans can work together to protect ourselves from a greater threat. We've shown you a path to peace. I strongly suggest you follow it." He looked down, like he could peer through the ship to the planet below. "Or do you need another demonstration, first?"

27

To whom it may concern,

Effective immediately, I hereby resign from my positions as a Lead Engineer, First Class, on Stepping Stone Station and as a Level 9 Covert Surveillance Analyst for the Krakau Colonial Military Command.

I am grateful for the opportunity I've had to serve under Admiral Pachelbel at Stepping Stone. I learned a great deal about practical ship and station repair. I will miss my team (with the exception of O. Susannah, whose hygiene leaves much to be desired).

My service to the CMC was equally educational. Thank you for teaching me the cost of short-sighted fearmongering and isolationism. I shudder to think how recent events might have flowed had the CMC been in command.

I look forward to my new position. Not only have we developed a previously unknown way of weaponizing A-rings, but my colleague Gabe has also engaged my expertise to attempt to construct a new personal combat weapon from old Earth designs: a saber made of light.

Though I believe it will instead need to be a form of looped plasma energy contained within a narrow magnetic field . . .

My future is hopeful, and the oceans of possibility are infinite.

Sincerely,

Johnny B. Goode
Chief Engineer (Probationary), EDFS Pufferfish

MONROE SAT AT MOPS' desk in the Captain's Cove. From the screen, Admiral Pachelbel glared in silence. Neither had spoken for—Monroe checked the time—almost four minutes.

Pachelbel broke first. "Do you trust them?"

"Do you mean the Preceptor and its representatives on Tuxatl, or the new Supreme War Leaders? And the answer is no." Monroe shook his head in disgust. "I've had to throw 'Supreme War Leader Cate' back in the brig because he was snooping through the *Pufferfish*'s systems, searching for more intel. But I've also seen parts of his proposed charter. It's heavily biased toward Prodryans, naturally. We'll need to sit down and fight that battle soon. But I believe his sense of self-preservation will overpower the drive to kill us all. He knows how close that bioweapon came to reprogramming his people."

"So do my superiors," said Pachelbel. "Just as they know how you withheld that weapon, the one thing that could have ended the Prodryan threat for all time." She sank back and blew a stream of bubbles, a display of unguarded weariness that shocked Monroe. "I assume you had a reason?"

"Two reasons. I meant what I said earlier. Even if the weapon worked, it would take time to spread through their population. I figure the only thing more dangerous than Prodryans united against us by a Supreme War

Leader is Prodryans united by desperation and vengeance."

Pachelbel blinked. "And?"

Monroe double-checked their connection was secure, then pulled up the latest report from Azure. "Our biochemist discovered a chain of five specific mutations that could theoretically result in a strain that's compatible with Rokkau neurons. It's a one in a billion event, and would only occur in a particular Prodryan genotype. But there are billions of Prodryans, which means the bioweapon would replicate tens of trillions of times. Over time, the Rokkau strain becomes a near certainty."

"Why Rokkau?" asked Pachelbel. "Of all Alliance species, they're currently the least able to threaten Tuxatl or anyone else."

"The Preceptor was able to sample a Rokkau directly. Azure believes she'll eventually find a path that would spread the weapon to humans, too. Possibly the Quetzalus as well—the Preceptor would have their biological data on file. And of course, there's a good chance the Preceptor scanned through our computer systems, including our medical records and databases, meaning they could have had enough information to tailor mutation chains to every known species in the galaxy. We just haven't found them yet."

"What would happen to the Freesail Jynx you agreed to escort to other worlds?"

"They'd be fine," said Monroe. "Better than fine. As the weapon mutated and the rest of us regressed or died out or whatever, the Jynx would be left with all that technology for themselves. Every planet would become a backup of Jynx genetic material, controlled by the Jynx."

"I see." Another long silence flowed between them.

"Peace is in reach, Admiral. All we have to do is grab it. I know there's been some grumbling about humans taking a position of power—"

"Grumbling?" Pachelbel scoffed. "Twenty minutes ago, Colonial Military Command officially named humans traitors to the Alliance. Four Alliance ships have reported attempted mutinies. I admire what you've accomplished here, but if you thought the rest of the galaxy would simply fall in line with your new Coalition—"

"One day ago, I thought the rest of the galaxy was about to kill each other."

"I think some of them would have preferred that," Pachelbel admitted.

Monroe snorted. "Admiral, Cate and Starfallen are in a precarious position. None of the clans have challenged them yet, thanks to what Tuxatl did to the *Destiny* and the rest of the former Supreme War Leader's fleet. But if they're going to survive more than a couple of days, the rest of the Prodryans need to see that this can work."

"Even if I wanted to help you, you know I don't have the authority to simply dissolve the Krakau Alliance. That would require a full vote of the membership, with review and approval from both the Judicial and Military Committees. We're talking about years of discussion and debate."

"Cate—I mean, Supreme War Leader Cate—has been going over the Alliance Charter. I'm pretty sure he's used it as a model for parts of his own, though he'd never admit it. But he also has a suggestion to hurry things along . . ."

He tapped the controls, looping Cate and Starfallen into the discussion. Starfallen had voluntarily joined Cate in the brig, where they'd been working nonstop since leaving Tuxatl.

Cate set aside piles of printed and electronic reading material and jumped to his feet. "Admiral Pachelbel. I assume Commander Monroe referred you to me so I could help facilitate the dissolution of the Krakau Alliance?"

"Something like that, yes," Pachelbel said dryly.

"Your Alliance Charter has extensive provisions for adding members, but none whatsoever for withdrawing," said Cate. "Presumably this was deliberate, another way to keep Alliance worlds ensnared in Krakau tentacles. For this reason, I have no doubt your Alliance lawyers are busy preparing arguments that Earth's withdrawal is illegal. However, there exists a principle of interstellar law known in ancient Human as clausula rebus sic stantibus. Put simply, it allows an agreement to be changed or terminated altogether in the event of drastic, unforeseen change. What could be more unexpected than Prodryans declaring peace in the face of a potentially greater threat?"

"I doubt the Judicial Council will accept that," said Pachelbel.

Monroe smiled. "With respect, Admiral, I don't think that matters. The JC can scream as loud as they want, but if the rest of the member worlds simply walk away—"

"Or fly away," Cate cut in.

"Or swim, yes," said Monroe. "There's not much the Krakau can do to stop them. All Cate did was provide legal cover."

"In other words," said Starfallen, "there's no need to fight over formally dissolving the Alliance. Cate's write-up has already been forwarded to the governments of your member worlds."

Cate raised his head and spread his wings. To Monroe's eye, he might as well have been posing for a statue. "After years of diligent spy work, I've finally succeeded in destroying the Krakau Alliance."

Behind him, Starfallen gave an apologetic, almost-human shrug.

"Given the state of the Alliance, our members may be hesitant to sign onto another such organization," said Pachelbel.

"I think self-preservation will motivate them," said Monroe. "Nobody wants humans and Prodryans working together unsupervised."

"That is . . . a terrifying thought," Pachelbel agreed. "I will be sure to share it with my superiors."

"And who knows?" Monroe glanced at Cate and Starfallen. "Maybe after a century or two, peace could become a habit. This could be the start of a Prodryan cultural shift away from war."

"Unlikely," scoffed Cate. "I have already begun developing our new long-term strategy for galactic supremacy. After observing your people and operations, I've concluded that Prodryan civilization is inherently superior. Our culture will continue to thrive and expand, while yours will inevitably collapse under the weight of its many failures and shortcomings, leaving us dominant."

Pachelbel let out a long, bubbling sigh. "The final item to discuss is Captain Adamopoulos' condition. I have medical specialists who want to study her, but we have no way of treating or curing her, and I know she would have hated being confined, poked and prodded."

"Agreed." Monroe turned away. He'd visited Mops in Medical twice, and both visits had left him feeling like he'd been shot in the chest. Last time, she'd roused herself enough to grab his arm. He and Azure had worked together to pry her jaw loose before she cracked her teeth.

It was that encounter, seeing the empty hunger in Mops' eyes and watching her gnaw futilely on his artificial limb, that had helped him realize she was truly gone.

"I've spoken with the crew," Monroe continued. "Once we transfer Cate and Starfallen to a Red Star Clan warship, we're going to take her home."

The last time Monroe had seen Wolf, formerly SHS Technician Wolfgang Mozart of the *Pufferfish*, she'd been packing her things to leave the ship, getting ready to join the Library of Humanity on Earth. Given Wolf's history of impulsivity and violence, Monroe had been dubious about her new life as a librarian—even in a library as unusual as this—but he'd kept those doubts to himself.

Seeing her now made him realize how wrong he'd been.

He hadn't recognized Wolf at first as she strode down a dirt path toward him and his shuttle. She'd trimmed her brown hair into fuzzy spikes. Dingy overalls covered an old EMC jumpsuit. Leather gloves were tucked through her belt. Sweat and dirt darkened her face, where she'd acquired two new scars along the jawbone.

But it was her movement that was most changed. For the first time, Wolf seemed . . . *relaxed*. Content. Always before, she'd come across like she was bracing for a fight with whoever or whatever looked at her funny. Here, she was at peace.

"Lieutenant Monroe! Or I hear it's Commander Monroe now?" Wolf grinned and clasped his hand. "Welcome back to Earth, sir. Sounds like I missed one hell of a mission."

"I take it you've received Gabe's recordings?"

"All of them. He sent back some great shots. I can't wait to see his footage from your next trip." Wolf's smile faded. "He also told us about the captain. Is she . . . ?" She gestured to the shuttle.

"She's on a grav stretcher in the back," said Monroe. "Azure sedated her for transport. We thought it would be less stressful."

"Good thinking. Ferals don't do well in tight confinement."

He knew she didn't mean anything by it, but hearing Wolf casually refer to Mops as feral made him cringe. He turned away and focused on sliding Mops' stretcher down the rear cargo ramp.

"We've got a hundred and ninety-six ferals on campus here." Wolf gestured to a chain-link fence in the distance. Beyond the fence, blocky-looking buildings of brick and concrete covered the sloping landscape. "It used to be a private college a couple centuries back. The Library restored two of the buildings for my team to use, but the rest is for them. We're in there every day, passing out food and medical treatment, breaking up squabbles, working to teach and reinforce certain behaviors. Like not eating my team."

"Sounds like the work suits you," Monroe said stiffly. He started up the path. The stretcher followed automatically.

Wolf walked alongside him. "Did you know they have personalities?"

"What?"

"You don't see it in the wild, but here where they're safe, secure, and well-fed, their personalities come out more. Take Lucy. She's a climber. We're always finding her up a tree or wandering the top level of the old parking garage. She's only fallen twice that I know of. Darcy, he's an asshole. He gave me these." She touched the scars on her chin. "Charlotte's one of my favorites. She's got a sense of humor."

"A feral with a sense of humor?" Monroe repeated dubiously.

"It's the humor of a drunk monkey, but yeah. Last month, one of our feeders, Benjamin, tripped and fell in the mud. Have you ever heard a feral laugh? I thought she was choking to death. I was about to give her a field trach when I realized what was really happening. The next day, she followed Benjamin around for more than an hour. When he was distracted, she *pushed him down*. Laughed even harder."

It wasn't behavior Monroe had ever seen from a feral human, but he didn't have Wolf's experience, nor had he ever seen a community of ferals in such a controlled environment. "What are you getting at?"

They stopped at a gate. A second fence stood three meters beyond the first. Wolf turned to face him. "The root word of personality is person. Ferals are still people. And Mops is still in there. We'll take care of her, sir. I promise. I'll start her in the old north dormitory. She'll have the whole building to herself for the first week to give her time to adjust to being back on Earth. I'll introduce her to the others a few at a time."

She grimaced and turned away. "Never thought I'd be processing anyone I knew. Especially the captain."

A guttural snarl came from behind the second fence. Without looking, Wolf flashed a middle finger and said, "Fuck off, Darcy."

That was the Wolf Monroe knew. He chuckled despite himself. "She'd be glad it's you looking after her. So am I."

"You're welcome to visit any time," said Wolf. "Or ping me for updates. It's not the most exciting life. They mostly wander around, chase the occasional squirrel or rabbit. Oh, but you should see them when it snows. Half of 'em want to roll in it, the other half want to eat it. I'll send you a vid."

"Ahem. Aren't you forgetting someone?"

"I was getting to that." With a sigh, Monroe removed the monocle and handed it to Wolf. "It should be compatible with your old implants."

"I don't understand." Wolf turned the lens over in her hand.

"Doc asked to stay here. To help you look after her."

Wolf blinked hard and brought the monocle to her eye. "I don't know what to say."

"Don't let him boss you around too much." Monroe's throat felt like he'd tried to swallow a rock. It was like losing yet another piece of Mops.

"What's next for you and the crew?" asked Wolf.

"We'll be taking the *Pufferfish* for monthly runs to Tuxatl for a while, transporting refugees. Nobody else wants to go near that planet."

"From everything we've heard, I don't blame 'em." Wolf snorted. "You think this peace with the Prodryans will hold?"

"The Supreme War Leaders are determined to keep their people as far from the Jynx as possible. With Starfallen balancing out Cate—"

"Can't believe that twiggy little shit of a lawyer is running the Prodryan Empire."

"Supreme War Leader twiggy shit, yes. He's seen firsthand what Tuxatl can do, both to Prodryan ships and to their species. I think the peace will hold. For a while."

"Good to know Mops' last mission was a success. And I'm glad we'll have some breathing room while we try to get Earth cleaned up." Somewhere beyond the fence, a bell chimed. The ferals immediately hurried away. Wolf waited for the last of them to leave, then unlocked the outer gate. "The bell is for snack time," she explained. "I had them ring it early today so Mops and I would have a clear path to the dorm."

She pushed the stretcher through the gate. "Good to see you, Commander. Try not to get blown up out there."

"I'll do my best. Try not to get eaten."

"Will do."

One day later, Monroe was skimming through the morning's briefing notes on his monocle as he made his way to the bridge. His AI also brought up the names and ranks of his new crew members so he could greet them in passing.

He'd paid for a substantial upgrade, merging the AI in his monocle with the one that controlled his prosthetics. It would take a lot more before the AI functioned on Doc's level, but it was a start, and his arm hadn't accidentally punched anyone since the upgrade. He was thinking of naming it "Ace."

A new message blinked for his attention as he entered the bridge. He skimmed it on his way to the center chair, then put in a call to the new chief of Shipboard Hygiene and Sanitation. "Problems, Kumar?"

"How the depths can a freshly refurbished ship get so dirty so quickly?"

"We have a crew of a hundred and twelve," Monroe reminded him. "That's a lot more dirt and waste."

"I think the increase is exponential," Kumar snapped. "Someone submitted the wrong supplies requisition order, so we don't have any of the equipment needed for processing waste material from our two Quetzalus techs. Azure's environmental circulation system is still calibrated for Krakau, not Rokkau. And someone tried to flush a Nusuran merkin on deck five and backed up the pipes."

"A *what*?" Monroe shook his head. "Never mind, I don't want to know. What do you need to keep us on schedule?"

"Two extra bodies assigned to SHS for the next twenty-four hours, and a commanding officer who can use his clout to get the rest of our supplies from Stepping Stone ASAP."

"Done." He pulled up the crew roster, picked two off-duty security personnel, and sent them orders to report to Kumar.

Grom sat coiled at Engineering, arguing with a Krakau tech over computer graphics upgrades. Rubin had taken one of the extra stations at the back of the bridge, where she was running checks on internal security. Gabe was on comms, working through another tutorial. The rest were mostly strangers.

"We've received clearance for our arrival in the Tuxatl system, sir," said Gabe. "A group of Freesail Jynx will be waiting near the Black Spire skytree. Two Black Spire Jynx have asked to join them. It should be a simple transport mission."

"Simple would be a nice change." Monroe double-checked their updated orders from the morning briefing. "We've got a couple of stops to make along the way. The clan of the former Supreme War Leader has begun dipping their wings in piracy. Starfallen believes they're going to hit Tjikko space next, so we'll be doing escort duty for a shipment of fungicide to the Tjikko's newest colony. But first, we've been asked to help the Glacidae deal with a centuries-old waste dump that just erupted into what they're calling a geyser of frozen garbage. Grom, this is your home colony, so I'll want you working with Kumar's team."

Grom shuddered, making their spines rattle, but said only, "Yes, sir."

"Captain Monroe?" Gabe glanced up from his tutorials. "Did you get a chance to submit my suggestions to the Coalition Organizational Committee?"

"I passed along your proposed names, yes."

"I really think 'United Federation of Planets' has a nice ring to it," Gabe continued. "Or maybe 'Galactic Republic.'"

"We'll see what the politicians decide." Monroe turned to Navigation. "Miranda, start plotting a jump to Tronginkaltok IV."

The green-skinned Krakau raised a tentacle behind her head in a passable backward salute. "Aye, Captain."

So far, none of the eleven Krakau crew had voiced

complaints about serving under a human. Not where anyone could overhear, at least. The Krakau had negotiated equal standing with other races in the new Coalition, but many Krakau felt equality was a step down. Some had even demanded Admiral Pachelbel be fired for her role in everything, demands Pachelbel had laughed off by announcing her well-deserved retirement.

Monroe stretched and touched a newly installed control on the side of his chair, another of Grom's unauthorized upgrades. The seat reclined, and the leg rest rose to support his feet. "Ace, how long before we can leave Stepping Stone?"

"Assuming Kumar's requisition is processed in a timely manner, we should be cleared for departure in approximately two hours."

"Look sharp, people. I want all pre-launch tests completed in the next ninety minutes," said Monroe.

"Yes, sir."

Monroe popped a new cube of gum into his mouth. It was time to show the galaxy what this Coalition could do.

Epilogue

Three Years Later

S HE TRIED TO SIT up. Her arms moved through warm water. Voices spoke in low tones, distant and distorted. Something slithered past her toes.

Cutis fish, whispered a distant memory. Another part of her mind suggested, *Food?*

The light grew brighter. She tried to cover her eyes, but some kind of binding held her wrists in place. She pulled harder.

Blurry shadows peered down at her. Strong limbs caught her hands.

The voices were louder now, more urgent. She recognized one—the food-bringer—and her mouth watered. She blinked and squinted until the shapes came into focus. Two were unfamiliar. The third had a scarred face, short hair, and a green lens over one eye.

She swallowed. Her mouth tasted foul, like a Krakau had taken a sauna in it.

"Mops?" said the food-bringer.

Mops. The syllable set off a cascade of other words long forgotten. She licked her lips and croaked, "Wolf?"

Shouting erupted from the figures. She flinched. Wolf spun away and snapped at the others. They quieted immediately.

Hands and tentacles steadied her as she sat up. Her heart was pounding, and her skin pimpled from the cold. This felt familiar, like memories from a dream. She looked down at the dingy water, watching the cutis fish dart about eating dead skin cells and other waste.

A familiar slick-skinned face, black mottled with blue, studied her closely. "How do you feel?"

"Tired." She flexed her fingers, trying to get the blood flowing. "Confused."

"This should help." Wolf brought a green object toward her face.

Mops jerked away.

"It's all right," Wolf said softly. She put the object into Mops' hand. "When you're ready."

She stared at the curved lens. Her hand moved automatically, bringing it to her eye. There was a quiet click, and half the world took on a faint green tint. Floating lights and symbols raced past, and a familiar voice spoke from a speaker in the side of her tank. *"Good morning."*

Her eyes filled with tears. "Doc?"

Memories flooded her thoughts: her crew, the *Pufferfish*, the war with the Prodryans, the Library of Humanity, Tuxatl . . . She clutched her head, feeling like she could drown in it all. One memory, more recent than the others, made her whirl and glare at Wolf. "You shot me!"

Wolf winced. "I was hoping you wouldn't remember that."

"In the ass!"

"It was just a tranquilizer," Wolf insisted. "I needed to bring you down so we could get you in for treatment. Even as a feral, you were too damn clever. You've caused my team no end of headaches."

A deeper voice spoke. "That seems only fair."

Mops squinted until the speaker came into focus. Monroe stood against the wall, arms folded across his chest, a wide grin on his face. Standing next to him was a short, furry Jynx.

"Monroe? And . . ." She stumbled over the name. "Argarrar?"

"I told you it would work." The old Jynx twitched her whiskers. "Hello again, Captain Mop."

"I believe *I* told *you* it would work," said Azure.

Monroe cleared his throat, cutting off Argarrar's response. "Azure's been on Earth for the past three years, working on the Krakau plague."

"The feral immune system kept destroying the cures we tried." Azure slapped a blood sensor onto Mops' arm, inside the elbow. "We needed a more robust delivery system, something that would mimic your biology and evade your defenses long enough to work. Do you remember Harkayé and how she tailored a chemical weapon to Prodryan biology?"

Azure's excitement was overwhelming. Mops struggled to stay afloat in a flood of memories. "I think so."

"I thought Argarrar might be able to do something similar to help us. She arrived two months ago, after Jagar returned home to Tuxatl."

Argarrar made a gagging noise. "I don't have a computer in my head, so I had to taste more than a thousand humans in order to grow a proper match. You ferals are filthy creatures. And so salty."

Mops looked down at the medical bracelet on her left wrist. Her vitals were normal—for a cured feral. "So it's not a true cure?"

"That's up to you, Captain." Wolf stepped closer, moving with quiet authority. "If you decide it's what you want, there's a second round of treatment that will reverse the effects of the Krakau plague."

"You'd be all but indistinguishable from a pre-plague human," said Azure.

"I turned it down." Wolf grimaced and cocked a thumb over one shoulder. "Why the hell would I want to be all soft and vulnerable like these clowns?"

Mops looked to where she was pointing. Kumar and Rubin stood by a wall, holding hands. Both had the warm flush brought by red blood flowing beneath their skin.

"You don't have to make any decisions today," Doc assured her. *"In fact, I doubt they'd let you. Not until*

you've gone through an absurd number of tests to gauge your physical and mental status. You'll have plenty of time to rest and recover and decide what you want to do."

She focused on Monroe. "Harkayé's weapon. The Prodryans. What happened after I—?"

"We finished the mission," Monroe assured her. "That was three years ago. Supreme War Leaders Cate and Starfallen, in cooperation with the Earth Defense Fleet, have done a good job maintaining peace throughout the Coalition. We destroyed the bioweapon shortly after the Battle of Tuxatl."

The Coalition?

Supreme War Leader *Cate*?

Mops focused on Monroe's uniform, trying to absorb one change at a time. She recognized the yellow rank stripes on his right shoulder. He'd been promoted. "Congratulations, Captain." The ship's logo was unfamiliar. It reminded her of a stylized deck mop. "What ship?"

"The same one," he assured her. "We just renamed her. The *EDFS Adamopoulos.*"

"The EDF wanted to continue the tradition of naming ships after dangerous Earth creatures," added Doc.

Words fled. Mops stared at the insignia until she finally managed a soft, "Oh."

"A therapist from the Library of Humanity will be meeting with you later today to help with your reacclimatization," said Azure. "You'll have temporary quarters in the north dormitory."

She nodded, still struggling to take it all in. It was like trying to drink the ocean. "And then what?"

"Whatever you'd like," said Monroe. "The EDF would love to have you back, if you want."

"Retirement is a perfectly valid option," suggested Doc. *"I'm told Admiral Pachelbel spends her days lounging in the hot springs of southern Dobranok."*

"Or you can stick around," added Wolf. "We've made some progress on planetary recovery, but Earth is still a hell of a mess."

Mops turned toward Wolf. Slowly, her lips tugged into a smile. "Sounds like you need someone to help clean it up."

Author's Note

In an ideal world, this book would have come out two years sooner.

Ever since my first book with DAW—*Goblin Quest*, way back in 2006—I've written about one book a year. I intended to continue at that pace when I finished *Terminal Uprising* and started on *Terminal Peace*.

Then in late 2018, my wife Amy was diagnosed with an aggressive form of lymphoma. For nine months she fought with everything she had. After multiple rounds of chemotherapy and other treatments, that fight came to an end.

I won't say she lost her fight. She got nine more months of life. She fought off cancer long enough to see our younger child finish Junior High School and our older child get her first job. She got to spend more time with family and friends.

Shortly after her diagnosis, I told my agent and editor I couldn't focus on the writing. Even if I had been willing to take the time away from my wife and kids, it's hard to write smart-ass space janitor humor when you're worried about tumors and blood counts and the next chemo treatment.

Both Sheila Gilbert, my editor, and Joshua Bilmes, my agent, told me to take all the time I needed. I'm incredibly grateful to them both for their patience, compassion, and understanding.

I talked a bit online about what we were going through. The love and support I received reminded me that I have the best readers, fans, and friends in the world. Thank you all so much.

Several months after Amy's death, I pulled up the draft of *Terminal Peace* and tried to pick up where I'd left off. It didn't work. I wasn't the same person I'd been when I started writing the story. This wasn't what I wanted, what I *needed* to write.

That changed when I added Mops' diagnosis to chapter one.

Mops' fight was one I could write. This was the heart of the story I needed to tell: the determination, the fear, the anger, and the utter unfairness of it all . . . And this time, I could give the story a happier ending. We deserve that, dammit. Even if we don't always get it.

Life is different these days, but I've gotten back into the writing groove, and I've been working on a new standalone fantasy that's just about complete. I'm hopeful the wait for that one will be much shorter.

I'll wrap this up with a request. If you're able, please consider donating blood or platelets. Cancer treatment is hell on blood counts, among other things. Amy wouldn't have gotten those nine months without the generosity of so many blood donors. (Plus, after you donate, you get free cookies!)

Thank you all.